JEFF IN VENICE,
DEATH IN VARANASI

JEFF IN VENICE, DEATH IN VARANASI

A Novel

GEOFF DYER

CANONGATE
Edinburgh · London · New York · Melbourne

First published in Great Britain in 2009 by
Canongate Books Ltd, 14 High Street,
Edinburgh EH1 1TE

2

British Library Cataloguing-in-Publication Data
A catalogue record for this book is available on
request from the British Library

ISBN 978 1 84767 270 4

Typeset in Sabon by Palimpsest Book Production Ltd,
Grangemouth, Stirlingshire

Printed in the UK by CPI Mackays, Chatham ME5 8TD

www.meetatthegate.com

for Rebecca

'For every step, the footprint was already there.'

Roberto Calasso

'Huge walls & towers & rocks & balconies – a prospect along the bend of the river like Venice along Grand Canal or seen from Judecca – finally to Manikarnika burning ghat . . .'

Allen Ginsberg, *Indian Journals*

Part One:
Jeff in Venice

'Alas, the movie wasn't much to speak of; besides, I never liked the novel much either.'

Joseph Brodsky, *Watermark*

'The deposed, the defeated, the disenchanted, the wounded, or even only the bored, have seemed to find there something that no other place could give . . . '

Henry James

On an afternoon in June 2003, when, for a brief moment, it looked as if the invasion of Iraq had not been such a bad idea after all, Jeffrey Atman set out from his flat to take a walk. He had to get out of the flat because now that the initial relief about the big picture had worn off – relief that Saddam had not turned his non-existent WMD on London, that the whole world had not been plunged into a conflagration – the myriad irritations and frustrations of the little picture were back with a vengeance. The morning's work had bored the crap out of him. He was supposed to be writing a twelve-hundred-word so-called 'think piece' (intended to require zero thought on the part of the reader and scarcely more from the writer but still, somehow, beyond him) that had reached such a pitch of tedium that he'd spent half an hour staring at the one-line email to the editor who'd commissioned it:

'I just can't do this shit any more. Yrs J.A.'

The screen offered a stark choice: *Send* or *Delete*. Simple as that. Click *Send* and it was all over with. Click *Delete* and he was back where he started. If taking your own life were this easy, there'd be thousands of suicides every day. Stub your toe on the way to the bathroom. Click. Get marmalade on your cuff while eating toast. Click. It starts raining as soon as you leave the house and your brolly's upstairs. What to do? Go back up and get it, leave without it and get soaked, or . . . Click. Even as he stared at the message, as he sat there on the very brink of sending it, he knew that he would not. The thought of sending it was enough to deter him from doing so. So instead of sending the message or getting on with this article about a 'controversial' new art installation at the Serpentine he sat there, paralysed, doing neither.

To break the spell he clicked *Delete* and left the house as if fleeing the scene of some dreary, as yet uncommitted crime. Hopefully fresh air (if you could call it that) and movement would revive him, enable him to spend the evening finishing this stupid article and getting ready to fly to Venice the following afternoon. And when he got to Venice? More shit to set up and churn out. He was meant to be covering the opening of the Biennale – that was fine, that was a doddle – but then this interview with Julia Berman had come up (or at least a probable interview with Julia Berman) and now, in addition to writing about the Biennale, he was supposed to persuade her – to beg, plead and generally demean himself – to do an interview that would guarantee even more publicity for her daughter's forthcoming album and further inflate the bloated reputation of Steven Morison, the dad, the famously overrated artist. On top of that he was supposed to make sure – at the very least – that she agreed to grant *Kulchur* exclusive rights to reproduce a drawing Morison had made of her, a drawing never previously published, and not even seen by anyone at *Kulchur*, but which, due to the fear that a rival publication might get hold of it, had acquired the status of a rare and valuable artefact. The value of any individual part of this arrangement was irrelevant. What mattered was that in marketing and publicity terms (or, from an editorial point of view, circulation and advertising) the planets were all in alignment. He had to interview her, had to come away with the picture and the right to reproduce it. Christ almighty . . .

A woman pushing an all-terrain pram glanced quickly at him and looked away even more quickly. He must have been doing that thing, not talking aloud to himself but forming words with his mouth, unconsciously lip-synching the torrent of grievances that tumbled constantly through his head. He held his mouth firmly shut. He had to stop doing that. Of all the things he had to stop doing or start doing, that was right at the top of the list. But how do you stop doing something when you are completely unaware that you're doing it? Charlotte was the one who pointed it out to him, when they were still together, but he'd probably been doing it for years before that. Towards the end that's how she would refer to this habit of muted karaoke. 'That thing,' she would say. 'You're doing that thing again.' At first it had been a joke between them. Then, like everything else in a marriage, it stopped being a joke and became a bone of contention, an issue, a source of resentment, one of the many things that rendered life on Planet Jeff – as she termed the uninhabitable wasteland of their marriage – intolerable. What she never understood, he claimed, was that life on Planet Jeff was intolerable for him too, more so, in fact, than for anyone else. That, she claimed, was precisely her point.

These days he had no one to alert him to the fact that he was walking down the street mouthing out his thoughts. It was a very bad habit. He had to stop doing it. But it was possible that, as he was walking down the street, he was forming the words, 'This is a very bad habit, I must stop doing it, it's even possible that as I walk down the street I am forming these words . . .' He glued his mouth closed again as a way of closing off this line of thought. The only way to stop this habit of forming the words with his lips was to stop forming the words *in his brain*, to stop having the thoughts that formed the words. How to do that? It was a major undertaking, the kind of thing you got sorted out at an ashram, not cosmetically at a beautician's. Eventually everything that is going on inside will manifest itself externally. The interior will be exteriorized . . . He made an effort to smile. If he could get into the habit of doing this constantly, so that his face looked cheerful in repose, then the exterior might be interiorized, he might start to beam internally. Except it was so tiring, keeping smiling like that. The moment he stopped concentrating on smiling his face lapsed back into its unbeaming norm. 'Norm' was certainly the operative word. Most of the people passing by looked miserable as a disappointing sin. Many of them, if their faces were anything to go by, looked like their souls were scowling. Maybe Alex Ferguson was right, maybe chewing gum ferociously was the only answer. If so, the solution was at hand in the form of a newsagent's.

Behind the counter was a young Indian girl. How old? Seventeen? Eighteen? Gorgeous, though, and with a bright smile, unusual in her line of work. Maybe she was just starting out, taking time off from her A-levels or whatever they were called these days, filling in for her surly father, who, though he spoke little English, had so thoroughly adjusted to British life that he looked every bit as pissed off as someone whose ancestors had come over with the Normans. Atman was always taken aback by his exchanges with this guy, by the way that, brief though they were, they managed to sap any sense of well-being he'd had on entering the premises. It was difficult to repress the habit of saying 'please' and 'thank you' but, as a reprisal, a protest, at the guy's refusal to abide by the basic courtesies, Jeff always picked up whatever he was buying – the paper, a bar of chocolate – and handed over the money silently. Not at all like that today, though. Jeff gave her a pound coin. She handed him his change, met his eyes with her own, smiled. Give her a few years and she would scarcely pay any attention to whoever she was serving, would just look up, grab the money and not try to make of the exchange anything other than the low-level financial transaction it was. But for now it was quite magical. It was so easy to make people (i.e. Jeff) feel a bit better about life (i.e. himself), so easy to make the world a slightly better place. The mystery was why so many people – and there were plenty of occasions when he could be counted among their number – opted to make it a worse one. He went away feeling happier than when he'd come in, charmed by her, even sort of aroused. Not aroused exactly, but curious. Curious about what kind of underwear she might have been wearing beneath her T-shirt and low-waisted jeans – exactly the kind of thinking, presumably, that many in the Muslim community – the *so-called* Muslim community – used as justification for the full-face veil. He had read, a few days earlier, that British Muslims were the most embittered, disgruntled and generally fed up of any in Europe. So why was there all this talk about the need for Muslims to integrate into British life? The fact that they were so pissed off was a sign of profound assimilation. What better proof could there be?

Chewing over this important Topic – at the last moment he'd opted for chocolate rather than gum – Jeff walked on to Regent's Park. The fact that he should, at this point, have returned home and got back to work meant that he kept going, walked through the park under the cloud-swollen sky and crossed Marylebone Road.

A creature of deep habit, Atman was programmed, the moment he set foot on Marylebone High Street, to go to Patisserie Valerie's and order a black coffee with a side-order of hot milk and an almond croissant – even though he didn't want either. Normally he came here in the mornings but now, in the post-lunch doldrums, it was too late for coffee, too early for tea (it was that time of the day, in fact, when no one wanted anything) and far too late to read the paper – which he'd read extra thoroughly, hours earlier, as a way of putting off writing his stupid think-piece. Fortunately he had a book for company, Mary McCarthy's *Venice Observed*. He'd first read it four years ago, after getting back from the 1999 Biennale, and had started re-reading it now – along with the other standard books on Venice – as preparation for the return trip. His almond croissant was the size and complexion of a small roast turkey and in the time it took to chomp through it he was able to read the entire section on Giorgione's *The Tempest*.

McCarthy reckoned there was 'a new melancholy in the chronic leisure' of the renaissance nobility. Could a similar melancholy be detected among the leisured ladies of Marylebone High Street? Apparently not. Like everything else leisure had changed with the times, had sped up. So there was actually a kind of urgency about these wives of investment bankers and hedge fund managers negotiating the brief interval between lunch and picking up their kids from the lycée or the American School. They had learned the lesson of leisure, the importance of contriving things so that there wasn't *time* to be unhappy. Back in the Renaissance time mounted up without passing so that sudden storms are forever on the point of breaking. Hence the melancholy that 'suffuses Giorgione's paintings, a breath of unrest that just fails to stir the foliage of the trees . . . It is the absolute fixity of his scenes that makes this strange impression.'

Atman hadn't seen the painting in 1999 but it was one of the things he was most looking forward to this time around (if he had the time): seeing *The Tempest*, gauging the painting – and the city – against what McCarthy had written about it.

Stuffed with pastry, tense with coffee, he left Valerie's and browsed through the Oxfam bookshop, all part of the normal pattern of a walk along Marylebone High Street. What was completely out of the ordinary was to find himself looking in the window of an expensive-looking hairdresser's. He had never paid more than ten pounds (with tip), had not had his hair cut anywhere but a barber's for thirty years, not since the unisex craze of the mid-seventies, and, most importantly of all, he didn't *need* a haircut. But here he was, opening the door, entering, taking the first steps towards doing something he'd been thinking about for years: getting his hair dyed. For a long time he'd thought of grey hair as a symptom, a synonym of inner dreariness, and had accepted it, accordingly, as inevitable – but all that was about to change. He shut the door behind him. The hair-conditioned interior smelled nicely, of product and potion, and looked conservative – not the kind of place where getting your hair dyed anything other than orange or pillar-box red marked you down as a hopeless square. It had the atmosphere, almost, of a clinic or spa. A man with shapeless brown hair – was it a subtly suggestive ploy that hairdressers so often looked like they needed a haircut? – asked if he had an appointment.

'No, I don't. But I wondered if you had a slot now.'

He looked at the appointment book, heavy and much-amended, a kind of Domesday book of the hair world.

'Cut and wash?'

'Yes. Actually, I was wondering . . .' He felt as embarrassed as a character in a 1950s novel buying French letters. 'Might it be possible to perhaps get my hair dyed?' The guy, who had seemed only marginally interested, at this point became more focused.

'Yes,' he said. 'Dyeing is an art like everything else. We do it exceptionally well. We do it so it looks real.'

'That's Sylvia Plath, right?'

'Indeed.' A hairdresser who quoted poetry. Well, this really was an upmarket place. Or perhaps this kind of thing came as standard in this part of London. Jeff would have liked to respond with some kind of counter-allusion but could dredge nothing up. He explained that he didn't want anything too radical, wanted it to be subtle.

'Like this?' the guy smiled.

'Like what?'

'Like mine.'

'Wow! Yes, exactly.' It was hard to believe his hair was dyed – it looked entirely natural and he still had a little grey at the temples. They moved into more detailed negotiations. It would cost a fortune but the great thing was that in ten minutes – he was lucky, the guy said, they'd just had a cancellation – Jeff was in the chair having his hair slightly cut and dyed . . . 'Discreetly, very quietly,' he thought to himself, but it was too late now to make use of this retaliatory bit of Plath: the man who'd welcomed him was evidently some kind of maitre d'; the actual dyeing was done by a young woman with multiple piercings (eyebrow, nose, a saliva-gleam of tongue stud), who preferred to work in silence. Fine by Atman. He was preoccupied, as he sat there, by the implications of coming out as a man who dyed his hair. It was the kind of thing you did if you emigrated to America, went to begin a new life in a place where no one knew your former grey-haired self – but he was reinventing himself on his home turf, in London, on Marylebone High Street. You grow older imperceptibly. Your knees begin to hurt perceptibly. They don't get better. Occasionally they get worse and then improve but they never get back to what they were before. You begin to accept that you have a bad knee. You adjust your walk to compensate and alleviate but, by doing so, you set the scene for lower-back pain. These things were complicated and sometimes impossible to fix. And now one of the symptoms of ageing – possibly not the worst, but certainly the most visible – was being dealt with, painlessly and quickly. It was as simple as that. All it took was money and a bit of time. Apart from that, you just sat under one of these Martian dryers, waiting, wondering if you should have opted for a lighter shade – or a darker one. Or just a trim.

The moment arrived, the moment of untruth. The silver foil was taken off. Jeff was tilted back over the basin. His hair was washed with almond-scented shampoo, rinsed. Flipped back into upright mode he was confronted, in the mirror, with his new hair. Wet, it looked *Thunderbirds*-black. Having it dried was like watching a Polaroid in reverse. The black gradually faded to a convincing shade of rejuvenation. It had worked! His hair was dark without looking dyed. He looked ten years younger! He was so pleased by the result that he could have spent ages gazing at himself adoringly in the mirror. It was him but not him: dark-haired him, plausibly youthful him. All in all it was the best eighty quid he'd ever spent in his life. (The only thing that could have made him happier was to have found a way to claim it back on expenses as necessary preparation and research for the Biennale.) And tomorrow he'd be on his way to Venice. Life was sweet, a lot sweeter than it had been three hours previously when he'd left the house as a way of putting off writing a stupid article – which still had to be written. If it hadn't been for that, if he didn't have to get back and write his stupid article, he'd have been tempted to drop in at the newsagent's again, to buy another Topic and see if that young Indian girl was still there.

Back home, back at his desk, the perennial question kept cropping up: how much longer could he keep doing this stuff for? For about two minutes at a time, it turned out, but eventually these two minute increments – punctuated by emails pinging in and out – mounted up. God, what a miserable way to earn a living. Back in the days when his hair was naturally this colour – or darker – it had been a thrill writing stuff like this, or at least seeing it in print was thrilling. The fact that his dyed hair had sort of rolled back the years brought home how little progress he'd made in the intervening decade and a half. Here he was, doing the same shit he'd been doing fifteen years ago. Not that that made doing it any easier; it just made it more depressing. As always he struggled to get anywhere near the required word length and then, after padding and expanding, ended up with too many words and had to expend still more energy cutting it back to the required length (which always turned out to be more than was actually published). Still, by eleven o'clock he'd finished, cracked it, done it. He celebrated with camomile tea – there were days of heavy drinking ahead – and the remains of *Newsnight*, amazed at how *grey* Paxman's hair had become.

Tomorrow he'd be on his way to Venice . . . More immediately, less sweetly, he was on his way to *Stansted*. With all the potential for cancellations and manifold failure – signals, points, engine – he'd allowed ample time for delays but, on this occasion, there were none; everything went smoothly and he got to the airport with time to spare. In this way the country's injury-prone transport system contrived to waste your time even when nothing went wrong. Ahead of him in the check-in queue was Philip Spender, a director at the Gagosian gallery, wearing his cream suit – his trademark cream suit – and expensive sunglasses perched atop his expensive haircut.

'Junket Jeff! What a non-surprise, meeting you here.'

'You too, Phil.' He was staring at Jeff's hair. 'You're looking good.'

'You too.' Spender was still looking at his hair. Jeff could see the question 'Have you dyed your hair?' bubbling away in his head unaskably at this pre-drunken hour of the day. But he *would* ask it at some point, probably at whichever time ensured maximum public embarrassment. They'd seen each other a couple of nights earlier, at Grayson Perry's opening at Victoria Miro, so the contrast between before (grey) and after (discreetly non-grey) must, in Phil's eyes, have been at its most marked and least discreet. They established where they were staying (quite near each other); parties they were going to (a lot of overlap, but Phil was going to some others as well, including an unscheduled, semi-clandestine Kraftwerk gig that Jeff had not even heard of, had no desire to go to, but which now preyed on his mind). This was it, the start of the Biennale proper: the onset of party-anxiety and invite-envy, the fear that there were better parties you'd not been invited to, a higher tier of pleasure that was forbidden to you. Once you got to Venice, this became still more acute. You could be at a tremendous party, full of fun people, surrounded by beautiful women, booze flowing, totally happy – but part of you would be in a state of torment because there was another party to which you'd not been invited. There was nothing to be done about it. Jeff was not really a player in the art world. He had a certain usefulness in terms of gaining publicity for galleries and artists but had no real value in his own right. He was the kind of person who could be bought relatively cheaply – a few glasses of prosecco, an Asian-inflected canapé – happy to be someone else's Plus One if that would get him into a party to which he would not otherwise have gained admittance. He was way down the totem pole but plenty of people were not even *on* the totem pole – and not everyone queuing up to check in was Biennale-bound. There were also families on the brink of riot, backpackers and a group of ruddy-faced Irish who looked like they'd booked tickets solely to get stuck into the duty-free.

'You know,' Phil said, as if reading his mind, 'flying has never been the same since Concorde was grounded.'

'Quite.' Where had that 'quite' come from? He'd never said it before. Must have been from reading a John le Carré novel a couple of weeks earlier. The Circus. Scalphunters. Babysitters. Quite. Perhaps Phil was a spy, working at Gagosian but secretly in the employ of White Cube. Actually, now that the idea of duplicity had entered Jeff's mind, it occurred to him that Gagosian was almost certainly having a party to which he had not been invited. What a shit Spender was, standing here chatting, all the time knowing that his gallery was having a party to which Jeff had been conspicuously uninvited. For the second time in as many minutes, Phil seemed to have read his mind.

'You're coming to our party, I hope?'

'When's that? I don't think I got an invite.'

'On Friday. You should have had one. I put your name on the list myself.' Typical: there he was thinking everyone was a total shit – an enemy agent – and it turns out they're considerate, thoughtful. The only shit was Atman himself, for being so suspicious, so ready to think the worst of everyone.

Phil clicked open his black, espionage-leather briefcase. 'There you go,' he said, handing over an invite. 'Take this one.'

'Thank you.' Jeff studied the invitation, noting the sponsor's logo – Moët, nice – and the time. Shit, it clashed exactly with the Australia party which, in turn, overlapped with a dinner he'd cancelled as soon as the Australia invite turned up. That was also part of the Biennale experience: not getting invited to things was a source of torment; getting invited to them added to the logistical difficulties of wanting to go to far more things than you had any desire to go to.

Another sign that the Venice experience had started here, at Stansted: he and Spender were both glancing over each other's shoulders, seeing who else was around. Jeff recognized several people in the various check-in queues that were in danger of merging into a single queue. Talking on her phone, rummaging in her handbag, Mary Bishop from Tate Modern spilled cigarette lighter and passport. The man next to her – Nigel Stein – bent down and picked up everything for her. Jeff waved to both of them. In fact, as he looked around, there were lots of people he knew, all looking around and waving at all the other people they knew.

In spite of its size, the queue was fast-moving. Jeff could now see, with some surprise, that the airline logo above the check-in read: 'Air Meteor: We Couldn't Give A Flying Fuck!' It was in exactly the same font, against the same yellow background, as the rest of the airline's graphics but none of the other counters boasted this interesting amendment. Moving closer he saw that this slogan had been stuck over the existing one, but so subtly and cleverly it was difficult to notice. Given how quickly it must have been done – airports, these days, were not the easiest places for guerrilla subversion or art pranks – it was extremely impressive. Maybe it had even been done by Banksy. Or perhaps, in the spirit of artistic collaboration and ironic brand-awareness enhancement, the airline had co-operated, let it go. Whatever the case, it was certainly fair comment. Airlines like Ryanair or EasyJet tried to dress up their no-frills status; Meteor basked in theirs. What you saw was what you got. More accurately, what you *didn't* get. This was budget flying taken to its limit. They had stripped away everything that made flying slightly more agreeable and what you were left with was the basically disagreeable experience of getting from A to B, even though B turned out not to be in B at all, but in the neighbouring city C, or even country D.

Spender checked in successfully. Turning back from the counter, he said he'd see Jeff on the other side, as if they were about to cross the river Styx. Jeff stepped forward, handed over his passport, answered the questions about security, said he had no bags to check in. The check-in woman asked to see his hand baggage. He held up the smaller of the two bags he was carrying and she went ahead and checked him in. Taking care to keep his other bag hidden from her, he turned away and headed towards passport control and security. With no larger aim in view, his life was made up entirely of little triumphs and successes like this. He had avoided checking in his bags, thereby saving an incalculable amount of time at the other end.

Boarding was a barely polite scramble, but such was the demand for a place near the front of the plane that Jeff succeeded in getting the ultimate prize: an exit-row seat. He stowed his bags, one of which was almost too large to get into the overhead bin, smiled at his neighbour and belted himself in for what promised to be an uncomfortable but festive couple of hours. The plane was filled with people who already knew each other, all on their way to the Biennale. It was like being on a school trip, organized by the art teacher and part-funded by a range of sympathetic breweries.

At the Biennale one entered a realm of magical excess. Champagne flowed like spring water. There were rumours that, at the Ukraine party, there would be a hundred and fifty thousand dollars' worth of caviar. Not like that here on the plane, of course. The cost-cutting was amazing, extravagant, even. No expense had not been spared. Getting rid of free meals and drinks was just the beginning of it. They'd skimped on the flight attendants' uniforms, on the design and graphics of the check-in counter, on the number of characters on the boarding pass, on the amount of foam and cushion on the seats. It was hard to imagine they had not skimped on safety features as well – why bother with a life raft when everyone knew that if the plane ditched in the sea you were fucked anyway? It seemed they had even budgeted on the looks of the flight attendants. The one doing the safety demonstration appeared to be suffering from an aerial equivalent of the bends. No amount of make-up – and there was a lot of it, caked on like the first stage in the preparation of a death mask – could disguise the toll taken by years of jetlag and cabin pressure.

As far as this particular flight was concerned, though, all went according to plan. The plane accelerated, succeeded in taking off, levelled out at the budget cruising altitude and, unless something catastrophic occurred, would land in Venice (or thereabouts) in less than two hours. Even a frequent flyer, hardened complainer and upgrade-seeker like Atman had to concede that, for a mere two hours, conditions on board were tolerable. He bought a Coke and a small tube of Pringles – 'Could I have a receipt, please?' – and began reading the press material biked over yesterday about Julia Berman, Steven Morison and their daughter, Niki.

Pretty standard stuff, really. They'd had an affair, she became pregnant, raised the kid on her own. Morison had pitched in with some money but continued his life as a globally successful artist, painting his pictures and porking whichever model or studio assistant took his fancy, the most recent of whom was only a couple of years older than his daughter, who was twenty-two and had her first record coming out (with cover art by her famous dad). Niki had

already been interviewed by *Vogue* but a 'rare' interview with
the 'reclusive' mum and a never-before-seen picture constituted some kind of scoop. All of this had to be arranged in
person, by Jeff, because, rather quaintly, Julia Berman didn't
do email. (As Max Grayson, his editor at *Kulchur*, had said,
'You're there anyway and it's such a simple assignment even
you can't fuck it up.') She was in her mid-fifties now; there
were rumours – and had been for years – of a forthcoming,
unghosted memoir. Jeff was to find out about that as well,
if possible.

In her day Julia had been famously beautiful, a sex symbol,
as they used to say. A nostalgic glamour still attached to her
even though there's actually nothing more tragic than these
old howlers having to trade on looks that have given way years
ago. Jeff had interviewed another of these crumbling beauties,
on stage, as part of the Brighton Festival. What a fright!
Smoking cigarettes, working through her gravel-voiced reper-
toire of classic anecdotes – the night she was on acid when
Hendrix puked in her fireplace!; the time she asked George
Best what he did for a living! – while the audience listened
politely, united by a single unspoken thought: ugh! She didn't
even have a memoir to promote. All she was publicizing was
the astonishing fact of her continued existence. Pathetic. So
what did that make Atman? Infinitely more pathetic, obviously, since his job was to provide cue lines for her greatest
anecdotes, a gig for which he received travelling expenses and
four complimentary drinks tickets. However much he despised
other people, when he did the math and added things up,
Atman always found himself more despicable still. Especially
since he'd asked if he could interview another of the guests at
the festival, Lorrie Moore, a writer he'd never met but whose
work he loved – and was told that, unfortunately, that slot
was already taken by someone else. The lesson was that he

was good for tittle-tattle but unsuited for anything serious; more *FHM* than *TLS*. As often happened the act of reading had sent him off on an inner rumble of discontent. He flicked further through the press cuttings and lingered on pictures of Julia taken by – he had to check the caption – none other than David Bailey. No doubt about it, she had been sensationally gorgeous. Slinky as a panther, with outsize purple bangles round her wrists and what used to be called bedroom eyes. No one had bedroom eyes any more (the phrase was almost as obsolete as 'a well-turned ankle'); they'd been rendered obsolete by the bedroom asses and bedroom thongs of the *Loaded* and internet era. Jeff had no idea what she looked like now. She had not been photographed for years – hence the last and most despicable part of his assignment: he was meant somehow to sneak an intimate picture of her. So, on top of everything else, he was supposed to be a pap without the advantages of a telephoto lens, just his own little digital camera with its 4x optical zoom. The biggest joke of all – the thing that made him more depressed than anything – was that at a certain level he was considered successful. People envied his getting assignments like this. One of the people who envied his getting assignments like these was Jeff. He bitched and griped but he would have bitched and griped even more if he'd heard that some other hack had got this junket instead. The writing – a so-called 'colour piece' – was a bore, going to see this old has-been in her rented palazzo was a drag, but Venice for the Biennale – that was fun, that was unmissable.

He crammed the cuttings back into his folder, read more of *Venice Observed,* dozed, and was woken by the captain announcing that they were about to begin their descent into Venice Treviso. Nothing very noteworthy about that; but when he went on to announce the temperature in Venice – thirty-six degrees – a gasp of astonishment swept through the plane.

Thirty-six degrees, that was – what? – ninety-five degrees Fahrenheit? That was *hot*!

Everyone assumed some kind of mistake had been made but as soon as they stepped onto the vibrating ladder down to the tarmac they realized how mistaken they'd been. It was like arriving in Jamaica in the middle of a heatwave. The heat immediately generated a kind of hysteria – a mixture of happiness and dread – among the British passengers. This was not what they had counted on. Some people on the plane must have received texts or calls from friends who'd arrived earlier, saying it was hot but this was . . . Jesus, this was *hot*! The heat bounced off the tarmac. The air was rippling and roasting. It was difficult to imagine anywhere hotter on earth. Cairo couldn't have been as hot as this.

As expected, Venice Treviso was nowhere near Venice – which made Jeff even more pleased to be one of the first people through immigration. He was ahead of the game, had stolen a march, was ready to go. Except getting his bags onto the plane turned out to have been a completely pointless bit of cunning. There was a bus waiting outside but it had been chartered specifically for their flight and would not depart until everyone had picked up their bags, cleared customs and boarded. He ended up spending a sweat-soaked hour pacing an arrivals lounge the size of a converted garden shed and the temperature of a sauna, before the bus, crammed with Biennale-goers, was ready to begin its crawl towards the city the plane had, nominally, flown into. Jeff was sat next to a red-haired woman he recognized but whose name he couldn't quite remember, a curator from the Barbican, who prodded her Blackberry for the entire length of the journey. For reasons that were unclear even to him Jeff did not own a mobile phone, let alone a Blackberry – which meant that he spent increasing chunks of his life in a state of suspended non-existence while other people took calls, checked messages and sent texts. It was impossible to read on the coach and there was nothing to see from the window. He had been longing for the flight to be over; now he was longing for the bus ride to be over. At what point would the longing for things to be over be over so that he could reside squarely in the present?

Not, it turned out, when the bus journey ended because he then had to struggle through the coach-crowded bus terminal, with his bags, in the baking heat. It was like being in the Italian version of an oily, hugely demoralizing art installation called *This Vehicle is Reversing*. Once he got on a vaporetto at Piazzale Roma, though, he was in Venice proper. What fun it was, going everywhere by boat – even though the boat turned out to be as crowded as a rush-hour Tube in London. The difference was that this Tube was chugging down the Grand Canal, through the miracle of Venice at dusk! Venice in the grip of an insane heatwave! Venice the city that never disappointed and never surprised, the place that was exactly like it was meant to be (just hotter), exactly synonymous with every tourist's first impression of it. There was no real Venice: the real Venice was – and had always been – the Venice of postcards, photographs and films. Hardly a novel observation, that. It was what everyone always said, including Mary McCarthy. Except she'd taken it a stage further and said that the thing about Venice was that it was impossible to say anything about Venice that had not been said before, '*including this statement*'. Still, there was always the shock that such a place did actually exist, not just in books and pictures, but in real life, with all the accoutrements of Venice-ness crammed together: canals, palazzos, gondoliers, vaporetti and everything. A city built on water. What an impractical but wonderful idea. Jeff had read several accounts of how the city came to be built but it still didn't make sense. Better to think that it just appeared like this, fully formed and hundreds of years old in the instant it was founded.

It was almost dark by the time he squeezed out of the vaporetto at Salute, the stop for his hotel (a five-minute walk, he'd been told) which turned out to be nowhere near the hotel – or at least the hotel, if it was nearby, was completely unfindable from this stop. If it hadn't been for the heat and the weight of the bags and a steadily mounting pressure in his bladder it would have been nice strolling around the neighbourhood, but the heat and the bags stopped it being a nice stroll and turned it into an exhausting yomp in a hundred-degree heat. Losing his bearings in the labyrinth of alleys, narrow waterways, bridges and little squares that all looked so much like each other, the five-minute walk took twenty minutes. The hotel, when he finally stumbled on it, was nowhere near where it was supposed to be and, at the same time, exactly where it was meant to be. Jeff produced his passport while the desk-clerk remarked on the incredible eat – eat that the bell-hop sought to counter by bringing, on a glinting silver tray, a glass of water so cold it made his teeth ache like metal.

What a relief to finally get into his pleasingly over-priced room (booked and paid for by *Kulchur* magazine). It was on the top floor and had a view of sorts – not of the lagoon or the Grand Canal, but of the roofs of buildings like the one he was looking out from. What a relief, too, that it was decorated in minimalist, boutique fashion – white sheets, blonde wood – not decked out in the rococo style of most Venetian rooms. *What a relief!* It was one of those phrases that buzzed around his head constantly, phrases that in music would have constituted the themes or motifs that wove in and out of a symphony, fading, disappearing for long intervals, but always eventually returning.

In the way of boutique hotels – and was there a decent

hotel in the world that did not designate itself boutique? – various books had been arranged in aesthetically-pleasing spots around the room. Naturally, they were all about Venice. The room was nicely air-conditioned, not something that he normally needed or used, but in these circumstances some kind of respite from the killing heat – the eat, as he now thought of it – was essential. Unfortunately, he was late for the dinner he was supposed to go to. It had been organized by *Modern Painters* magazine and though it was usually a good idea to avoid these big sit-down dinners – they ate into one's evenings – this had seemed a perfect way of easing into the Biennale. Well, nothing to be done about that. If he went now he'd only be in time for dessert and would be unable to make the quick getaway he was counting on in order to go to the Iceland party (a much sought-after invite: Björk was going to be there, might even be DJing) near the Campo Manin. He called the editor on her cellphone, left a message, apologized, blamed the plane, the bus, the time difference. He stripped, showered, put on a fresh shirt, underwear and socks, left the hotel and ate quickly on his own – dreary salad, bread that might once have been fresh, home-made ravioli – at the trattoria a couple of doors away.

The concierge had assured him that if he took a vaporetto one stop, across the Canal to Santa Maria di Giglio, Campo Manin would be only a short walk after that. And, amazingly, he was right. Jeff found the palazzo easily, arrived at the perfect time, just as the party was filling up. There was the thump of decent-sounding music from inside but, with temperatures still in the eighties, everyone was outside in the courtyard. He took a bellini from a waiter – his first of the Biennale, the first, in all probability, of very many – and drained it in a couple of gulps. Always awkward, arriving at these big parties, before you see people you know, so he traded the empty glass for a full one, the last of its kind on the tray. He'd almost guzzled that as well when he spotted Jessica Marchant, wearing a kind of Bridget Riley Op Art blouse. They clinked glasses. Jeff complimented her on the blouse and congratulated her on the novel she'd published a couple of months previously. Half the people Jeff knew had written books, most of which he'd not even attempted to read. The majority of the ones he *had* started he'd not had the patience to finish but he'd whizzed through Jessica's in a state of constantly increasing admiration. It seemed a good omen, that the first person he'd encountered in Venice was someone on whom he could lavish praise. The problem was that doing so made Jessica look so distinctly uncomfortable – had he been too fawning? – that she immediately turned the tables, asking him about his long-awaited book.

'I was hoping everyone had forgotten about that. Including the publishers. I just never did it.' This was every bit as honest as his admiration for Jessica. Write journalism for long enough and a publisher will eventually suspect that some article that you've written contains the seed of a possible book. A letter forwarded by *Esquire* had led to a phone call, which had led to a lunch, which had led to a contract to write a book on . . . He pushed the thought from his mind. Even back then he'd had no desire to write such a book but had hoped that the contract and advance – minuscule though it was – would impel him to do so. And it had. For about a month. There then followed six months of fretting before he more or less abandoned the book and went back to writing nonsense for magazines. When he heard that his editor was leaving, Jeff congratulated himself on having, effectively, gained a small amount of money for nothing. Except for a brief call from his editor's replacement, no one at the publishers seemed to expect anything from him. And he'd not even had to pay back the advance. Perfect. The only mistake he'd made, in that first flush of enthusiasm, was to tell people he was doing the book. Hence the current conversation. He explained that he had given up, abandoned it.

'I don't blame you,' Jessica said. 'It's hell writing a book.' So many people ended up, inadvertently or deliberately, making you feel bad about yourself (many people thought Jeff was one of those people) but Jessica always made you feel OK, normal. It was as if she had put her arm round him and said that they were in the same boat.

'It really is, isn't it?' he said. 'I don't know why everyone seems to be doing it. But what about you and here? Are you writing about the Biennale for someone?'

'For *Vogue*,' she said. Well, that was one of the reasons for writing books. You got offered gigs like this. As happened, Jeff's admiration immediately became tinged with jealousy even though, aside from a few details – accommodation, fee, and the nature of the article – they were here for the same purpose, were having the same experience. That was the thing about the Biennale: it was a definitive experience, absolutely fixed, subject only to insignificant individual variation. You came to Venice, you saw a ton of art, you went to parties, you drank up a storm, you talked bollocks for hours on end and went back to London with a cumulative hangover, liver damage, a notebook almost devoid of notes and the first tingle of a cold sore.

They were joined by David Kaiser, a film-maker (i.e. someone who made telly programmes), and Mike Adams, an editor at *Frieze*. Jessica knew them both too. The Kaiser was just back from Saudi Arabia, 'a truly vile country, worth visiting if only to have an experience of unsurpassable vileness'. The experience of going without alcohol for a week had had a profound effect on him.

'It was like being in the desert and seeing a mirage,' he said. 'Every few seconds, whatever I was doing, whoever I was talking to, I'd zone out. All I could see was a pint of beer. The climate is very conducive to drinking, obviously, and you can't do it.' Mike and Jeff shook their heads in disgust, nodded in sympathy. This was a story, evidently, with a strong human-interest angle, even though it wasn't the main point of the story. The main point of the story was how the Kaiser had discovered he was a Muslim. 'I was confronted by a member of the police or the committee to promote virtue. He didn't say anything, no "*Salaam ali Kuhn*" or anything like that, just "Have you read the Qu'ran?" I said, "Yes, I have." He said, "Did you read it properly?" I said I thought I had, yes. He said, "Then you are a Muslim. Good." End of conversation. Implacable logic.'

'And all the time he's speaking to you,' said Mike, 'all you're thinking about and seeing is this big, chilled Heineken in a frosted glass, right?'

'Not necessarily a Heineken. Sometimes a Budvar.'

'But always a lager? Never a real ale?'

'It was too hot for real ale. But let's not get bogged down in specifics,' he said. 'There's a larger point here.'

'I thought we were already in receipt of the lager point,' Jeff quipped. 'How much bigger can this story get?'

'The point is that it took this trip to Saudi to make me realize that, all things considered, for the last thirty years, I have loved beer, if not more intensely then certainly more constantly, than anything else in my life.'

The Kaiser was forty-six so that sounded about right. There was no opportunity to dwell on this expression of faith, however. In accordance with the laws of social physics the group of four had begun to draw others into its conversational orbit: Melanie Richardson from the ICA, Nathalie

Porter who worked at *Art Review*, and Scott Thomson, whom Jeff had known, off and on, for more than a decade. During that time, while other people changed jobs and advanced their careers, Scott had continued working at the same undemanding job (interrupted by lengthy periods spent travelling) as a sub at the *Observer*. That was how he earned his living but his true vocation was to be a perpetual convert, every few years embracing a new enthusiasm so wholeheartedly that it completely cancelled out whatever he'd previously set so much store by. His latest craze, though, was the same one he'd been evangelizing eight months ago: Burning Man, the big freak-out in the Nevada desert. He'd been for the first time a couple of years ago and was going again in August. It was, he said now, 'a life-changing experience'. Scott had said exactly the same thing the last time Jeff had seen him, at a party for the Frieze Art Fair, and he was happy to take his word for it. Not Mike, though.

'In my experience,' he said, 'the thing about life-changing experiences is that they wear off surprisingly quickly so that after a few weeks you emerge from them pretty much unchanged. Nine times out of ten, in fact, it's precisely the life-changing experience that enables you to come to terms with the *un*changingness of your own life. That's why those novels are so popular, you know, the ones that culminate in a day or an event that will "change all of their lives forever". It's a fiction.'

'God, *you* don't change, do you, dude? Cynical as ever.' Credit where it's due: Scott (who was always calling people 'dude') had not taken offence; in fact, he was laughing as he said this whereas Mike, while not being aggressive exactly, had spoken somewhat severely.

The slight tension generated by this exchange was broken by a guy in a blue linen jacket, who backed into Jeff, spilling his drink. He half-turned round and Jeff instinctively apologized. No self-restraint was required; this was how the aggressive impulse manifested itself. In its way it was a triumph of evolution, of cultivation. Jeff's frustration simmered constantly; confronted with a recalcitrant piece of equipment – a frozen computer, a jammed printer – it boiled over, but in social situations it always transmuted itself, without effort, into its smiling opposite.

Someone tapped him on the shoulder: Jeff recognized him instantly, actually knew him quite well, but his name, for the moment, escaped him. Like a witness scrutinizing a police photo-fit of a suspect, Jeff registered the details of his appearance – broad nose, short brown hair, white shirt emphasizing tanned complexion – but they refused to add up to a name, an identity. Jessica and Melanie were talking to a guy in a blue Bob Marley T-shirt and pale jeans. Mike and the Kaiser had wandered off. The original little group, having acquired a gravitational mass, was dispersing, fragmenting into new groups. Ah, this was Venice, this was a party ... A party where there were a lot of nice-looking women, all decked out in their Missoni and Prada dresses.

'Plenty of nice-looking women here,' said ... What the fuck *was* his name? Before Jeff had started racking his brains, trying to dredge up his name, he'd been thinking exactly the same thing but, said aloud, this completely accurate observation took on a surprisingly coarse quality. It suggested that your life was spent in a woman-less pub, empty except for a few men gazing forlornly into their pints of aptly-named bitter. Blotting out this image, Jeff took a sip of his womanly bellini.

'There really are,' he said as they stood there, bellinis in hand, looking. Of course it was nice, being at a party full of nice-looking women, but the real value of this situation – a party full of nice-looking women – was that it meant there would be one woman who was stunningly gorgeous, who was radiant in a way that only one man in the party – Jeff, hopefully – could properly appreciate. And so it proved.

It was her hair he noticed first: shadow-dark, falling to just below her shoulders. She had her back to him. She was tall. She was wearing a pale yellow dress, sleeveless. Her arms were thin, tanned. She was talking to a shaven-headed man in a striped shirt. The guy whose name Jeff still couldn't remember was talking about an artist he'd not heard of who did these drawings of trees that took forever to do and looked exactly like photographs – that was the *point* – even though they were drawings. Jeff nodded but all his attention was focused on the dark-haired woman in the yellow dress. She was still facing away, still chatting to the shaven-headed guy in the striped shirt, but he knew that when she turned round she would be beautiful. There was so little doubt that he was not even impatient to have this prediction verified. All he had to do was stand and wait. So he stood there, glass in hand. The shaven-headed guy was laughing at something another shaven-headed guy had said. A woman came up to her and touched her on the shoulder. She turned round, smiling when she recognized her friend, whom she kissed on the cheek. Without being able to make out the details of her face, Jeff knew that he had been right. As she stood chatting with her friend he saw her dark eyes and pronounced cheekbones. Her hair, parted in the middle, was almost straight. To the impartial onlooker her face may have appeared too bony, slightly equine; that was it, the flaw that clinched it for him, the flaw that was not a flaw. He was no longer listening to what was being said, just standing there gawping. He tore his gaze away from her, focusing again on his companion, who was no longer talking about the photographs that looked liked drawings of trees or whatever it was. It occurred to Jeff that he had entered

31

the *vague* phase of his life. He had a vague idea of things, a vague sense of what was happening in the world, a vague sense of having met someone before. It was like being vaguely drunk all the time. The only thing he was not vague about was the woman in the yellow dress, who – he glanced over at her again – was still chatting with her friend. The guy with the maddeningly elusive name was still speaking. Jeff was listening, trying to listen, but he was also calculating how he might introduce himself to the woman in the yellow dress, who, when he looked back to where she had been standing, was nowhere to be seen. The reason for this calamity that was not a calamity was that she and her friend had come over, were saying hello to Frank. Frank! That was his name, Frank Delaney. Of course it was. The woman he *wanted to meet* had just come over and revealed the identity of the person whose name he *wanted to remember*. What was happening? Was this a day when he could not make a false move, when he only had to think of something to cause it to happen? This was the kind of luck that drove people mad, convinced them that God was telling them to do terrible things, to assassinate presidents or celebrities.

It was now just a matter of time. Jeff had only to stand there, smiling, holding his empty bellini glass and, in seconds – assuming Frank could remember *his* name – he would be introduced to the person in the room he most wanted to meet. Up close he could see that the yellow dress had a faint pattern. She was wearing no make-up – or at least had applied it so skilfully that it was invisible – and a thin silvery necklace. He guessed that she was in her early thirties. Her eyes – laughing at something Frank was saying – were brown. Frank made the introductions. Her name was Laura, Laura Freeman. He shook her hand, her thin hand. On her middle finger was a large yellow ring, made of perspex. Her friend was called something that, in his excited state, Jeff forgot the moment it was said. Anxious to make a good impression, he focused his attention on this friend while Laura talked to Frank. How was she enjoying Venice? Where was she from? He asked the questions but was incapable of listening to the answers or of preventing his gaze straying back to Laura, who glanced in his direction, once, while he was looking at her. When Frank said something to the friend, Jeff seized the opportunity to address his first remark to Laura. It didn't matter what this remark was. It could be ditchwater dull. The important thing was to say something, anything, to get the ball rolling. He looked at her but there was only one thing to say. If he said anything else it would be a lie, and since he couldn't say what he wanted to say – you're beautiful and unless you have a voice like David Beckham's, I'm going to be in love with you in less than a minute – he said nothing. She was waiting for him to speak and he just looked at her. She was tall, five-ten, maybe. A couple of inches shorter than Jeff. Beneath the thin strap of her yellow dress he could see the white strap of her bra. She had small breasts. A voice in his head was saying, *Act normal, act normal, say something* normal. *Don't act like a nutter.* She came to his rescue.

'So, when did you get here, to Venice?' He watched her form the words. It was the most normal question in the world and, although it didn't break the spell, it at least enabled him to function normally again.

'Just now, a couple of hours ago. How about you?'

'Yesterday.' She was American.

'Where are you from?' He was speaking. They were having *a conversation.* This was how it was done: she said something and he said something back. It was easy.

'Los Angeles,' she said. He wanted to say *I'll move there tomorrow,* but managed to ask if this was her first Biennale.

'Second. I came last year. Two years ago.' He nodded enthusiastically. Two years ago. It was amazing that a simple statement of fact could be so magical, so *interesting*. 'How about you?'

'I was here once before, four years ago.' As far as Jeff was concerned, this was just about the most fascinating conversation he'd ever had, but it could not go on like this. At some point he would have to break out of the loop of pleasantries. She looked at him as if she were waiting, possibly for him to say something interesting, and if that did not happen then she would be waiting to find a way of extricating herself from this non-conversation. Without thinking he said, 'I love your dress.'

The effect was, simultaneously, to relieve the pressure in his head and – since this remark carried a suggestion of sexual appreciation, was so close to a declaration of love for the person inside it – to drastically increase it.

'Thank you,' she said. Jeff realized that she was fully aware of the effect she was having on him. Instead of further inhibiting him, it enabled him to relax.

'It's a great dress,' he said. 'But, frankly, it wouldn't be anything without the shoulders. And most importantly of all . . .' She raised her eyebrows enquiringly, uncertainly. To have said 'breasts' would have been so crude as to have destroyed whatever vibe may have been germinating between them but, though his head routinely swarmed with crudity, he had never intended to say anything other than what he did say: 'The collarbones.'

She was visibly relieved – he wasn't a complete jerk! – and flattered.

'Well, thank you again.' He had spoken honestly. Her shoulders were not wide; they were bony but strong-looking.

'I suppose I should return the compliment.'

'Please. Don't feel you have to.'

'No. I want to. I really do.'

34

'OK. Maybe the shirt.' He held out his arms, a gesture that was part display and part shrug.

'It *is* a nice shirt.'

'Thank you. Look, I know I had to drag that out of you but, well, it's my favourite shirt. I feel it's so . . .'

'Blue?'

'No.'

'Wrinkled?'

'No. Though I admit I could have folded and packed it more carefully. No, the word I was looking for was "manly". Sorry, I shouldn't have said it. You were right on the brink of getting it anyway.'

'Was I? I thought I was going to say "cheap-looking".'

'A synonym of manly. Whereas your dress is expensive-looking.'

'Which is a synonym of . . .?'

'Exactly.' Wow, he was really in the swing of things now. There was no trace of that earlier paralysis. If anything, he was feeling too full of himself.

'Fifty dollars from a thrift store,' she said.

'Really? It looks like it cost, I dunno, twice that.' A waiter came by. 'Would you like a bellini?' Jeff asked, gallantly. They took one each, depositing their empty glasses on the waiting tray. These opening exchanges out of the way, they talked Biennale logistics, where they were staying, and for how long (she was leaving on Sunday). It gave Jeff the chance to look at her more closely, to note the mole high up on her cheek, her earrings (small, gold), her full lips. Frank and Laura's friend turned back towards them.

'We're going over to see if Bruce Nauman will grant us an audience. Will you come too?' Frank had addressed both of them. Under normal circumstances Jeff would have jumped at the chance to suck up to such a big-hitting artist but now – even though he forced himself to say nothing – every molecule of his being was screaming *We'll stay here, Frank, thank you.*

'We'll stay here,' said Laura.

'See you back here,' said her friend.

'What was your friend's name?' asked Jeff, watching her follow Frank.

'Yvonne.'

'Yvonne, that's right. Of course.' He was so relieved to have gained this time alone with Laura that he was unsure what to say, eager to lure the conversation back in the direction of her dress and his shirt, metonyms – if that was the word – of manliness and womanliness. Instead, rather dully, he asked what she did.

'I work in a gallery.' The impulse he'd had earlier, to move to LA, reasserted itself. What did this say about his life, his situation, that he could be so ready, at the drop of a hat, to chuck everything in? Probably that the 'everything' was in fact nothing.

'What about you? What do you do?'

'Journalist. I'm freelance. If it was a proper job, I'd pack it in and do something else, but freelancing *is* the something else that you do after you've packed in your job so my options are kind of limited. It's that or retirement – from which it is at times pretty much indistinguishable.'

'Actually, I *am* quitting my job. Though the gallery doesn't know it yet.'

'What happens then?'

'I'm going travelling. I'm doing what kids do when they're twenty. It's just that I'll be doing it more than ten years too late.' So, he'd been right, she was thirty-one or thirty-two maybe. Nothing was escaping him tonight. He hadn't been as sharp – as *un*vague – as this in years.

36

'Where are you going?'

'Oh, you know. The places everyone goes. South-East Asia. India.'

What was wrong with him? Minutes after contemplating moving to LA he was ready, now, to go backpacking through Vietnam, Cambodia and Thailand. Lacking any larger ambition or purpose meant that you clutched at whatever straws came your way. If she'd said she was thinking of moving to Romania, he'd have signed up for that too. Or Mars, even.

He said, 'Have you been to India before?'

'Once. To Goa and Kerala. This time I want to go to Rajasthan and Varanasi, Benares.'

'They're the same place, right?'

'Exactly.'

'From the Sanskrit, isn't it? *Nasi*, place. *Vara*, many. Place of many names.'

She laughed. She had perfect teeth, quite large: American teeth. 'I have absolutely no idea whether that is extremely impressive or complete *Ben* as in bull, *Ares* as in shit. Which means it's probably both.'

They clinked glasses. He watched her lips touch the rim of her glass, watched her drink. No smudge of pink was left on the glass; she was not wearing lipstick. He took a gulp from his own glass. The act of drinking served as a reminder of the heat from which it was intended to bring relief.

'My God,' she said. 'Is it ever hot!' She pressed the glass to her head. He could see her armpit, shaved. The glass left a few beads of moisture on her forehead.

'Tomorrow will be even hotter, apparently.' He had nothing particularly in mind by this meteorological observation, but it carried the vague suggestion of less clothes, shedding layers, sweat. Underwear, nakedness. Heat. 'Actually I got that wrong. The people at my hotel don't call it heat. It's eat. And tomorrow it's going to get otter.'

'The eat will be otter?'

'Exactly.'

'Really? I feel like the whole place could just, like, evaporate overnight.' Such a thing seemed quite possible. It was easy to imagine waking up to find the once-watery city stranded and stilted in foul-smelling mud, the lagoon turned into an expanse of nothingness, a moist brown desert in which the last few fishes flapped and gasped. On the positive side it would be an opportunity to give the canals a scrub and do much-needed repair work on the foundations. Surprising, in a way, that something along those lines had not been proposed as an art project, like a Christo wrap. Assuming it was temporary and reversible, it would probably turn out to be a tourist attraction.

Laura was saying, 'Nice to write, though . . .'

'Oh, it's not proper writing. It's just . . .' He shrugged, paused, wondering if, with all the words of the English language available, there was a way of completing the sentence without recourse to the one that sprang immediately to mind. But there wasn't.

'Bollocks,' he said at last. In the long interval of expectation the word doubled both as a description of his work and an exclamation of resignation to the fact that he had been unable to dredge up an alternative.

'Ah, bollocks,' she laughed. 'The very essence of the English.'

'You're right. You have freedom and the pursuit of happiness. We have . . . bollocks to it.'

'You're writing about the Biennale ?'

'Yes. Plus, you know that singer Niki Morison?'

'Steven Morison's daughter, the artist?'

'And of Julia Berman, the mum, who is here at the moment.

I have to interview her and get her to hand over this picture of her by Morison. A drawing. The editor of the magazine I'm writing for is obsessed by this picture even though he hasn't seen it.'

'What's so special about it?'

'No idea.' Jeff could think of nothing else to say. The absurdity of his job, of the stuff he wrote, extended its reach to taint any words he might use now. Again, she came to his rescue.

'But you write mainly about art?'

'Not really. I'm not a very visual person.' That was it – his best shot. He'd come up with this line before coming to Venice, had decided it was going to be his big joke of the Biennale, to be repeated at every opportunity. What he hadn't counted on was being able to try it out, for the first time, in such perfect circumstances, to such devastating effect.

'Me neither,' she said. Oh, no. She was perfectly serious, she *meant* it, hadn't realized he was joking. She was an earnest Californian. His disappointment must have been obvious – maybe he had even been silently mouthing the words to himself – because she punched him on the arm.

'Joking,' she said. Shit! He'd been out-deadpanned. She'd taken his best shot, thrown it right back at him.

'Sorry. Like I said, I only just got here. I'm a bit off the pace still.'

'OK. Let's backtrack. You write about art?'

'Sometimes. Celebrities. Interviews. Profiles. Features. The usual—'

'Bollocks?'

'Got it in one. Have you spent time in England?'

'London. Stratford. *The Tempest*. Oxford. The Cotswolds. Portobello Road. Hoxton. I did it in a day and a half.'

'Well, I guess you saw pretty well everything. It's a small country.'

'Difficult to get around, though.'

'Foolish even to try. Especially on a Sunday. Did you come across the words "engineering works" and "bus replacement service"?'

'I flew into Stansted from Pisa on a Sunday. They said we should take the Stansted Express train. They sold tickets on the plane – even though there was no train. The train was actually a bus. It cost a fortune—'

'And took forever. Welcome to England.'

In terms of what had been said, nothing much had passed between them, but these few words had carried an enormous weight of expectation. It was just a fluke, just luck, but the air between them was charged. She was beautiful, anyone could see that, but perhaps he was the only person here who could have felt that beauty as *a force*. He desired her – not sexually, not yet; that was too specific, would have diminished the scale of his longing – and he would not have done so were the feeling not reciprocated at some level. He could take no credit for this. It just happened. They could have met anywhere, anywhere in Venice in the course of this weekend, or anywhere else in the world in the years to come, and the result would have been the same. They could have said anything and nothing would have changed. Everything would have turned out the same.

Frank and Yvonne came back over, accompanied by a guy called Louis something. They were all amped up from meeting Bruce Nauman but the party was winding down. There was talk about what to do next. Everyone was enthusiastic about going somewhere else. Except Laura. Jeff was surprised to hear her say that she was tired, was going back to her hotel. He wondered if this was a strategic move to get away from the group and back to her hotel – with him – but, evidently, she had nothing of the sort in mind. She wanted to go back to her hotel. As they prepared to leave he was able to say, unheard by anyone else, 'I'd love to see you again.'

'Me too.'

'Shall I phone you? At your hotel?' She shook her head. Because of the pause in the middle of his question, he was not sure whether this shake of the head meant *No, not at the hotel, call me on my cellphone*; or *No, don't* phone *me at my hotel* (with the possible implication *Come visit me there instead*); or even – though this seemed a remote possibility – *Don't contact me in any way, ever.*

'Would you like to meet somewhere?' he said. 'Or perhaps I could call for you at your hotel? Where are you staying?' These three questions came tumbling out one after another, but really they were all the same question. He hoped he didn't sound desperate, but such a possibility was not out of – in fact, was probably implicit in – the question.

'None of the above.'

'Really?' So he'd got it completely wrong. There'd been no energy passing between them. It had all been coming from him, in such abundance that it bounced back and was now running down his face, like egg, or ego.

'But I hope we do see each other again.'

'OK, I admit it. I'm baffled.'

'I hope we see each other again this week. In Venice. But it's nice, don't you think, to introduce an element of chance into things?'

'That depends on whether I run into you again or not.'

'Well, I think you will. There are lots of parties.'

'So many that we might be going to different ones. Which ones are you thinking of going to? Just out of interest.' She didn't say anything, but the way she looked at him meant that it was Jeff's turn to speak again. 'I hope I do see you again.'

'Me too,' she said. Unsure what else to do, he just stood there. 'You see,' she continued, 'if there's no chance, then there's no . . . Well, let's put it like this, if we meet again it will seem nice, romantic, even. Don't you think?'

'Yes. But, you see, I'm English so I go into this with a different mindset. I assume that we'll miss each other – bollocks! – and I'll spend the rest of my life wondering what would have happened if we hadn't.'

'That's even more romantic.'

'But a lot less fun. And at a certain point romance turns to tragedy.'

'How's your memory?'

'Not that great, to be honest. Why?'

'Because, earlier on, I did actually mention where I was staying.'

'Did you?'

'Yes.'

'Did I say "tragedy"? I meant farce.' He racked his brains. 'You know I've got absolutely no recollection of that.' Had she really mentioned it? 'Why don't you just whisper it again now, in passing? I'm almost certain to forget.'

'If I tell you where I'm staying, you'll be hanging round there all the time.'

'No, I won't.'

'You will. I'll step out of reception and there you'll be: "What a coincidence, just passing by . . ." It's just that you'll have been passing by for the last two hours.'

'You really think I'm that interested?'

'I really think you're that kind of person.'

'You're right. That's exactly the kind of person I am.'

'Cunning?'

'Desperate.' A particularly clever remark that one; by saying the word he cleared himself of the charge.

She leaned forward, kissed him on the mouth. He could not remember the last time a simple kiss, in public, fully clothed, had been so saturated with longing. But whose? And for what? Impossible to say. He thought, for a moment, that she might change her mind and invite him back to her room after all, but the purpose of the kiss was to confirm that she was leaving.

'And you're really not going to tell me where you're staying?'

She shrugged. There was nothing to do except watch her leave. Dark hair falling to her shoulders. Bare arms. Her back, her ass, her legs, her ankles, her cute white sandals.

The vacuum left by the vast, unrealized promise of this encounter meant that his gathering excitement turned immediately to anxiety. He replayed bits of their meeting – odd words, moments, glimpses – but lacked the concentration to turn them into anything other than a source of torment. A single word started beating like a tattoo in his head: shit, shit, shit. But – shit! – he shouldn't have been thinking like that. He was happy, he had that animating – i.e. anxiety-inducing – sense that it was occasions like this that made life worth living. The immediate solution was to walk to the bar and grab another bellini. One of the very last on offer, it turned out. A few moments later the waiters stopped serving. He saw Dave Glanding, went across and laid his hand on his shoulder. He'd known Dave for almost twenty years. Technically, this made him one of Jeff's oldest friends. And he was, at least in the sense that Cyril Connolly had in mind when he said that old friends are all but indistinguishable from enemies. Dave was part of another loose group of people going to Haig's Bar. Phil Spender, still in the trademark cream suit he'd been wearing at Stansted, was coming. So was the Kaiser. Melanie too, with other people from the ICA. There was an interval of milling around while everyone waited for everyone else, then they all trooped out of the party, drunk, full of the excitement of the first night of the Biennale.

Because of the heat and the mass of people, everyone at Haig's Bar had spilled out onto the piazza, as far as the Gritti and the Grand Canal at one end and, at the other, the gleaming white façade of Santa Maria del Giglio. The Kaiser went inside and bought a round of drinks, beer mainly. Jeff was surrounded, now, entirely by people from London, many of whom he saw at art openings and book launches: home from home, Soho in a Renaissance setting with a heatwave thrown in. Lots of women in nice dresses too, but without this one woman in her yellow dress the night was abruptly devoid of promise. How quickly the world got narrowed down to one person, to one woman. Even the most inveterate womanizer must have succumbed to periodic pangs of monogamy. He was happy here, he was having fun, but, having met Laura, he also had a gnawing sense of lack, had to keep reminding himself to tune back into the conversations that were bubbling all around.

Jane Felling came over and joined the group. She and Jeff had slept together a couple of times, years ago. They'd never officially gone out together, which meant that they had never split up either. She was here with her new boyfriend so Jeff had to suppress his tendency, when drunk, to flirt somewhat crudely with her. Or maybe not, since she started flirting with him.

'You're looking extremely handsome tonight, Jeff,' she said, kissing him on the lips.

'So are you, Jane. Pretty, I mean.'

'Your hair looks different.'

'I'll be honest. I had it dyed.'

'It suits you and it's very subtle. I knew something had happened, but couldn't work out what.'

It was surprising how little impact having sex with someone could have on your relationship with them. Or at least it was surprising how something that usually defines a relationship can sometimes make so little impact, leave almost no trace, become just another part of the rough and tumble of metropolitan life. Jane was reminiscing, too, with Phil and the Kaiser, about the circumstances of her first 'date' with Jeff.

'If you could dignify it with that word,' she said, putting her arm through his. 'We went to . . . Actually where did we go? I can't remember.'

'The French House.'

'That's right. Anyway, we had this lovely dinner. He was charming and witty and I thought he was definitely worth a shag. And when the bill comes, what did he say? What did you say?'

'"Can you claim this back on expenses?"' This supposedly showed Jeff in a poor light, but it was one of those occasions when he felt rather proud of himself.

'Classic Atman,' said the Kaiser, slapping him on the back.

'And the great thing was,' said Jeff, 'a), she could, and b) . . .'

'I shagged him anyway!' They clinked glasses amid much laughter all round. To be honest, it was not the first time they had showcased this anecdote together. After a certain number of drinks, it was always favourably received. Still, he was glad Laura wasn't around to hear it. There was something too London – maybe it was that word 'shag' – about it.

'Well, I can repay the favour now,' he said. 'Who would like another drink? On *my* expenses.' Silly question. *Everyone* wanted a drink.

In the bar, waiting to get served, Jeff decided that, following the example of Tracey Emin's *Everyone she'd ever slept with* tent, if he were an artist he would build a one-to-one scale

45

model of all the booze he'd ever poured down his gullet. Beer, wine, champagne, cider, the lot. Christ, he'd need a gallery the size of an aircraft hangar just for the beer: the pints, the tins, the bottles. It would be a portrait not simply of his life but of his era. Some of the brands he'd started out with had since disappeared: Tartan, Double Diamond, Trophy, the inaptly named Long Life. And it would be international too; not just the domestic beers, but the ones you swilled when abroad – Peroni, for example, five of which he ordered from the busy barman. The bottles, when they were handed over, were cool rather than chilled. Jeff asked if there were any colder ones to be had.

'Even the magnificent fridges of Venice are struggling to cope with the heat and the insatiable demand for cold drinks that it generates,' the barman replied, in epic English. Jeff took the coolish drinks outside to the waiting, thirsty Londoners.

Jane's new boyfriend, Mark, had joined them. One of the people who'd asked for a beer had disappeared so he gave the spare one to Mark. He was one of those guys, not particularly good-looking, not particularly anything, but as soon as you saw him you liked him. Jeff took a slug of his lukecold beer. When Mark got drawn into conversation with another group of people, Jane said, 'You know what I love about him?'

'What?'

'He's so easy-going.'

'I know what you mean. I love easy-going people. Even though I know I'm not one myself. Perhaps that's why I like them so much.'

'There's something so manly about it.'

'I used that very word only a short while ago, in a different context, but I know what you mean. The corollary of that is there's something so *un*manly about being uptight.'

'You're lovely, though.' She kissed him on the cheek.

'Thank you, Jane. You too.' And that was it. She went off to join Mark, but what a pleasant little exchange it had been! So much so that he decided to head for home. There were still four days to go; it would be wise to make it back to the hotel on this, the first night, without getting totally fucked up. And tomorrow he had a lot to do, all of which had to be done while keeping an eye out for Laura. He said goodbye to various people, waved to others and began walking.

Within minutes he was lost. Confronted with sudden dead-ends and bridgeless canals, he kept coming across other lost souls, squinting into maps beneath dim lamps. At one point a sign indicated that if he turned left he would come to San Marco and that if he turned right he would come to . . . San Marco. We rely on signs to make choices for us – or at least to enable us to make choices. This sign made a nonsense of itself. It might as well not have been there. Where it was meant to clarify, it succeeded only in confusing. Or did it? Perhaps it announced some larger truth about Venice: whichever way you went, even if you tried to avoid it, you would end up in San Marco. Whatever you did, whichever way you turned, the result would be the same.

In certain states – if you were exhausted, desperate for bed, on your last legs – the city's impossible geography could have driven you insane, but tonight it was fine, it was fun, part of being in Venice, having the Venice experience, the same experience everyone else was having. Still, Jeff was relieved when, without warning, miles from where he'd left it earlier in the evening, his hotel obligingly appeared. The night porter was asleep – always difficult to tell whether this was a job best suited to people suffering from insomnia or prone to narcolepsy – but attained consciousness for long enough to hand Jeff his key.

The a.c. had made his room as chilly as a fridge. He flicked it off and the silence thickened by several degrees.

He dreamt he was asleep, not in his room but by the side of a canal, a wide, fast-flowing Venetian canal. The city looked even older than it really was, more decayed and dirty, rubbish-strewn. He was woken by something pulling at his arm, tugging at him. Then the tugging grew painful, sharp. He opened his eyes to see a dog, with ancient eyes, chewing his arm. He tried to fend it off with the other arm but there was no other arm, only the one that was in the dog's bloody teeth. In the dream he was awake but he could not wake from the dream in which the dog was biting his arm, threatening to sever it. Or perhaps he was being unfair. He was soaking wet. Had the dog dragged him out of the canal, saved his life? Impossible to say. He woke up from the dream, bathed in sweat. He was in his room and there was no dog, just the canal-damp sheets.

The sun was roasting the roof of the hotel (which was also the ceiling of his room). Sharp light peered in through the shutters. It felt like the afternoon but, looking at the clock, he saw that it was only 7.45. He was hungover, dazed from the dream, far from rested and far too excited about the various things the day held in store to stand any chance of getting back to sleep.

He flicked on the a.c. again, opened the curtains and shut-ters. In a flash, the room was filled with enough sunlight to power a small town. He directed a yellow rope of piss into the toilet, catching a glimpse, as he did so, of his new, dark-haired self in the mirror. Shit, with his hair like this he looked five years younger than he had a week ago. Hangover and lack of sleep made him feel five years older so, once every-thing was factored in, he had come out quits. He showered, shaved, brushed his teeth, put on shorts and a favourite T-shirt – infinitely faded, blue, with a discreet Element skateboard logo – and headed out for breakfast.

It was already desert-hot outside, but what did it matter? He was in Venice, happy to be alive, happy to be on the lookout for Laura, glad to be in Venice – which was already up and running and probably had been for hours. Fruit and veg were being sold from barges, or whatever they were called, a few gondoliers were punting for business along the canals. People were looking out of windows, shouting and waving. Barrows of produce were being wheeled through the narrow streets. It was like being in *The Truman Show*. Every day, for hundreds of years, Venice had woken up and put on this guise of being a real place even though everyone knew it existed only for tourists. The difference, the novelty, of Venice was that the gondoliers and fruit-sellers and bakers were all tourists too, enjoying an infinitely extended city-break. The gondoliers enjoyed the fruit-sellers, the fruit-sellers enjoyed the gondoliers and bakers, and all of them together enjoyed the real residents: the hordes of camera-toting Japanese, the honeymooning Americans, the euro-pinching backpackers and hungover Biennale-goers.

One of whom was walking aimlessly but with great purpose, looking for a café where he could get exactly the breakfast he wanted and to which he could return every day. *It* needed to have fresh orange juice, good coffee (easy enough in Italy), half-decent croissant or cornetti (almost impossible), and he needed to be able to consume all of this while seated in the shade with a view of some kind of piazza (but not one of the really big ones, where the price of a coffee could leave you clutching the bill and saying two words – '*How* much?' – to yourself over and over, in a state of uncomprehending shock).

He found such a place quickly, on a tiny square, with a

view, at the end of a long, tree-ornamented street, of the Giudecca Canal. The coffee was sensational and by hooking out the honey – which he hated – he was able to turn the cornetto into a tolerable croissant. Someone had left a copy of *La Repubblica*, which he sort of read. The big news, understandably, was the eat. *Che caldissimo*! Only nine-thirty and already it was as hot as noon.

It was a mistake ordering coffee *and* orange juice. Returning to the hotel to pick up everything he needed for the day, he had to trot the last hundred yards and sprint up the stairs to make extravagant use of his en suite bathroom. Considerable though it was, the relief at having made it – just! – was short-lived. The phone began ringing while he was still sitting on the toilet.

'Pronto.'

'What is this "pronto" shit?'

'Oh, hi, Max. I was trying to go native.'

'Well, I've been trying to ring you for ages.'

'I've been out. For breakfast. What time is it there? I didn't think you got into the office so early.'

'I'm on my mobile. Why don't *you* get a mobile? You're the only person in the world who doesn't have a mobile. And you're supposed to be a journalist.'

'I don't know. I find the prospect of choosing one rather daunting. The phrase "call plan" makes me anxious.'

'I'll tell you what's making me anxious. This interview. Have you spoken with her yet?'

'I only got here last night.'

'So you *haven't* spoken to her yet?'

'I left a message,' Jeff lied.

'And how is she meant to respond to that message, if you don't have a phone?'

'I do have a phone. In fact, unless I'm very much mistaken,

I'm talking on one now. Let's see. It's got a mouthpiece you speak into and—'

'Very funny.'

'Yes, yes. I'm even hearing a voice in my ear, the voice of someone from another country who I'd rather not be speaking to. That clinches it. It's definitely a phone.'

'We've got to get this interview. Understood?'

'Roger that.'

'And the picture.'

'Affirmative.'

'You really are a wanker,' said Max. Then he hung up. How pleasant it was, dealing with someone with whom you had a working relationship going back almost fifteen years. Such a relief to be able to dispense with distracting pleasantries and irrelevant chit-chat. As a belated but symbolic riposte, Jeff flushed the toilet.

It was too early to go to the Giardini – but the perfect time to walk to the Accademia and see Giorgione's *Tempest* ahead of the crowds. Like everywhere else in Venice the museum was undergoing renovation but it was open – and there was no queue. A sign at the ticket desk announced SORRY WE HAVE NO AIR CONDITIONED. Another sign, smaller, in Italian, said something about Giorgione's *La Tempesta*. Bollocks . . . There was a simple rule of museum-going: if you had only one day free in a city, that would be the day the museum was closed. And if it *was* open, then the one piece you wanted to see would be out on loan or removed for restoration. But no, the sign simply explained that, due to renovation, *La Tempesta* had been moved, temporarily, to Room XIII. Jeff headed straight there.

No one else was around. He had the room and the painting to himself.

To one side of the picture a young mother is breast-feeding

an infant, gazing out of the painting, meeting the eye of whoever is looking at it. Presumably she has just bathed in the river separating her from the elegantly dressed young man wedged into the bottom left-hand corner, leaning on a staff, gazing at her. He looks at her; she looks at us, looking at them. Whatever is going on, we are implicated in it. Behind them, in the background – though it isn't really background – a bridge spans the aquamarine river. Beyond the bridge a landscape-city crouches under the gathered clouds. A white bird, perhaps a stork, perches on the roof of one of the buildings. The sky is a wash of billowing, inky blue. A single line of white lightning crackles through the storm.

'The stoppage of time in Giorgione has a partly idyllic character. But the idyll is charged with presentiment,' McCarthy had written. 'Something frightening is about to happen.' This, Atman saw now, was slightly misleading. It was not only impossible to say what that 'something' was – let alone whether that something might be 'frightening' – it was impossible to tell whether it had happened in the past or would happen in the future, or would not happen at all. There was no before and no after, or at least they were indistinguishable from each other, interchangeable. Apart from that, what he saw now confirmed how precisely she had fixed the painting in words. It was, as she insisted, the stillness that produced the sense of unrest.

The museum may have had no 'air conditioned', but it was cool compared with the heat lying in wait outside. Jeff bought a litre bottle of water from a kiosk and a three-day pass at the Accademia vaporetto stop. The vaporetto, when it arrived a few minutes later, was jam-packed – with artists. Handsome and well-mannered Wolfgang Tillmans was talking to old blood head, Marc Quinn, whose latest work – a giant metal orchid – could be seen as the boat passed the Peggy

Guggenheim Collection. As Jeff made his way to the front of the boat he passed Richard Wentworth, wearing a panama hat and a striped blue shirt, looking like he was starring in a TV adaptation of a novel about an artist who was also one of the Cambridge spies.

'Thought for the week,' he said as Jeff squeezed by. 'Art *world*, music *business*. What does that tell us?'

The distinction was somewhat lost on Atman: a seat at the front had become vacant and he was determined to occupy it. Someone else was even more determined and Atman was left standing but at least here, at the front, the motion of the boat generated a parched breeze. As they chugged past San Marco, several vaporetti passed by, heading the other way. On one of these he spotted Laura, leaning on the rail, wearing a white dress. Yes, surely it was her. She was holding what he guessed was an umbrella, yellow, rolled tight as a stick. He couldn't make out the number of the vaporetto, didn't know where she was going, only that it was in the opposite direction to him. He looked at his map, tried to calculate quickly where she might be heading, but it was impossible. She could have been going anywhere. He stared at the wake spreading out in a V behind the vaporetto. How to regard this failed sighting? Either as a good sign because it suggested that it could turn out to be a frequent occurrence. Or maybe – like those occasions in London when you come out of a party late at night, see a cab immediately, just fail to attract the attention of the driver and then find yourself marooned for hours – this was his one and only chance. A chance that was also a non-chance.

People say it's not what happens in your life that matters, it's what you *think* happened. But this qualification, obviously, did not go far enough. It was quite possible that the central event of your life could be something that didn't happen, or something you *thought* didn't happen. Otherwise there'd be no need for fiction, there'd only be memoirs and histories, case histories; what happened – what actually happened and what you thought happened – would be enough.

All that remained of the other boat's wake was a slight swell passing under the wake of his own vaporetto. It was like a double annulment. They had passed each other like ships in the day.

Jeff disembarked at San Zaccaria, where he had to pick up his accreditation from the Biennale press office. He'd been warned to expect huge queues and a wait of several hours in the blistering sun, but there were only a few people ahead of him. One of whom was Dan Fairbank, turning away from the desk, press pass in hand. This was somewhat unexpected since, last Jeff had heard (two weeks previously), Dan was working as a director of commercials. Spotting Jeff, anxious to avoid any public exclamations of surprise, he came over and explained, *sotto voce,* that he had contrived some kind of eligibility for a press pass, 'to gain ingress to things I might otherwise not have the patience to wait to see'. Moments later Jeff was called forward to the accreditation desk and Dan made his egress.

Smiling, wearing red, aspirational glasses, the young woman dealing with Jeff's application was full of enthusiasm for her job, eager to make sure that this important journalist had all the information he could possibly need, even though he was only interested in whatever it was that would get him in – grant him ingress – to as many things as easily as possible. Biennale society was completely hierarchical. At the bottom were the members of the public, who, at this stage, had access to nothing and, for these few days at least, were conspicuous by their absence. At the top were the artists and the curators from the big institutions and the famous commercial galleries, then the collectors, then the journalists and critics, then an army of liggers. To keep track of and help maintain this admittedly flexible caste system – a journalist like Jeff was really just a successful ligger, a ligger with accreditation; come to think of it, many of the artists were liggers with paintbrushes or cameras, and the curators were liggers with power – a wide variety of passes was available, only the very highest of which granted you access everywhere, at any time, to anything. Beyond that, at the very peak of the celebriarchy, was the super-VIP level, where to be in possession of any kind of pass except that bestowed on you by your wealth or fame – by a self-evident entitlement to go exactly where you pleased – was itself a token of exclusion.

As Jeff was issued with his basic, no-frills press pass he had a sudden and brilliant idea.

'Perhaps you could tell me,' he asked, 'if my colleague Laura Freeman has picked up her accreditation yet.' She was not a journalist, but, like Dan, she may have signed up as one to reap the benefits of a press pass. And if she *had* signed in, then it might be possible to discover her hotel and, possibly, her cellphone number. While the assistant happily went through the computer to check the name, Jeff stood anxiously by, the excitement of adding significantly to his hoard of information about Laura supplemented by the thrill of his own cunning, the private-eye sleuthiness of it all. Such animation was short-lived, however. No one called Laura Freeman had registered.

'Ah. Well, thank you anyway,' he said. The assistant had been more than simply helpful. She'd added that extra bit of charm to which a man of Atman's age was uniquely susceptible: the suggestion that she was doing this not because it was in her nature or in her job description, not even because she was well-disposed towards him, but because she found him attractive. Whether she really did was as irrelevant as it was unlikely; what mattered was that her manner – flirtatious simply because it was so abundantly pleasant – made it possible to entertain the idea. Had he not been so preoccupied with thoughts of Laura, he might have tried to put this lightly to the test – a drink later, perhaps? – a test which would, almost certainly, have yielded a negative result. As it was he thanked her for her help, wished her a nice day and the whole exchange concluded with big smiles on both sides. It was like a version of the scene at the newsagent's in London, re-written and re-located to Venice.

All-important press pass in hand, Jeff stepped out into the sci-fi heat. Perhaps it was this new press pass that provoked a surge of professionalism: he went straight to the *tabaccheria* nearby and bought a phone card so that he could call Julia Berman about the interview. The temperature appeared to have soared another ten degrees while he'd been inside the press office. Under the perspex canopy of the pay phone it was hotter still. The phone rang for a long while. He waited for a human or a machine to answer, then hung up and dialled again. Same thing. He felt enormously relieved. He had done his best to secure this much-needed scoop. He had rung and rung – twice! – and still there was no answer. He had tried everything to track her down, with no luck, so he was free now to get on with the dozens of other things he had to do, the most important of which was going to the Biennale – while all the time keeping an eye out for Laura.

Near the leafy entrance to the Giardini students and young artists handed out flyers for exhibitions of their own, alternative, semi-underground versions of the Biennale with music, DJs. The Giardini was already crowded by the time Jeff got inside, less than an hour after it had officially opened.

Patriotically, his first stop was the British pavilion, given over to Gilbert & George. In the 1980s, the critic Peter Fuller had conducted a vituperative crusade against Gilbert & George, seeing in them a threat to everything he held dear. By the time Fuller was killed, in a car crash, he must have realized it had all been in vain, for Gilbert & George were poised to become godfathers to several generations of YBA hustlers – and now they had been honoured by having the British pavilion to themselves. The work, needless to say, was as weary as some harmless sin, the same old brightly-coloured, stained glass-looking nonsense they'd been doing for years, but the way Jeff looked at it (the only way one could look at it): who gave a shit? They were never going to do anything new, but so what? There was no point kicking against this affable pair of pricks.

From there he should have gone about things in a systematic fashion, ticking off each of the national pavilions in an orderly sequence, but there were already queues of art immigrants waiting to get into Canada and France – whose pavilions were next to Britain's – so he skipped them and started dropping into places in a completely haphazard fashion. From G & G he went to the Norwegian pavilion, which featured a wall of yellow and black Op Art circles. Except they weren't circles, they were targets, dartboards, an entire wall of them. Some distance away there were large cardboard boxes of green and red darts, which you could aim at the wall, gradually altering the overall pattern and distribution of colour. Jeff had just aimed the last of a handful of red darts when someone called his name and threw a dart in his eyes. Shit! It was Ben Jennings – doing that old trick of unscrewing the dart so that the flight fluttered harmlessly and frighteningly against Jeff's face.

'Wanker!'

'Excellent, isn't it?' said Ben, reassembling the dart. 'Jackson Pollock meets Jocky Wilson.' He was wearing a pale blue shirt, already navy with sweat under the arms. Years ago he had been something of a man about Soho, a wit, a Kenneth Tynan in the process of formation. Now, fifteen years down the line, he was regarded – even by a hack like Jeff – as a hack who had never had the discipline or application or talent to fulfil whatever promise he had shown. Not that he seemed to mind. He was happy attending the various art fairs of the world – Art Basel in Miami, Basel itself, the Armory in New York, Frieze in London, Berlin – and banging out gossipy stories about them. Jeff tended to assume that he disliked him but, in his company, always found himself warming to him, partly because he suspected that, behind the charm and bonhomie, Ben might be desperately unhappy with the lot he was ostensibly happy with. Still, he always managed to have a good time. Last night, for example, he had been 'disco-dancing until four in the morning'. It was pathetic, it was unbelievably immature, but even now, aged forty-five and counting, Jeff felt his heart sink when he heard that someone had been out later than him, had been having more fun than him, even when he'd been having fun himself and had decided, of his own free will, to call it a night. Other people's ideas of a good time underwent well-established changes as they got older. They ended up raising children, buying sheds or playing golf. Jeff had proved remarkably constant in his pref- erences. He'd liked drinking, taking drugs, going to parties and chasing after women who – another sign of constancy – ideally, were not too much older, now, than when he'd first started doing so. In recent years a bit more time was spent at home, zonked out in front of the TV, but that wasn't something he *wanted* to do, that was just recovery time. On occasions he was bored rigid by his idea of a good time, but nothing had come near to displacing or replacing it. And he'd never got to the stage or gone through the phase of being passionate about his work except in so far as he had always felt passionately averse to it. No wonder he had such ambiguous feelings about Ben: he was like a ruddier, portlier version of Atman himself. It was quite possible, he reasoned, to like someone you disliked and vice-versa.

'I thought I might have seen you at the Iceland party last night,' Jeff said. They both picked up more darts and stood side by side, chucking them, aimlessly, at the wall of unmissable targets.

'I was at a dinner for Ed Ruscha.'

'That was last night? I thought it was tomorrow.'

'There's one tomorrow as well.'

'So, every night there's an Ed Ruscha dinner?'

'And – one hundred and eighty! – probably a breakfast every morning.'

They threw the last of their arrows. Ben said he had it on good authority that later this afternoon, at the Venezuelan pavilion, chocolate-covered cockroaches would be served. With that they went their separate ways, Ben to the Swiss pavilion and Jeff to an installation by a Finnish artist whose name – Maaria Wirkkala – meant nothing to him.

A simple wooden boat was adrift in a frozen sea of broken, multi-coloured Murano glass – discards and fragments, presumably, from the factories near Venice. Painted a dull red, the interior of the boat was gradually filling up with water dripping from the ceiling. Every now and again – so infrequently Jeff wondered if he was imagining it – the boat rocked slightly. He was transfixed by this, glad that he'd seen it right at the beginning of his tour, before he became punch-drunk, sated and oblivious.

Australia and Germany were packed, so it was a relief to

come to Uruguay, where there were no queues, no crowds – and no art. They'd hung a few rags on washing lines but, even by the low standards of some of the other pavilions, this was pretty derisory. And they weren't giving away any free stuff either. Many pavilions were handing out free canvas bags, some of them rather elegant, all very useful (for stuffing in free bags from the other pavilions). Produce a press card and some places would throw in a lavish catalogue as well, but the Uruguayans were not playing the game at all.

In the compressed geography of the Giardini Uruguay was bordered by the United States, featuring Ed Ruscha's long, horizontal paintings of buildings, some in colour, some in black and white. Fine, good, seen that. Jeff went briskly from pavilion to pavilion, using his little digital camera as an aide-memoire to be consulted – in tandem with the catalogues – when he wrote his article. Extraordinary – there was all this art and yet there was very little to see, or very little worth looking at anyway. Some of it was a waste of one's eyes. Good. Because even though there was nothing to see, there was a lot of it to get round and Jeff had to at least poke his nose in at everything. Quite a bit of the work on display could have been designated conceptual, in so far as the people looking at it were conceived as having the mentality of pupils at junior school. Fair enough, except most of it looked like it was *made* by someone in primary school, albeit a primary school pupil with the ambition of a seventeen-year-old Russian whose widowed mother had saved every ruble to get him into a tennis academy in Florida. The work may have been puerile, but the hunger to succeed of which it was the product and symbol was ravenous. In different historical circumstances any number of these artists could have seized control of the Reichstag or ruled Cambodia with unprecedented ruthlessness.

Within a very short time the pavilions all started blurring together: it became impossible to recall, with any certainty, which art was to be found in which pavilion. The big, bright, psychedelic druggy paintings were in the Swiss pavilion. The video shower, tiled with monitors so that you were surrounded, on three sides, by a torrent of images – tennis, porn, news, Formula 1, cheetahs, football, more porn, breaking news, wildlife porn, deserts, bushfires, boxing – was Russian. But the red plastic castle – you stepped inside and it was like being in a red world – which nation's world was that? Not the same nation, obviously, that had come up with the completely blue room. Nothing but blue in there. No corners, no angles, no shadows, just blue nothingness. It was a highly abstract environment, a space of light, even though there was no obvious source of light except for the blueness that was everywhere, all around. Atman had entered this installation at a time when it was completely empty. The only corporeal thing in the room was him, but that was enough – he was enough – not to *ruin* the experience but at least to severely qualify it. The fact that he was here, in the midst of it, meant that it was not the non-corporeal experience it came tantalisingly close to being. He sat on the floor so that he would be less conscious of the body he was dragging round, nearer to dissolving into directionless, sourceless blueness. Still, it was pretty cool and came closer than anything he'd seen to what people – or Atman, at any rate – wanted from art, a space where you could trip out, lose yourself: installations raised to the level of complete immersion. Ideally, the perfect art installation would be a nightclub, full of people, pumping music, lights, smoke machine and maybe drugs thrown in. You could call it *Nightclub*, and if you kept it going twenty-four hours a day it would be the big hit of the Biennale.

As Jeff made his way from pavilion to pavilion, he kept

running into people he knew, some of them from last night, some of whom he was encountering here for the first time. Most had hangovers. After Haig's had stopped serving, at two, some diehards had gone on to the Bauer, which had been so packed the terrace was in danger of collapsing into the Grand Canal. Everyone had their favourite pieces, their recommendations and aversions, and everyone had an assortment of free bags. No one else had seen the rainy Finnish boat in its sea of shattered glass. It was as if Jeff had hallucinated it. The more he told people about it, the more that boat meant to him. Scott Thomson was adamant that the art here lagged a million miles behind the art at Burning Man. Bottles of water and fans were being handed out. Some people suffered from the heat more than others, but everyone agreed that the heat was unbelievable. They stood in the warm shade of trees, fanning themselves, drinking water, clutching their free bags and catalogues, comparing plans for the evening, feeling relieved and vindicated when it turned out they were going to the same parties. They said goodbye and then ran into each other half an hour later, on the way to the Spanish pavilion, enthusiastic about Serbia, delayed by the airport-level security checks for Israel. Jeff bumped into still more people he knew and recognized lots that he didn't – Nick Serota chatting with Sam Taylor-Wood, Peter Blake talking to himself (nothing unusual about that, half the people here were glued to their mobiles), and someone who may or may not have been the actress Natascha McElhone – but he never saw the person he most wanted to see, never caught a glimpse of Laura.

At a pay phone, he tried Julia again. This time someone answered.

'*Buongiorno*. Hello. Is that Julia Berman?'

'Speaking.'

'Ah, good. My name is Jeffrey Atman. From *Kulchur* magazine.' At this point she would, ideally, have said, 'Yes, indeed. How are you?' Failing that, some kind of encouraging noise – 'uh-huh' – would have been helpful. But there was nothing, just the faint sound of breathing, breathing that sounded irritable. 'I'm sorry to call you out of the blue like this. But not entirely out of the blue, I hope. I think my editor, Max Grayson, has been in touch with you?' More breathing. 'About my perhaps doing a short interview with you about, well, about your life and your daughter's record? That kind of thing.'

'What was the name again?'

'Jeffrey Atman.'

'And the magazine?'

Tempted to say *Razzle* or *Cheeks*, he responded politely and accurately, '*Kulchur*. With a "k" and a "ch".'

'I think I do remember something about that.' Her accent was English, slovenly posh. Jeff waited for her to continue but it was, evidently, his turn to speak again.

'So, um, if it wasn't too inconvenient, could we perhaps do the interview sometime in the next couple of days?'

'When would you like to do it?'

'Whenever and wherever would be convenient for you.' A gamble, this. There were plenty of times that would be extremely inconvenient for him, but it was part of the etiquette of being an interviewer that you had to let the interviewee call the shots. It made them feel important and being important hopefully made them more amenable – though, in practice, as often as not, it just made them feel even more important, which manifested itself in their being extremely difficult.

'How long would it take?'

'Not long at all, if you're busy.' He had been doing this kind of thing for long enough to realize that there was no need to spend hours conducting an interview. You could cut it down to twenty minutes and still have enough quotes to cobble a half-decent piece together – and half-decent was still twice as good as it needed to be. In any case, he had better things to do in Venice than spend his time listening to this old has-been (a euphemism, generally, for a never-was).

'Tomorrow is impossible, so perhaps today. Quite soon. At about four o'clock?'

'Perfect,' said Jeff, meaning it.

'Could you come here?'

'Yes, certainly. Um, where are you?' She gave him an address – completely meaningless – and instructions on how to get there.

Her directions were unambiguous and easy to follow. Having taken a vaporetto from Giardini to Campo d'Oro, Atman arrived at her building exactly on time. He pressed a metal bell, unable to hear if, somewhere within, this action manifested itself as a ring. There was no sound of movement, no footsteps or doors opening. He waited, was about to try again when he heard a lock turning. The door opened. It was so bright outside that he had trouble making out the figure shrouded by the darkness within. As his eyes adjusted he saw long dark hair, threaded with grey, a thin face whose ageing was indicated not by a softening of features but by the skin being stretched more tightly over the skull. She held out her thin hand, asked him to step inside, into the cool. The door clanged behind them. She was wearing a knee-length dress, blue. He followed her up the dark staircase – she was barefoot – to a third-floor apartment. It was large and airy, simply furnished, but he had no opportunity to look around as she led him straight out onto a terrace. There was a small metal table, painted white, and two chairs, shaded by a large canvas umbrella. She asked what he would like to drink. Sparkling water was fine, he said, and she went back inside. The view was of a small canal, and some other apartments, all with their own terraces.

She returned with a bottle and glasses piled with ice, each topped by a slice of lemon. The ice creaked and cracked as she filled the glasses. The whole thing was like an advertisement for the word 'refreshing'. He took a gulp.

'Very refreshing,' he said, stupidly, before hunting for his Dictaphone in the collection of bags he'd amassed at the Giardini. 'Have you been to the Biennale yet?'

'Not yet,' she said. 'Tomorrow.' He told her about the things he'd seen so far, the dartboards, the Finnish boat slowly filling up with water on its journey across the sea of coloured glass. He found the Dictaphone.

'Would you mind if I recorded our talk?'

'That's fine.' He placed the machine on the table between them, pressed *Record*.

'It's, um, voice-activated,' he said. 'How cool is that?' It was another stupid remark and, as such, he was happy to have made it. Years ago he had tried to impress his subjects with how astute, on the ball, up to speed and generally smart he was. This, he had learnt, was a mistake. Interviews worked much better if the subject thought you were a complete numbskull. They let their guard down, became more expansive, actually tried to compensate for your manifest failings. Not, he began to suspect, that that was going to make much difference here. She was not unfriendly, but she was entirely business-like. Interviewees generally tried to charm you; she did not bother. But she did pour more water into his glass. She wasn't interested in him – interviewees never were, they were only interested in how they would appear in print – but she seemed equally uninterested in herself.

'Perhaps I could start by asking you about Niki's record.' He found himself squirming as he spoke. 'What do you think about it?'

'I like it,' she said. He waited for her to continue. She didn't.

'Would you like to expand on that a bit?'

'I like it a lot. They're nice tunes. I like the lyrics too, some of them.'

'Any ones in particular?'

'I can't remember them off-hand, but I think she has a nice turn of phrase.'

'What about the recording? I see that you actually sing backing vocals on one of the tracks.'

'That was sweet of her to ask me. Obviously I can't sing for toffee, but it doesn't matter because there's so much else going on you can't really hear me.' *For toffee.* It was years since he'd heard that expression.

'Well, I like it,' he said, even though he had not yet bothered listening to the presumably crap CD that the PR had biked over to his flat with an urgency appropriate to desperately-needed blood. 'Um, is it the kind of thing you listen to normally? I mean, what kind of music do you like to listen to?'

'I like older music. I'm showing my age, but I like Bob Dylan. I like The Doors.'

'Did you ever meet Dylan?'

'No. I saw him at Blackbushe in nineteen seventy whenever.'

'Eight. Me too. Great, wasn't it?' This was it, the breakthrough, the moment they discovered they had something in common even though it was the thing that everyone from twenty to seventy had in common: an interest in Bob Dylan. With a bit of conniving on Jeff's part, the interview could now genuinely become what it always tried to masquerade as: a chat. 'I was at Earl's Court too.'

'I didn't make that.'

'Who else do you like?' he asked, resisting the temptation to go completely Dylanological.

'Tangerine Dream,' she said. 'Van der Graaf Generator.' He couldn't tell if she was joking.

'Did you ever see Van der Graaf?' he asked, responding in kind.

'I knew Pete Hammill slightly.'

'*Did* you? What was he like?'

'He was nice. A nice, well-read, well-mannered English boy.'

Jeff said, '*H to He Who am the Only One.*'

'*Pawn Hearts,*' she said back. He thought she was about to laugh, but she didn't quite.

'There's another one, but I can't quite remember it.'

'*The Least We Can Do is Wave to Each Other,*' she said.

'Of course.'

'*Aerosol Grey Machine.*'

'My,' said Jeff, 'you really know your Van der Graaf.' He had had versions of this conversation – different groups, same format – dozens of times, but always with men. Having it with a woman was a different, altogether more thrilling experience.

As if reading his mind, she said, 'This is a rather strange interview. Is *Kulchur* with a "k" and a "ch" a progressive rock magazine?'

'Unfortunately not. Be great if it was, though,' he said, conscious, suddenly, that he was having a good time. And the interview would turn out fine. Or would have done had she not reached forward and turned off the Dictaphone.

'Do you like to smoke grass, Jeff?'

'Sure.'

'Good. To be honest with you, I'm somewhat of a pothead, though I'd appreciate it if you didn't put that in your piece.'

'Absolutely.'

She went back in to the apartment, giving Jeff the opportunity to begin slightly regretting that confident 'Sure.' Back in the twentieth century he had enjoyed smoking grass, but with the new millennium dominated absolutely by super-strong skunk, he had pretty well given up on it. In the 1980s getting stoned on sensei had been fun, but getting bombed on skunk – and with skunk, there was no possibility of getting anything other than bombed – was a different experience. It was like a conduit to dread, to heebie-jeebies paranoia.

She returned with a bag of grass. Jeff tried not to appear nervous.

'Uh, one thing,' he said. 'I don't smoke tobacco.'

'Me neither. This is nice Jamaican grass. Not that horrible skunk.'

'Oh, good,' he almost shouted with relief. 'I hate that.' What an amazing time he was having in Venice. Everything was working out so well.

'It's terrible, isn't it? God knows what it's doing to the minds of these kids who smoke it all the time.'

'Quite,' he said, for the second time in as many days.

She rolled a small thin joint, took a hit and passed it to Jeff. He did the same, passed it back. He became pleasantly stoned. They were pleasantly stoned together. The light was brighter, sharper. The canal threw shadow patterns on the yellow wall opposite. In fact, he was very stoned, but pleasantly so. This was what being stoned used to be like.

'So, about Hawkwind,' he said.

'Now, remember, nothing about getting stoned in your article. No little nudges or winks.'

'I promise.' His throat was burning. He took a big gulp of water whose sparklingness made his throat sting, briefly, even more. 'Moving on, reluctantly, from seventies prog rock, maybe you could tell me a little about Steve Morison.'

'Charming man. Quite good artist. Total cunt.' This is dynamite, Jeff thought to himself, unsure, moments later, whether he had in mind the interview or the grass. 'But, needless to say, I wouldn't want you to quote my saying that either.'

'Oh, OK. You mean the whole of the answer or just the last part?'

'No, just the first two parts.' They both laughed. This was turning out to be *fun*.

'What do you think of his work now? Back in the sixties, he was so revered. I wondered how you felt it had stood up to the passage of time.'

'I think it was extremely variable. His best is on a par with some Hodgkin.' Jeff looked at her closely, hoping to penetrate her sunglasses, to see her eyes, to see how this remark had been intended. Hodgkin, in recent years, had become a complete joke. Jeff waited for her to expand on Hodgkin, but she went back to Morison. 'And the earlier, figurative stuff is good. He had a knack of capturing the way people stood, their relationship to their surroundings. And if there *were* no surroundings, then just the way they stood in relation to themselves. Out of that there was a kind of psychological intensity that was very difficult to articulate but that was definitely there. Everyone could see it or sense it even though there was nothing – absolutely nothing – interior about the scene. It would be as objective as a photograph.'

'Yes,' said Jeff. Though impressed by the analysis, he was having trouble remembering how it had begun. That was the beauty of recording interviews, though. It was like an external memory. Except, he realized now, he had forgotten to turn the Dictaphone back on.

'Fuck!' He reached forward, pressed *Record*.

'Naturally you don't expect me to say all that again, do you?' she said.

'No, no.'

A motor boat went by, the canal swooshed and churned in its wake, making the shadow-swirls on the wall coil into life again.

'Was it . . .? Bringing up Niki on your own. You lived partly in France and partly in London. How was that?'

'Fine. We had a lovely apartment in Paris. A reasonable flat in London. We weren't short of money. Niki was an easy-going child.'

'What about you? What were you doing? Apart from bringing her up, I mean.'

'I didn't have any impulse to do anything much. I wrote a few articles. I had vague ideas about writing a book, but never got round to it.'

'There was talk of a memoir.'

'Oh, yes, I did a few little things, but I didn't have the application and there was nothing I wanted to get to the bottom of. So there was nothing to sustain me and nothing to propel me. And although I had a few famous friends, I actually felt too loyal to them, or too affectionate, to say anything interesting about them. You know, that kind of book always works best when there's some kind of betrayal involved. I had no interest in betraying or score-settling. And the idea of writing didn't interest me enough. So I just swanned around. Tell me, do you get bored?'

'Me? Yes, all the time.'

'That must be an advantage. You see, I've never had any capacity for boredom. I'm like one of those people you see in India or Africa, sitting by the roadside, staring into space. I can just do nothing all day long and I'm quite happy. And I've never had any ambition. Not even in its most basic, negative form of envying other people's success. I think that's why I've had so many friends, I was really delighted for them to get on when so many of the other people around were measuring themselves against how everyone else was doing. I'm sorry, am I speaking too much?'

'No, not at all. This is great, actually.' Jeff glanced towards the Dictaphone to make sure it was recording, to make sure that, by turning it on, he had not accidentally turned it off. Such things, he remembered, had a way of happening when you were stoned.

'All of which applies particularly, presumably, to Niki?' He was sharp as a pin! As Paxman!

'Yes. It was obvious she was going to do something. If it hadn't been music, it would have been art or writing. Something like that. She had just enough discontent. Unlike me. I've always sat very comfortably in my own skin.'

It was true. She was just sitting there, comfortably, talking about herself but not in an egotistic way, imparting inform-ation about this person who happened to be herself. And it was easy to see why she had so many friends. She was easy to be around. She made you feel at ease – a thought that immediately made Jeff feel ill at ease, anxious about how to broach the subject of the picture Max had requested and which, in its way, was more important than everything that had gone before. The shadow of Julia's building was stretching across the wall opposite like a plimsoll line suggesting, as it moved slowly upwards, that cargo was being loaded onto this neighbouring house, causing it to sink slightly into the water. He turned off the Dictaphone.

'Great. Thank you. That will work really well.'

'That was painless.'

'Good. The only other thing – and again it's something I think Max Grayson, my editor at *Kulchur*, mentioned. The picture of you by Steven. They were hoping you might agree to let them reprint that with the article.'

'You want to take the picture with you?'

'Not necessarily. Whatever's easiest for you. If you prefer, they could arrange a courier or it could be scanned and sent electronically. But, well, it would be great if I could at least see it.'

'And would you mind if I asked what was in it for me?'

'No. In fact, one of the things I've been asked or authorized to do is to agree a fee with you.'

'So?'

'A thousand pounds?'

'It's strange, this is one of those situations when I could be difficult.'

'You'd certainly be within your rights.'

'What if I just asked for more money? Money that, by the way, I don't even particularly want but, well, that *is* what you're meant to do, isn't it?'

'Absolutely, yes. How about fifteen hundred? To be honest, that's the limit. Top dollar, as they say.'

'Let me go and get the picture.'

She went inside again. He stood up and walked a few paces. He was still very stoned and it was still incredibly hot. The combination made him sit down again, under the diffused glow of the umbrella.

Julia came out with a folder, which she untied, revealing a yellowish, thick piece of paper. She flipped the folder over, opened it again and there was the drawing. She was naked, her legs apart. Between her legs was a scribble and blur of lines. She had lovely breasts – and it was obviously her. The face had the same prominent cheekbones, the same strangely blank expression. Even her hair was pretty much the same. It was easy to imagine that, if she undressed now, he would see roughly the same body as the one in the picture.

'My,' he said. He looked at her face in the drawing, but was unable to look at the face of the person who had handed it to him. There was the startling fact of the drawing showing her naked, but there was also an unsettling psychological quality to the picture – the quality she had commented on earlier. She was letting this man, her lover, look at her and draw her. To gaze at their lover, naked: it was what men had always wanted to do. If the man was an artist – or just a teenager with a camcorder – then what he painted or filmed was not simply what he saw but the unchanging strength of that desire, that hunger to see . . . But in her face there was an absolute indifference. Any love in his gaze was unreciprocated. Instead there was just a blank. Look all you want, her expression said. You can see everything and you will see nothing except what I have in common with every other woman on earth. One only needed to look at the picture for a few moments to know that the relationship was not going to endure. And presumably Morison knew this, either while he was doing it or, failing that, as soon as he had finished. Maybe that didn't matter, to either of them. Maybe the moment contained and recorded in this piece of paper was enough. But if that was true, then why was there such a sense of loneliness about the drawing: not hers – she was calm and perfectly still – but that of the person looking at her, the artist himself?

'A hypnotic relation between the subject and the spectator is established in all Giorgione's pictures. This derives partly from the motionless, arrested scene, and partly from the unwavering look in the eyes of the portrait subject . . . The stillness produces the unrest.'

'It's . . .' He cleared his throat. 'It's a remarkable picture.'

'Yes.' He handed it back to her. She returned the picture carefully to the folder, which she tied neatly together. 'So I think you understand that I wouldn't want to give it to your magazine – any magazine – either for a thousand, fifteen hundred pounds or . . . Or however much.'

'I agree,' said Jeff. 'It's a very private picture.'

She looked at him. 'You're not a very dedicated journalist,' she said. 'But you are an understanding one. That must be a disadvantage in your line of work.'

He shrugged.

'Will your editor be as understanding?'

'I don't think it's a sackable offence. Especially since I'm only freelance and so, strictly speaking, don't have a job from which I *can* be sacked.'

'That's reassuring,' she laughed.

Their meeting was over. They descended the cool stairs. She opened the door. Jeff thanked her, was about to shake her hand when she leaned forward and kissed him on the cheek. There was nothing sexual about it, but neither was it the standard continental air-kiss that was as conventionalized as a handshake. There was an intimacy about it that could not be accounted for, either by their getting stoned together, or because of the interview or because of the picture that he had just seen. He said goodbye, stepped out into the fierce heat, and heard the door shut jarringly behind him.

He walked back to the vaporetto stop at Campo d'Oro thinking, for the tenth time that day, that it was even hotter – otter – than it had been earlier. The vaporetto came quickly and was unusually empty. If nothing else, he was getting fantastic value out of his three-day pass. He stepped aboard, found a seat at the back and reached into his assortment of bags for the Dictaphone, wanting to listen back to what he had, to check the quality of recording. Instead of the Dictaphone, he pulled out his digital camera. Fuck! He had forgotten to take her picture. He had failed to come away

74

with the drawing and he had forgotten to take her picture. Of the three things he was supposed to have done, he had failed or forgotten to do two. And the one thing he'd not forgotten to do – the interview – had been sabotaged by forgetting to turn the fucking Dictaphone back on for the best part of it. He looked in his bags again: at least he still *had* the Dictaphone. He was in a panic, torn between getting off at the next stop, going back, ringing the door bell again and asking if she wouldn't mind, if it wasn't too much trouble, if he could . . . As with the email he hadn't sent the day before coming to Venice – 'I just can't do this shit any more' – he knew, even as he contemplated doing so, that he would not get off the boat, would not go back, would return to London empty-handed and would get told by *Kulchur* that they did not want him to do this shit any more because he could not be trusted – he could hear Max's voice rising – *to do the simplest fucking thing that he was asked – not asked, commissioned, paid – to do!* He knew also that as soon as he was told that they did not want him to do this shit any more he would realize how desperately he wanted to keep doing this shit that he did not want to do any more. He wished he was not stoned, wished he could think clearly. That was something else he remembered about getting stoned, one of the reasons he'd gradually stopped doing it: there always came a time, when you were stoned, when you wished you weren't stoned, when you needed to not be stoned, needed to think clearly. Venice was sliding past, glinting and greeny-gold, watery. Many of the grand palazzos were adorned with large banners publicizing Biennale-related art events and exhibitions. Glancing round, he saw that the vaporetto had filled up as it had stopped at whichever stops it had stopped at since he had got on at his stop, was actually very crowded. Well, what could he do now, about the photo that he had not taken? Nothing. The best thing was not to think about it, not to worry.

A lot of people got off at Accademia, but even more piled on. The boat pulled away and passed under the bridge. As it emerged on the other side he saw Laura on the low arch of the bridge, leaning on the rail. Birds slid and swooped, over the bridge and under. She was wearing a white dress, was shading herself from the sun with a parasol – ah, so that was what it was, not an umbrella, of course it was not an umbrella. If she had been looking down at – or even along – the canal, she would surely have seen him; but she was looking – smiling – at the person she was talking to, a man, a guy Jeff's age or a little younger. It was obvious, even from this glimpse, from the way she was facing him, the way he held himself in relation to her – one hand on the bridge rail – that they were not in the midst of a walk through the city together; no, they had just bumped into each other. All of this passed through Jeff's mind in less than a second. He could have called her name. He was still debating whether this was or was not the best thing to do when it became – gradually and suddenly – too late to do so. Too late! Calling out her name had ceased being an option and had become a source of regret.

He got off the vaporetto at Salute, returned to the hotel and took the lift up to his room. He spent five minutes under an almost cold shower and lay on the bed in a thick, eminently stealable robe. Feeling only the faintest aftermath of stonedness – what a relief! – he looked through one of the Venice books provided by the hotel: a lavish edition of Turner's pictures of the city. They were all full of light dissolving into itself, water and light, melting into each other, colour becoming light, sunlight going down in flames, over the water. Some were so diluted as to be just washes of almost-colour. Although the city was instantly recognizable, the idea of Venice being insubstantial, a shimmering dissolution of light and water with everything turning into air, was at odds with Jeff's experience of being here. The thing that struck him about Venice was how *substantial* it was. And not just the place, but the people. This wasn't a town where, over time, generations had been born, lived and died. No, there was the same set of characters there had always been, a constant and unchanging population who simply changed their clothes according to the epoch they were living through. Each individual remained stuck at a particular occupation and age till the end of time. The old guy running the grocer's next door – Jeff had stopped in there to buy bottles of water three times the size and a fraction of the price of the ones in the hotel mini-bar – had been the old guy running the grocer's for thousands of years. The chamber maid had been a chamber maid forever. They were just there. And so, evidently, was the city they inhabited. It was the most *there* place on earth, and had been since time began, since long before it allegedly came into existence. Maybe the lost city of Atlantis didn't disappear beneath the waves so much as reappear above them, morphing into Venice as it did so. OK, there was the water, that was liquidy and aquatic, obviously, an agent of dilution and dissolution, but the main effect of the water was to make the buildings seem, by contrast, extremely tangible. Not only did Venice look like it had been around forever, but – despite all the stories about how the city was sinking by however many centimetres a year – it gave the impression that it would be around forever, that it might be the only place standing after a nuclear strike Turnered the rest of the world into a blazing melt of frying water and scorched air.

* * *

It was an unusual night in that there was no dinner for Ed
Ruscha. The reason there was no dinner for Ed Ruscha was
because there was a *party* for Ed Ruscha. Jeff only realized
this – that the party at the Peggy Guggenheim Collection was
actually in honour of Ed Ruscha – as he checked the thick,
heavily embossed invite on his way over. By the time he arrived
there must have been a thousand people stuffed into the garden
and hundreds more – the great uninvited – trying to get in.
It was as if the government of Venice had fallen and the last
helicopters were about to take off from the Guggenheim before
the victorious armies of Florence or Rome occupied the city.
Invite in hand, he was ushered through the gates by the scrupulously polite security. Inside, everyone was belting back bellinis
as usual. The waiters were struggling to cope with the insatiable demand for bellinis. There was barely room to move
and around the drinks tables it was mayhem. Jeff had got it
into his head that risotto had been promised. He assumed
he'd got this idea from the invite, but there was no mention
of it there and, at present, no risotto was in evidence. In view
of the numbers, producing risotto was an absurdly ambitious
and labour-intensive undertaking, but it seemed that Jeff was
not alone in expecting risotto. The risotto and its potential
non-appearance was, in fact, the chief topic of conversation
in the garden. People were counting on risotto to line their
stomachs; a lack of risotto would have a significant impact
on their ability to belt back bellinis. From the balcony of the
gallery itself a bearded American ambassador or cultural
attaché was pleading for calm, or at least trying to get everyone
to quieten down for a few minutes so he could give a speech.
When the hubbub subsided, the bearded dignitary welcomed
Ed Ruscha, praising him to the skies, explaining what an
honour it was to have him here and what an important artist
he was. At the end he asked everyone to raise a glass to Ed

Ruscha, which, though fair enough, was pretty superfluous since the only time during his speech people had stopped raising their glasses was while getting them refilled by the much put-upon bar staff. And then the doors to the gallery itself opened. This was it! The risotto, obviously, was now being served. There was an amazing stampede as people seized on the idea that the risotto moment was imminent. Jeff was perfectly placed. He surged up the steps and found himself in the galleries, confronted not by vats of creamy risotto but art, paintings and sculptures from the glorious heyday of modernism – Duchamp, Max Ernst, Picasso, Brancusi – when it was impossible to believe that there would come a time when all people cared about was free risotto to mop up all the free bellinis they'd been swilling in the garden. Like a flood, the crowd of people kept finding new levels within the building. Suddenly Jeff was out on the terrace, faced with the back of Marino Marini's statue of a guy on a horse – or some kind of creature anyway – with a kind of turd-tail sticking out of its bronze bottom. The rider's arms were stretched out horizontally, crucified by air or, perhaps, by the splendour of the view of the Grand Canal. As Jeff squeezed past he saw that, just as his mount had this stiff little tail at the back, so the rider had a stiff little dick sticking out at the front. He had no opportunity to ponder the significance of these details. Such was the intensity of the search for risotto that, within minutes, the terrace was jammed solid. Drinks were being served out here too, and so were some appalling bits of pastry, dried up old things, like samosas but not as spicy. Jeff manoeuvred his way to the drinks table, where he spotted Ben.

'Any sign of the risotto?' he asked.

'You know, I don't think there's going to be any risotto,' said Ben. He looked really cast down. Jeff could empathize with that. He was pretty devastated himself, even though he had taken the precaution of eating several slices of pizza on the way over.

'They lure you here with the promise of risotto,' he said, 'and there's no fucking risotto.'

'It's not even like there's a limited quantity, available on a first-come, first-served basis.'

'There's absolutely none.'

'All there is are a few miserable bellinis.'

'Rather a lot of bellinis, in fairness. In fact, you've got two in your hands.'

'They go down a treat, don't they?'

'They slip down,' said Jeff, finishing his. Since they were pressed right up against the drinks table, he scooped up a couple more.

A glass in each hand, Ben and Jeff made their way to the edge of the terrace, taking in the commanding view of the Grand Canal. The sun was sinking Turnerishly, about to disappear behind the buildings on the other side of the Canal. The vapour trails of planes converged there too. Almost directly across from them was the Gritti. It looked a bit boring, being there, compared with being here. People on vaporetti were looking up, wishing they were either up here, chucking free bellinis down their throats, or sitting on the terrace of the Gritti, paying for them through the nose.

'The thing about a bellini,' Jeff said to Ben, 'is that it's actually an extremely refreshing drink.'

'In these conditions one couldn't wish for a better drink.' It was the Kaiser who said this, so there were three of them now, with six drinks between them. The problem was that they went down such a treat that in no time at all it would be necessary to start barging back to the drinks table for refills.

'I just wish they came in a bigger glass,' said Ben.

'Good point,' said Jeff. 'It's so stingy, serving them in these little fuckers.' He had said it as a joke, or at least that's how he'd begun saying it, but by the time he'd completed this remark its truth was so glaring that he felt genuinely annoyed. Especially since the poxy little glasses were empty. He was girding his loins, preparing to head back to the drinks table, when, in one of those magical Venice moments, a waiter appeared with a jug of bellinis. The three of them stuck their hands out, watched as the waiter filled their greedy pairs of glasses.

'Didn't the Buddha say that you should take whatever was put in your begging bowl?' said Ben.

'Wise words!' Moved by the serendipity of the moment, they clinked their begging bowls and sipped their drinks, sipped in the sense of gulped. Although a bellini was, as Jeff had claimed, a refreshing drink, the heat was stifling, impossible to keep at bay. A kind of mania was in the air. Atman closed his eyes and gave himself over to the noise around him, the din of voices, the pandemonium of conversation and laughter, the remarks and questions in several languages, the popping of prosecco bottles and the clinking of glasses, the jokes and the laughter sprinkled over everything. It was a representative sample of what people having a good time sounded like. They could have recorded it and sent it off to some distant part of the solar system to sonically illustrate what social life on Earth – or high-quality freeloading, at least – sounded like. Jeff opened his eyes and there he was, gazing out over the Grand Canal. It was like waking up and finding yourself in a more wonderful dream than any you'd had while sleeping. What a city, what an utterly sensational place! Someone tapped him on the shoulder. He turned round.

It was her. Laura. The same person. But dressed differently.

Of course she was dressed differently. There was so much

to see. Her hair, her face, her dress and the small yellow badge – with words too small to read – pinned to her dress. The overwhelming happiness of the moment made him suddenly confident, freeing him to say,

'You found me! You see. I said you would.'

'Weren't you meant to be looking for me?'

'I realized the only way to do that was to let *you* find *me*, to stop looking. But at some level I never stopped looking. I was looking out for you just now in fact – but in the wrong direction.'

Now was the time to bend and kiss her. On the lips. He didn't feel nervous about it at all.

'I'm glad I found you,' he said.

'So am I.' Up close like this he could read the words on her badge: MY SAFE WORD IS OUCH.

'Have you been having a good time?'

'Yes. What about you?'

'I've got to say, everything has worked out perfectly.'

'Did you go to the Giardini?'

'Yes. But what time were *you* there? That's the interesting thing.'

'I guess I got there at about one-thirty.'

'What about on the bridge of the Accademia, at about six?'

'Yes, I think I was there about then. Why didn't you come up?'

'You were talking to someone. And there wasn't time to get off the vaporetto. Also, you know I was doing that interview with Julia Berman? I ended up getting stoned with her, so it was all a bit strange. I was a bit discombobulated.'

'You got stoned?'

'And as a result of that, I forgot to get the drawing. Oh, it's a long story. Did I tell you about the picture last night?'

'You mentioned it. But the interview was more important, no?'

'I don't know. Maybe. I saw the drawing Morison did of her, but she wouldn't give it to me.'

'What was it like?'

Had he unconsciously arranged the conversation so that he would be able to say that it was of a woman, naked, her legs open? Or was there nothing *un*conscious about it?

'It was of her. Nude, lying down, looking at Morison, who was drawing her.'

She raised her eyebrows. 'And?'

'It just didn't seem appropriate to take it.'

'Was it a good picture?'

'Yes, I think it was. There was an intensity about it. It was really quite powerful.'

'You're not going to say something boring about "the male gaze" are you?'

'I was actually,' he said, looking at her. 'Did you only say that to make me look at you?' Which was all he wanted to do for the moment, a moment that, as far as he was concerned, could last forever. To look at her in this red and gold dress. To look at her and wonder about her underwear, to wonder about her naked . . . Clicking back to the present, he said, 'What about you, though? What did you do after that? After you were on Accademia bridge.'

'This is more like an interrogation than a conversation.'

'I can see it is in a way. A similar urgency in the wish for answers. There's so much I want to know. Like what you did after Accademia.'

'I went to buy glasses. I needed sunglasses.'

She rummaged in her bag – a Freitag bag, mainly red.

'I love your bag,' he said.

'Me too. You know what I most love about it?'

'Let me look.' He looked at it while she rummaged, even peeked inside slightly. 'The fact that it's got a zip,' he said.

'Without the zip, its beauty would be diminished by its lack of practicality.'

'Very good.'

'Did you think I'd just say "red" or something?'

'Oh, no. I had no doubt you'd say zip. That's why I asked. To make you feel astute. The other great thing about this bag is it's got a separate compartment.' She showed him. 'With another zip.'

'Worlds within worlds. Also cuts down on rummaging.'

'Cuts down on,' she said, rummaging in her bag. 'but can never eliminate completely.' With that she produced her new sunglasses. She put them on. They were the bug-eyed ones that make every woman look like Kate Moss or the girlfriend of an England footballer. There was no doubt about it: this was one of the great eras for women's sunglasses. They were fantastic sunglasses. He could see her eyes through them, could see himself reflected in them and, behind him, the buildings of Venice.

'Try them.'

He took them from her, looked through them. In the fading light the sky glowed as it does when there is a bank of clouds with the sun shining directly on them so that they become a glowing black screen. It was like a storm was coming – a storm of gold-green light.

'Fantastic,' he said, handing them back. 'Speaking of fantastic, what about this dress? The one you were wearing last night was great. But this one – it's the most beautiful dress in the world. You could wear it to the Oscars.'

'Too short. But thank you.'

'Where did you get it?'

'Ah, the interrogation resumes. In Vientiane.'

'I'll be honest, I don't know which country that's in.'

'Laos,' she said, pronouncing it so that it rhymed with 'how'.

'You know what my favourite thing about it is?'

'What?'

'The sleeves.'

'There aren't any.'

'Bingo!' They clinked glasses.

'What about the piece you're writing?' she asked. 'Have you found anything to say?'

'It's impossible to say anything about Venice that's not been said before,' he said, cleverly.

'Including that remark,' she said, even more cleverly. That line gave him pause; her next floored him completely. 'So,' she asked, 'did you get any risotto?'

'No! Not a grain.'

'You're kidding.'

'No, *you're* kidding. There isn't any.'

'You're right. There isn't *now*. But I had a ton.'

'Where were they serving it? I can't believe this has happened. I find you and I realize that I've lost the risotto. By confirming its existence, you've confirmed my missing out on it.'

'I'm sorry to be the bearer of bad tidings.'

'How was it?'

'Very nice. Pea. Pea risotto.'

'Fuck! I love that shit! I don't suppose there's any left?'

'They were clearing it away just before I came out here.' He stood there dumbfounded. 'I'm sorry for your loss,' she said.

'I'm glad for my find,' he said.

There was something so obviously heartfelt about this that the conversation stalled until Laura said, 'So, how was Julia Berman? Was she like some kind of older-woman fantasy come true?'

'She was really nice but, to be honest, I've reached the age

85

where even fantasies about older women involve women younger than me.'

'Very good. Actually, while we're on the subject, how old *are* you? Roughly.'

'Um, forty. Ish.'

She held up her fingers, counted on them. Looked startled, looked at him. Recounted desperately, looked at him in horror.

'No, no. It can't be.'

'Very funny.'

'You look good. Ish. For your age.'

'I've got to tell you something.'

'What?'

He bent down and whispered. 'For the first time ever. Two days ago . . .' He paused. 'I dyed my hair.'

Laughing made her spit a mouthful of bellini back into her glass.

'I had my suspicions,' she said.

'You did?'

'No. just kidding. It looks great. Like it's not dyed. So, you've been getting stoned on the job.'

'I know. I'm sorry, I feel I've let everyone down. Including myself. How about you?'

'Do you mean have you let me down or do I feel I've let myself down?'

'I mean do you like getting stoned? California must be very conducive to smoking dope.'

'California is very conducive to everything.'

And so, at this moment, was Venice. Speedboats and low-slung taxis were pulling up, across the canal at the Gritti, and here, at the Guggenheim, but they were now taking more people away than they were dropping off. The party had passed its peak. There was plenty of booze and plenty of people still drinking it. Under normal circumstances the party could have continued, in full swing, for hours, but this was the Biennale, there were lots of other parties to go to and as soon as a party began flagging it quickly fizzled out. If the tacit theme of every conversation had been what fun it was to be here, the implied subject, now, was where to go next. There was a general move towards the exit. They joined a group going to a party given by a Russian collector at the something palazzo – Jeff was not invited but Laura had an invite for two. At some level this was his destiny in life: to be a Plus One. It was probably worth trying to change his name by deed poll, to Plus One.

They left the Guggenheim and rambled through the alleys and lanes of Venice. A couple of members of their party went missing almost immediately. As they were passing the Accademia stop a vaporetto pulled up so they scrambled aboard, only to get off at the next stop, San Toma. Jeff didn't care where they went. They came to the palazzo where the party was being held and were admitted, all eight of them, without let or hindrance. It was essentially the same party as the one they had left. Same scene, different setting: a hot courtyard, lots of people drinking.

Except, scandalously, the drinks were not free. Unbelievable but true! You were expected to *pay* for them. Jeff was already at the makeshift bar when he discovered this outrageous breach of party etiquette. Eager to make a good impression, he was about to buy a bottle of prosecco when the barman's attention was diverted by a guest who claimed to have been short-changed. In that moment of distraction, a bare arm reached past Jeff, swiped a bottle from the ice bucket and instantly disappeared. He glanced round, saw Laura's discreetly retreating back, one arm raised above her head, a finger wagging him to follow.

By the time Jeff had located some clean glasses the bottle was openly steaming, ready to be poured.

'You're something else,' said Jeff.

'She's terrible, isn't she?' said a man he had not quite met. 'One day she is going to get into all sorts of trouble. In the meantime, here's to Laura.'

Jeff joined in the toast, secretly fearing that she could get *him* into trouble, could smash his heart as easily as she had pinched the prosecco. Shared between many, the hot chilled bottle only lasted a few minutes. When someone went off to buy a replacement, Laura turned to Jeff and said, 'Don't you think it's time?'

'Yes, I do. Definitely. But, um, for what?'

'That we had a conversation about the art.'

'What art?'

'Very funny. What did you see?'

Jeff told her about the Finnish boat in the shattered glass (she'd missed that), the fun dartboards, the blue room, the video shower . . .

'Overall, though?'

'Overall, I was walking around and saying to myself, "It's of a banality that beggars belief."' He hadn't been thinking this at all, but he was thinking it now, as he said it.

'But that's completely wrong, isn't it? Because we aren't actually amazed by the banality. We've come to expect it. It's reassuring, a stamp of quality. We've sort of invested in it. It's like we're living through a conceptual breakthrough. It's really exciting. People keep wondering how long it can go on for, when the bubble is going to burst. The thing is, the bubble *has* burst but it keeps expanding anyway, even after it's burst. It's like the discovery of a new law of physics.'

'Quite unusual, hearing someone from a gallery talk like that.'

'I know. That's why I'm getting out. I'm going to become a hedge fund manager instead. In Varanasi.'

'I wish I was a hedge fund manager. Or at least I wish I knew what hedge fund managers do.'

'They collect art.'

'Do you have a collection?'

'A few small things. Gifts from artists whose shows I worked on. What about you?'

'Not really. Not art. I like owning things so much that I resist collecting anything except books. Books and Dylan bootlegs.'

'How about me?'

'How d'you mean? Are you asking me if you collect Dylan bootlegs?'

'No.' She raised her glass to her lips, took a sip. 'I meant, would you like to own me?'

'I spent my twenties in the 1980s. The days of the feminist terror. If a woman had said that to me in 1984, it would have been the most flirtatious thing imaginable. But it would probably have been an ideological trap.'

'I'm a trap. A honey trap.'

'Are you? I've always wanted to get caught in one of those. Back in the eighties, they didn't have them. Or at least they had the traps, but not the honey. It was more like a Vegemite trap.'

This pleasantly ambiguous topic of conversation was brought to an end by the arrival of more prosecco, more people and a different, more heated discussion, about Turner and Venice. Having looked through a book devoted to exactly that subject earlier in the day, Jeff felt confident of contributing but it was impossible to get a word in.

Dave Glanding was saying, 'Turner came to Venice—'

Maria Fielding was saying, 'The Last of the Fighting Temeraires or whatever it's called . . .'

You could say anything at this point in the evening. It didn't have to make sense and you didr't have to wait for the other

89

person to finish what they were saying before you said it, but, by the same token, no one had to listen to what you were saying or wait for you to finish saying what you were saying.

'Constable—,' said a woman Jeff didn't recognise, but that was as far as she got because the Kaiser was saying, 'There's only one artist in the Biennale I care about.'

Unusually, there was a pause as everyone waited for the result of this declaration.

'Bellini!' he said, raising a glass in acknowledgement of the enthusiastic applause with which this remark was endorsed. At some level everyone agreed and some agreed at every level. Evidently, this was a free-fire zone in which a conversation that made perfect sense dissolved into another conversation that flowed on perfectly sensibly from the previous one even though there was no connection and the previous one had been perfectly nonsensical anyway. Jeff had no chance to join in, but was reassured by everything he'd heard – reassured by the way that lots of people were far more drunk than him. Relatively speaking, he was as sober as a slightly tipsy judge.

The conversation spilled over into another unexpected topic: where to go next. It was decided to go to a different party, quite nearby, at the Palazzo Zenobio. Laura and Jeff left with the rest of the group, but the Zenobio was so crowded that no one was being allowed in until someone from inside left: the zero-sum maths of *one in, one out*. There followed another enthusiasm-draining interlude of milling around. The Kaiser and a couple of others said they were calling it a night – calling it a night in the sense that they were going to Haig's Bar. Just across the canal was the so-called Manchester Pavilion, a bar. Laura, Jeff and the rest went there instead.

A lot of the people in the bar had nothing to do with the Biennale – backpackers who happened to be in Venice, who had not been to any parties, for whom the anxiety of invitation was as alien as lumbago – but there were plenty of art people as well. Some of these art people were friends of the art people in Jeff and Laura's little group, which, having suffered a slight numerical falling-off, merged with this new group and was soon back to full strength again. Suited Jeff perfectly: the more people there, the easier it was to be left alone with Laura.

They took their beers and sat outside, on the warm steps of the humpbacked bridge over the sleeping canal. With all the talking that had been going on, it felt as if this was the first drink of the night Jeff had actually had the chance just to *drink*, to sip and enjoy for its own sake. Everything prior to this had just been fuel, chucked on the conversational pyre.

They sat quietly. He noticed again the things he'd been noticing all evening. She was wearing pink flip-flops with no heels. Beneath one ankle was a patch of red skin, rubbed raw by another pair of sandals. Her bare legs were tanned.

Laura said, 'How many times have you been in Venice?'

'Twice. The Biennale two years ago and once before, ages ago, when I was twenty-one. I was on my way to meet a friend in Corfu. I slept outside the station. Which was fine except the cops woke everyone up really early so I spent the day trudging round, exhausted, occasionally buying a slice of pizza to keep me going. I was only going to Corfu, but I was travelling on an InterRail pass – you know those things? – because it was cheaper. So the second night, instead of sleeping outside the station, I went to Florence on a train, slept all the way, and then got a train straight back and slept some more. I was still exhausted but I sort of saw the city, in the brief intervals when I could keep my eyes open.'

'Why didn't you get a room?'

'They were so expensive. I was on my own. It seemed an incredible indulgence.'

'How cheap!'

'I know. But I've learned my lesson. Guess where I'm staying this time?'

'Where?'

'In a *hotel*.'

She was on a slightly higher step, sitting with her feet discreetly together, but as she laughed he caught a glimpse of white knickers that set his heart racing. The history of sex is the history of glimpses: first ankles, then cleavage, then knees. More recently, tattoos, navel rings, tongue studs, underwear, Laura's underwear . . . Whenever she shifted position slightly, he hoped to sneak another look up her dress.

Laura said, 'Are you trying to look up my dress?'

'No! Not now. Now I'm making a real effort to look you in the eye. But a few moments ago I was, yes.'

'How old did you say you were?'

'Early to mid-forties-ish. But some things are timeless. You're fourteen, you want to look up women's dresses. You're forty, you want to look up women's dresses. You're seventy, you've got one foot in the grave, but you're hoping, even as your gaze turns towards heaven, that you might get one last chance for a look up a woman's skirt. Hemlines go up and down, but nothing really changes.'

Jeff felt, after saying this, as if he had made a speech, a statement of belief. Perhaps he had. They sat quietly again. Then Laura said, 'Shall we go quite soon?'

'I'm ready to go now.'

'C'mon then.'

They stood up, left their bottles on the steps and began walking. He put his arm around her shoulders. Her arm went around his waist. They walked through the cat-deserted alleys and lanes, along canals, through waiting piazzas.

'What do you think the chances are of finding your hotel?' said Laura.

'I'm not sure. But the incentive for doing so is considerable.' They consulted the map frequently – torn now from careless folding. They sought guidance from a patient man out walking his dog.

'*Sempre dritto*!' he replied unwaveringly, 'Straight ahead!'

Within a hundred yards it became impossible to continue straight ahead. A turn had to be made and that turn must have been a wrong turn. Further mistakes were made. Dead-ends loomed without warning. Bridges that were supposed to serve as short cuts failed to appear, but after twenty minutes of zigzagging and backtracking they came to the hotel. The night porter handed over the key. No eyebrow was raised.

The room, when they entered, was cool. Laura went straight into the bathroom. The white door closed behind her. Jeff heard water running, the sound of the toilet flushing. He took off his Birks, looked at the closed white door, saw it open again.

'Can I use this?' She was holding up the little toothbrush provided by the hotel.

'Of course.' The door shut again and he stared at it again. When it opened and she came out he went in and brushed his teeth with his own brush. He came out. She was not lying or sitting on the bed. She was standing by the desk, leaning against it, looking through the book of Turner's paintings of water-coloured Venice. She closed the book, put it down on the desk. He moved towards her and they were kissing. It was like a kiss from hundreds of years ago, when people had no hope of experiencing such a thing until their wedding night. Everything that came after was implied by these first moments of their kiss. He touched her face, her hair fell over his hands, over his face. As they kissed he pulled her dress up around her thighs. Her hands were on his back, beneath his shirt. She eased forward so that he could pull her dress up over her hips then leant back again on the desk. Looking down he could see, plainly now, the white underwear he had glimpsed earlier. His hands moved up the unbelievable softness of her legs, the inside of her thighs. He touched the cotton between her legs, pressed it against her. She had unbuttoned his shirt. Her fingers, as they moved up his ribs, sent charges down his spine. He reached behind her back, tugged down the zip of her dress, slipped it off her shoulders. He undid her bra and bent to kiss her breasts. One of her nipples was pierced with a silver ring. The sight of that sent his blood surging. His hands were on her nipples, both growing hard, flicking the nipple ring very slightly. He bent his head and took her nipple in his mouth, the silver ring clacking loud against his teeth. They were kissing again. He pulled her underwear aside and slipped his fingers inside her. He stepped back and knelt in front of her, kissing her stomach. Her hands were by her sides, on the desk. He licked down her stomach and then moved lower so that he could smell and see her. She reached down to hold her underwear aside. He stayed there motionless, inhaling deeply through his nose, exhaling through his open mouth. Only his breath touched her. Neither of them moved. He tilted his head and she moved from the edge of the desk, bending her legs slightly until she was almost touching his tongue and then was. She kissed his face with her cunt, moving over his mouth, moving in synch with him. He moved his thumb inside her, inside and out, then his fingers. She pressed down harder against his face, then reached back and pulled her dress over her head, tossed it onto the bed. He stood up and they kissed again, the smell of her on both their faces. She was naked except for her white underwear. She began unzipping his trousers, reached inside his underpants. They shuffled towards the bed. He took off his trousers and underpants and she bent down to remove her knickers. As she did so he saw, just below her hipbone, a

94

small tattoo of what he thought, at first blush, was a shark. But it was a dolphin, of course, leaping bluely out of a line of saw-tooth surf.

They were both naked now, sitting on the bed. Her pubic hair was thick, very dark, soft, trimmed into a narrow strip. She was kissing his stomach and he was licking her stomach until his face was between her legs and her mouth was around him. He moved his left arm between her legs, using it to ease her legs open and bury his face in her. He saw, for the first time, her asshole. She had taken him more deeply into her mouth, wet as her cunt in his face. They stayed like that, moving easily in rhythm until she was coming, coming on his face, as his come washed into her mouth.

They disentangled their legs and arms, feeling, he suspected, a little self-conscious now about how their faces had ended up in each other's genitals. Intimacy is not consistent or uniform; it has its own delays and lags. He was also wondering, slightly, about the etiquette of what had just happened. Were they supposed to have fucked? Laura, evidently, was thinking along the same lines.

'So, are you going to fuck me now?'

'Maybe not *right* now,' he said. She was smiling and then they were kissing.

'Your face smells of pussy.'

'Your face smells of come.'

'Shouldn't that have gone, "Your face smells of come, *bitch*"?'

'You're right. But I've got that whole post-coital tenderness thing going on at the moment.'

'Me too. I love the way you licked me.'

'I love the way you sucked me. And I love this,' he said, touching her nipple ring. He meant it, of course, but what he really meant was that there was so much to love.

They lay side by side, took it in turns to drink, awkwardly, from one of the big bottles of water he'd bought earlier. Jeff said, 'You know, it's amazing, isn't it? You meet a woman and you talk to her and then she lets you do this *stuff* to her, stuff you've basically been interested in since you were about thirteen. And she doesn't just *let* you do this stuff. She *wants* you to do this stuff. And she wants to *do* stuff to you. It's just great.'

'Why are you telling me this? Of all people.'

'I had to share it with *someone*. And you were the only person here.'

She handed Jeff the water and rolled over, onto her stomach. He saw again the tattoo of the dolphin he had glimpsed earlier. His hand followed the notches of her spine down the length of her tanned back.

'When did you have the shark done?'

'It's a dolphin, idiot!'

'I told you, I'm not a very visual person.'

'Five years ago. In San Francisco. Do you like dolphins?'

'In some ways I envy them.' He put the water on the bedside table, touched the dolphin and then stroked her legs and ass. Slid his fingers between her legs. He was feeling turned on again.

She said, 'Are we still talking about stuff?'

'Possibly.'

'So, what stuff are we talking about now?'

'We're talking about how lovely it feels, having my fingers in your cunt.'

'It does feel lovely,' she said. 'Yes, do that.' Her legs opened more. He could see what his hand was doing.

'Like that?'

'Hmm. Do you have condoms?'

'Yes.' She turned over, onto her back. They kissed.

*　　*　　*

96

In the morning they ate breakfast – orange juice (great), coffee (perfect), cornetti (tolerable) – in the same place he'd gone to the day before. They were sitting in the shade, on gleaming silver chairs, wearing sunglasses, looking down the tree-adorned street with its glimpse of the Giudecca Canal. This was it: happiness. The same happiness experienced many times before and not just in Venice: by people in other cities, on other mornings like this. To look at her long, tanned legs was to feel their smoothness against his hands, his lips. Jeff asked, 'What would you be having for breakfast if you were at home?'

'A full English. Eggs. Bacon. Beans. Black pudding.'

'Do you know what that is?'

'Isn't it shit fried in sheep's blood or something?'

'Other way round.'

'Actually, I'd be having orange juice, coffee and croissants.'

'You can get all this in LA? Must be quite a city.'

'The orange would be decaf.'

Jeff was looking through the newspaper, which confirmed what they – what everyone – had suspected: today was going to be even hotter than yesterday.

'There's an article here,' he said, glancing up. 'It says that men are biologically programmed to read the newspaper at breakfast. What d'you think? Any truth in that?'

Laura was dipping the last of her cornetto into her coffee, brushing her hair behind her ear with her other hand. He folded the newspaper away – a manly, breakfastly gesture. She said, 'You're in a good mood.'

'I'll give you one guess why.'

'Because you're not sleeping outside the station?'

Little birds kept landing on their table, pecking at crumbs. Laura shooed them away. They were a nuisance and possibly a health hazard too. Laura rummaged in her bag, the same bag she'd rummaged through the previous night, before they'd slept together. Eventually she produced a much-amended print-out of her schedule.

'What day is it today?'

'Friday.'

'Shoot.'

'What is it?'

'I have to meet my boss for lunch. Which means I should be going. I have to go to my hotel and change.'

'Change? Into an even nicer dress?'

'Maybe not. Unfortunately, this one has come spots on it.'

'Sorry. That's so rude of me.'

'I forgive you. Also, I need new underwear. Look.' She nodded her head, cast her eyes down and opened her legs slightly. She was naked beneath her dress. 'Isn't it terrible, though? As a culturally aware person, that gesture has been sort of ruined by Sharon Stone.'

'I still enjoyed it,' he said. 'But what a difference ten hours makes. Last night you were accusing me of looking up your dress and now you're asking me to.'

'It's a privilege, not a right.'

'Last night you said I owned you.'

'I said, "Would you *like* to?"'

It happened that, as they were having this conversation, Jeff was also spooning honey from his cornetto.

'The freaking honey trap,' he said, holding up the spoon.

'What are you going to do with that?'

'I suppose, at the risk of appearing vulgar, I should lick it off. But I hate honey. That's why I've hooked it out.' He lay the honey-sticky spoon on the plate.

'What about you?' Laura said. 'What do you have to do?'

'I don't need to change. I'm happy with what I'm wearing, thanks.' Another instance of shyness, modesty: at the hotel, as they were dressing, he had opted, in spite of the heat, for trousers instead of shorts. 'I just have to go to the Arsenale. Can we meet there later?'

'I'm not sure what time I'll be able to get there. Maybe two? If I can't make it by then, I'll phone.'

'I don't have a phone.'

'You don't have a phone?'

'No, but I could call you.'

'I don't have one either.'

'Now, that really is a coincidence.'

'Don't you need a phone in your line of work?'

'Probably. Don't you need a phone in your line of work?'

'Definitely.'

'We must be the last two people in the world not to have a phone. Castaways.'

'Not a problem, though. If I'm not at the Arsenale, at the ticket desk, by two, assume I'm not coming. In which case I'll meet you at Accademia, on the bridge. At four.'

'Perfect. Shall we get more coffee?'

They ordered two more cappuccinos, two more juices, two more cornetti. In addition to the birds a wasp was buzzing around the table, attracted, bee-like, by the honey. Fiona Banner, the artist, walked briskly past. With her jet-black hair and big-framed glasses, she looked like she was in disguise – as herself. Jeff waved, but she didn't see him.

He would have been happy to sit here for the rest of the day, the rest of his life. Laura said she had to get going. He paid the bill and they kissed goodbye.

'I'm tired,' she said.

'So am I.'

'I wish we could take a nap.'

'Well, I'm free.' Her arms were around his neck.

'I'll see you later. Arsenale at two—'

'Or Accademia at four.'

He watched her go, her hair shadow-dark in the sun, her feet moving lightly.

Relieved that he didn't need to repeat the previous morning's post-breakfast dash, Jeff decided to walk to the Arsenale, through Campo Santo Stefano and San Marco. To say he had a spring in his stride would be an understatement. He swaggered through Venice as if he owned the place, as if it had been created entirely for his benefit. Life! So full of inconvenience, irritation, boredom and annoyance and yet, at the same time, so utterly fantastic. What an absolutely, sensationally brilliant planet it was! Wobbly with fat, a woman in a white T-shirt looked at him uncertainly. He must have been doing that thing again, mouthing out his thoughts. But who cared when they were thoughts like these, thoughts that actually contributed, in their small way, to making the world the excellent, happy place that it was?

It took a while to get to Piazza San Marco, so lovely in photographs or at dawn, so pigeon-congested once the day got going. It was especially crowded in the south-west corner. Especially around *Jeff*. He was being barged from the side, from the left. A young guy – handsome, in his late teens, possibly east European – was speaking, in such heavily accented Italian that Jeff couldn't understand what he was saying. He was wearing sunglasses. He bumped into Jeff again, was still speaking. But what was he saying? It made no sense. Maybe it wasn't even Italian he was speaking. Jeff felt something bump against his right hip, on the other side from the guy to his left, who was still talking in this confusing language that may or may not have been Italian. What . . . ? Shit, he was being pickpocketed. That's what was happening. He yelled, '*Ladro*!' and pushed through the crowd, clearing some space. All eyes turned, first on him and then on the guy who had been speaking to him and then on his accomplice, both of whom were moving quickly out of the way. Jeff felt in his pockets. Money, vaporetto pass, press pass . . . Everything was where it was meant to be. The two would-be thieves were still in view, conscious of the accusing stares of the crowd. Jeff was suddenly exultant. They had tried to rob him and had failed. Feeling invincible he called out, in English, in the direction of the two Albanians – or Serbs or whatever they were.

'Call yourself pick-pockets? You couldn't steal the piss from your mother's cunt.' As soon as the words were out of his mouth, he felt suddenly un-invincible, frightened that this was an insult so grave it would have to be avenged immediately, that their honour demanded they come back and stab the person who had uttered it. Fortunately, it seemed their English wasn't good enough to understand what had been said. Not so the elderly Italian next to Jeff, evidently a connoisseur of invective, who clapped him on the shoulder and said, '*Bravissimo! Bravissimo!*' Looking bewildered and fearful – their fear of getting lynched was greater than Jeff's of getting stabbed – the two culprits slunk off, looking harmless, poor, foreign and hopelessly outnumbered. Some tall Africans were nearby, selling knock-off Prada bags. From their long-limbed, indifferent demeanour it was impossible to tell where their allegiances lay. Did they feel solidarity with their poor Slavic brothers, on whom the fury of the mob could so easily have been unleashed? Or were they enjoying the opportunity to affirm, however passively, their own relative law-abidingness, to show that while it may not have been strictly legal to be flogging leather goods that no one wanted they were, in the larger scheme of things, honest tradesmen, starting out on the road to what might turn out to be a legitimate career in retailing?

Jeff emerged onto the Riva degli Schiavoni – or the promenade, as he seasidely thought of it. It was still crowded, with tourists and the stalls catering for them, but after a hundred yards it became pleasantly quiet. The view of the sea or the canal – he wasn't sure at what point the one turned into the other – was obstructed by huge yachts: the *Ecstasea*, the *Neptune*, the *Sea Breeze*, a name that alerted everyone to the fact that there was none, that the baking city was becalmed in windless heat.

Along with the national pavilions at the Giardini, the Arsenale was the other key component of the Biennale: a selection of work by artists from around the world, chosen or commissioned by the director of the Biennale and united (allegedly) by some kind of theme. That this theme was impossible to discern from the apparently random array of art on display did not diminish the experience – or not Jeff's experience, at any rate. There was a ton of stuff to see: paintings, installations, photographs, video streams, sculpture (sort of), even, quaintly, the odd drawing. He breezed through it all, taking it all in, even if, much of the time, he took nothing in. He'd been watching a video loop of a kid playing keepy-uppy in the bombed-out ruins of a city – Belgrade, it turned out – for five minutes before he noticed that it wasn't a football he was dribbling around: it was a human skull.

A few minutes later, out of the corner of his eye, he spotted some colour photographs of tanned naked flesh. Porn! That was the great thing about the art world these days – you were never far away from Adults Only, sexually explicit, hardcore, triple-X material. Except, as he moved closer, they turned out to be the opposite of porn. These were full-colour pictures of a woman giving birth. Blood everywhere, the intestinal-looking umbilical cord and, finally, the fluid-smeared, crumpled little alien baby. Ugh! That stuff should be banned. It was deeply offensive. It could put you off sex for life. And not just sex. It could put you off *life* for life.

Needless to say, these pictures – like all the other photographs on offer – were the size of *The Raft of the Medusa*. So what if they were just snaps of someone jerking off in a leather armchair in an apartment in Zurich? So what if it was just a half-eaten, pre-packaged egg-and-cress sandwich abandoned on the seat of a bus shelter in Stockholm? So what if it was a portrait of the artist's sour-faced grandmother pushing her shopping trolley round a poorly stocked supermarket in Barnsley? Blow 'em up big enough and they looked . . . Well, they looked like shit, frankly, but they looked like art too.

As at the Giardini, there was a constant flow of people to greet and compare notes with: what they'd seen this morning, what they'd got up to the previous night. Never one to kiss and tell, Jeff would have liked nothing more than to boast and brag and generally yell from the rooftops about his adventures of the night before but he managed, somehow, to restrain himself. Everyone he met was more hungover than they had been yesterday and some had got their hands on free T-shirts as well as free bags and catalogues. The most resolute were even getting stuck into the free bottles of Asahi that were already being handed out from ice-crammed bins, strategically located.

Stretched out on cushions and orange and red rugs under a blazing jungle of neon, Scott Thomson waved to him to come on over. Since everyone else was respectfully walking round or briskly through the installation, Jeff expected him to get thrown out by security but Scott called out, 'C'mon dude, it's allowed.'

Jeff walked over and joined him on a pile of comfy cushions, gazing up into this mad tangle of neon allsorts and illuminated chillis and plastic bananas and God knows what else.

'This is more like it, isn't it? This is a *bit* like Burning Man,' said Scott.

'They have this kind of stuff there?'

'Loads of it. But more far out. You'd probably get some kind of performance thrown in as well. Or at least a bunch of people making out or serving cocktails.'

'Who's the artist?'

'Jason Rhoades. And all these signs—'

'Yes, what are they? Mexican beers or something?'

'No, man. Synonyms of pussy.'

Jeff looked again, tried to decipher and isolate the red, blue and purple letters: House Under the Hill, La Tortilla, Hombre (what was that all about?), Rinkly Stinkly, Bank, Birdy, Filthy Hatchet Wound (jeez, what sort of sick fuck had come up with that?), Lovely Meal, Pink Panther . . . There must have been a hundred more of them, but he got the point.

'And what's the piece called?' Scott shrugged, handed him the guide and pointed to the title: *Tijuanatanjierchandelier*.

'Quite a mouthful.'

'There you go: you've come up with another synonym.'

Funnily enough, last night . . . Jeff didn't say the words, but his face must have been beaming some kind of message of gleeful well-being.

Scott said, 'You know that expression "a shit-eating grin"?'

'Yes?'

'That's exactly how I'd describe your face now. Haven't seen you look this happy in years.'

'I haven't *been* this happy in years,' said Jeff, liking Scott more than he had for years. He would gladly have continued the conversation, but it was almost time to see if the source of his happiness had turned up for the first of their possible rendezvous. He got up to go, smiled goodbye to Scott. Now that the ice had been broken, quite a lot of other people were sitting and chatting in the midst of the installation.

Jeff waited for Laura at the ticket desk till ten past two, hoping they'd be able to relax together in the neon lair of *Tijuanatanjierchandelier*. Then he waited ten minutes more. She was not going to come. He was about to plunge back into the Arsenale when, some way off, he saw a bunch of Africans selling their knock-off bags in the bright heat. Even here, they were at it, hustling their wares! They really were irrepressible – and optimistic. What were the chances of *selling* bags when they were being given away free all over the place? But people were buying them, or at least showing an interest, entering into negotiations about price, quality and the possibility of discounts for bulk purchases. And a surprising number of people were filming or taking photographs of these happy Africans and their prospective customers. That's what caused the penny, eventually, to drop. The Africans were a work of art, a real-life installation, simulating the outside world the way their bags simulated the Prada and Louis Vuitton originals, thereby raising questions about authenticity, value, commodification, exploitation and several other things, probably, that didn't spring immediately to mind. Porn that was childbirth; a football that was a skull; commerce that was art: nothing today was quite what it seemed. And though it may have seemed as if Jeff was absorbed completely by the conceptual implications of the Africans and their bags, this was itself a form of dissimulation and disguise, camouflaging the fact – from himself as much as anyone observing him – that he was contriving a way of waiting a little longer for Laura. Eventually, though, he had to accept that she was not coming and, with a final look behind, headed back inside.

He soon spotted something he'd missed first time around:

photographs of celebrity academics and intellectuals, lecturing, hosting seminars and generally making the life of the mind look, if not glamorous, then certainly lucrative. There was Linda Nochlin contemplating 'The Glory and Misery of Pornography' in a colloquium in Paris; there was Eric Hobsbawm explaining how history means never having to say you're sorry; and there was Edward Said – so handsome, cuff-linked and dapper it seemed Richard Gere had already signed up for the biopic – guiding a group of adoring students through the minefields of orientalism, late style and why the Oslo Accord sucked the big one.

Under normal circumstances he wouldn't have had the patience to sit through videos, but today, feeling tired, he was glad to flop down in darkened rooms and let them take their course, even though many of them, of course, had no course to take. One showed a woman, filmed from behind and slightly above, silhouetted against a river. She did not move, but her coat and hair moved in the breeze. In front of her a grey blur of water moved slowly from left to right, filling the entire screen. Every now and then bits of garbage drifted by: bottles, clumps of branches, plastic bags. At one point a large lump floated past. It was impossible to tell what it was, but it looked like some kind of animal, a dog or a cat perhaps. The river kept flowing, hazy, trash-strewn, endless. Bird shadows darted over the water. Atman watched for a long time, continued to do so even after the tape had looped back, returning the river to the place where it had begun.

Another video showed a shaven-headed boxer shadow-boxing, ducking and diving, throwing punches at a woman who stood absolutely still. He never quite hit her, but his fists came within inches of her impassive face. She never flinched but, like the laundry woman, a few strands of her hair moved in the draught left by his blows. At one point, when he missed her only by millimetres, her nostrils flared slightly. He bobbed and weaved, protecting himself at all times, probing with jabs, making that boxerly snorting sound through his nose, looking for openings and then unleashing a brutal combination of blows, a flurry of lefts and rights, uppercuts and hooks, shots to the body, the face, the head. And all the time she stood there impassively, unharmed and lovely.

From the vaporetto he saw Laura in the middle of the Accademia bridge, talking to a man he did not recognise. By the time he got off the boat, the guy she'd been speaking to was nowhere to be seen. He walked up and stood in the place her companion had been standing. She was wearing a white dress. She raised her parasol a few inches. More of her face came into the sun. Her hair was pinned up, making her neck seem longer, her cheekbones more pronounced. She raised the parasol still further. Her eyes were lit up by the sun.

'Come into my shade,' she said. He moved towards her and she lowered the parasol again so that their faces were in the shade. He kissed her on the mouth. She smelled slightly, and tasted, of cherries.

'It's nice in here,' he said. It was like being in a capsule, insulated slightly from the world.

'Yes. The eat is otter than ever. But it's fractionally cooler under here.'

From her Freitag bag she produced another bag – polythene – of cherries. 'Have one.' She held a cherry by its stalk in front of his mouth. He closed his lips around it like Tess in the Polanski film. She tugged the stalk free. Then she took one for herself so that she was left holding two stalks while they chewed. His hand was on her hip, near her tattoo. Beneath the fabric of her dress he could feel the slight ridge of her underwear. She turned him towards the canal. They gazed out together, at the terrace of the Guggenheim, the nameless palazzos, the idle gondolas, the hitching posts like barbers' poles. He said, 'Did you get to the Arsenale?'

'My lunch was put back till two, so I went straight over there after changing. I was sure I'd see you there. Then, at one-thirty, I had to leave.'

They compared the things they'd seen. There must have been so many near-misses when they'd almost bumped into each other: she'd spent ten minutes in the vaginal neon of *Tijuanatanjierchandelier*, had seen the shadow-boxing and the river videos . . . It was a shame, but it didn't matter because they were here now.

'What about now?' Laura said. 'Is there anything you have to do?'

'Nothing at all.'

'So, shall we stroll?' Without waiting for his reply, she began walking. He fell in step beside her.

They walked through the Campo Santo Stefano and into a tighter network of shopping streets, where it was too crowded to hold hands. A very small shop specialized in gloves, displaying them in such a way that it looked as if they were praying to be purchased. They crossed a bridge spanning a small canal, in which there was a log jam of gondolas. One of them had a single occupant, sitting in his throne-like seat as if he were Genghis Khan, belatedly coming to terms with the futility of a life devoted to conquest. The passengers in the other boats all shared a diluted version of the same expression, one that reluctantly acknowledged that, in agreeing to travel by gondola, they had been sold one of the oldest pups in existence.

They came to a shop selling glasses, vases and lights made of glass, all decorated with dots, swirls and streaks of bright colour: the most beautiful glasses in the world, surely, and probably the most expensive as well. A small glass – the size a very small orange juice would come in – was eighty euros. There was a moment of shocked disbelief and then, almost immediately, the idea of a glass costing eighty euros began to be assimilated. Dostoevsky might have had these glasses, these prices, in mind when he defined man as a creature who got used to things.

'It seems a lot for a glass,' said Jeff, 'but I guess there are plenty of people in Venice this week who can afford them.'

'It's not about being able to afford them,' Laura said. 'It's about being able to not worry about breaking them. Besides, what does it mean to be able to afford something? It's a way of externalizing and gauging how much you desire something.'

They stood staring at these inessential, very desirable glasses.

'D'you know,' she said, 'I'm going to buy one for you.'

'No!'

'Yes. And not only that. You're going to buy one for me.'

'Am I? Ouch!'

'Yes. But the condition of doing so is that we don't care at all about breaking them. Obviously we'll wrap them in paper on the plane, and we won't put toothbrushes in them, but we'll use them whenever we feel like it. And you know how that will make us feel?'

'I'm tempted to say poor, but I think the correct answer is rich. Mainly, though, I'm relieved that you're not going to steal them.'

She led him into the shop. It was a wonderful shop, but just being in it made him feel clumsy, bullish. A careless gesture could prove extremely expensive. Anxious that even staring too hard at the glasses might cause cracks to appear, Jeff tried to look at them *gently*.

The glasses were all different, but they were so uniformly beautiful that choosing became somewhat arbitrary. For Laura he picked one that had a swirl of red and white, as if a scoop of raspberry ripple had been imprisoned in the glass. For him she chose one that was pale blue with tiny bobbles of orange. They paid. The sales assistant wrapped their glasses in pink tissue paper, handling them as if they had just been plucked from the tomb of Tutankhamen and might shatter on contact with the coarse air of not-the-afterlife.

Outside, Jeff noticed that they were right next door to Prada. For a moment he worried that a precedent had been set, that having bought each other an amazingly expensive glass, they were now going to up the stakes still further, splashing out on even more expensive clothes.

'So,' said Laura, 'let's go and use our new glasses.' Jeff's instinct was to squeak out 'Where?', but he forced himself, instead, to say 'Sure' and, once again, to fall into step beside her.

'Are we allowed to put them in a dishwasher?' he said, as they walked.

'Of course. They get no special privileges. They're just glasses, not shrines to be worshipped.'

'I suppose there is another problem,' he said. 'Are all other glasses going to seem inferior to these? Will drinking out of a normal champagne flute seem like drinking out of, I don't know, a jam jar or something?'

'If everyone felt like that,' she said, 'we would never even have evolved to the point where we drank out of jam jars.'

They walked on, through a reassuring part of town where the shops were selling normal things at normal prices.

Laura said, 'Do you know where we are?'

'Not exactly.'

'Do you know where we're going?'

'No. But I'm certainly interested in finding out.'

Five minutes later he did. At the end of an alley was a small but grandly-named hotel, the Excelsior. Laura picked up her key from the woman at reception, who greeted her with a big smile and took no interest in her new friend. In the tiny lift – a squeeze even for two – Laura pointed to a sign, covered in plastic and taped neatly beneath the maintenance certificate and said, 'Check out this piece of conceptual art.'

'PLEASE BE SO KIND AND DO NOT SCRATCH THE PLASTIC COVER. WE LIKE TO BE AS ENVIRONMENTALLY FRIENDLY AS POSSIBLE, BUT IF YOU SCRATCH THE COVER WE HAVE TO REPLACE IT.'

'You're right,' said Jeff. 'It should be in the Arsenale.'

Her room was small, dominated by a white double bed it was impossible to evade or ignore. She washed out the new glasses, crushed the pink tissue paper and threw it into the bin.

'What would you like for the inaugural drink? There's all the usual mini-bar stuff, plus I bought some pomegranate juice and soda because of the heat.'

'That would be great.' It was a relief, in the afternoon, to be free of the obligation to consume alcohol.

'If we break these glasses now we can think, "Wow, that was an expensive pomegranate juice." That way the pressure's off. Chin chin.'

They clinked glasses carefully, kissed. Delighted, evidently, at finding themselves in such luxurious vessels, the pomegranate and soda fizzed enthusiastically.

'You taste of pomegranate.'

'So do you.' She bit his lower lip. Her mouth opened. They were kissing again. He had never loved kissing anyone as much. Then – it was impossible to tell who instigated this – they manoeuvred in such a way that he was kissing her thighs while she licked his stomach. He lifted up his hips so that she could tug his trousers down. She pulled his prick from his underpants, began licking along its length. He pulled her knickers – white again – over her hips and off. He was unsure what to do about her dress, bunched around her middle. She sat up and pulled it off. Her smell – and his desire for her – was stronger than the night before. He breathed in that smell and pressed his face between her legs. She moved over on top of him. Drips fell from her, into his mouth. She sat back, twisting his nipples, rubbing herself in his face. His face gleamed with her smell. He reached up so that he could pull gently on her nipple ring. She disengaged herself from him, lay back on the bed, her legs raised.

'Now fuck me,' she said. He reached for his trouser pocket, for the condoms. 'You don't have to use a condom. I have a cap. I didn't have it with me last night.' He moved on top of her. His prick slipped into her cunt, her tongue into his mouth.

He began moving inside her. It was like nothing he had ever experienced before. She had opened herself to him at a non-physical level that increased the intensity of the physical sensation of their bodies moving together. He was conscious of being inside her, but it was like an *out of body* experience. The word that insistently came to mind, afterwards, as they lay in each other's arms, was unusable in a way that 'cunt', 'cock' or 'fuck' once were: communion. She was licking her fingers, moistening them with the saliva from her mouth and his, arching her back, pushing her hips towards him.

'I'm coming,' she said. Her wet finger pressed into him and, a moment later, he too was coming, joining her, coming inside her.

They lay still.

'Well,' he said. 'That was most agreeable.'

'Wasn't it?' she murmured. When his prick slid from her, they moved onto their sides, in each other's arms. He felt himself drifting to sleep.

He woke up just ten minutes later, his arm numb under her

neck. She was waking too. His arm, as he disentangled himself from her, pinned and needled back to life.

'You're the thinnest person I've ever slept with,' she said. 'It's like making love to an ironing board.'

'There must be some culture in the world, possibly an ex-Soviet republic, a very poor place suffering from a dearth of consumer goods, where that is the greatest compliment a woman can ever pay to a man. Wherever it is, I am going to find that place, ideally with a view to taking up permanent residence.'

'That is where I'm *from*,' she said. They kissed. He continued lying on the bed while she got up to take a shower. He watched her walk into the bathroom: small hips, thin, long back. He heard the toilet flush and the noise of the shower. She emerged from the bathroom with a white towel wrapped round her and he took her place in the steamy shower. When he came out she had put on the same white dress that she had worn that afternoon. He helped her with the zip and the hook at the top.

They left the hotel and walked to an almost empty trattoria that, in a few hours, would be crammed, hectic. Neither of them wanted wine, just fizzy water. Jeff asked for risotto; Laura ordered a veal cutlet.

'A strange and potentially controversial choice,' he said, 'though I can see why, after stuffing your face at the Guggenheim last night, you can't face any more risotto.'

'Actually,' said Laura, 'there's something I have to tell you about that night.'

His stomach flipped. 'What?'

'I lied about the risotto. There wasn't any.'

'No!'

'I overheard you and your friend talking about it.'

'Why, I oughta . . .'

'It's funny, no one says that any more: "Why, I oughta."
We should start a campaign to bring it back.'

'You're right. We oughta.'

'We otter.'

While Jeff tucked into his pea and mushroom risotto – even
more satisfying in the wake of Laura's confession – she told
him about an exhibition she hoped, one day, to curate. Having
seen the look of stunned disappointment on the faces of so
many gallery-goers, she aimed to take the bull by the horns
with a show called 'Is That *It*?' featuring works by some of
the most consistently disappointing artists of the day. Soon
they were trading titles for a series of related exhibitions:

'This, That and "The Other".'

'Something of Nothing.'

'Next to Nothing.'

'Slim Pickings.'

'Climaxing with a symposium of curators and critics,' Laura
said. 'Something along the lines of "Now Talk Your Way Out
of That".'

It was fun, talking like this, but Jeff had the nagging sense
that they were talking themselves out of what he most wanted
to talk about: how they were going to spend the rest of their
lives together. They ordered another bottle of mineral water.
He watched her eat a strawberry gelato for dessert. They each
had an espresso.

After dinner – and how nice it was eating early, like pensioners
– they walked through Venice in the hot evening, holding
hands. He'd read somewhere – it was another of those things
that practically every writer-visitor remarked upon – that
Venice was a narcissistic city, always looking at itself in the
mirror. What he saw reflected everywhere was his – their –
well-being. The city was radiant with reflected happiness.

They had both been invited to the Australia party, on Giudecca. They stopped at Jeff's hotel briefly, so he could change, and then walked to the vaporetto at Zattere. Twilight was falling. In the church behind them the bells started up, tumbling over each other, becoming a torrent of sound. The wide stretch of water separating them from Giudecca glowed darkly with the surplus light absorbed in the course of the day. Then it dulled, grew dark, as dark as the sky – navy blue and then Atlantic-black. The vaporetto chugged into view, the first stars appeared.

They got off at Palanca and walked west a couple of hundred yards. The party was packed by the time they arrived. Or at least the terrace was packed. As had happened on the previous two nights, the heat had driven everyone outside. Every few seconds there was the pop of a new bottle of prosecco being opened; bellinis were being prepared in vast quantities. It was, in other words, exactly like every other Biennale party except Jeff had turned up at this one with Laura, was arriving with the woman he'd met at the first party on the first night and slept with after the party of the second night. He took a couple of drinks from a tray, passed one to Laura, who was immediately greeted by a friend. In turn Jeff was greeted, not by a friend but by Graham Hart, art critic for the *Observer*. Either he'd been here for a while or he'd not waited till he got here to get his snout in the bellini trough. It wasn't just difficult to understand what he was saying; it was difficult to tell where one word ended and the next began. What emerged from his mouth was an undulating torrent of what was obviously language, but which had no capacity to convey information. That was not the only thing to emerge from his mouth. He sprayed slightly as he spoke and a blob of spit landed on Jeff's lower lip. He could feel it there, wet and alien, but out of good manners refrained from wiping it away. To have done so would have been to acknowledge what they both preferred to ignore: that Graham had spat on him. Graham was sweating profusely, more than all the other guests who were also sweating profusely. He mopped his forehead with an old-fashioned handkerchief.

Gradually Jeff grew acclimatized to what Graham was talking about, namely the prodigious amount he'd had to drink in the course of the day, but his ability to understand served only to confirm the lack of any desire to listen. Fortunately Graham was so far gone he didn't mind – probably didn't even notice – when Jeff sidled away. One of the reasons he was keen to get away was because he worried that Graham was a prophetic mirror. Was *he* like this when drunk? Was Graham a premonition of how he'd be a couple of hours and a dozen bellinis down the line? What must the world seem like to the ex-drinker, the teetotaller, the permanently sober, recovering alcoholic, surrounded on all sides by pissheads and drunks? It was a horrible prospect, enough to drive Jeff back to the bar. On the way he bumped into vehement Monika Weber, who presented a cultural affairs programme on German TV. She asked if he was going, tomorrow, to the exhibition curated by Jean-Paul. Jeff had completely forgotten about this show, but said he would be going, yes.

'I am going for one reason,' she said. 'I want to go just to tell him how much I hate him.' It was an excellent plan, one Jeff immediately fell in with. He was more than happy to tell Jean-Paul how much he hated him, even if he didn't actually hate him, could scarcely remember who he was. There was no opportunity to clarify things. Having spotted other people they knew, both he and Monika continued in their respective directions. In some ways the Biennale was like *A Dance to the Music of Time* condensed into four days: the same people cropping up, expectedly and unexpectedly, generally looking somewhat the worse for wear.

Jeff grabbed a drink and retreated from the bar, jostled and jostling as he did so. It had gone from being crowded on the terrace to being very crowded, impossible to move, difficult to drink without spilling bellini over your neighbour. And the area outside the party, as more and more people clamoured to get in, was almost as crowded as it was inside. Jeff was congratulating himself on this, on being one of those *at* the party rather than one of those trying to get into it, when someone tapped him on the shoulder: Laura, not looking any the worse for wear.

'Guess what I've just been given?' she said.

'A bellini?'

She shook her head and whispered in his ear.

'A gram of cocaine.'

'No!'

'Yes.'

'How did that happen?'

'I bumped into a friend. He'd forgotten my birthday and wanted to make it up to me.'

'Nice friend.'

'Shall we have some?'

'Most definitely.'

'Come on then.'

They pushed through the crowd to the bathrooms. Surprisingly, there was no queue and no one to spot them stepping inside. He locked the door and rolled up a ten-euro note while Laura arranged two neat lines with a Visa card. She snorted up one and he quickly followed suit.

'Very nice,' he said, folding away the note. 'Thank you.'

'Actually, I need to pee.'

Unsure whether she was asking him to leave or simply making an announcement, Jeff said, 'Let me watch.'

She pulled up her dress and pulled her knickers down to

her knees. Unconcerned by his being there, she began pissing immediately. Jeff held his hand between her legs, feeling her piss run hotly over his hand while she did so. He was on the brink of asking her, later on, when they were back at the hotel, to piss on his face but, even in the midst of the rush of coke, worried that this might lie outside the realm of her sexual enthusiasms – on reflection, he wasn't even sure it lay within the realm of his. He ran his hand under the tap. They came out of the toilet together, sniffing, glowing, unnoticed.

He'd been in a good mood before; now, with the chemical taste of coke trickling down his throat, he was in a *really* good mood. Unfortunately this surge of good feeling coincided with seeing Charles Hass, whose arm was in a sling. Jeff was about to introduce him to Laura but she was already talking animatedly to Yvonne, the friend she'd been with on the night they met. So Jeff was stuck with him.

'So, Charles,' he said, 'what's been happening to you? Very briefly.' Unfortunately so much had been happening to him it was not at all compatible with brevity. His injured arm was the latest instalment in a bad run of luck that extended back to the last time they'd seen each other – what? – a year ago? First, his wife had left him. Six months later his mother died and then, within a month of burying her, he was knocked off his bike by a taxi and had broken his arm. Hence the sling. How did you cope with such an unfortunate series of occurrences? By just plodding on, presumably. It actually took less effort to keep plodding on, putting one foot in front of another, than it did to lie down and stop. You kept on going. The ploughman homeward plods his weary way, even after a freak accident, even after the plough has run over his arm, severing it at the elbow. You pick it up with your good arm and head home as fast as possible, undeterred by all the pain, inconvenience and gruelling physiotherapy that lie ahead if – and it's a huge if – you're lucky enough to get the arm sewed back on. You keep plodding on. What else can you do? The only alternative is to not plod on. But you might as well keep plodding on as sit down and not plod on. As Charles told Jeff more about this terrible run of luck, he found himself transfixed and increasingly distressed by it, distressed by the possibility that something of the kind could be coming his way, hot on the heels of the run of incredibly good luck he was in the midst of now. He was aware of a wave of self-pity, heading towards him, about to crash over his head.

'Nothing bad will ever happen to me, will it, Charles?' he said.

'No, I'm sure it won't.'

'Are you sure?'

'Well, you can never—'

'Promise me. Promise me that nothing bad will ever happen to me. I need to be reassured.'

'I promise.'

'Say it like you mean it,' he said. 'Swear on your mother's grave.'

Charles looked at him harshly. Jeff knew he had gone too far, but the only way to get out of this situation was to go further. He gripped Charles's good arm. He implored him, looked him in the eye. By now the fear of something bad happening had gripped Jeff as he had gripped Charles's arm, so much so that it was as if he had gripped himself. He no longer knew if he was joking. Everything began as a joke – or some things did anyway – but not everything ended as one. Some things began as jokes, but ended up not being funny at all. If he wasn't careful, something terribly unfunny could befall him here. He could get punched in the face by Charles, especially now that he was no longer gripping his good arm.

He tried, instead, to get a grip on himself, but it was no good: the thought of Charles punching him in the face had turned into a general level of threat, a premonition that at some point in the coming days someone would hit him for something he had done or not done, something he should have done or had neglected to do.

'The thing is,' he said, 'I don't have the resources to deal with anything bad happening. I'm hanging on by my finger-nails as it is.'

'Let's change the subject,' said Charles.

'Great idea,' said Jeff. A waiter came by, bearing a tray with a single full glass of champagne. Jeff grabbed it – with his arm in a sling Charles, even if he'd had his eyes on it, never had a chance – and took a huge swig.

'So, anyway, how are you?' said Jeff, suddenly in good humour again, so much so that he laughed aloud at this little joke. 'You see, I've learned from your example. There I was, seriously depressed a few moments ago, but I had the tenacity to butch it out, to hang on in there. And I'm glad I did. I've pulled through and am having a fine old time again here at this party, shooting the breeze with a friend whose glass, I note, is tragically empty.' Jeff clinked it with his full one anyway. What a rollercoaster ride life was. He really was feeling great again. Unlike Charles, who looked distinctly down in the mouth.

'Come on,' said Jeff. 'I know I went off on a bit of a downer a few minutes ago, but I feel fine now, honestly. And I know that, technically speaking, I should have offered that glass of champagne to you but, well, it was a fifty-fifty ball and at that moment I felt I needed it more than anyone else in this entire city.'

Charles turned away. Jeez, he'd had a real sense of humour failure. Not that it mattered, because here was Valerie Sacks, in seriously high spirits, blahing drunkenly on about the man next to her – Pavel Something. They shook hands, but Jeff didn't catch the rest of his name.

'He's Polish,' she said. 'A count.'

'Between you and me, though,' slurred Graham Hart – where had he sprung back from? – 'I think the "o" is silent.' Count Pavel Whatever seemed not to have picked up on this vicious slur, but Jeff was quite keen to get away from this little group. Especially when he saw Laura heading towards him. My God, she was radiantly beautiful, high on coke, and, fifteen minutes previously, he'd had his hand between her legs while she pissed. And now she'd come and put her arm around his waist. Life was too good to be true! His whole life was validated by the last couple of days in Venice. He'd never made a mistake in his life because everything, even the mistakes, had led to his being here now. That was the thing about life. You couldn't cherry-pick the good bits. You had to say yes to the whole package, all the ups and the downs, but if the ups – the highs – were like this, you'd sign up willingly to the downs because, by comparison, they were nothing, so irrelevant he couldn't even remember them.

While Jeff had been busy behaving insensitively to poor Charles, Laura had been getting invited to a party on a yacht. A yacht moored nearby, just a couple hundred yards away, on Giudecca. A bunch of people were going. It was being hosted by James Hofman, a German, and his parties, apparently, were always excellent. After the scale and clamour of this party, the idea of going to a smaller party, *a party on a yacht*, was immensely appealing. Especially since, in the course of the following half hour, the booze showed signs of drying up. Jeff didn't actually want anything else to drink, but the knowledge that the drink was running out had the effect of draining all momentum from the party. It began thinning out and then, once it became obvious that it was thinning out, thinned out still more rapidly. It was time to go.

In characteristic Venetian fashion, the yacht was a lot further away than it was meant to be. They walked so far – past Zitelle vaporetto stop – that they thought they'd somehow missed it, but here it was, at last, docked near the Cipriani.

They bounded up the gangplank, greeted by a crew member in an all-white sailor's outfit.

'Permission to come aboard, sir?' Laura asked, throwing in a salute for good measure. She had gauged their entrance perfectly. The party was not just *on* a boat; it had a nautical theme as well. Guests, as they stepped aboard, were asked to remove their shoes but, in compensation, were issued with white officers' hats.

'It suits you,' Jeff told Laura.

'You too, cap'n,' she said. Their host, Herr Hofman, stood to attention, welcoming them aboard. With his beard and German accent, he looked like the commander of a U-boat. It was easy to imagine him, eyes pressed to the periscope, firing torpedoes into the merchant convoy and not being at all scrupulous about picking up survivors. Not that there was anything cramped and oily about this vessel. It was exactly what one wanted from a boat: Roman Abramovich on the cheap, but still superbly expensive. You could imagine – something about this boat was making Jeff think in terms of movie scenarios – being out on the Caribbean or the Mediterranean with a load of overweight gangstas and hookers in bikinis, being served Cristal and, after a lunch of some endangered species of freshly-caught fish, unlimited quantities of top-quality cocaine. Much nicer, tonight, though, when all the people aboard were part of the international art crowd, intellectuals, artists, connoisseurs and appreciators of the fine things in life – which meant, basically, that everyone wanted to drink champagne and snort coke. It was a relief to be spared the tedium of the fish course. A relief, too, to be within a few feet of dry land so that they could jump ship whenever they wanted. James was a quite charming man in that his conversation consisted, almost entirely, of telling Laura and Jeff what a pleasure it was to have them aboard. He could not talk to them for long, however: there were other guests he had to welcome aboard, other people who had done him the honour of coming to his little party.

Kitted out, camply, in the white uniform of a naval rating, a tanned waiter offered Jeff and Laura champagne. Glasses in hand, they went below deck – if that was the term – and into the lounge. Even in this relatively spacious boat, Jeff had to stoop through the doors. A few people were dancing to down-tempo music.

A pleasing side-effect of taking drugs is that once you have had some you access, as if by magic, the drug *scene*. You go out looking for magic mushrooms, spend an hour stooped over in a field, eat the few you eventually find, and suddenly, obviously, they're all around, pleading to be picked. It was the same here. Still animated from the line they'd had at the previous party, Jeff and Laura were chatting again with their host, in the lounge, when he asked, quietly, if they would like to join him in the bedroom for 'a little cocaine'. There were four or five people already in there, sprawled on the white bed or in chairs, talking, drinking, wearing their naval hats. James ushered them in and shut the door carefully behind him. At the foot of the bed was a mirror with a small amount of powder that he arranged into three lines, two of which were ample for Laura and Jeff. Politely they left the biggest for James, but this, evidently, was insufficient for a man of his considerable appetite. He quickly supplemented it with another fatter and longer one. As soon as he had snorted this,

James said again what a great pleasure it was to have them aboard but, if they would excuse him, he felt he should attend to his other guests. With that he stood up and left the room, shutting the door carefully behind him. Wow, Jeff was thinking to himself, this is not just the drug scene, this is the *yacht* scene. I'm part of the drug-yacht scene! And what a great scene it was to be part of. It was so great that he was unsure whether he wanted to stay here in the bedroom, be in the lounge dancing, or up on deck enjoying the heat of the maritime night. Laura was more decisive. She touched his hand and suggested they re-join the party. They smiled goodbye to the other people in the bedroom and stepped outside, shutting the door behind them as James had done.

They went up on deck. San Marco sparkled across the dark water. The boat swayed only slightly. James came towards them, smiling, his arm around the shoulder of a man wearing a white cowboy shirt (with black trimmings) and dark jeans – an outfit that looked frankly out of place in this nautical context. James must have been buzzing with cocaine, but the only apparent effect it had was to make him still more formal and correct in his bearing.

'Would you allow me to present to you Mr Troy Montana?' Jeff half expected James to click his heels as he made this intro-duction. (He was prevented from doing so, presumably, by the fact that he was wearing deck shoes.) Not that there was anything uptight about him. No, he seemed thoroughly at ease. It was just that his ease manifested itself in courtesy of a kind rarely seen these days, especially among those wired on coke. Was this the very summit of Euro-sophistication? Or perhaps – and it may have amounted to the same thing – he was one of these people (Jeff had encountered them occasionally before) who took cocaine to *relax*. Mr Montana, whose outfit matched his name if not his surroundings, was clutching a bottle of champagne. He refilled Jeff's glass, which had emptied itself with inexplicable rapidity. Spotting the opportunity for a belated witticism, Jeff asked, 'So, Troy, were you invited, or did you just sneak aboard on your wooden horse?'

As soon as he said this, Jeff worried that it had come out sounding rude rather than witty. Difficult to tell. Everything was becoming a bit smeary at the edges. He had to make sure that it didn't get smeary in the middle as well. Troy didn't laugh, but he didn't take offence either. Perhaps he'd not even heard. From his repeated sniffing, he had evidently been enjoying James's hospitality, and was in no mood to listen. He was a curator. Next weekend he was going to Documenta and, the following weekend, to Art Basel – or vice-versa. From where Jeff was standing – on a yacht, in Venice – this was a fantastic prospect: two more weekends exactly like the one he was currently in the midst of. Yes, please. He had to ask Troy to remind him of the name of his gallery, then forgot it again the moment he had been reminded. Jeff was in danger of forgetting everything as soon as it was said, even when he was the person saying it. Not that it mattered. Troy was proposing that they went to see what was happening below deck.

The music on the sound system was heavier, funkier, than before. Laura said she needed a glass of water. As they were stepping towards the galley, James summoned them into the bedroom again. It was the same scene as before, with dimmer lights. As James began chopping out more lines, Laura said that they should use some of her own stash, but he waved the suggestion aside.

'No,' he said, as soon as he had snorted up a line. 'It is my pleasure. Please.' He really was an advert, James, for the civilizing effects of cocaine. Laura helped herself to another nose-full and Jeff followed suit, motivated by a hunger that had already been thoroughly assuaged. James introduced them to some of the other people in the room, including a couple sitting in a chair, who, until that moment, had been kissing passionately. They did not appear to resent the interruption. Jeff saluted them both and shook hands with one or two other people in the immediate vicinity. Unconsciously, he was aping James's style of extreme formality. It actually made conversation easier, leaving him free to concentrate on how *incredibly high* he was feeling. Except, as soon as he did that, he had a great urge to start blahing on about how *incredibly high he was feeling* and jumping round like Diego Maradona in his Neapolitan pomp. His heart was beating wildly, his legs felt trembly, but, in James's presence, he felt a compulsion to behave as if he had just enjoyed the benefits of a complimentary healing session at an exclusive spa on the Pacific coast of America. Through the door the music was audible as a deep, but not intrusive, thump. There was the sound of laughter, all around, talk in several languages. He made room for Laura on the bed. Her cap was tipped back on her head. The couple who had been kissing earlier were kissing again. There was a knock at the door and a young woman of uncertain nationality came in and curled up next to James. The vibe was poised midway between the relaxed, sleep-over atmosphere that you got with a bunch of strangers on ecstasy in an uncharacteristically well-upholstered chill-out space and the franker physicality of the early stages of what might turn into some kind of sex party. Either way, Jeff was too amped to find out what might happen next. He and Laura stepped outside, where half a dozen people were dancing, including cowboy Troy. The music was louder than before. Laura's eyes were shining. Her bare feet moved lightly over the colourful, oriental rug that demarcated the dance floor. More people joined in and soon a nice little dance party was happening.

Dancing freed Jeff from the state of serial distraction to

which coke made him prone, but eventually, after another glass of champagne and several conversations (of which he could not recall a single word), he was on deck again, crowded with people drinking and talking. He leaned on the rail, looking back at the light-rimmed horizon, as though taking his watch on the bridge of a destroyer. A woman in a sparkly green dress was standing next to him. They smiled, but did not speak. The black water was splashed with light, reflected stars. A speedboat powered by, causing the yacht to rise up and rock in its wake. The night was thick with heat. Unlike grass, cocaine did not enhance – or even lend itself to – the lyricism of the moment. Still, he was thinking to himself over and over, if this is not my idea of a good time I don't know what is. I am having an unbelievably fantastic time, he said to himself. I am having the time of my fucking life! The last six or however many hours it was were like a concentrated version of everything he had ever wanted from life. What more could one want? The thing about this life is that you just don't know what's going to turn up, what's going to come your way. Christ, he had arrived at the Tom Hanks philosophy of life, part *Forrest Gump* and part *Cast Away*. It was exciting, coke, but it didn't give you much in the way of profound thoughts, he thought. The thing about Tom Hanks was that all his films, not all of them but the quintessential ones, were about wanting to get back home. *Saving Private Ryan*, *Cast Away* and – this was the one that elevated the point to the level of universal truth – *Apollo 13*. And that was their shortcoming, because life, at its best, was about wanting never to go home, even if that meant spinning off into outer space. Having said that, perhaps it was time to go, to go back to the hotel. But he didn't want to go yet. He was still having a good time, still having the time of his life, or at least he thought he was. Maybe he did want to go. Maybe, although he was still having a good time, or thinking he was having a good time, he was ready to have a different good time. Still feeling high, he was conscious of not feeling as high as he'd felt a short while earlier, when he'd been feeling far higher than he wanted to feel, a feeling whose passing he somewhat regretted. He recognized these post-euphoric symptoms of cocaine, every impulse turning instantly into its opposite. The thing was not to have any thoughts at all, not to fall into the kind of wired-up reverie that made you feel like a dog chewing its tail. How did people ever become addicted to cocaine? He wasn't sure he even *liked* it – though not liking something did not necessarily mean one did not want more of it. He ran that sentence through his head again, untying the tangle of nots. He held up his glass of champagne and looked through it at San Marco, bubbling away greenly like an underwater city. He took a big gulp and turned round. He leant on the rail, tilted his cap back on his head like some swilled-out rummy in a Hemingway story. James, he saw, had emerged from the bedroom, was mingling agreeably with his guests again. Laura too, talking to a guy of about his age, wearing a pale linen jacket. She spotted him and walked over.

'Let me tell you about linen,' she said. 'After a certain age, it makes a man look ten years younger. Up until that age, it makes him look ten years older.' It was an excellent point, but Jeff was struggling, slightly, with the complexities of the arithmetic involved. He made a mental inventory of his wardrobe, relieved to discover that, as far as he could remember, he didn't own a single item of linen. This bit of stocktaking may have taken longer than he realized. Laura was saying, 'I'm wondering if it's time to leave.'

'What time is it? Oh, you don't have a watch either.'

'It's three,' she said. 'I just asked someone.'

'Three! How did it get to be so late? Let's go.'

'D'you want to?'

'I don't know. Do you?'

'I'd like to stay *and* go.'

They decided to go, even though they didn't know if they wanted to. They found James, who thanked them for coming to his little drinks party. Laura handed back her cap but James said they should both keep them as souvenirs. So they descended the gangplank and walked along the quay like two sailor buddies on shore leave, looking for fights, hookers, tattoos.

Jeff's arm was around Laura's shoulder. The moon was nowhere to be seen. Perhaps it was the wrong time of the month. Its absence now made him conscious of its non-appearance earlier in the day, at the Biennale.

'You know what was lacking in the Arsenale today?' he said.

'What?'

'Photographs of the moon, of space. That's what I love more than anything. Pictures from the NASA archive. The Apollo programme. Extra-Vehicular Activity. Space walks. The Lunar Module. Earthrise. The blue of earth against the infinite black of space.'

It was a valid point even if, conversationally, it proved a void.

They'd given no thought to how they were going to get back home, back to the mainland – if that's what it was called. At the Zitelle stop they consulted the timetable and, after much deliberation and concentration, worked out that a vaporetto was due in twenty minutes. Which meant, since walking was so nice, they could continue on to Redentore, the next stop. They walked on, their arms around each other, hips bumping occasionally together. The dark water lapped against the quay. A satellite passed overhead, silvery and quickly.

A crowd of people was already waiting at Redentore when they arrived, followed, minutes later, by the vaporetto.

They sat outside, at the front of the vaporetto. Another clear, calm night. The lagoon was flat, still, dark. The air, as the boat powered forward, was hot on their faces. It was like being on an open-air spaceship, surging through a sea of stars left reeling in its wake.

In the morning they returned to the place where they'd eaten breakfast the day before, where Jeff had eaten breakfast on his first morning in the city.

'I can't help it,' he said, as they drew near. 'I'm programmed to keep coming back to the same place. Ideally, in fact, to the same table. Which, I see now, is free!'

They sat down. The sun bounced off the silver chairs and the cutlery. Jeff had spent ten minutes in the bathroom, sluicing out, excavating and blowing his nose in order to get it functioning again. And he had a headache. If he hadn't been so happy, he would have been feeling irritable from tiredness and a combination-hangover. (The kind of sleep you had after coke – if you were lucky enough to get to sleep – was devoid of any component of rest, as if the brain kept gurning away while it was notionally asleep.) Laura seemed fine, not even particularly tired – or at least she didn't look it. In a nice, wifely gesture she passed a newspaper for him to look at, but the print was too black and the paper too white.

'So, what about Cap'n James?' he asked. 'About six months from rehab?'

'Maybe so,' said Laura. 'Which means these are the best six months to know him.' They ordered more water, more coffee, extra glasses of orange juice. Best of all, Laura produced aspirin from her trusty bag.

After breakfast they crossed Accademia and walked to

Laura's hotel so that she could change. He used the bathroom and then lay on the bed, watching her undress and dress, starting to feel better. She had put on a navy blue dress, a halter neck that left her long back almost bare.

'Ready?'

'That would be putting it a bit strongly, but at some level I suppose the answer is yes.' He got off the bed, slipped his feet into his sandals, followed her out of the door.

There were a lot of Biennale-related things scattered around the city that neither of them had yet been to. Fortunately the one they most wanted to see, James Turrell's *Red Shift*, was also the nearest, by the Rialto. It was part of a larger exhibition, but they skipped the other stuff and joined the queue for the darkened room.

At first it looked like just a red painted rectangle, luminous against a dull background. Then, as they sat down and watched, it changed – but so subtly that it was impossible to tell how or when it had changed. The red became a slightly different red, a bit darker or brighter or something. The shape remained the same but, as the colour altered, so the edges of the frame became less rigid. There was a pulse in the changing redness. The surface of the picture was completely flat and infinitely deep. They sat without speaking. Time melted away, registered only in terms of the light and colour changing, to purple, to a deeper purple, a purple that was almost blue and then *was* blue . . . They were perhaps ten feet away from the light but there was no distance. The colour, the light, touched them. The cycle was beginning again. They stood up and reached into the flat surface of the red, but there was nothing there. It was impossible to feel the back or the side of the light source. Their hands stretched out, suspended in the shifting red that was no longer quite red. It was an illusion, but because it was an illusion this did not mean it was less real than anything else, than things that were not illusory.

They were disoriented when they stepped outside again. The red square of light was still pulsing in Atman's head as they boarded a vaporetto at Rialto. The fact that they didn't know where it was going changed the vaporetto from a bus to a cruise ship. Neither of them said anything about the Turrell.

For the first time since Jeff had been in Venice, inspectors came and checked everyone's tickets. Being in possession of properly validated, three-day passes suddenly seemed a significant achievement, something to be proud of.

'We can spend all day on a vaporetto, if we want,' Jeff said smugly.

'Yes,' Laura said. 'Though if we did, we'd be a), bored out of our fucking minds and b), completely seasick.'

They chugged under the Accademia Bridge, past the Gritti and the Guggenheim Collection and San Marco. Eventually they passed beyond Giardini and out into the lagoon, which may even have been the sea proper. Sky and sea opened up. Gulls wheeled overhead. The boat managed to keep fractionally ahead of the pursuing wake. Bits of a wave – the wake of another boat motoring by in the opposite direction – managed to splash aboard for a moment or two. There were various buoys or markers to indicate channels. Someone had dived from one of these: his feet could be seen as he plunged into the sea. At another marker a hand – bright red – emerged from the sea: artworks, of course, life-sized sculptures.

From time to time Laura consulted the map. Eventually she said they should get off at the next stop.

'What's here?'

'San Michele,' she said. 'A cemetery.' He could see it now: like Böcklin's *Isle of the Dead*, but symmetrical and neat, and not at all foreboding.

After so long on a boat, the land swayed like the sea. Laura put up her lemon parasol. With the sun so bright, it glowed as if illuminated. All the women, surely, wished they had a parasol, and all the men must have wished they were with the woman who had one. They walked through the gates, entered the curving walls of the island. Beyond this they found themselves in the larger grounds of the cemetery. It was crowded with graves, crammed with flowers. Laura said, 'Diaghilev is buried here. And Stravinsky.'

The first sign they saw, though, was for Ezra Pound. Within the white arrow indicating the way to his grave, someone had written, in black felt tip: 'J Brodsky'. Strictly speaking it was graffiti, but it was very civic-minded too. Officially you were directed towards Pound, but someone had taken it upon themselves to update the canon through a bit of guerrilla action. Pound now led, inexorably, to Brodsky. Jeff had never read Brodsky, but knew he was a big deal, that there were growing numbers of people for whom he – Brodsky – was a bigger attraction than Pound. They came to another sign indicating Pound's grave. Once again, the same person had written 'J Brodsky' in felt pen on the arrow.

It was Pound's grave they saw first, a flat tomb with his name in Roman characters: EZRA POVND. Quite a few flowers. Always good to see the grave of a celebrity, even if it's someone you aren't especially interested in – but it was difficult, these days, to imagine anyone except academics getting excited about Pound. Or maybe he'd got that wrong, maybe there were still kids in their bedrooms, all fired up with the promise of modernism, intent on making it new – whatever the 'it' was.

Brodsky was nearby, within spitting distance: a headstone with his name in Russian and English and his dates: 1940–1996. It wasn't a mess exactly, but there was a touch of Jim Morrison and Père-Lachaise about the scene. There were a couple of tealights, empty except for a last smear of candle wax, and some postcards with messages. Laura picked up one of them. It showed the Grand Canal, but the writing on the back was too blurred by rain and faded by sun to read. A yellow Post-it had been almost completely wiped clean by the elements. It was impossible to say what language the vestiges of words were in, let alone what they had said. By the headstone itself was a little blue plastic bowl, half-full of Biros and pencils. Most of the pens were caked with mud; at a push one or two might have been usable – not to write a poem, but good enough to jot down a phone number.

Laura rummaged in her bag and added a shiny new Biro to the pile. Now someone could write something longer. She even added a few pages from her notebook. The future was a blank page, ready for whoever came after Brodsky and wanted to have their say.

'In India these kids are all the time running up to you,' Laura said. 'All they want and know how to say is "School pen?" They just say it as a question: "School pen?" It's the cutest thing. It's lovely, if you have a pen to give. If you haven't, you feel mean as Scrooge.'

They walked on. It was hot under the parasol, but cooler than not being under it. Diaghilev and Stravinsky were next to each other. At Diaghilev's tomb a similar practice of appropriate tribute was in operation. Pens had been left at the poet's grave; here, people had left ballet shoes. There were three in total, three halves of three pairs, two left and one right. Lots of messages too. Stravinsky's tomb was bare. No one had left a violin or piano or anything.

They waited on the quay for the vaporetto. When it came they squeezed to the back of the boat, watched the island of the dead slide away behind them. After a few minutes there was nothing to see except a thin line of land surrounded by sea and parched sky.

They disembarked at Giudecca, just in time for lunch, minutes before the restaurant stopped serving. A waiter showed them to a table sheltered by an umbrella, right by the water's edge: the perfect setting for food of quite stunning mediocrity. The salad was a bit of condemned lettuce, bright tomato halves and grated carrot. The penne with tomato sauce was the kind of thing you could knock up in ten minutes, slightly better than the Heinz stuff Jeff had eaten as a kid. A more basic meal was hard to imagine.

A barge went by, carrying cement mixers and a big crane. It was followed, as they settled the bill, by a ferry the size of a recently spruced up council block, big enough to completely blot out the view of mainland Venice. A vessel of the high seas, it was out of all proportion to everything around. It simply could not have been any bigger. There were cars, vans, trucks onboard. People too – a whole floating city. The letters on the side – MINOAN LINES – were big enough to be seen from space.

The wake generated by the passage of this monster ferry flung itself at the quayside as they walked, hand in hand, past the men who were fishing nearby. Nothing about their posture suggested any hope of ever catching anything. In some vaguely oriental way Jeff wondered if you only ever became a proper fisherman when the idea of the catch became wholly irrelevant. Or was that the moment you were reincarnated as a cod or, if you were lucky, a dolphin – ideally, the one on Laura's ass? The water, as they walked, was pure glitteringness. Whoever said that all that glitters is not gold was right because the water, golden in the sunlight, glittered, so much so that one might have thought it did nothing but glitter – but it did, of course; it swayed and rocked, actions which produced the glitter. While they waited for a vaporetto across to the mainland, Jeff remembered he had his camera with him.

'Can I take your picture?' he said.

'Sure.'

'I forgot I had it with me. I should have taken one of you at Brodsky's grave.'

Laura was standing by the water's edge, not using the parasol.

'Make, I don't know, some kind of gesture.'

'How about like this?'

'Just standing there does not constitute a gesture.' Or maybe it did.

'Like this?' She did not move a muscle.

'Perfect.' He pressed the button, took the picture. She was standing there, in her blue dress, next to the blue water. He held the camera so she could see the digital image of herself. She looked quickly, without interest.

'You don't like having your picture taken?'

'I had a boyfriend who was always filming and photographing me,' she said. 'It was so boring.'

At the mention of this boyfriend, Jeff felt a stab of jealousy. Still, he would have liked to take a peek at the pictures this photographer-boyfriend had taken. Seeing a man walking by with an expensive-looking camera round his neck – it had a large lens and the wide yellow strap supporting it had the word CANON written in clear letters – Jeff asked if he'd take a picture of the two of them together with his own, more modest device. They took off their sunglasses and stood with their arms around each other, smiling while the photographer composed the shot with more care than was necessary. Birds skittered by. The shutter whirred. Jeff thanked the photographer and took back his camera. It was an ordinary photograph, a snap of a couple in Venice, water and sky in the background, holding their sunglasses, smiling: proof, if nothing else, that they looked like this, had been here together.

Back on the mainland, Laura said they should go for a drink at the Gritti. As they made their way there, Jeff became conscious of something which had previously escaped him: the omnipresence of Vivaldi. *The Four Seasons* was being played in a church. A busker was playing *The Four Seasons*. It was impossible to go more than a few hundred yards without hearing one of *The Four Seasons*.

'Is Vivaldi *from* Venice or something?' he asked.

'If he isn't, they're certainly making up for it.'

'It makes you really hate Vivaldi, doesn't it?'

'It makes you really hate Venice.'

At the Gritti a table had just been vacated and they assumed their place on the terrace. The view was magnificent, especially of the various boats going by, full of people taking pictures of the privileged few – men chewing on cigars, women muttoned up in Prada – fortunate enough to be drinking on the terrace of the Gritti. There were also a few younger, less affluent-looking people, here for just one supremely expensive drink and all the nuts they could scoff. Jeff thought of having a Campari and soda and then, as usual, changed to a beer. The drinks came with small plates of large green olives, hazelnuts, a few cheesy whotsits and three exotic canapés: sashimi and blueberries, tomato and mozzarella (not so exotic) and cucumber and caviar, all on little discs of catholic bread. Every few minutes a taxi pulled up at the jetty and people stepped, regally, onto the terrace before disappearing inside. This was sophistication of the tried and tested, old *scuola*. Conversation, in such circumstances, defaulted to a pleasant sequence of murmur and assent. Just as you had to raise your voice to make yourself heard above loud music so, here, you had to come down to the level of the jazzy jazz being played very quietly on the hotel's 'sound system', as faintly as an insect in the vicinity of your ear. Still, it was pleasant being here, looking across at the terrace of the Guggenheim, where, two nights earlier, they'd been swilling bellinis, looking at the terrace of the Gritti. After all the party-going it felt quite novel to be sitting in a bar where you had to pay for drinks – especially when they could be claimed back on expenses.

'Don't look now,' said Laura, pausing for effect. 'But Jay Jopling and Damien Hirst have just arrived.' Jeff waited a few discretionary seconds before turning round to see this all-powerful pair step out onto the terrace and then go inside. Less grandly, a man came rowing along the canal in a *sandolo*, standing up and rowing at the same time. Jeff knew it was a *sandolo* because Jan Morris, in her book, had helpfully provided a list of the different types of craft ploughing the waters of Venice. Laura said it was the kind of thing you expected to see on the Ganges – an impression heightened by the rower's shaved head, tanned skin and loose, all-white outfit. He made slow but certain progress, unperturbed by the larger craft speeding past him in both directions. Even so, the lack of a seat seemed an absurd oversight. It was difficult to see how the provision of a seat could have done anything except improve his lot.

Hoping for another glimpse of Hirst and Jopling (who were nowhere to be seen), they paid and left, began walking back towards Jeff's hotel. On the way they bought a bunch of bananas and ate them, two each, sitting on a low wall by the side of an unknown canal. The bananas were cool inside, in spite of the incredible heat.

'You look like a monkey,' Laura said, watching him eat.

*   *   *

Back at the hotel Laura brushed her teeth with the disposable brush that she had used before, the first night they had spent together. Jeff lay on the bed. The red message light was flashing on the phone.

'You know,' Laura said, emerging from the bathroom, 'we still have the coke that Martin gave me. Shall we have some?'

'Sure, let's.'

She rummaged again in her Freitag bag and chopped up two lines on the pale chest of drawers. Jeff could see her face in the mirror above the chest and, unreflected, the back of her head, her hair, her back, her ass, her legs. She moved aside and gestured to him to help himself. He snorted up one of the thin lines and sat down on the bed again, watching as she leaned forward, enough to stretch the fabric of her dress tight around her ass.

'What are you looking at?' she said, straightening up.

'In a word, you. In two . . . ' he hesitated.

'Yes?'

'Your ass.'

She leaned forward, sniffing. He looked up and met her eyes in the mirror. The combination – of coke and conversation – was making his heart beat hard. A spectrum wobbled in the mirror's bevelled edge.

'And what were you thinking while you looked?' she said. It was the mirror that was enabling them to have this conversation. It was not them talking, it was these two reflections, leading an autonomous life of their own.

'I was thinking that I would like to walk towards you and put my hands on either side of your dress, on the hem.' He stood up, walked towards her, placed his hands on either side of her dress. He pressed his prick against her. She pressed back against him slightly. 'And then I would pull your dress up, slowly. Very slowly.' Inch by inch a little more of her

139

tanned skin was revealed. 'Until I could see the first glimpse of your underwear.' As her dress rode up over her hips, he saw the blue cotton of her underwear. They stood exactly as they were, silently, not moving. He looked up once and saw her looking at his eyes, which immediately focused again on the little triangle of dark blue disappearing between her buttocks. He bent down slightly so that he could stroke the back of one of her legs.

'Then,' he said, stroking the inside of her thighs, first with one hand and then with the other, going close to but not quite touching the blue fabric between her legs, 'then I would kneel down between your legs so that my face was level with your ass.' He knelt down, his face inches from her. He reached up and felt her knickers, wet. Hooking his finger through them, he pulled them to one side. She leaned further forward. He pulled her buttocks apart slightly with both his hands. The sight of her asshole – neat, almost hairless – made his cock harder still. He licked her ass several times and then pulled her buttocks apart and pushed his tongue inside, feeling it throb. She pushed back against him. He held her hips, pushing his face into her, pushing his tongue into her. Her asshole tasted of nothing. She reached down and began touching her cunt. He unzipped his trousers, heard her say, 'Fuck me like this.'

She stepped out of her dress. He stood up, saw her face and breasts in the mirror again. His prick slid inside her. When she bent further forward he could no longer see the reflection of her face, only the downpour of her hair, her long back. She spread her feet further apart, reached her hand between her legs again. He rubbed a finger around her wet asshole. She pressed back against him more strongly. He eased his finger inside her, her ass pulsing tightly as she came, as he came.

They stood still for a while. He opened his eyes. Her face swam into view again in the mirrror, saying, 'Let's lie down.'

They collapsed onto the bed, calm from sex, jazzed up from coke. It was difficult to know what to do now. Under normal circumstances they might have dozed, but that was out of the question so they just lay there. Then Laura got up, said she would take a bath, which seemed like a great idea. While it was running, she opened the mini-bar.

'There's a little bottle of white wine in here,' she said. 'Shall we have some?' That seemed like a great idea too. She opened the bottle and poured two glasses. She was naked still. His eyes moved over her.

'It's a shame we haven't got our special glasses,' he said, but they clinked the ones they did have.

'I know. It's like drinking out of a jam jar,' said Laura, heading for the bathroom.

Jeff got up from the bed, seized by an urge to write a bit of his article on the Biennale. This impulse evaporated almost as soon as he sat down at the desk and opened his laptop. His head was full of excited feelings, but his brain was completely empty, devoid of the thoughts that were racing through it, all except one: Laura's ass. What was it about women's assholes? Where did it come from, this irresistible desire to stick one's fingers, cock and tongue up them? Shit was horrible, revolting stuff, but women's assholes . . . Maybe he should do a five-hundred-word op-ed piece on that, how the only thing in life contemporary man loves more than eating pussy is licking ass. He felt like a Roman emperor in the age of room service. He wanted to beat his chest Tarzan-style but, in the circumstances, there was nothing to do except turn on the TV. This was the unique freedom, the supreme indulgence of the hotel room: not the opportunities for afternoon sex, for snorting coke and licking ass, but the freedom to put the telly on at any time of day, to watch anything (basically nothing) without shame or guilt. If he spent more time in hotel rooms, he would never read another book. If the whole world lived in hotels, no one would read anything more demanding than the in-room dining menu. He channel-hopped until he came to a compilation of footage of sporting disasters: skiers tumbling down slopes, matadors getting tossed by bulls, motorcyclists cartwheeling through the air. It wasn't seeing people get *hurt* that made it so compelling. No, the hurting part was awful, but there was something idyllic about the mid-air interlude, before they landed and messed themselves up. If the earth hadn't been so hard, or gravity a less potent force, it would have been fun to get thrown twenty feet into the air as a result of a mistake on the piste or track . . . Even the telly, which was what you resorted to when you had no ability to concentrate, could not hold his attention. He got up, gazed out at the scorched roofs, the invisible gravity of sky. Laura was calling from the bathroom, asking what time it was, what time they had to go out. Shit, it was six already. They ought to be going in half an hour, he called back. So far today it had been as if they were in Venice on holiday, for their honeymoon, even. They had gone sightseeing, had not run into anyone they knew; now, suddenly, they had to be back in Biennale mode. There were parties to go to, friends to see, bellinis to be drunk – and, gallingly, the phone was ringing.

'Max, greetings!'

'How did you know it was me? Have you got caller ID on the hotel phone? Is that why you haven't answered all day?'

'No. I've been out. I just *hoped* it was you and, like a dream come true . . . '

'OK, to cut to the chase—'

'Did I say "dream"? Excuse me, I meant nightmare, of course.'

'Very funny. So, what happened?'

'It's all worked out really well,' Jeff smirked. 'And the interview was fine too.' Smirk turned instantly to frown as he tried to think how best to respond to the inevitable next question, about the picture he hadn't got and the photo he hadn't taken.

'And . . .'

'Yep, all fine,' he said. 'But listen, I've got to go. I'm going out to meet her now, to do the picture. I'll call you tomorrow, OK?'

Max must have been in a hurry too. Jeff was able to get off the phone without clarifying – in the sense of deliberately clouding – things any further. Laura emerged from the bathroom, naked, her hair turbaned in a towel. It was a very homely moment, like being married.

That might have been why, as they walked to the party (Jeff didn't know where they were going, he was following Laura like a puppy), he had the sense of not feeling completely up for it. By the time they got there, had queued up and got inside, this had changed to the extent that he felt completely not up for it. He wanted to ask about their future, about when and where they might meet again, but to have done so would have been a distraction from the perfect present that still surrounded them. But it would not do so for long. They were running out of time and, at the back of his mind, he was conscious of the problems awaiting him when his time here *had* run out, when he was back in London without the picture and photo and without having paid adequate attention to the art he was meant to be writing about. Not that that was his main concern. Far from it. As far as he was concerned, the Biennale had always been more about the parties than the art. It's just that tonight, instead of going to a party, what he'd most like to have done was to have gone home (i.e. back to the hotel) with Laura and lain on the bed while she wiped her cunt with his face. Desirable though this may have been, it was, for the moment, impossible. The whole point of coming to Venice was to go out, to go out to parties like this, where, if everything went like a dream, you might end up going home with someone . . . His thoughts were grinding away pointlessly, as they do when you're tired. Why, when everything had turned out so perfectly, more perfectly than he could ever have dreamed, was he fretting like this? Because a residue of cocaine-fuelled excitement, overlying a deeper sub-stratum of tiredness, was turning into all-purpose anxiety. It was as if the grey roots of his hair were already growing back. The answer, obviously, was to drink more bellinis to calm himself down and snort more coke as a way of waking himself up.

And it worked, sort of. He and Laura did a line each in the toilet and came out together, sniffing, glowing. Anxiety turned instantly to excitement, albeit excitement with an anxious edge. Dance music was booming away on the sound system.

'That sounds familiar,' he said. 'D'you recognize it?'

'It's a Paul Oakenfold remix of Nigel Kennedy playing *The Four Seasons*,' said Laura. He didn't know if she was joking, but it certainly sounded plausible.

Monika came over and said she had not told Jean-Paul how much she hated him because she realized that she actually quite liked him after all. Jeff said this showed a weakness of will and that, if he saw him, he was going to tell him he hated him anyway, irrespective of how he personally felt about him. He introduced Monika to Laura, who introduced him to someone whose name he didn't catch because, at that same moment, Phil Spender came up to him. He apologized to Phil about not making it to his party, the party he'd been so anxious to go to and which, he remembered now, he had completely forgotten about until two seconds ago. Ditto the secret Kraftwerk gig. For his part Phil wanted to know about Jeff's hair. Had he dyed it? Jeff admitted he had, yes.

'Join the club,' said Phil. Ha! So they were all at it! They did a semi-ironic chest-bump, taking care not to spill anything on Phil's still-pristine cream suit – amazing, really, that it had stayed the course. To Phil's left, he spotted Jane. And, nearby, Jessica and the Kaiser. He knew loads of people here and recognized lots more, possibly from the preceding nights' parties, possibly from just this one. Factor in the people he knew but failed to recognize . . . Everyone was here, including people he was meeting only now, for the first time, people he was yakking away at and who yakked back at him, saying things they'd said a few minutes earlier, just as Jeff found himself bound to an ever tightening loop of incessant repetition. Whoever they all were, tonight was the last night they were all here, in Venice together, swilling bellinis, even though some of them had already left, this afternoon. The Biennale – or at least this part of it, the *vernissage* – lasted an incredibly short time. While you were in the midst of it, it was so relentless it seemed like it went on forever. You craved a night off, an evening in. But you couldn't afford to do that because, at the same time that it went on for a long time, it also went on for an incredibly short time, was over before it had even begun. No sooner had it started than it was over, moments after it had started. There he was, grinding away again. He'd noticed this lately, about drinking and drug-taking. Doing either was like shining a UV light into his brain, illuminating its burned-out circuitry. Over the years great stretches of cognitive processing had been ruined, laid waste. Under normal conditions the full extent of the damage was hidden from view, but it took only a bit of bingeing to reveal the inner disintegration. A few years from now his brain would be like damaged coral, like brain coral, in fact, brain-damaged coral, lifeless, colourless, dead. Hair you could fix, dye, but the brain . . . At the very least he was going to have to start taking supplements: memory stimulants, serotonin boosters, neuron steroids. In the meantime, spying an approaching waiter, he held out his glass, his begging bowl. The act of doing so enabled him to regard his brain troubles in a new, less troubling, more optimistic light. When he was young he had prided himself on *being clever*. Walking down the street, not even thinking anything, just walking along like every other moron, he'd had a distinct sense of how *clever* he was. He'd never done anything with that cleverness except write stupid articles and make occasionally clever remarks, most of them not even clever. He just *felt* clever, and it was a good feeling, feeling clever. Now he felt, with equal conviction (and rather more evidence), that he was entering the stupid years. The stupid years complemented the vague years. They went together. The vague years and the stupid years were the same years and they had already started. Well, bring them on. Forgetting everyone's names – as those adverts in the newspapers were always reminding you – was embarrassing, but apart from that, being stupid was fine, like a premonition of enlightenment.

In his pocket he had his little digital camera. He got it out, intending to take what would turn out to be one of those pointless, universally disappointing pictures of a party in red-eyed progress. When he turned it on, the camera was still in *View* mode. The screen showed not the scene moving around him, but the picture from earlier in the day, of him and Laura on Giudecca. He pressed the optical zoom, eliminating himself from the frame, focusing on her face and then just her eyes, continuing to do so until they were not eyes at all, just an exploding galaxy of pixels.

Laura's flight was at two in the afternoon. It was eleven in the morning now. He lay on her bed, head aching, holding a tissue to his bleeding nostril, watching her pack. The white dress, the red and gold one she had bought in Laos (a place he'd never visited but which he now knew how to pronounce), the navy blue dress – all were folded neatly into her wheelie. It was like an awful inversion of a striptease, but it was worse than that too, like watching her prepare things to take with her into the afterlife – the after-Venice life, the after-him life – and leaving him for dead. If it had been him, he would have tried to change the return flight and, if that was impossible, would have just blown it out, bought another ticket for a later date. But she was going, had almost finished packing.

They had swapped email addresses and phone numbers, but had no plans to meet again. The traditional way of these things was that men came and went, leaving women weeping in their wake, but he was the one being left behind and, if he was not careful, he could easily start weeping. The prospect of crying brought with it a related thought, of his dyed hair dripping blackly down his forehead, running down his cheeks like a girl's mascara. Yesterday afternoon he'd felt like a Roman emperor, capable of anything; now, with his nose bleeding, his mouth a sour desert, his head parched and fried, he felt like sobbing, wailing. When he was seventeen he'd read *The French Lieutenant's Woman* and had been much impressed by John Fowles's distinction between the Victorian point of view – I can't have this forever, therefore I'm miserable – and the modern, existential outlook: I have this for the moment, therefore I'm happy. It had stayed with him ever since but it seemed absurd, now, to have any pretensions to existential contentment. In 2003, in his mid-forties, he had got in touch with his inner Victorian. In Venice he discovered that he was the last Victorian.

He heard Laura zipping up her bag, the same sound – but coarser, louder – as her dress being unzipped by him, for him. It was luck, just luck, the way they had clicked sexually – but as soon as luck revealed itself in that way it was changed into something different, something that made it impossible to believe that it was only luck.

'A present for you,' she said, handing him the wrap of cocaine. 'There's a bit left.' He needed that like he needed a hole in the head, which he didn't need at all because he felt like he already had one. His head, in fact, felt like nothing but hole, but at least his nose had stopped leaking blood. He chucked the wad of tissue into the trash.

'And don't forget your glass,' Laura said. There it was, standing on the chest of drawers, expensive and delicate, looking exactly like the blue and orange shrine she'd said it wasn't. He stood up, wrapped it in a page of newspaper and put it in a plastic bag.

Laura came over and kissed him on the mouth. Their arms were around each other. Her hair smelled slightly of city. She didn't mention the future, when they might meet again, and neither did he. The reason he didn't was because she hadn't. Did she refrain from doing so because he had said nothing? He couldn't know for sure but he felt, reasonably or not, that he was taking his cue from her. A strange, modern form of intimacy – not Victorian at all – that made it easier to lick someone's ass than to ask when you might see them again. *When will I see you again?* The crap pop song, by whichever crap group it was, started going round and round in his head, his empty, thought-crammed, empty head.

'Well, as I said before,' he said. 'That was most agreeable.'

'Wasn't it?'

'Personally, I found it so agreeable that I would love to do it all over again.' There, he had said it, or was, in a manner of speaking, saying it.

'Me too.'

'Do you have any idea when that might be?'

'No. But soon, I hope.'

'You know, this time we can't just leave it to chance, can't just hope to run into each other.'

'I know.'

'It worked in Venice, in a small town, but on a global scale I think it's just, you know, the odds are stacked against it.'

'You're right.'

Holding her against him, he could feel his cock growing hard, even now, when everything was so close to becoming just memory. Or the opposite of memory: a longing for something that would soon be impossibly remote.

'I could come to LA,' he said. 'Or I could come to meet you wherever it is you're going to be, when you go travelling.'

'That would be nice.'

'So, we'll email.'

'Of course.'

They had been holding each other while they had been speaking. Now the time came to let each other go, for him to pick up her wheelie and his glass, to leave her room and squeeze into the lift and look at the pointless sign about not scratching the plastic cover.

Laura settled her bill, checked out. She was walking to the coach station, but they were saying goodbye here, in the little courtyard in front of her hotel, the grandly-named Excelsior. They kissed again. He breathed in the faint smell of her hair that was still new to him, new and already familiar. Then she began trundling her case in the direction of the station and he began walking.

Where? It didn't matter. He was alone in Venice, walking through the stifling heat. She had gone, and he had gone from Plus One to Minus One. There was nothing to do except stroll, so he strolled through the crowded, empty city. It was like swimming in the sea, when you go from a patch of warm water to a band of chilling cold. One moment he was in a busy, densely populated area and then he was in completely silent streets, deserted except for sunlight. It would have been a relief, now, to have encountered the Serbian pick-pockets, to have fought them and let them chuck his body into a canal. But he didn't see them or, thankfully, anyone else he knew.

He'd been tired from the moment he woke up, exactly as he had been after sleeping outside the station when he'd first come here, years ago. After strolling for an hour, he reached the pitch of weariness encountered only in dreams, those dreams when you are walking and walking and getting nowhere. He was in the death zone of tourism, where stroll turns to trudge, where every step requires the effort of ten. The air was filling up with the pleasant pealing of bells. As he approached the source – a church he'd not seen before – it became an avalanche of gold noise, pouring over him, tumbling into his dry head.

He continued walking through streets that became increasingly familiar . . . Because, he suddenly realized, he was near the Palazzo Zenobio and the bar that termed itself the Manchester Pavilion! What a stroke of luck! Now he knew what he could do: he could get a beer. It was like being in an advert for lager, or a Venetian remake of *Ice Cold in Alex*. Beer! He crossed over the Ponte del Socorso, the humpbacked bridge where they'd sat after the party at Zenobio that was too crowded to get into, the exact same steps.

'Are you trying to look up my dress?'

The bar was open, but quite deserted. Even taking into account the fact that it was a Sunday afternoon, it was surprisingly empty. Staff were stacking chairs on tables. It had the look of a place that had been looted.

'What's happened?' Jeff asked.

'We run out.'

'Ran out of what?'

'Drink.'

'You mean there's nothing left to drink?'

'Si, nothing.'

'Nothing?'

'*Niente*. Is all gone. Beer, wine, whisky. Finito.' He seemed exhausted, proud, amazed and a little appalled by what had occurred. He had, evidently, never experienced anything like this. Or expected it. If an English football team had been playing in Venice, then he might reasonably have assumed there would be a huge demand for booze, but he had seriously underestimated the insatiable thirst of the international art crowd. Jeff was disappointed, obviously, but at some level it was a situation to relish. He had heard of such things happening, but this was the first time he had ever seen and – to give himself a little credit – played a tiny part in a bar being drunk dry. Clearly, there was no point in staying. Everyone who had come here had concluded the same thing. Like parched locusts, they had descended on this bar, drunk it dry, squeezed every last drop of alcohol from it and had then moved on elsewhere. Many people had already moved on, not just to another bar but to other cities, other countries. It was still, ostensibly, a bar but it was a place, now, of abandoned meaning. The atmosphere was woebegone, an architectural equivalent of a fearful hangover. It was as if an atrocity had been committed, something shameful that no one cared to remember but which permeated the walls, the floors and all the fixtures. It seemed quite possible that a curse had now fallen on the place, that it would never again enjoy the dizzy heights of the last few days when the booze flowed and flowed and then ran out, leaving in its wake an emptiness that could never be filled, an after-taste of waste and pointlessness. He thanked the barman and left, feeling more exhausted than ever.

He bought a bottle of Ferrarela from a grocery shop and walked on, looking for a place to sit down. There were lots of places to sit, but he kept going until, utterly exhausted, he sat down by any old canal, not even a particularly scenic one. A tennis ball was bobbing in the water. He took out his expensive, lovely glass, filled it with sparkling water and glugged it down. He did this repeatedly until both bottle and glass were empty. Then he just sat there, legs crossed, like a yacht-owner turned mendicant who had lost everything except for this exquisite blue and orange reminder of his former life of luxury. All very well to think, as he had the day before, or two days ago or whenever it was – he felt like he'd been in Venice forever – that those wonderful, high moments made all the other moments worthwhile. Easy to think like that while you were in the midst of those moments, when it was all but impossible to remember the other moments, moments like this, when it was – already! so soon! – becoming difficult to remember those great, all-redeeming moments.

A pigeon gawked by. He watched as it pecked and twitched its way across the ground. It looked incredibly stupid, as if it were barely capable of carrying out its species-specific duty of being a pigeon. Just being a pigeon exhausted everything of which it was capable. It didn't even know how to fly, it just hopped. To that extent it wasn't even a bird, just a pigeon, a non-bird.

A boat went past, loaded with broken chairs and logs. Water lapped up the steps. An Italian family came towards him, mother, father and a dark-haired girl of five or six, bouncing along on something like a space hopper in the form of a kangaroo. She sat on its haunches and hung onto its front paws. Evidently this unusual mode of transport delighted the parents every bit as much as it did the child riding it. Holding hands, laughing, they greeted Atman warmly, happy that a stranger could enjoy the sight of their daughter bouncing along on her kangaroo-hopper, could share their happiness. Atman grinned back. It was completely adorable. There was even a pouch, with a little baby kangaroo peeking out. If it had been possible, he would have climbed right in there, into the pouch, and gone bouncing along with them.

After the family and their kangaroo had passed from view, he didn't know what to do so he picked up his glass and started walking again. He passed through the Campo Santa Margherita, at pains to ignore the irritating mimes, painted silver, doing their motionless statue thing.

Eventually he came to a small piazza – not even a piazza, really – hemmed in by three churches, cheek by jowl. Two of them were bright white, and one of these – one of the white ones – was the Scuola Grande di San Rocco. Feeling as worn out and used up as he did, the prospect of paying just five euros to get out of the heat and into the cool darkness of a church – with a massive helping of Tintoretto thrown in – was a welcome substitute for a drink in the Manchester Pavilion.

After the blaze of daylight, stepping into the interior was like blacking out. He had a quick scan around the ground floor and trudged up the stairs. Too bad the idea of the church tended to go hand in hand with a not inconsiderable thrust of verticality, that the notion of the bungalow had never really taken root in ecclesiastical design. He plodded onwards, climbing a stairway to chiaroscuro heaven. It was all happening up here. There was a lot to take in. Way too much. Walls, ceilings: every inch was crammed with prophets, angels and tough-guy saints. Everywhere you looked, figures came looming out of the muscle-bound darkness. Everything loomed out of the darkness. Wow, Tintoretto really painted up a storm in this place. Jeff's knowledge of the sources was a little sketchy;

beyond the fact that these were biblical scenes, he was completely in the dark. As far as he could make out, Tintoretto had compressed the best bits of both Testaments into one building. In a way, though, it was an easy book to compress, the Bible. Basically, things were always getting hurled – out of the light and into the darkness – or were ascending – out of the darkness and into the light, of which there was not a vast amount. Bearded prophets, swirling drapery and billowing clouds – it was all go up there. In marketing terms, though, the pitch seemed fundamentally and horribly flawed: the idea that we could be bullied into paradise.

Looking up at the ceiling was making Atman's neck ache. Then he noticed a few people walking around holding little wood-framed mirrors the size of portable TVs. He picked one up from the stack on the other side of the hall, the other side of the world in a sense. The first thing he saw was his own face looming out of the biblical swirl in the background. The mirror was like a square halo. Cubist. The halo, the mirror, the ceiling – the background – all loomed darkly. Everything blazed with light, but only because, in such a dark place, any bit of light, however scarce, was somehow sacred. As far as the weather was concerned, a devastating flood or torrential storm seemed a distinct possibility. He scanned the room. Apart from a couple of quiet Japanese, he was now the only person here. He flopped down into a chair, put down his glass, and emptied the remains of Laura's wrap onto the mirror. Using the leaflet explaining how Tintoretto had done all this knock-out painting, he tapped the coke into a rough line. Surrounded by the mirrored darkness, the powder seemed whiter than ever, white as a cloud. He took another quick look around, dipped his head to the mirror and snorted it up. Partially blocked with dried blood, his nose made a sound like a pig snoring. Ha! He saw his pupils – already large from the darkness – dilate further. This made the art of the past really come alive. Now everything really loomed and reeled. It was like staring up from the bottom of a well. There was nothing but dark and light, and everything was reeling. Swirling, looming and reeling. Everything loomed and everything swirled, and the swirling and the looming were one. And the paintings, he saw now, were explicitly – in the sense of allegorically – about getting high. Guests at the Passover looked like they were crowding round a table wanting to snaffle up more than their fair share of whatever was on offer. The halos of illumination around the saints' heads were like comic-book signifiers, signifying that of all these holy men were getting loaded.

With renewed energy Atman passed into the adjoining room, one whole wall of which was devoted to the crucifixion. Quite an epic. Everything reeled, still, but now, as well as looming and reeling, it converged. What appeared to have loomed could now be seen to converge, and it all converged here. This was the point of it all. A bit confusing, though. Ah, but now he understood: what he'd thought was a guy pointing an incredibly long spear at one arm of the cross was actually a rope – one of two, in fact – pulling up the cross with one of the thieves nailed to it. The weather, which had been unsettled in the other paintings, was catastrophically bad in this one. Giorgione's tempest was just a shower in a teacup compared with what was happening here. No rain was falling, but everything was drenched. Light was drenched in darkness.

He was still holding the mirror. He looked at his own face – old, excited, crumpled. He sat back on one of the chairs and gazed at this huge helping of art. It really was a mad painting, great if your idea of great painting was maximum action and maximum atmospherics on a maximum scale, which, at that moment, seemed a pretty good definition of maximum greatness. This was high concept art, all right, and there was no doubting who was the star of the show, the focus of everyone's attention. Everybody in the painting he was looking at was looking at the crucified Christ, even the two thieves who were getting crucified alongside him, even people like the guy on the horse, who was looking at something else. Atman didn't know how long he sat there, staring at this painting, not having any thoughts about it, willing on an epiphany that never came, never happened, just seeing it, looking at it. Perhaps that *was* the epiphany, surrendering himself to what he was seeing.

Then, as happens, he'd had enough seeing and got up to go.

It wasn't just a shock, stepping outside, it was like getting resurrected. Bright daylight still. The world hadn't ended, the sky was the same deep blue. The eat was otter than ever. How quickly these little jokes took up residence – and how quickly they became sad, how sad they quickly became. He started walking again, past a woman in black, on her knees, begging. He dropped a couple of euros into the squat Pringles tube she was using as a begging bowl. When he came to a half-decent canal, he sat down beside it and didn't weep. Nothing was moving. Leaked oil had left a few threads of rainbow in the water. The air was stifling, he was drenched in sweat. He took off his damp shirt and sat there, bare-chested and skinny, trousers rolled up above the knees. Having done that, he was tempted to strip down to his underwear and walk straight into the canal, as if it were a long and stagnant paddling pool.

A gull swooped low over a passing water-taxi, a dead pigeon in its beak: an ill and not terribly hygienic omen. Maybe it was the pigeon he'd seen earlier. He lay back uncomfortably and looked up at the nothing sky. An aeroplane passed overhead, leaving a fine vapour trail in its wake. Slowly it expanded, becoming a line of powdered whiteness against the empty blue.

156

Part Two:
Death in Varanasi

'*This is not the river,*
it's an explanation of the river
that replaced the river.'

Dean Young

'*And to think that while I play with doubtful images*
the city I sing persists
in a predestined place in the world,
with its precise topography
peopled like a dream.'

Jorge Luis Borges, 'Benares'

T he thing about destiny is that it can so nearly not happen and, even when it does, rarely looks like what it is.

It's just a phone ringing routinely at three in the afternoon (not alarmingly in the middle of the night) and the person on the other end is not telling you that the results of your blood test have come back positive or that your girlfriend's partly clothed body has been discovered floating in the Ganges. That would be handy, that would lend narrative continuity and drive – albeit of a not very novel kind – to the purposeless drift of events. But no, it's just an editor at the *Telegraph* asking if you can go to India at short notice, to write a travel piece about Varanasi.

'Should be really nice,' she said. 'Business-class flight to Delhi. Short wait for a connecting flight to Varanasi. Five nights at the Taj Ganges. I'd do it myself, if I could get away.' The trip had been set up for one of her regular contributors, who had fallen ill. ('You'd have thought he could've waited till he got there, like everyone else,' she said.) That's why she was calling at the last minute like this. And she only wanted twelve hundred words. There was nothing I had to do in London in the coming week . . . So I said yes, OK, I'd go.

Two days later, the night before I was due to fly out, I ran into Anand Sethi at an opening for Fiona Rae at the Timothy Taylor Gallery. I'd known him slightly when we were both

students, ages ago. These days he was a banker (and therefore an art collector). He'd grown up in Bombay and had
been to Varanasi several times, was going back in the spring,
in fact.

'Where are you staying?' he wanted to know.

'The Taj,' I announced grandly, knowing that the Taj chain
was one of the most luxurious in India. Apparently not. Anand
shook his head. The Taj was on the outskirts of the city, so
I'd be commuting to the ghats every day. And the traffic in
Varanasi was terrible. The only place to stay was the Ganges
View. It was, he said, one of the great hotels of the world. I
made a mental note of the name even though, at this late
stage, nothing could be done about changing hotels. I had an
impulse to contradict or counter-boast in some way. Before I
got the chance to mention that I was flying – was being flown
– business class, Anand told me that he had bought a couple
of Rae's paintings, including one the size of a garage door.

Anand was completely wrong about driving in Varanasi. The
traffic is not terrible at all. It is beyond any idea of terrible-
ness. It is beyond any idea of traffic.

The journey from the airport to the hotel was fine. It was
terrifying, chaotic, dangerous, but it bore some kind of relation to journeys I'd experienced previously, in other places.
The Taj was set in a verdant tropical park, complete with
badminton and tennis courts. Other than that I noticed very
little about it, just checked in, showered and changed. I was
jet-lagged, full of exhausted energy, hungry, impatient to see
the city. I ate daal and rice – I am capable of living off daal
and rice for months, have done so, in fact, in London – in
the hotel's India-themed restaurant and arranged with Jamal,
my guide, to be driven into town. The car was one of those
sturdy white Ambassadors, praised, in every article or book

about India, for their sturdiness, whiteness and reliability. For a few minutes after leaving the hotel all seemed quite normal – crowded, busy, noisy – but nothing more than expected. Then everything began to converge, contract and – this was the interesting part – accelerate. The roads shrunk; the volume of vehicles increased. Through the window I saw what seemed to be a house built around a tree. Branches protruded through the windows. When I bought my flat in London the survey had warned that there was a tree growing on the pavement fifty feet away, that its roots might cause subsidence or interfere with the foundations. And here was a house whose entire living room must have been filled with the trunk of a big old tree, like something built by Frank Lloyd Wright, something that leaked in a downpour and became quite soggy during the monsoon. Jamal, meanwhile, was telling me about motoring protocol in the city.

'You need three things if you are driving in Benares,' he said. 'Good horn, good brakes and good luck.' He said it spontaneously, in an off-the-cuff style that had obviously been honed in the course of picking up hundreds of new arrivals.

'A seatbelt might be handy too,' I said. It was the last thing I said for some time because Sanjay, the driver, I realized now, had just been warming up, idling, girding his loins for what lay ahead. I am no stranger to the mighty traffics of Asia. I am a veteran of the perma-jams of Manila, the jihad of Java, the full-metal frenzy of Saigon, but this was something else. Cars, rickshaws, tuk-tuks, cars, bikes, carts, rickshaws, motorbikes, trucks, people, goats, cows, buffalo and buses were all herded together. The sheer quantity of traffic was the sole safeguard, the only thing that prevented a stampede. At one point we came to a roundabout and went round it, clockwise; others went round it anti-clockwise. Given the ability to do so, everyone would have done neither, would have just roared over it. The din of horns rendered use of the horn simultaneously superfluous and essential. The streets were narrow, potholed, trenched, gashed. There was no pavement, no right of way – no *wrong* of way – and, naturally, no stopping. The flow was so dense that we were rarely more than an inch from whatever was in front, beside or behind. But we never stopped. Not for a moment. We kept nudging and bustling and bumping our way forward. Given the slightest chance – a yard! – Sanjay went for it. What, in London, would have constituted a near-miss was an opportunity to acknowledge the courtesy of a fellow-road-user. There were no such opportunities, of course, and the idea of courtesy made no sense for the simple reason that nothing made any sense except the relentless need to keep going. From the airport to the hotel, Sanjay had used the horn excessively; now that we were in the city proper, instead of using it repeatedly, he kept it going all the time. So did everyone else. Unlike everything else, this did make sense. Why take your hand off the horn when, a split-second later, you'd have to put it back on?

As we burrowed more deeply into the city, the nature of the journey changed again, taking on the quality and dimensions of a procession – especially once we entered the strip leading down through a market, heading to the river. The action on the road was first matched and then exceeded by what was happening on either side of it, by the blare and frenzy of display, of frantic buying and selling, loading and unloading. This particular phase of the journey – the driving phase – was coming to an end. Everything was piled up. Everything was excessive. Everything was brightly coloured and loud, so everything had to be even brighter and louder than everything else. So everything blared. There was so much of it, all blaring so loud and bright, that it was impossible to tell exactly what this everything was made up of, what it comprised. It was just a totality of bright, noisy, blaringness.

Eventually the press of people, animals and cars became too much, even for Sanjay. Our sturdy Ambassador could have kept going forever, of that there could be no doubt. All it needed was the road, but it had run out of road. Even the road had run out of road. It was impossible to move. The noise, when I opened the door and squeezed out, increased markedly. Jamal was supposed to accompany me, but I insisted that I would be fine on my own, that he could wait for me here. With that I joined the throng of people flowing towards the river.

After the claustrophobia of the streets, my first sight of the mighty Ganges and the sky stretching over the opposite bank was a glimpse of another, more spacious world. The steps down to Dashaswamedh ghat were lined with beggars waving silver bowls, empty except for grains of rice and the odd coin. They were the lucky ones. Some didn't have bowls. They were the lucky ones too. Some did not have hands.

Beyond the jostle was what seemed like a view, across a narrow ocean, of an empty continent, desert-dry. It was like arriving at the world's first-ever seaside resort. This resort, evidently, was in serious need of repair, but its popularity was undiminished. Whatever else had happened to Varanasi, it had never fallen into ruin – and never would. Even if every building in it collapsed, it would not be a ruin. The sky was holiday blue. Banners fluttered in the breeze. There was uncompre-hended meaning everywhere, I could see that. The colours made the rainbow look muted. Lolly-pink, a temple pointed skywards like a rocket whose launch, delayed by centuries, was still believed possible, even imminent, by the Brahmins lounging in the warm shade of mushroom umbrellas. Were they imparting wisdom to disciples or just chatting with pals – India was losing to South Africa in a test match – about

167

the cricket? Enlightened or completely out of it? Both? Even the fake holy men – and I'd been warned, by Jamal, that many of them were wholly fake – were genuine. And everyone was so friendly. I'd only been here a minute and someone was wanting to shake my hand. It was like being a celebrity or a visiting royal. Except he didn't want to shake my hand at all. He wanted to demonstrate the massage he was hustling. He was kneading my hand and wouldn't give it back. While he was doing this, a woman was shoving her silver bowl under my nose so that I could sniff at the few grains of rice in it. A boy insisted I took a boat ride. Another insisted I took his boat instead. I was the tallest person around, towering over everyone like a radio mast, broadcasting the fact that I had just arrived in Varanasi, was new to India, had no idea how to cope. I was easy prey, fair game: the kind of person who could be taken for a boat ride, who was ripe for a massage. I got my hand back and walked on, trying to look as if I had been here for weeks, was no stranger to lepers, was in no hurry to see bodies being burned at Manikarnika ghat.

That's where I was hurrying, to see bodies being burned. (On arriving in a new place, it's no bad thing to simply do what everyone else does.) I could see the fires burning. From this distance they were just bonfires, as if a festival or party, though still in progress, had passed its peak. I made a note in my notebook: *Late afternoon. Flames in sunlight, by the river. Slow smoke. People drifting through the smoke, moving in sunlight. Behind all this, the spires of temples, one of them tilting precariously.*

The whole operation at Manikarnika was really labour-intensive, like one of those Salgado photographs of peasants toiling on the mountainside – a mountainside, in this case, that had been so thoroughly worked over that it was no longer a mountain. There were great stacks of wood, higher than houses, forever getting added to and denuded as logs were weighed out to fuel the never-ending need for fires. Barges arrived, crammed with logs that were carried up the shore, so big that only one or two could be carried at a time, slung like animals, stiff and heavy, over the shoulders of the men carrying them. The wood was stacked, chopped, weighed and carried down to the water again, probably weighed again. Each cremation required a ton of wood. Ton in the sense of a lot, not a specific unit of measurement. Smoke smudged the sky, blackening the temples and buildings crowded round the fires. Cows chewed on soggy marigolds, picking through the ash at the river's dark edge. The water was sooty and dark, burned. Some dogs were there too. Half a dozen fires were burning, tended by the men who worked here. People were standing around talking while, all the time, wood was lugged back and forth and fires were prodded with branches. It was like watching the dawn of the industrial revolution, as it might have occurred if there were no industry and a vast surplus of manpower, all employed in the service of death.

Jamal had told me that you were not allowed to take pictures but, beyond this, I wasn't sure about the general etiquette of the place, how close you could get to the fires. To the left was a large smoke-grimed house, from the balcony of which several tourists were watching. I'd only glanced up there when a boy in a tattered Planet Hollywood T-shirt was offering to show me the way, leading me there. By the time you have shown the first flicker of interest in doing, seeing or buying anything in India, someone will have read the signs and acted on them, will be trying to turn this wish – for interest is a wish, a desire, and, as such, constitutes demand – into a reality, to his or her financial advantage. I only learned this later. Now, when he said 'Come,' I followed.

'No pictures. No cameras.'

'I don't have camera,' I said, making it clear that I was not a newcomer, not just off the boat, not Japanese. But I followed the boy's down-at-heel flip-flops up darkened stairs, to an empty room with a balcony where I'd seen the other tourists, who were nowhere to be seen.

'View,' said the boy, as if he were issuing a command the way he had earlier instructed me to 'Come.' Again, I obeyed. I had a good view of the fires, the river behind them, but I couldn't actually see any bodies, just piles of logs, flames, and the milling crowd – including the tourists who, a few minutes earlier, I'd seen up here. I looked around to see if anyone else was here now. Just the kid in his blue Planet Hollywood T-shirt, who joined me, looking out from the balcony at the cremation ground. And a couple of friends of his, who appeared on the other side, my left. Older than him, and rougher-looking. This was a hospice, one of them explained. A place where people came to die. I nodded and smiled and looked back at the river, and he said the same thing again.

'That's good to know, but for the moment I'm happy living,' I said. 'Thank you.' It was the first joke I had made since being in India. The comment about the seatbelt had not been a joke and neither, really, was this, but it made a change from only saying 'Hello' and 'No, thank you.' The kid talking to me, an old-looking teenager, had something wrong with one of his eyes. It was like he was cross-eyed, but not in the normal way.

'This is hospice,' he said again. 'People come here to die. People look after people who come here to die.' I nodded, took a different tack.

'That's good,' I said.

'Give donation,' said his friend, clarifying the situation. For a hospice, the atmosphere was surprisingly threatening. I handed over a ten-rupee note and turned back to the river.

A corpse, wrapped in a red shroud, was carried down to the banks by mourners, chanting, chanting something, chanting. I couldn't understand what they were saying, chanting. They dipped the body in the river and . . . But it was no use, the guy with the wonky eye – both eyes were wonky, that was the thing, so they sort of cancelled each other out – was tugging at my sleeve. This time he had an old hag by his side and she must be given a donation as well, because she was a nurse, nursing the sick people who had come here to die. I reached into my pocket and pulled out a note. A hundred rupees – relatively speaking, a fortune. I handed it over and started to leave. Five rupees would have been fine, but the hundred had turned me into a mark. They were tugging at my sleeve again, the two older kids, and the kid with the Planet Hollywood T-shirt. There was another so-called nurse – and she wanted a hundred rupees too. Inflation in India can be instantaneous; suddenly a hundred rupees was the going rate. But for what? For being allowed to get out of here alive?

'For nurse,' said the other older kid, the one with nothing wrong with his eyes.

'If she's a nurse, I'm Florence Nightingale,' I said with a big smile. I had hit a rich vein of humour in this dingy place, but this was obviously not the occasion to mine it more deeply. I made for the exit, unsure what was going to happen. Nothing did. They made a symbolic attempt to bar my way, but did not try physically to stop me.

In the gloomy interior everything had felt quite sinister, but as soon as I was outside, in the angled sunlight, it was difficult to tell what, exactly, had been going on. Had the guys been threatening? Were the old women really nurses? Even if they weren't, they looked like they needed one.

By the river was a kind of viewing platform where tourists

– including the ones I'd seen earlier – were watching the cremations. I went and stood near them, feeling safe again. Everything was intensely ritualized and completely ad hoc. Head shaved, wearing only a length of white cloth, a thin man led a group round an as yet unlit pyre, sprinkling oil over the shrouded body. I assumed they were mourners, but there was nothing mournful about them. A few minutes later the wood was lit. The shaven-headed man and his friends stood around and watched, joking and chatting. No one could accuse Hindus of being killjoys. The only people with funereal faces were the tourists, us. A pair of charred feet were sticking out of a collapsing pyre. One of the *doms* chucked more logs onto the body of this ex-person and prodded the feet back into the flames. I was still unsure how close you were allowed to get to the pyres, but no one gave a damn, really. A Japanese woman moved almost as close as the mourners, as if she were the widow who, in a loyal display of grief, might join her dead husband by throwing herself on the fire. Her interest, actually, was quite disinterested. She just wanted to see, like the rest of us, only more boldly. Over her shoulder I glimpsed a head dripping fat into the flames. The skull became gradually apparent. There was more chanting. Another body was being carried down to the river. Cows munched the wilted remains of flowers. The ashes of earlier funerals were being raked through. Then they were shovelled towards the river. The body that was about to be burned, the one that had just been brought down, was being dipped in the river: an after-the-fact baptism – of fire.

The sun had gone. So, almost, had the light. The fires burned more brightly. Darkness was falling. The river blackened. Candle flames floated downstream, a fleet of yellow stars.

Continuing my policy of doing whatever everyone else was

doing, I left Manikarnika and joined the boatloads of tourists for the daily ceremony at Dashaswamedh ghat. We were joined, in turn, by kids selling the little candle-coracles that looked so nice as they drifted by. They were all selling the same thing and all saying the same thing:

'Five rupees. Father, mother, sister, brother. Good karma.'

I bought a couple, lit them and watched them wobble and float away. They were lovely, and it was lovely, at first, being on the crowded water in the faded light, waiting for things to begin. Almost as soon as it began, though, the ceremony became disappointing. You didn't have to be a particularly discerning tourist to see that this was an exhausted pageant, drummed up for tourists, a *son et lumière* with a cast of hundreds. Any significance it was supposed to have had been drained, possibly a long time ago or maybe just yesterday, or even now, right before our eyes. The event had bled itself white, but each night it had to bleed afresh, which only made it seem more stale and bloodless. It was like trying to glimpse, in a performance of *The Mousetrap*, the ravaged majesty of *Macbeth*. The air was frantic with bugs, dense with harshly amplified chanting, the sound of conches and the clamour of bells. I left before the end, before it had even got going.

I was back at the river before dawn the next day, just as the sky turned grey. It was a lot colder than I expected. Icy. But not cold enough to deter the hundreds of people who had come to bathe in the Ganges. Right on time, the red sun boiled up through the river mist. The world, having disappeared overnight, was coming into existence again. The far bank remained vague, a greyness without substance: formless, qualityless.

Together with other tourists from the Taj, I was on a boat, drifting along the river as people bathed, said prayers, offered *puja*. I say 'drifting', but we were actually going upstream, rowed by a boatman who had to work hard to keep us moving. The effort kept him warm. He'd taken off his sweater and was wearing a short-sleeved red shirt. The rest of us were all in anoraks or swathed in blankets. Wrapped in our blankets we gawped at the skinny, shivering, near-naked Indians, some of them quite fat, men and women, young and old, bathing in the freezing river. We assumed it was freezing, coming from the Himalayas, though none of us touched it to find out. The only thing we wanted on our hands was the anti-bacterial handwash that we all carried. There were four of us from the Taj – the more adventurous of the guests, in that we had come down to the ghats without a guide. We had with us just our warm clothes, cameras and a driver waiting. Jean and Paul were a Canadian couple, in their fifties, open-minded as an expanse of snow. Mary was a Dutchwoman, in her late thirties, nice enough but exuding a loneliness doomed to exacerbate and extend itself indefinitely. The expression 'She's not my type' had a kind of universal applicability: she was not anyone's type. She'd been told that dolphins lived in the Ganges and could occasionally be seen.

'That seems hard to believe,' I said. It was a negative thing to say, but it was not intended negatively, and it was not the last word on the subject anyway because Jean had heard the same thing from someone who had actually seen them.

The walls and windows of the riverside palaces loomed and blazed anciently in the horizontal light. The fact that the light is horizontal does not mean that the buildings are ancient. The light is horizontal, but the buildings are not ancient. The light is ancient, the buildings are not. None of them is older than the eighteenth century. The history of Varanasi is the history of how it gets razed to the ground and rebuilt, razed to the ground and rebuilt. No sooner has it been rebuilt than it looks like it's on its last legs. Every atom of the air is saturated by history that isn't even history, myth, so a temple built today looks, overnight, as if it's been there since the dawn of time. *Every morning is the dawn of time*, I wrote in my notebook. *Every day is the whole of time.*

Most of the ghats had their names painted in faded, bright letters: Chousatti ghat. Ranamahal ghat. Munshi ghat – where some kind of film or pop video was being made. The brightness of the sun wasn't bright enough. Extra lights were brought in to make the scene blaze whitely. Kshameshwar ghat, with a faded yellow temple standing unfilmed in front of it, looked dull by comparison. A sign, also yellow, at Chauki ghat, read: 'Ganga is the life-line of Indian culture'. The temple at Kedar ghat was painted in pink and white vertical stripes; the steps leading down to the river were horizontal bands of pink and white: Op Art of a kind. The edge of the temple roof was crowded with gods painted the colour of toys, jostling for position, looking out at us as we gazed, admiringly, at them. Dhobis were in the river up to their thighs, thwacking sheets and clothes on rocks, beating them into a state of submissive cleanliness. Ten yards upstream was Harishchandra ghat, the other cremation ground. Much less of a spectacle than the one at Manikarnika. Not many people. A few dogs picking through the ashes. With only one fire burning, Harishchandra's identifying feature was a square yellow and black structure. It resembled a squat lifeguard's tower but, like everything else, it was a shrine or temple or both.

'I've got to say,' said Paul, 'if it'd been up to me, I'd have done it the other way round. Put the cremation site downstream from the laundrette.'

'Me too,' I laughed. But I was also remembering the philosopher who asked, rhetorically, 'Where did logic come from?' From illogic, of course. In this sense, illogic was upstream from logic. We were heading upstream.

A boat sidled up alongside our boat. The man was selling those little candle dishes that I'd seen floating down the river the night before.

'Good karma,' he assured us, but no one in our boat wanted any karma, good or bad. A man of uncertain age was in the river up to his shoulders, praying, oblivious to the cold. Next to him a white-haired man was washing himself thoroughly, using a polythene bag as a flannel. We rowed past the UP Pollution Control Boat. No longer part of the solution, it was rusting away into the river, becoming part of the problem. Behind it, on the steps of Jain ghat, was a mustard-brown temple that was not doing any business at all; behind that, a pale blue structure that looked like the exterior of a municipal Lido.

The other members of our expedition were taking the boat back to Dashaswamedh. I got out at Assi, the last of the ghats on the city's curving riverfront. Most of the other ghats were made of concrete steps, but Assi was just a bare mud bank sloping down to the river. Spotting me walk up this slope, a man hurried over to ask if I wanted a boat.

'I've just got off a boat,' I said. Even as I said this, I realized the irrelevance of my response. All that mattered was that I was not on a boat at the precise moment the question was posed. I was therefore available, a potential boat-taker. No calculation had been made as to the chances of the offer of a boat being taken up; the important thing was to lodge the offer before anyone else was able to. Sound-wise, the clamour of bells from a temple competed with Indian pop music being played over a sound system pushed beyond limits that were yet to be absolutely established.

The sun was warm now. A goat jogged by, white except

for the feet and legs, which made it look as if it were wearing dainty black socks. There was a little row of shops and a guest house with families of beggars sitting outside, still cold from the night. The air smelled of wood smoke.

It was only eleven but, having been up since the dawn of time, I was in need of lunch. I ordered daal and rice at a place with moulded red chairs on a terrace overlooking the river. The opposite bank was no longer quite as insubstantial as it had appeared earlier. A few other people arrived, one of whom sat at the table next to mine. He was in his early thirties, hair cut army-short. His arms were tanned, roped with muscle. He was wearing a navy WKCR T-shirt, faded jeans and aviator shades. Below the shades, on his right cheekbone, was a U-shaped scar. All of this, together with his bright smile, gave him the look of an actor playing the part of someone who had begun undercover work for the CIA. We said hi, asked each other the usual stuff: where we were from, where else in India we'd been. He ordered the same as me, the daal and rice that had arrived at the table after he sat down. I washed my hands carefully with anti-bacterial handwash, said I hadn't been anywhere else, had come straight to Varanasi from London.

'Jumped right in the deep end, huh?' An American could probably have placed his accent, but to me he sounded simply American. He was originally from a small town in Illinois, but now lived in Oakland. He'd been in Chennai for the music season, during which time there were seventy concerts a day of south Indian classical music. It was amazing, he said. After a fortnight he felt like he didn't want to hear another note of music for the rest of his life. I asked which musicians he'd seen. He mentioned a lot of names I'd not heard of, and one or two that I had. I'd listened to quite a few musicians who'd been influenced by Indian music but, for me, 'Indian' was a vaguely defined part of the broader, much-derided classification of 'World Music'. Eager to impress, I ran through the few names I did know: Shankar, Talvin Singh, Trilok Gurtu . . . I said I'd seen Nusrat Fateh Ali Khan play at the Hackney Empire in 1990. I mentioned Ry Cooder and the record he'd done with an Indian guy whose name I couldn't remember.

'V. M. Bhatt,' he said, not showing off, just helping out. 'And I'm Darrell, by the way.' After we'd shaken hands, a waiter brought his lunch and we both sat there, spooning up our daal in companionable silence. I liked him. There was a steadiness about him.

When I'd finished eating, Darrell pulled a thick history of India from his bag, asked if I'd read it. I glanced through the battered pages, he continued eating.

'No, I haven't,' I said. 'How is it?'

'I'm finding it a struggle. The only thing that's keeping me going is the phrase "Indo-Gangetic Plain". I just love that phrase.'

'Me too,' I said. 'It's just . . . It's one of the great place names.'

'It makes you really want to go there, doesn't it? To the Indo-Gangetic Plain.'

'D'you think we're actually in it, even as we speak?'

'You mean we're having a conversation about the Indo-Gangetic Plain in the Indo-Gangetic Plain? How cool is that?'

'Thing is, I'm not sure exactly where it is. It's so big, it's difficult to say where it ends.'

'Or begins.'

'It's everywhere.'

'It's nowhere.'

'It's . . .'

'The Indo-Gangetic Plain.'

From that moment on, I knew we were going to become friends.

After lunch we walked to a bookshop where, as well as books, lots of classical music CDs – sitar, sarangi and vocal – were on sale. Darrell flicked through a copy of Allen Ginsberg's *Indian Journals*. There were several pages of photographs, including one of the bearded, bespectacled poet on a moldy balcony in Varanasi, shaking hands with a nimble monkey, betraying no signs of speciesism (Ginsberg, I mean; the monkey approached the human with evident wariness).

'You like Ginsberg?' Darrell asked.

'To be honest, I've always thought of him as a bit of a tosser.' Like a wise monkey, I should perhaps have kept my opinion to myself, but Darrell bought the book anyway.

Next door to the bookshop was a travel agency, where Darrell had to make arrangements for train tickets. He was planning on being away from Varanasi for a few weeks, after which he was going to return for a longer stay, at the Ganges View.

'A friend in London recommended that hotel,' I said.

'It's super nice,' he said. 'Right along from here.'

We said goodbye outside the bookshop. Given how little time we'd spent in each other's company, I was surprised to feel so disappointed that he was going away. I said I hoped I saw him again, before he left.

'Bound to,' he said. 'It's a small town. Or at least the tourist bit is. The Ganges View is just a few doors down. Go take a look.'

We said goodbye again and I walked up the steps to the Ganges View. From what Anand had said, I expected a Maharajah's converted palace, or a boutique version of the Taj Mahal, but it looked like quite a homely place. The man at the desk was so gentle he seemed reluctant to speak, as if to utter words was an expression of violent intent – or, more basically, to risk a red explosion of the *paan* he was chewing. He consulted a piece of paper the size of a desktop, which can have made sense to no one but him. From the way he scrutinised it, I wasn't sure it made sense even to him. It had been arranged, sensibly enough, with room numbers along the top and dates down the side, but within this simple grid everything had been rubbed or crossed out and written over. There were two ways of looking at him looking at it: like a fortune-teller trying to discern the future from the random patterns of tea leaves in a cup or like an archaeologist confronted with some palimpsest in which the mysteries of an extinct civilization might be deciphered.

'We have room from Tuesday,' he said.

'Tuesday,' I repeated. I lost my bearings for a moment and had to ask what day it was today.

'Today is Saturday.'

That's right. Today was Saturday and Tuesday was the day I was due to fly back to Delhi, and from there to London. I asked if I could see the room. He said that although a room would be free, he did not yet know which room. Then he gestured to me to go inside, to take a look. On the first floor was a warm terrace, rimmed with potted flowers, large, with a view of the river. The opposite shore had acquired further definition, some kind of shape. A middle-aged couple was eating lunch. Right next door were the brown stupas of a couple of temples. A couple of parrots, green as limes, were sitting on a telephone wire. Everything was part of a couple, but that was fine.

I peeked in a room, went back down the stairs and said I would take it. This was not strictly true. I intended flying back to London as planned, but my ticket was changeable and it is always a good feeling, keeping one's options open.

He wrote my name in the column – if I had understood things correctly – for Room 9, even though this did not mean I would definitely be in Room 9. I said I would see him on Tuesday and he nodded, Indian-style, by shaking his head.

I walked back along the ghats I'd passed earlier, on the boat. It was like strolling along the seafront at Hove, but there was more to see. A dog chewed what I thought was a chunk of wood but was actually the head of another dog, or maybe a fox. The dhobis had finished bashing their laundry. At several ghats the steps were covered in drying saris, the size of bright carpets on stairs. Whether they were cleaner now than before they were washed was difficult to say. Being damp, the dust clung to them. People kept asking me if I wanted a boat and I kept saying no. The man I'd seen from the boat was still there, praying, tranced out in the Ganges. He could have been there for weeks, years, even.

I was trying – partly for my own sake, partly as research for the article I had to write – to get a rough idea of the sequence of the ghats, what each looked like, what went on at which. Mahanirvani was easy: it jutted out in a large concrete apron and was the place where buffalo roamed. They mooched around rather than roamed and a boy whose job it was sometimes gave them a thwack with a stick. Being water buffalo, the proximity of the river was a big plus. They took it in turns to kneel in it, or sit, and there were some cows too. Probably they did not even know there was such a thing as grass. As far as they were concerned, this was the prairie, only inedible. It wasn't a prairie, though, it was a cricket pitch and a skinny boy was stationed on the boundary, in amongst the cattle, to stop the ball flying into the Ganges for a six. The ball was a tennis ball, mud-brown and soggy, and the kid bowling looked like he meant it, but the kid batting meant it even more, and there was quite a wait while the ball was fished from the river by the kid who was meant to have stopped this happening. The whole scene was a persuasive essay on the decline of cricket in England.

Some of the buildings faced outwards, enjoying the view. The one at Dandi ghat had its back turned to the river, like the outside of a football stadium whose team, recently relegated, played in orange and pale blue. The palace behind Karnataka State ghat had the tragic grandeur of a disused bingo hall. The sense, on this stretch of the ghats, of hard times – of mass entertainment and faded glory – extended to Harishchandra, the cremation ground with the yellow and black lifeguard's tower. A couple of fires were smouldering and the golden trash of shroud and marigold at the water's edge appeared to have been there an age. The water looked left behind, lifeless.

I passed Kedar ghat, the temple with the pink and white stripes. The white stripes were actually pale blue, it turned out. The offers of boats had not stopped all the time I was walking.

Something was happening up ahead. A commotion, a crowd: the film shoot I had seen from the boat. Large screens and lights were being hauled into place. The camera was on rails. In the midst of all the activity it was difficult to tell who was part of the production and who were extras and who was just watching. Next to the busy work of the film set, apparently oblivious to it, a holy man sat in front of a small orange shrine. He had grey hair and a beard that looked like it was made out of the fur of a long-haired animal, mythical in origin, close to extinction and completely incontinent. A dozen listeners sat, cross-legged, on a blue tarp. Their teacher had before him a presumably sacred book the size of a comprehensive, if slightly out of date, road atlas. When I say slightly out of date, I mean from a time before there were cars, when there were no roads – or atlases. The director called out instructions to his crew, his actors, the extras. More screens and lights were assembled. One of the actors was playing the part of a holy man. He was a healthier-looking, more expensively dressed version of the bearded holy man a few paces away. His hair and beard were obviously fake; they looked like human hair, but not the hair of this particular human. Red-assed monkeys swarmed and squealed over the building behind the shrine, clambered down on to its orange roof. One of them swung down and tried to grab the sacred road atlas from the guru. The monkey was quick, but insufficiently strong. The book dropped from his paw and the guru continued his instruction. As he did so he took, from a plastic bag, what looked like an old turd but was actually a very overripe banana and tossed it in the direction of the monkey. The monkey grabbed it and scampered back up to the roof of the shrine. The director called 'Action' and the monkey peeled and ate his banana directly above the head of the guru. The scene from the movie involved one of the actors standing still while, behind him, a young woman in a green sari slinked shyly past. The actor playing the holy man had nothing to do with this scene; he was just hanging around. The director said, 'Cut.' Fed up with his banana, the monkey dangled down and – there was no satisfying him – snatched one of the marigold garlands from behind the guru's head. It now began to seem that they were a double act, that instead of instructions in navigation some kind of lesson in evolution was being enacted. We began as thieves, swinging from trees and stealing whatever we could lay our paws on – books, bananas, marigolds. Then, over time, we learned to sit cross-legged and talk and listen, and the urge to pilfer and steal gradually diminished. In the larger scheme of things, the fact that some of us went on to make films or write poems called 'Howl' was irrelevant. The monkey was sat on the orange shrine, head cocked to one side, as if he might begin to see the error of his ways. He looked like he was listening, but he may have been taking the piss or wondering where his next banana was coming from. The director said 'Action' again and the same scene was shot again. The girl in the green sari slinked past. The male lead looked at the camera with a completely gormless expression on his face. The monkey grew bored and went ricocheting up the walls of the building. The holy man continued mumbling his instruction.

I took an auto rickshaw back to the hotel. We'd only travelled a few hundred yards when the driver stopped so that he could pick up a purple pile of tiny aubergines from a friend. Immediately something smacked into the back of us. I thought nothing of it, assumed it was a collision – a car or another tuk-tuk crashing into us – but it was actually a policeman, a traffic cop, whacking the back of our tuk-tuk with his baton: Varanasi's robust implementation of a red route. We roared off again. It was a different experience to being cocooned in a car. Travelling by Ambassador was like being in the armour-plated discomfort of a Humvee. This was a whole new ball game. Actually, it was more like a video game. I was too tall, obviously. Once I had folded myself into the seat, I could see almost nothing until it was within a few feet or inches of smashing us to pieces. In addition to everything else – the competing traffic, the oncoming traffic, the din, the fumes, the noise – the journey was also a steeplechase. We were always crashing over some kind of speed hump or into a trench. It would have played hell with the suspension, but since the suspension had been shot to hell years ago it made no difference. Nothing made any difference, so we rode roughshod over everything. Everything except a manhole, completely uncovered. We veered round it in the nick of time even though the hazard was clearly indicated – by a half brick placed inches from the rim. Cars, buses and tuk-tuks reeled into view and shrieked past. I've never had any enterprising ideas, but it occurred to me that there was scope for a simulated version of this experience, a computer game called *Varanasi Death Trip* or simply – in homage to Scorsese and De Niro – *Tuk-tuk Driver*. The idea would be to travel from the Taj Ganges to Manikarnika without getting crushed, losing a limb or having your nerves shredded.

I ate dinner in the attained safety of the Taj and then had a beer in the bar: a Kingfisher with a slightly oily taste, from a clear bottle. There were only a handful of people there, no one sitting at the bar, no one to talk to. Perhaps with the solitary drinker in mind, the hotel had provided a selection of books about Varanasi. One of them was called *End Time City*, a book of photos by Michael Ackerman. It took some adjusting to: the buildings looked familiar, but the pictures were in black and white, and the most obvious thing about the place I'd spent the day walking round was its colour. It was probably the most colourful city on earth. To get rid of the colour was to create a place that, in some ways, was not a place at all but a stunned reaction to it. They were like pictures of the inside of the photographer's head while he was here, or later, while he was remembering it, or while he was asleep, sweat-drenched and dreaming about it. There were monkeys, sad-looking and thoughtful, aware, even if they did not yet know it, that if other things died then they would too. Sure enough, a few pages on, there was one of them, dead as a loved dog, coins scattered over it. People crouched, reading, behind the bars of a cage or temple. Normal life in a place where the idea of normal was as exotic as a monkey sleeping on your shoulder. Streets in the sense of the gap between buildings where you could walk or chuck garbage or live, or not. A face evaporating in a fire. Shaved heads, a blur of animal. Things no longer alive, vultures the size of turkeys. Rags that must have been clothes. Cloth imprinted with the divine, stained. The pictures were stains. Time was a stain. I took a gulp of beer. They weren't there just to be looked at like photos, these pictures. They accosted you, lunged and reeled at you. Some were like daylight after emerging from a dark lane, others were as impenetrable as an alley after hours sightseeing in bright sun; the best were both. After looking at them for a while, the colours of the actual city – the pink and orange and vermilion, the blue of the sky – drained away, got forgotten, reduced themselves to the nothing glare of a light bulb, the white glow of cotton, the gleam of sun on water or an eye, gleaming, and the black of everything else, the night that never went away, that lurked, waited.

I went walking in those lanes the next day, in colour again. I had my neat little digital camera, but ended up not taking any pictures, even though everything was crying out to be photographed. Many of the lanes were only wide enough for two people to walk side by side, but bikes, motorbikes and cows managed to squeeze past too. That was something I was beginning to realize about India: there was always room. Even when there was no room, there was room. The sort of opposite was also true: however slender the lane on which you found yourself, there was always a narrower lane leading off to an even narrower alley. Eventually, when this stopped being true, there was a dead-end or an alley leading back to a lane that seemed, by comparison, the size of a major thoroughfare. It was difficult to believe that this web of lanes and alleys had ever been mapped. There was no need. Everyone knew where they were going, and how to get there. Most people were there already. Women in red and yellow saris flickered by like load-bearing flames. Shops, stalls and people sleeping were squeezed into every cranny and shadow. Everyone was busy going about their business, even if that business was just sitting. Sitting or dusting – a waiting game, essentially. People who looked like they were lazing around, doing nothing, sprang into action the moment any kind of sale seemed possible. This was true even if they were asleep, using their arms as numb pillows. If they had carpets to sell, then it made sense to sit on a stack of them. Most of the trade came from within the community of stallholders. They were always buying things from each other: food, tea, sweets. One of the things they were always buying was money. No one had any change. So if a tourist wanted to purchase a souvenir or a fun toy for his kids back home in Washington or London, then a boy was sent off to another stall to buy some smaller denomin-ations of note. In this way a minor transaction created enormous ripples of economic activity that spread through the whole neighbourhood, animating it, generating interest. I didn't yet have any hash to smoke – was not sure I would even want to – but I bought, on spec, a small pipe. The guy had dozens of them, several of which were completely blocked. I paid with a fifty-rupee note and – after a boy was dispatched – received in change a twenty that looked like it had been unearthed from the bottom of a compost heap. I loved that about India, the way that, in spite of everything, stuff retained its value. In another life, I could quite happily have worked here. There was something seductive about spending your time tending a stall that was both workplace and pub, the place you hung out with your friends, without your wife, without beer, and often without customers. If you didn't have a wife, it was less appealing, obviously. Then you had to rely more on the solace of the newspaper. The spectacles worn by certain men – thick lenses, black plastic frames – lent the act of reading these newspapers a most scholarly air. Wherever a newspaper was being read, however great the surrounding commotion, there was the contemplative air of a reference library. Pages were turned. The sun was directly overhead. Spears of light made the shadows darker. Soldiers in khaki sweaters sat cradling rifles with wooden butts, the kind of weapons associated with the Second World War. Nearby was a large sunlit courtyard, where a game of badminton – doubles – was being played. It was surrounded, on three sides, by steep green walls where monkeys paid no attention to the game. They were interested only in bananas and there were no bananas to hand.

Shortly after this I found myself outside a temple – I didn't know which one, only that it was not the big one, Vishwanath, with all the airport security: metal detectors and searches. That's why there were so many soldiers around: because Vishwanath, the Golden Temple, and a mosque were practically on top of each other, goading the faithful, inciting them to live in peace. It was the old 'neighbours from hell' scenario, raised to the level of intense theological principle and proximity. There is no God but God, says the one place. There are millions of them, says the other. The fact that people were able to get along in harmony for years did not mean that, at the drop of a hat, they would not be at one another's throats. Hence the soldiers.

I took off my sandals and stepped inside the temple. The tiled floor was wet underfoot. It was a dark, rather wet, not entirely clean-looking place. There was an assortment of gods tucked into little niches and an even larger assortment of kids eager to explain who they all were. Ganesh was there, draped with marigolds, with a black face and beady eyes, eyes made

188

of beads. Ganesh, one of the boys explained, was the god of good fortune – and it was easy to see why. He looked as if he couldn't believe his luck – half elephant and he still gets to be a god! That's the thing about Hinduism, though – everyone is in with a shout and there is always room for another god. Garuda (part eagle) was there and so was Hanuman, the monkey. Hinduism is the Disney of world religions. The gods all have their consorts, and the gods and their consorts all have their own private form of transport: Vishnu travels by eagle (Garuda), Shiva by bull (Nandi), Kartikeya by peacock . . . The list and the permutations of the list are endless, impossible to keep track of, but it seems safe to assume that even the 'vehicles' (whom one would have thought capable of taking care of their own travel arrangements) have their vehicles, that Garuda occasionally rides an owl or tortoise. And Ganesh, the elephant, how does he travel? By mouse, of course.

If there is one thing the great monotheisms have in common, it is the lack of a sense of humour. Is there a single joke in the Bible or the Qu'ran? Hinduism, I saw now, was a joke, but it was not just a joke; it was completely ridiculous. And it didn't stop there. It did away with the idea of the ridiculous by turning it into an entire cosmology! I didn't really know if this was true about Hinduism, but here, in this Hindu temple, the notion of the ridiculous became suddenly sublime.

It was only a small temple. My tour was soon complete. I gave some old rupees to the boys who had shown me round, stepped out into the remembered sun. My sandals were where I had left them. I was pleased to have them on again, to not be walking barefoot through the dusty, shit-splattered lanes of Varanasi. The invention and development of footwear was so obviously a good thing that my happiness, the spring in my step that derived from being comfortably shod, was accompanied by a corresponding draining of enthusiasm. What, a few moments earlier, had seemed such a persuasive notion – that ridiculousness might be the animating principle of life – seemed, in the face of this more pedestrian idea of progress, abruptly . . . ridiculous. No sooner had I thought this, than I'd suddenly had enough of walking. I wanted to go back to the hotel, to play *Varanasi Death Trip* again.

I bought a can of Coke (to get more change) and struck a deal with a tuk-tuk driver (who had none). I hoped to avoid saying the name of the hotel – an immediate incitement to hyper-inflation – but did not know the name of any other landmark in the vicinity. So the Taj it was, or should have been – but after five minutes we lurched off the main road.

'What are you doing?' I shouted. I wasn't angry, but I had to shout to make myself heard above the noise of the tuk-tuk and the other traffic. 'Why are we going this way?'

'Main road closed,' he said. The main road may have been closed, but it was hard to believe it could have been in worse condition than these side roads. They weren't roads at all, just dusty lanes, unpaved, full of rubble, trash-strewn. We made another turning, into a smaller, even less roadworthy road, through what was evidently one of the poorest parts of the city. That's probably not true: there are endless degrees of poverty. Compared with some areas, this one might have been relatively affluent, desirable, even. A couple of happy-looking pigs were rooting through a mass of garbage. Some of this rubbish had been compacted down into a dark tar, a sediment of concentrated filth, pure filth, filth with no impurities, devoid of everything that was not filth. The layer on top of this comprised a mulch of rotting vegetables from which a suitably adapted creature could conceivably derive a vestige of nutrition. On top of this was an assortment of browning marigolds, bits of soggy cardboard (not automatically to be discounted as a calorific source) and freshish-looking excrement (ditto). The whole thing was set off with a resilient garnish of blue plastic bags. In its way it was a potential tourist attraction, a contemporary manifestation of the classical ideal of squalor. I was quite excited by it, was tempted to ask the driver to stop so that I could have a better look, perhaps even take a picture. Before I had a chance to do so, he had stopped. Because the tuk-tuk was surrounded by a swarm of kids. There are plenty of dirty kids running around Varanasi, barefoot in ragged T-shirts, pestering tourists for rupees. But these kids, it became immediately clear, were worse off. Even by the standards of the penniless, they were poor. By the standards of the dirty, they were filthy, as filthy as the pigs nosing around in the garbage. It was even possible that what I had taken for a rubbish tip was actually their playground, perhaps even their kitchen. There was nothing charming about them, but they were kids, kids with teeth and eyes and thin arms, and, as such, there was – or could have been – something charming about them. They were hyena children, urban prairie dogs, wild, feral creatures. More accurately, they were like the detached, highly animated parts of a single swarming entity with dozens of eyes and multiple arms and hands, all of which were reaching into the tuk-tuk, grabbing at my bag, my camera, my arms, my pockets. The tuk-tuk driver looked frightened. Fortunately I'd had some small experience of this before, in Naples, when a gang of ten-year-olds had robbed me. Back then I hardly knew what to do; by the time I had figured out what was happening, they had made off with my wallet. Now, keeping my bag firmly between my legs, I lashed out as spitefully as possible, using elbows, fists and forearms to hit anything that came near me while taking care not to hit anyone in the face. It was unlikely that they had parents, but I did not want the daddy of any of them to appear on the scene, wanting to know why this rich tourist had bloodied his little boy's snout. Swatting and jabbing, clutching my belongings and guarding my pockets, I ordered the tuk-tuk driver to keep going.

'Drive on!' I shouted with all the imperial authority I could muster. 'Drive on!' The engine fumbled into life. Hands were still grabbing and snatching. Unable to get anything more substantial, they resorted now to pinching my flesh. The tuk-tuk began to move. 'Faster!' I roared, never ceasing to punch and parry. 'Run them over if necessary!'

We accelerated noisily away. A projectile – a stone or a brick, conceivably a lump of dried shit – thumped on the roof of the tuk-tuk, but we were in the clear. The driver said nothing. I said nothing. It was not clear whether he had deliberately, as they say in thrillers, 'set me up', whether he was complicit in the ambush or as much the unwilling victim as myself. Certainly he had looked alarmed. Anyway, I was safe now. It occurred to me that a version of this incident could usefully get worked into the *Varanasi Death Trip* software. I twisted round and looked back. I could still see these hyena children by their patch of garbage. They were hopping round excitedly holding something aloft – something that flashed in the sunlight – as though it were a trophy, the spoils of a raid. I checked my belongings: I still had my camera, my iPod; my money belt was still around my waist. And then I realized: they *had* made off with something. The object I had seen them waving excitedly in the air was my can of Coke.

The next day I made another new friend – or at least had another conversation. A long flight of blue and white steps near Shivala ghat led up to the Mother Rytasha Bookshop and Café. At the top, sitting on one of two white chairs, was Andre Agassi. Not Agassi as he is now (or was a few years ago, at the time of his retirement): shaven-headed, loveable; a duck-waddle Buddha with a two-fisted backhand. This was Agassi in his rebelliously marketable early twenties: long hair, earring, baseball cap, unshaven. I sat down on the other seat, unsure if he worked here or was simply a customer. A bit of both, it turned out. His friend Chandra ran the place and he came by and hung out and helped. He sounded American, his name was Ashwin, and the resemblance to Agassi – I could not help mentioning it – was not entirely fanciful. Like Agassi, he was of Persian descent.

'But you're American?'

'In this incarnation.'

'How about previous ones? Do you know where you were from in them?'

'From God.'

'Sticking, for a moment, to this incarnation, where are you from in America?'

Ashwin was from California, had been in Varanasi four weeks. Right now he was just back from volunteering at one of Mother Rytasha's eye camps in Bangladesh, where inexpensive operations for cataracts and other easily curable conditions were performed. I had not heard of Mother Rytasha, so he fetched me an illustrated book about her. She had pale skin and looked like her nose had been worked on by the same surgeon who'd done Michael Jackson's. It was impossible to say how old she was. Obviously, she was a force for good. All of the money she raised went entirely on doing work for the poor. Ashwin had met her in Santa Fe, where she was doing some work on the rich, fund-raising. He had gone with all the usual scepticism, but when he had seen her, he had felt this emanation from her of pure love. Even so, he was not convinced. He went away. Then, later in the day, he came across her again. She was sitting with friends in a park, under a tree, and once again she had looked at him and he had felt her love – not love for him, love for everyone, for the world, just love – filling his heart. Through his love for her, he had found God.

'Which particular god?' I asked. I did not mean to sound cynical, but we were in India, there were lots to choose from, and some kind of clarification seemed essential. He pressed his hands together and raised his eyes to the . . . heavens, I suppose you would call them.

'The god of love,' he said. It was a good, non-sectarian answer. I couldn't fault it, but at some level I did fault it of course. He told me more about Mother Rytasha and the things she did, all of which – there was no doubt on this score either – made the world a better place. Even so, there was something about the blissed-out look in Ashwin's eyes that made me think of heavy doses of Prozac or Zoloft. The love he was full of – genuine, absolute, unconditional, commendable, life-enhancing – was all that stood between him and the nervous breakdown that, like the night in Ackerman's pictures, lay in wait. The love would keep it at bay but, eventually, would leave him more susceptible to it. Part of me even hoped I might be here to see it happen.

Still, it had been nice drinking a Coke and hearing him talk. We shook hands, said we'd see each other around.

I checked out of the Taj and into the Ganges View. I called the airline, cancelled my existing booking and got confirmed on another notional flight to London a couple of weeks from now. I was in no hurry to leave Varanasi, but I was glad to be changing hotels. The excitement and noise of the daily journey to and from the ghats had become a chore – a commute – and I had grown bored with the sanitized comfort of the Taj. I was so happy to be at the Ganges View that I spent the whole of the first day on the terrace, ordering lunch and drinks, reading. Or trying to.

I'd bought a pile of books on Hinduism from the Harmony bookshop – the shop I'd been to with Darrell – but found it difficult to concentrate on them. However hard I tried, I could not keep track of who was who and what was what. It was impossible to tell if the person in one part of a story was the same one in another part, a few pages later. Everyone was an avatar of everyone else. No one was just themselves. Shiva, Vishnu, Krishna – they were all each other. It was like a world in which Thor, instead of banging his hammer and turning back into frail Don Blake, was re-ignited as the Human Torch (who was also Doctor Doom) or – even more bafflingly – into a guest star from a rival mythological system: the Green Lantern, say, or Lois Lane. (A surprising oversight on the part of Marvel that the super-heroic potential of Hinduism was so under-utilized.) Even when they were not each other, they were always turning themselves into something else to punish a rival or get themselves out of a jam. Since their powers were unlimited, the jams in which they found themselves could never generate much suspense. The names were essential – nothing was more important than the names – but they were infinitely flexible, shared. Another problem was that the epic antics of these gods – all those yarns about eggs the size of planets, drops of water forming great lakes, the blink of an eye shutting out the sun, errands lasting tens of thousands of years – were exactly the kind of things I'd always had trouble reading. After a fling with Gabriel García Márquez, I'd come to detest even a hint of magic realism in fiction. As soon as I came to a passage in a novel where the trees started talking to each other, I gave up on the spot. Compared with what went on in the Hindu myths, trees talking to each other seemed like scrupulous reporting, documentary. This was magic realism without any vestige of the real. Maybe you had to absorb it all as a kid, and just get lost in the fabulousness of the *Mahabharata* or the *Ramayana*, and then, as a result of that early exposure, your brain would be configured or formatted in such a way that it all made a kind of sense that was simultaneously allegorical and literal, fantastic and believable. For me, obviously, that possibility was long passed.

Perhaps I'm being too hard on myself, though, because I did learn a few things. Most of the books had glossaries, and although I didn't understand all of the terms, it was good to see where things like Shakti (the group formed by John McLaughlin, Shankar and Zakir Hussain in the 1970s), Rasa (the restaurant in Stoke Newington), Samsara (as in 'Escape from', the trance club) or Surya (as in Surya Samudra, the resort in Kerala) derived their names.

Thanks to Kerouac, Ginsberg and the Beats, notions of karma and dharma had become common currency, but words like *moksha*, *bhakti* and *rocana* were new to me. Terms like these didn't lend themselves to straightforward translation because they were ideas that did not have an equivalent in our limited western consciousness. One concept that did make sense was *darshan*: the act of divine seeing, of revelation. This was what Hindus went to the temple for: to see their god, to have him or her revealed to them. The more attention paid to a god, the more it was looked at, the greater its power, the more easily it could be seen. You went to see your god and, in doing so, you contributed to its visibility; the aura emanating from it derived in part from the power bestowed on it.

It was an easy idea to grasp because of its secular equivalent, the worship of celebrity. The more celebrities were photographed, the stronger their aura of celebrity became. I'd once seen David Beckham step off a coach at La Manga in

Spain. Obviously, I'd seen photographs of him before and now the cumulative effect of having seen all those photographs was making itself felt. The flash of camera lights made him radiant, glossy, divine. I saw him in all his Beckhamness and Beckhamitude. Someone who had not seen the thousands of pictures, who was not familiar with the changes of hairstyle, the viral spread of tattoos (including the misspelt bit of Hindi on his forearm), would not have seen him in this way. But maybe the point of view of that hypothetical and implausible onlooker – the person who didn't know they were seeing David Beckham – was more revelatory, at the very least, more interesting, than that of the rest of us who understood exactly who and what we were seeing. Here in Varanasi, the ill-informed tourist did not see the same city that the thousands of pilgrims saw, the pilgrims who came here and the ones who lived here. But this was not to say that the visitor was not capable of his own form of *darshan*. Even if I didn't know what I was looking at, I could still see. And if ever somewhere was designed with the eye in mind – there was probably a Sanskrit term meaning exactly eye-in-mind – then Varanasi was that place.

Next morning there was nothing to see. The river, the ghats, even the sky, had disappeared. A dense fog obliterated everything except a few vague details: the blurred shape of the temple next door, dark figures moving in the street below. I dressed and went down to the ghats, heard people coughing before I saw them, a few feet away. Boat rides were still being offered even though, with nothing to see, there was no point in taking one. Then I did see something: a boat, emerging from the haze as if returning from the realm of the dead or the undead. There were two passengers, swathed in grey blankets. After a while they drifted away again and merged silently into the larger, greyer blanket of fog. There were a few squares of colour – the yellow of a sign, the blue of a wall – but infinitely subdued and dampened, shadows of their usual selves.

The mist cleared, unnoticed, before midday, making the afternoon seem even brighter than usual. A kingfisher appeared on the wall of the Ganges View terrace, eager to be seen, to re-exist. The sky, when I went out again, was busy with kites. At Munshi ghat I noticed a small blue shrine, the size of an emergency phone on the side of a motorway. In the middle of the shrine, where the phone would have been, was an orange blob, a worn blur of a shape. Within the general roundness, it was possible to make out the lump of a body and the smaller lump of a head, but more rounded, less defined than a Henry Moore version of an Indian god. Who was it? Ganesh? It could have been any of them. There was not even a residue of definition, but this did not suggest that its power had been diminished or had shrunk; the sense was that its essence had become more concentrated. The feeling was not of erosion or diminution, but of withdrawal. The god, whoever it was, had retreated into itself. By reducing itself almost to nothing, by coming so close to that which could not be identified as itself, it had became more nakedly itself. I felt sure of this, even though I did not know who or what I was seeing.

'Who is that?' I asked a boy.

'Hanuman,' he replied instantly. Because he recognized the monkey god (because he could *see* that it was him?) or because he knew that this is what the blob was, because he knew that this blue shrine was the place – one of the places – where Hanuman lived? The questions were irrelevant. They were the same. This orange, blurry blob was Hanuman.

'Very powerful god,' the boy added. The fact that his identity was not in doubt, that the boy had not hesitated to say his name, was proof of that.

I took a boat home. Kites flew over the city, like embers floating over a bonfire.

The fog reappeared the following morning, and the morning after that. In addition to the fog, temperatures had plummeted throughout northern India. Newspapers were full of reports about freezing temperatures – 'as the mercury plummeted . . . ' – and travel disruption. Flights were cancelled and there were severe 'delayments' to all destinations. Trains from Delhi arrived in Varanasi ten hours late. Kite-flying was adversely affected.

Once the fog had gone – after the initial novelty had worn off, I was glad to see the back of it – the volume of kites in the sky increased daily. There were kite strings everywhere. In their thin, resilient way, they had tied up the entire city. The oars of boats were wrapped in them. It was impossible to walk more than a couple of steps without becoming tangled in them. They flailed from every tree and dangled from every telegraph pole like broken wires.

I saw many of the same people, the same kite-flying kids, the same hustlers, the same boatmen. Older, more affluent-looking tourists stayed only a few days before moving on to Agra or Kerala. I rarely saw any of them two days running. The backpackers stayed longer, and the longer they stayed the more closely they conformed to an international standard of scruffiness. Quite a few had dreadlocks anyway, some – like Ashwin, whom I bumped into a couple of times – opted for turbans that had started out as sarongs. The women wore shawls to protect themselves from the daytime sun and the evening chill, and also as a concession to local standards of modesty. Most of these travellers were in their twenties, here for enlightenment, yoga, charas-smoking, spiritual growth, liberation. They were apprentice seekers, and in Varanasi there were dozens – probably hundreds, possibly thousands – of gurus and guides to help them bust out of the prison of the ego or get fast-tracked to enlightenment or wherever else they wanted to go. Most would return home several pounds lighter (the weight and the currency), but otherwise vastly enriched by the experience; some would go seriously off the rails – Varanasi's reputation for sending people nuts rivalled its reputation for making them ill – and a few, in time, would turn into versions of the older guys who were here, guys my age, many of whom looked like they'd done a decade or more in Goa. They often had the slightly hardened look of men accustomed to spending evenings on their own, reading *Mr Nice* or selections from Gurdjieff. Like me, they were often to be found on the terrace of the Lotus Lounge, eating excellent pancakes, drinking cappuccinos (the best in Varanasi) or chai. We nodded at each other but, like blacks at an otherwise all-white cocktail party, tacitly avoided forming any kind of alliance because that would have exacerbated our mutual status as age-outcastes. Not that the young people were unfriendly – they were just young. Even that is not right; it's not that I felt they were young so much as I thought how old I must appear from their point of view. In their shoes, I would not have paid any attention to a man of my age. I'd have been concentrating all my energies on persuading the young girls in their T-shirts and shawls that there was no danger of my standards of modesty being offended by any behaviour, however licentious.

These young people may not have been here for sex, but they were certainly here for death. They were as keen to see corpses being burned at Manikarnika ghat as the next person – me, for example. I'd never seen a dead body before, but in Varanasi the procession of death was endless. I got used to seeing mourners carrying litters through the streets, chanting *'Rama nama satya hai . . . Rama nama satya hai . . .'* taking the body to the river, dipping it in the Ganges. The random details that had caught my eye that first afternoon were part of an unvarying ceremony, re-enacted dozens of times every day. The mood was never sombre because the dead did not appreciate displays of grief. The man with the shaved head, dressed only in a white cloth, was the chief mourner. Having his head and eyebrows shaved was part of a ritual that left him suspended between the living and the dead. He led the other mourners five times around the unlit pyre, anti-clockwise (because, in death, everything is reversed). He was the one who poured sandalwood onto the pyre, before lighting it from a sacred fire that never goes out, that has burned since the world was created, here in Varanasi, at Manikarnika ghat, where it will end, except it will never end, any more than the journey from life to death will end.

It took hours for a body to burn. Near the end of the cremation the chief mourner cracked open the skull with a bamboo pole, releasing the soul from the body. Finally he tossed a pot of Ganges water over his shoulder – always his left shoulder – to symbolically extinguish the embers of the pyre. Without looking back, he walked briskly away. It was over. The soul had begun its journey to join the ancestors on the far shore. That journey would last eleven days, days of mourning and feasts. On the twelfth day, if all had gone well, if all the rituals had been correctly observed, it would arrive, safely.

The fact that the far bank was deserted made it easy to believe that the journey was more than a physical one. The reason the far bank was empty, a young boy with an old face explained, was that if you died over there you would be reborn as a donkey.

On this side, meanwhile, the area around the cremation

ground was always dense with activity. The journey from life to death never stopped, and nothing stopped here at the ur-departure lounge. Funerals were always in progress, but there were always other things going on as well: arguments, kite-flying, card games, music, yoga, bathing. A few yards beyond the cremation ground was Varanasi's leaning tower of Pisa: a temple that had collapsed or subsided in the mud of the river's edge. If it had once been painted Prayag-pink, now it was the dull, neglected brown of riverbank mud. From some angles it looked as if it sloped only slightly; from others it seemed on the brink of toppling over completely. I'd thought its vulnerability might have made it a particularly auspicious place to worship, but this, apparently, was not the case. It was, however, impossible to conclude that it had become entirely obsolete, that its power had been completely cut off simply because it had fallen on hard times. It was just an old temple that had gone on the wonk and was left to its own devices. Like a volcano which was somehow neither active nor extinct – nor anything in between – it still looked good in photographs. As such it remained viable, did its bit, brought something to the table. If it had a name, I did not know it.

The far side of the river, with all its changes, formed the constant backdrop to my days. At first light it was pure poten-tiality. As the lava-lamp sun floated clear of the horizon and wobbled through the grey haze, it became insubstantial other-ness. Gradually it was possible to make out the difference between the sandy foreground and the greenery behind it. At night everything disappeared. It made me think of the day when the sun first went down, when there was no guarantee that the earth would emerge again from the darkness that had descended on it. Even now, all these years later, with all the precedents for a tomorrow, it seemed that the other side did not just reappear but had to be painstakingly re-created again overnight, day after day.

The *Hindustan Times* (Lucknow) was exemplary in its vagueness: 'This year the festival of Makar Sankranti is being celebrated for two days due to some astronomical reason.' The banks at Assi and other ghats were packed with people waiting to take a dip on these, the first auspicious days of the new year. The street outside the hotel was crammed with beggars and those dispensing alms to them. It was still chilly in the mornings but, because it was a holiday, the sun shone more brightly.

'It's windier too,' I said to the boy tagging alongside me.

'Because is kite-flying day,' he said. Of course. Just as every god had his or her vehicle, so there was no effect without a cause. Makar Sankranti was the climax of the kite frenzy that had taken over the city, but flying kites was only part of the fun. It was also about catching or capturing them, sometimes with the aid of a pole, or cricket bat – anything that came to hand. Kites were chased among the dozing, resigned, indifferent buffalos, content to chew on flowers or, failing that, to graze on their own shadows.

At Manikarnika, a kite flopped down onto one of the pyres and, not surprisingly, burst into flames. What was surprising was that it had come down there in the first place. Hot air was supposed to rise, but evidently the normal laws of physics were reversed here. Seeing an opportunity to break free of the endless ups and downs of its existence, the kite took the plunge, seized this once-in-a-lifetime opportunity to crash and burn.

I looked at books about Varanasi, but there was more to learn than I could ever hope to take in. It was where Shiva had decided to live. It was where the world began. Crossing places –

tirthas – were sacred, certain crossing places were especially auspicious, but the whole of Varanasi was a crossing place, between this world and the next. Basically, there was no place on earth more worth visiting even though, in a sense, it was not of this world. I had read somewhere that Lourdes is not Lourdes for the people who live there. The same probably went for Mecca: where did the people who lived there go for a pilgrimage? But it was not true of Varanasi. Varanasi made going anywhere else seem nonsensical. All of time was here, and probably all of space too. The city was a mandala, a cosmogram. It contained the cosmos.

And it contained me: the longest-residing guest at the Ganges View. I was the only person conscious of this status for the simple reason that no one else had been there as long. If you arrived on a Tuesday, say, you simply saw that a number of guests had already settled in by the time you arrived. You could not have known that I had seen them all arrive, even as you had now arrived, and would see them depart, even as I would see you depart, world without end.

I had been at the Ganges View long enough to see that Anand Sethi was right: it really was one of the great hotels of the world. The reason for this, as the owner, Shashank, explained, was 'because we don't really know how to run a hotel'. The idea behind most hotels, especially luxurious ones, is very simple: to leech money out of guests. Every desire and whim can be catered for in an instant – and comes with a whopping surcharge. In the course of my stay at the Ganges View I'd eaten dozens of lunches, breakfasts and dinners, had ordered endless juices, teas and dozens of bottles of water. Wondering what all this might be costing, I asked Kamal – one of the smiling, gentle Nepalis who worked here – if they were keeping some kind of record of what I'd consumed. No, I was supposed to have kept a record, but they had forgotten to give me the piece of paper on which this record was kept. Kamal duly produced the relevant paper and said I could start from today. As he handed me the paper, I heard a rustling behind me. When I looked around I saw a rat scurrying out of sight, behind a wardrobe.

'Don't worry,' said Kamal. 'He is guest too.'

In the main room of the hotel was a portrait of Shashank's father, in his thirties, looking suave in a suit. It was like one of those paintings in films where real eyes peep through the painted eyes, spying and monitoring. Dinner was served here, in a semi-communal way that encouraged interaction among the guests. As different people came and went, bonded and dispersed, so the vibe of the hotel changed. At any time, different combinations and nationalities held sway. For a few days the French were dominant; there would be a group of six of them at the big table for dinner, chattering away in French, somehow making the rest of us feel that we were in France, wishing we weren't. Then, after they left, Americans would be in the majority and the hotel would be animated by their friendliness and perfect manners. Occasionally, there would be a lone Japanese, or Indians, some Germans, interested Scandinavians, lively Italians. Then there'd be a phase marked by its lack of defining character or cogency, when it was just a mixture of people from all over the place: mainly singles, the odd couple. Always, whatever the nationality, at least one person was sick and spent the day languishing in their room, unseen and unhappy. Everyone had come from somewhere and was going somewhere else. Everyone had had experience of trains and fog, delayments. Everyone had favourite places and places where they had fallen ill. We all had anecdotes and knew something that everyone else also knew.

I ate dinner in the hotel every night. It was nice meeting

people, and sometimes we sat around talking after dessert, but these dinners never turned into more than dinners. If you wanted an early-evening beer on the terrace, one of the boys would go out to the market to buy a bottle of Kingfisher, but no alcohol was allowed in the house itself. For people used to running their social lives on booze, the lack of wine at dinner meant that once the food was eaten the experience was pretty well finished. It was still too cold at night to sit on the terrace drinking beer. So we said goodnight, went to bed early and read under blankets in our rooms, eager for another dawn.

It was not a lonely time, though. Because the Ganges View was more expensive than most of the other places on the river, the guests tended to be a little older, or at least the ages were more mixed. It was easy for me to pass myself on from one group to the next, like a baton.

Even so, I was overjoyed when Darrell came back to Varanasi. I'd only spent a couple of hours with him, but when he appeared on the terrace one afternoon – 'Hey, buddy!' – it felt like the return of a long-lost friend. His hair was cropped short as before, as if it had not grown at all in the intervening weeks. He was now staying here at the Ganges View, albeit in an entry-level room. Until a better option became available, he had to settle for a windowless cell at the back of the hotel ('in backside', as they say in India). We ordered black tea and talked about where he'd been and what had been happening in his absence. It was as if we were in a diner in his dusty hometown in the Midwest and he had ventured out into the wide world while I had stayed put, pumping gas or working in a hardware store.

On the way back to Varanasi he'd stopped off at Bodhgaya, where the Buddha had gained enlightenment. Darrell had gone for a five-day retreat, but only lasted one night. Vibrationally, it was one of the most intense places he had ever been to –

and he couldn't wait to leave. Everyone in Bodhgaya was a monk or beggar or tourist, and there were loads of each. There were counters in the town, he said, where you were given ninety rupee coins for a hundred rupee note so that you would have something to give to ninety beggars – and that wasn't nearly enough to go around.

'What I liked about it,' he said, 'was that the mark-up was so easy to calculate. Ten per cent.'

'I wish I'd known you were coming,' I said. 'I'd have asked you to bring some coins back for me. You can never have too much change in India. You could have taken a cut to make it worth your while. Another ten per cent.'

'Trouble is, ten per cent of ninety is nine. So right away the math is becoming more complex. We are down now to eighty-one.'

'And suddenly, from my point of view, it starts looking like not such an attractive deal. Maybe you'd have to settle for just five per cent.'

'Five per cent of ninety? I'd struggle with that.'

'It's true. We're getting into fractions.'

It was nothing, just a bit of chat. But it was the first conversation of its kind that I'd had in ages, the first time I'd been able to talk with someone who had an instinctive understanding of another kind of maths that people often find difficult to grasp: that it's possible to be a hundred per cent sincere and a hundred per cent ironic at the same time. This was the kind of conversation I could feel at home with. It made me think that, despite what I said about not being lonely here, it had been a lonesome time.

From the day that Darrell returned, my time in Varanasi was subtly changed. In turn, *our* time was completely transformed by the arrival, shortly afterwards, of Laline. She was travelling alone, beautiful, friendly, Indian (we assumed – she *looked* Indian and we heard her speaking Hindi with Shashank), and Darrell and I ate dinner with her on her second evening here. Her hair was dark, long. She was wearing tortoiseshell glasses, white T-shirt and trousers, and a cosy blue cardigan. There was a superficial nervousness about her manner – her eyes flickered around the room, she scratched, absently, at her forearm – and yet she seemed completely unnervous. She was from Bangalore originally, had moved to London with her parents when she was five, grew up in Hounslow. In the course of this trip, she'd been to Bangalore and to Hampi (Darrell had been there as well) and, most recently, Lucknow, where there was an interesting museum.

'As far as I know,' Laline said, 'it's the only museum in the world where, in order to enter, you have to buy a ticket for the zoo.'

Our friendship with Laline was accelerated by an incident involving another new arrival. Her name was Francesca, she was Italian, and our dinner with her was dominated by a long debate about Islam and women who choose to wear the veil. Francesca was very anti-veil. So was Laline, so were Darrell and I, so it was not as if we approached this divisive issue from fiercely polarized points of view or radically different cultures. No, the reason the debate went on so long was solely down to the way Francesca pronounced 'veil'. For her, it was terrible to be forced to wear the veal. The veal was a symbol of the absolute subordination of women. Rather than correcting her, Darrell, Laline and I also began talking about the veal, contriving ways of keeping the veal debate going.

'So, you don't think the veal is just a matter of personal taste?' asked Darrell.

'The veal is obviously an ethical issue,' I said.

The longer this went on, the more difficult it became not to laugh. Eventually Laline said, 'It's so obviously a dreadful thing . . . ' On the brink of being consumed by laughter, she was finding it difficult to complete the sentence and had to begin again. 'It's so obviously a cruel thing . . . I don't know why, as an issue, veal is even on the menu.'

There was a brief moment of calm before a storm of laughter broke simultaneously over the three of us. Once we had given in to this long-postponed laughter, we found it impossible to stop. Francesca sat there, bemused and confused, waiting for an explanation we were incapable of attempting without redoubling the hilarity of the situation. When the explanation was eventually forthcoming – from Laline – Francesca took it in good part, sort of, but the damage had been done: we had conspired against the new arrival, excluded her, and the laugh we'd had – a monstrous, all-consuming laugh that quickly grew beyond our control – was entirely at her expense. She had not planned on remaining long in Varanasi and the veal-veil gag did not encourage her to extend her stay.

Laline, like Darrell and I, had no plans to go anywhere else. This was great news for me. If you have been spending a lot of time on your own, meeting people you like can be as exciting as falling in love. I had liked Darrell from the moment I met him, but now things were even better for the simple reason that there were three of us. I've never enjoyed the serve-and-volley of seeing friends on a one-to-one basis. If there are just two of you, something is always goading the conversation towards a heart-to-heart – not in order to lift the veal on some hidden but essential truth, just to keep the ball rolling. In a trio, the three of you are the ball and it never stops rolling. And because we were all staying in the same hotel, we never arranged to meet; we ran into each other on the ghats, at the Lotus Lounge or, failing everything else, back on the terrace of the Ganges View. So our relationship had the quality of a happy accident, constantly renewed and extended.

It is a convention among travellers that you tend not to ask each other what you do for a living. As a result you become extremely curious, trying to extrapolate back from how they are now to what they do or did back home. (I don't remember how I learned that Darrell was an industrial designer – and since I didn't know what this involved, I was none the wiser anyway.) Laline was the exception to this rule, revealing on only her third day that she worked in television, for a production company, and had taken time off to travel in India. After spending a morning on the ghats and in the lanes, she had come up with an idea for a six-part series.

'It's a reality TV show,' she said. 'Someone from Health and Safety is sent to Varanasi to enforce UK standards. In the first episode we watch him going about his business, making inspections and so on. Then, over the next five, we watch him crack up.'

We were on the terrace, the three of us, drinking beer before dinner. We clinked glasses. I told them about my idea for *Varanasi Death Trip* and we clinked glasses again. From similar small beginnings, this was probably how the British East India Company had come into existence. The move from drinking a couple of bottles of Kingfisher to the establishment of the British Empire – a vast swathe of exploitation and accumulation – seemed a historic inevitability.

In a related piece of entrepreneurial ingenuity, we had discovered a place just off the Shivala Road where you could buy beer at seventy rupees a bottle. The hotel charged two hundred rupees, a mark-up that was entirely reasonable. Because of the numerous temples in the area, nowhere near Assi was permitted to sell alcohol, so every request for beer involved a special errand. Even so, three for the price of two was impossible to resist and so, when Darrell and I found this place, it made sense to buy in bulk. We stumbled on it by accident, drawn by a scrum of bodies who looked like they were buying crack. Actually, they were scoring bottles of hard liquor through a tiny gap in a carefully guarded security grille. Next door was the less fortified, more sedate sister outlet where beer was sold. The following evening we bought ten large bottles apiece, came clanking home on a rickshaw and stashed them in our respective fridges. At this rate, we could flog beer to fellow-guests for twice what we paid and still undercut the boys in the hotel by sixty rupees. Once we'd got that hustle up and running, we could start moving in on other rackets.

'Gambling.'

'Boats.'

'Dope.'

'Whores.'

'Marigolds?' Laline asked sweetly.

'Fuck marigolds, man. Cremations – that's where the big bucks are in this town.'

Another bond between the three of us was our loathing of the crusties who gathered on the steps just down from Assi ghat. I sometimes saw them walking to or from wherever it was they were staying, but these steps were where they spent most of their time. They walked slowly, gently, as if the idea of hurrying or urgency were a sign of being trapped in some inferior version of your current incarnation. From the sadhus they had developed the trick whereby vacancy could be taken as a mode of superior awareness, gormlessness of wisdom, near-catatonia as enlightenment. Being stoned helped, of course, and although I never saw them smoking, it was safe to assume that they were all mashed all day.

One of the women was actually extremely attractive, or would have been were it not for the dirty blanket and air of cultivated squalor that clung to her. She had luminous eyes, olive skin, dreadlocks (naturally) and delicate ankles. If she'd washed her hair and dressed up a bit – not in designer clobber, just the clean, casual gear of the international traveller – she would have been immensely desirable. Like that she would have retained some of the feral quality that had, at present, overwhelmed all others. It took only the smallest hop of the imagination to picture her as an NYU undergraduate, a well-heeled JAP who did yoga, ate only vegetables and consented quickly to anal sex. Once this leap had been made, I realized I had been wrong about her feral quality, for there was nothing wild or savage about her. She looked dirty, yes, but her main quality was of obedience, submission. She had about her the slightly bovine quality of the convert to a cult: happy, fulfilled, completely accepting of the identity in which she had enrolled.

It says something about our relationship that I told all this to Laline – it was actually she who supplied the anal-sex gag. We were friends; the idea was to keep each other entertained. She was extremely attractive, but we were just friends, in the same way that Darrell and I were friends – though not, it turned out, in the way that she and Darrell were friends.

There are certain men who, without ever making any attempt to attract them, always seem to have beautiful girl-friends. It simply happens. I don't mean successful, ambitious men for whom getting what they want is second nature, who acquire women as part of a general rapaciousness. No, the kind of man I have in mind often lacks drive and ambition. That lack of effort, the absence of any kind of pushiness in either the worldly or romantic realm, is probably part of their attraction.

Except on one occasion – so exceptional it had made me feel like a different person – I'd never had that 'if it happens, it happens' attitude that seems almost to guarantee that something will happen. Without the desire – or maybe ambition is a better word – to render myself attractive, without cultivating all the things that made me attractive to women, I was not attractive to women. And this holds true for most other men too. That leaves a tiny minority, laid-back, often good at yoga, not even particularly funny, usually completely lacking in vanity, whom beautiful women gravitate towards. Darrell was like that, with the considerable bonus of a GSOH thrown in. The one thing he lacked – a lack so crucial that it appeared to undermine this little idea of mine – was . . . a girlfriend.

I found him easy to be around. I liked spending time with him. I enjoyed his company. I could see how, for a woman, this translated very easily into desiring him. And Laline could see this too. So I was able to observe my theory in the process of being proved right.

If Darrell was a type of man I'd always been fascinated by, Laline was the kind of woman I had often fallen for. She was funny. She had long, dark hair. She made the cheap, nothing-special clothes she wore look like they were made by a designer whose name, a few years down the line, would be known by cool people in London and New York. She had a lightness of spirit. The way she treated everyone with whom she had any dealings – rickshaw drivers, waiters, other guests – was unfailingly considerate, patient. Her relation to the world was completely non-hierarchical. She remembered the names of all the boys working in the hotel, chatted with them in Hindi (that, she assured us, was nothing like as fluent as we imagined). She was beautiful, but I lacked whatever it was that might have attracted her to me, part of which was the urge to render myself attractive to her. One of the reasons for this was because she and Darrell were obviously attracted to each other.

It is strange when two people fancy one another, when liking turns into reciprocated desire: it is tangible. You can see and feel it as a physical force, a kind of gravity. Even when they were talking, on opposite sides of the table, not touching, their arms were reaching towards each other. When they spoke, their lips were on the brink of touching, just through the words they used. I looked on. I didn't mind.

The Ganges View had a good supply of Indian classical CDs, which could be played on the little boom-box in the dining room. Gradually Darrell siphoned this house supply of CDs onto his laptop – already well-stocked with Indian music – some of which, in turn, he transferred to my iPod. This was a breakthrough – and not only in terms of the amount of music to which I was exposed.

Every morning on the ghats I came across people facing the rising sun, Indians and travellers alike, meditating, or doing yoga. No wonder yoga and meditation flourished here. It was an evolutionary necessity – a way of getting a bit of peace and quiet. The only place to go was in: you had to go in to keep the outside out, to keep it at bay. Tuning out meant you could be left alone for twenty minutes or so. And since those twenty minutes were so pleasurable, it was a logical next move to take it further and try to zone out forever, to regard the external world as no more than an irritating distraction and intrusion.

Not being a meditator or a devotee of yoga, I started using my iPod to similar effect: listening to Indian music as a way of keeping the din of India at bay. It didn't always work. Walking along, insulated by headphones, deaf to the offers of 'Boat?', meant that my attention had to be gained in other ways: by pokes, pulls and prods. In order to avoid getting asked if I wanted a boat, I took a boat. An hour-long journey: perfect for losing yourself in a *raga*. But I was aware, after only a few minutes, of the boatman's lips moving. To ignore him was simply too rude. I took off my headphones. Every boatman, however limited his English, also wishes to serve as a guide. And so, pointing to the sign saying Jain ghat, he announced 'Jain ghat.' I smiled, put my headphones back on. The pattern repeated itself at every ghat. The sign was pointed out and its name pronounced. I gave up on the music, sat there on the boat I'd only taken in order to listen to music, letting him intone the many names of the ghats.

When it worked, though, it was bliss, like inhabiting a campaign designed to expand the Apple brand into some as-yet-untapped realm of the global unconscious (i.e. market). As the boat drifted past the darkening ghats, I was caught in the ebb and sob of the sarangi. Sultan Khan was playing the *raga Yeman*. The current was strong enough for the boatman to do little but steer. Twilight was falling. Candles floated alongside the boat. The far bank had disappeared. Soon the stars would happen. The city curved along the western bank of the river. It could have been the coast of any popular tourist area – Amalfi, say – during a power cut, with just a few lights in homes equipped with generators, but with the unceasing fires of Manikarnika ghat in the distance. Tugged along by the sarangi and then urged on by the tabla, we passed a dead cat, floating in the water like a dark log.

The state of the dogs of Varanasi was a source of constant, horrified fascination to all visitors. But in a city full of mangy dogs, one was unquestionably the mangiest, the worst in show. He hung out near Manikarnika and was covered in sores that rendered him incapable of sitting still. Instead he contrived ingenious ways to scratch various parts of his body. By 'various parts of', I mean 'entire'. Even his tail was raw. Practising a form of kundalini yoga, he gripped his tail in his jaws and dragged it through his teeth as if trying to skin it. Head and ears he scratched with a back leg. His back he rubbed against the step behind him. His existence consisted of the awful Samsara of itching and scratching, itching and scratching. Fur had disappeared completely in places, leaving huge patches of pink, horribly human-looking skin. It was as if a botched reincarnation had taken place, as if the dog he were destined to become was still partly the human he had been – or vice-versa. And so his considerable physical torments came to seem the manifestation of what was obviously the far worse psychological malaise of being suspended between two lives, two species.

The monkeys, by contrast, were perfectly at ease in their own skins, at one with their monkeyness. I was walking with Darrell and Laline, near Munshi ghat, when a gang of them came steaming along, like a mob of nightmares.

'The wild bunch,' said Darrell.

'The dawn of the ASBO,' I said.

'The return of the repressed,' said Laline.

They were all these things. They were the opposite of gods, but one of them was a god. I had seen the orange blob of him, on the verge of abstraction, in his blue shrine at Munshi ghat. The three of us stood back, made way, while the monkeys bounded along, tore down some laundry that was hanging up to dry, and then leapt up the sheer walls of a building. It was as if the Grand National had been transferred to another species and taken to a vertiginous extreme. There were several fallers, but they all bounded back and continued their rampage.

'It's like *Sands of the Kalahari* or something,' Darrell said, but in a way it wasn't. Everyone agreed the monkeys were dangerous; no one ever suggested doing something about them, let alone wiping them out, exterminating the brutes. If it came to an all-out war, there could be only one victor; like this, in a guerrilla war, they were harassing us and winning constant, small, usually banana-related victories. Although the monkeys had a bad reputation, I never saw anyone get directly harmed – attacked, scratched or bitten – by one. Apart from contributing to the general climate of disease, they livened the place up a bit – though, God knows, if there was one thing Varanasi didn't need it was livening up.

Ever since I had first seen them trying to steal his sacred road atlas, the monkeys had been twinned in my mind with the holy man preaching by the film set. And now, a few minutes after the monkeys passed from view, we came across him again, at Tulsi ghat. He was having terrible trouble with his voice. He could hardly speak. Laline said this incapacity was probably the result of over-exerting himself in the course of the furious row she'd seen him involved in – about money, naturally – the day before. Whatever the cause, today he just rasped and croaked. Occasionally he coughed, an invocation to the soothing god Strepsil. The people listening to him could barely hear a word, but this didn't matter because he wasn't using words: he had gone beyond them to a post- or pre-verbal realm of croak, grunt and rasp. It didn't look like he was saying anything nice. Any enlightenment he was in receipt of and imparting to others seemed of a harsh, dark nature. The usual stuff, presumably: do this, don't do that. Or perhaps I'm being unfair. Maybe he was a storyteller and his stories were about being nice to animals and wives and not bearing a grudge lest you be reborn as a termite mound. Or perhaps he was telling the story of his own life, of what had brought him to this hoarse pass. A shadow of his former oratorical self, he was still a venerable figure, able to work the crowd, to compel attention in the face of competition, not all of it stiff.

The crusties, for example, who, back at Assi, were treating anyone who was interested – and quite a few who weren't – to one of their so-called performances. The woman I sort of fancied – the woman who, if circumstances had been entirely different, I would have fancied – was part of the performance in some unspecified way, even if she was not actually doing anything. Her hair was tied back with a length of dark ribbon. She had a gold nose-stud, full lips, dark brown eyes. One of her friends was playing a three-stringed instrument that I did not recognize but which, evidently, was of such limited technical and expressive range that competence on it could be obtained in ten minutes, mastery in an hour. At one point, he asked her to pass him his bag. He used her name: Isobel. For me, this was the highlight of the performance, worth the price of free admission alone. The bag was embroidered yellow and black, decorated with dime-sized mirrors, which lit up, as she handed it to him, with flashes of hair, face, sky. Her fingers were long, ringless.

Another guy was blowing a didge. A couple of others played drums of various kinds – though not the tabla, of course; the tabla is complicated. They had drawn a crowd but, in India, this is no sign of even rudimentary ability. It is simply to say they were in India, for India *is* a crowd. There were plenty of people around and, as long as their gaze was turned in the direction of the scruffs, they constituted an audience.

So, Isobel . . .

There were some proper concerts too. One of them was held in a large marquee behind Tulsi ghat, illuminated by white and green fluorescent tubes. Lal, Darrell and I sat down near one of these tubes and immediately wished we hadn't. The lights attracted a dreadful swarm of bugs. In anticipation of the concert, we'd all got stoned beforehand and this intensified the horror of the swarm-storm. We moved to more distant seats and then sat back and watched the next lot of unfortunates take their turn at being swarmed at.

The audience could not have been more mixed: Indian and western, Sikh, Muslim and Hindu, men and women, young, old and unbelievably old, possibly even immortal. I spotted Ashwin and we waved to each other as if it were the nineteenth century and we were at La Scala for an opera. There was no sign of Isobel. Being stoned might have played a part in this, but I was conscious that this occasion was somehow significant for Laline and Darrell and their relationship. In several ways – all of them, apart from the unavoidable fact of their shared knowledge of Indian classical music, infinitely discreet – both were with each other more than either was with me. Earlier that day, as I was coming back from Manikarnika in a boat, I'd glanced up at the terrace of the Lotus Lounge and seen them there, arms round each other. As the boat skulked upstream, I looked up from time to time like some sad fuck in a Henry James novel, relieved that they'd not seen me seeing them.

At the centre of the stage was a carpet, as thick with colour as the floor of a forest in autumn. More colour was provided by garlands of flowers and the paintings of Shiva on the backdrop to the stage, all bathed in the warm light of candles. The concert was preceded by a long series of speeches and tributes as various pandits and gurus were introduced to the audience. No one showed any signs of impatience to move on to the nominal purpose of the evening: to listen to music.

When the musicians took to the stage, Laline – sitting between Darrell and me – warned that this should not be interpreted as a sign that music was in any way imminent. Just getting comfy took a while. The singer was wearing a dull green sari. She must have been sixty, was grand-looking, stern, hefty. She supervised the tuning of the tampura, sipped water without letting the bottle touch her lips, and waited. The sarangi was tuned (no small feat;

learning to tune the sarangi takes as long as it does to learn to play most instruments), the tabla was tuned. Or at least that's how it seemed. But it wasn't the instruments that were being tuned, Laline whispered; it was the musicians, tuning themselves to the *raga*. Then the singer introduced the first piece.

Within minutes of starting to sing, she was transformed. It was like hearing a girl, dark-haired and lovely as the gopis Krishna had spied on from his tree-top hideaway. I had no idea what she was singing about, could not even tell when the words stopped being words and became just syllables, gliding sound. Her hands reached into the air above her as if the notes were growing there and, as long as they were picked endlessly, over and over, would always be there. Music people talk about perfect pitch, but what her voice made me think of was perfect posture: hair as long and straight as a supple back; bare feet moving so lightly they scarcely touched the ground. Her voice promised absolute devotion; but then the note was stretched further still, beyond this, until you wondered what you would have to do to be worthy of such devotion, such love. You would have to be that note, not the object of devotion but the devotee. Her voice slid and swooped. It was like those perfect moments in life, moments when what you hope for most is fulfilled and, by being fulfilled, changed – changed, in this instance, into sound: when, in a public place, you glimpse the person you most want to see and there is nothing surprising about it; the pattern in the random, when accident slides into destiny. A note was stretched out as long as possible and then a little longer; it continued, somewhere, long after it was capable of being heard. It is still there, even now.

*   *   *

Laline and I were walking by Mahanirvani ghat in the fading light. The first candles were floating downriver. A cricket match was in progress. We stood and watched for a couple of overs, were about to leave when the batsman swiped the ball high into the air. It was coming in my direction, three feet above my head, towards the Ganges. I jumped up and caught it, one-handed. The ball smacked wetly into my fingers and stuck there. In the realm of myth, I had grabbed a blazing comet from the sky and stopped it in its tracks. Even now, on a Tuesday afternoon, in poor light, it was a spectacular catch. There were cheers and applause, from Laline and from the players and the scattered spectators. The batsman was clapping. I raised my arms to the sky, still holding the dirty ball, basking in the praise that was my due. Then I threw it back to the bowler and we continued walking to the Ganges View.

I was glad Laline had been there to witness and corroborate my catch. It is not enough to perform a god-like action. It must be seen – ideally, by the gods. I wasn't sure of the extent to which *darshan* was a reciprocal idea. Of course the gods needed to be seen, but did they also like to watch? Were they spectators too? Did they look at us with all the love and awe with which we – or some of us – regarded them? If that was the case, then the earlier comparison with Beckham and celebrity was faulty. For the one thing celebrities are not free to do is to *look*. The sunglasses they are obliged to hide behind are the symbolic expression of the blindness to which they are condemned by always being looked *at*. On my first day at the ghats I'd felt like a visiting royal and, increasingly in the weeks that followed, I'd been conscious of living like a celebrity, of being the object of constant curiosity and scrutiny. I may have despised them, may have done nothing to deserve such attention, but this was something I had in common with the crusties. There was lots to see, there was more to see in ten minutes here, in godly Varanasi, than there was in a week in ungodly London, but there were plenty of things and places one thought twice about doing and seeing because of the quite amazing commotion it generated. I am not being vain or deluded. There were occasions when even the simple task of trying to take a rickshaw caused a turf war of bidding. A visit to the Durga temple had made even routine sight-seeing seem more hassle than it was worth.

The temple was only a ten-minute walk from the hotel, was painted bright red, was so unmissable that it was hard to believe it took so long to find it. Inside the temple compound a sign said that non-Hindu gentlemen were not admitted into the temple itself. That was frustrating, but I was assured immediately that it was OK, I could go in. All I had to do was take off my shoes. The person who told me this claimed he was one of the priests, a Brahmin, but he looked and acted more like a janitor. A janitor who had been sacked or made redundant years earlier, but kept turning up for work anyway because he had nothing else to do and nowhere else to go. Before showing me the inner temple, he took me into a small, foul-smelling shrine. Paste was daubed on my forehead. Then someone else appeared, another janitor-priest who, despite my protestations, insisted on draping a garland of marigolds around my neck – the source, I realized, of the foul smell. It was as if they had been marinated in urine and then allowed to rot for several days. For the privilege of having this rank thing hung around my neck, I was expected to pay, naturally. I had only a hundred-rupee note, but managed to insist on fifty rupees change – no small achievement in a situation where change is not simply unavailable but practically inconceivable. The two janitor-priest-hustlers indicated that I should place the garland on the *lingam*, which I was happy to do.

I was glad to be rid of the stinking thing. They then began ushering me towards the actual temple but, eager to avoid whatever horrors and hassles awaited in there, I climbed into my sandals and fled.

Everything about the experience had been revolting. The rotten smell of the marigolds clung to me – the smell, I thought to myself as I stomped back to Assi ghat, of a religion that was primitive, dark and dank. It was ridiculous to aspire to the mindset that made it possible to see these rituals as sacred. No, this was a phase through which the species would eventually pass. It was like entering some backward part of the human psyche. And if it seemed like that to me, now, how must it have appeared to the missionaries who arrived here bearing the message of Christianity – clean and bloody, dreary as a Sunday in Wales – in whichever century it was that they came? The idolaters with their mumbling jumbo and their *puja* must have seemed scarcely less horrifying than Apaches with warpaint and the scalps of pale faces hanging from their bareback saddles.

At Vats Yaraj ghat was a sign that read 'I LOVE MY INDIA'. I often felt like calling out 'Me too!', but after that visit to the Durga temple it just bugged the shit out of me. Literally. I had picked up some kind of bug and was always having to dash back to the hotel to use the toilet. It was nothing too serious, nothing compared with what some tourists were suffering. People in the hotel were dropping like flies. Actually, that's not the right expression at all, for the flies were thriving. And how could they not? In my teens there'd been a craze for offensive T-shirts and posters that urged you to 'Eat shit – ten million flies can't be wrong'. Maybe the posters originated here, for there was shit everywhere in the City of Light (as Varanasi had once been called). Every kind of shit: animal (monkey, goat, cow, buffalo, dog, bird, donkey, cat, goose), vegetable (the abandoned marigolds formed a stinking mush) and (last but not least) human. In certain auspicious places there was probably even god shit. Prahbu ghat, where the dhobis pounded their laundry into submission, also doubled as a default toilet ghat. It was horrible walking along there. The sight entered your eyeballs and the stench entered your nostrils. I felt like writing a sign next to the 'I LOVE MY INDIA' sign: 'If you love it so much, then don't shit all over it'. Surely it was in everyone's interest to introduce and enforce a law to prevent people from shitting on the ghats. Surely, however poor and ignorant people were, they could be educated not to shit in the middle of what was, effectively, the promenade. Before you could do that, of course, you had to make sure there were alternatives, that there were toilets for them to shit in. Surely nothing could be more important, more basic than that. (The number of times, in Varanasi, in a place where so little could be understood for sure, that one's thoughts – one's indignation, irritation and outrage – began with that word, 'Surely'!) One way or another, however scrupulously one washed one's hands, held one's nose and kept one's mouth shut, one was destined to ingest shit. How had the connection between disease and excrement not been made? How could a culture with a horror of pollution be so indifferent to the most offensive form of pollution? However hard you tried to remain healthy, you inevitably fell ill. There was no avoiding it. Something was bound to have a bug in it – and how could it not, in a city where shit and animals and humans were heaped on top of each other? Magazines and papers were full of articles about the modernity of India – about the bars and clubs of Mumbai, about how Chennai was thriving, how Bangalore was the Silicon Valley of the east – but, aside from internet cafés, there was little sign of that here.

There were days when I felt like I was turning into the protagonist of Lal's reality TV idea, when I thought that Varanasi should be razed to the ground, built over in the name of health and safety, hygiene, progress. It was on one such day that I decided to take the bull by the horns. I walked to the edge of the river, undid my zip and pissed in the Ganges. That's right: *I pissed in the Ganges*. I was desperate, I had to piss, but it was also a protest of sorts, highlighting the ludicrousness of worshipping a river while simultaneously polluting it. Pissing directly into the river was more hygienic, all round, than pissing – and shitting – on the ghats and letting it drain into the river. It was early evening, there was no one around, but all the time I was pissing – it was one of those epic pisses that seem never to end – I was waiting for someone to notice and something to happen, for shouts followed by blows, or for blows unannounced by shouts. But nothing did happen. No one did anything. If people noticed – and they must have done; it's impossible to do anything in India without someone noticing – and took offence (as they must have done), they decided to let it go.

If that piss had seemed never-ending, it was brief compared with the incessant, relentless, unstoppable demand for money. Every social exchange was a prelude to commerce. Some social exchanges consisted entirely of commerce. At its most rudimentary level, a child would say 'One rupee', so that the demand for cash constituted a form of greeting. At the next level, one would be greeted – '*Namaste!*' – and then there would be a request for money, or the offer of a service. Other times, a few lines of conversation would precede the offer of services. Generally speaking, the more protracted the build-up, the more insidious the whole deal – and it always was a deal – would become. We would have a chat about things, a boat would be offered and the man would say 'Come', even though a price had not been agreed. Occasionally it would seem that, for once, you were really having a conversation – about places of interest, about people to avoid, the bad people operating in the neighbourhood – until, eventually, the transactional motive kicked in. The masters of this art were like classical musicians, indefinitely extending the *alap*, elaborating and exploring the *raga* without precisely identifying it until its nature became clear – except, in this case, the *raga* was always the same: *raga* Boat, *raga* Rickshaw, both variants of *raga* Rupee, one of the few *raga*s, perhaps the only one, not tied to a particular season or time of day. No, this great overarching *raga* could be played constantly, at any time, and was suitable for all moods. It was so disappointing, the way one's relations always came down to the bottom line of people wanting your money, never more nakedly than in a temple. It meant you viewed any conversation, even those – for there were a few – conducted with no ulterior motive at all, with suspicion. I tried to extricate myself from conversations at the earliest opportunity, before the subjects of boats or visits to shops or factories came up. I tried to avoid having conversations at all. I avoided meeting people's gaze. I looked anywhere to avoid getting caught in the web of cash transaction.

These frustrations were reminiscent of the time, in my thirties, when I made the mistake of moving to Oxford for a few years. There was, allegedly, a vibrant intellectual life going on somewhere in town, presumably behind the walls of the venerable old colleges, but I never penetrated that scene and ended up languishing on the acid and vegan fringes of society. In Varanasi there must have been a world of poets, intellectuals and thinkers but, unable to gain access to – or even locate – this tier of society, I was left to play my part, grudgingly, in the eternal *jugalbandi* of tourist life: 'Boat, sir?' 'No, thank

226

you.' 'Rickshaw, sir?' 'No, thank you.' 'Very cheap.' 'No, thank you.' East meets west. Fusion: *Raga* Rupee; *Raga* No Thank You.

This phase of irritation and annoyance came to a head when I was queuing up to use the ATM in the lobby of a bank in the middle of town, just up from Dashaswamedh. The noise made queuing stressful. What made it all the more stressful was the way that, strictly speaking, it was not a queue at all; at the same time it was not *not* a queue. A total free-for-all, a non-queue or scrum, I could have handled, but this was the worst of both worlds: a sort of queue in which the principle of the queue was neither completely ignored nor adhered to. Several times the tall German in front of me had allowed people to push in front of him. Just as 'queue' is not quite the right word for what was happening, so, neither, is 'push'. People didn't push. Somehow, they just got in ahead of him. There was a guard at the door, but he was doing nothing. Really, he was just a pillar in a blue uniform.

'If you let people push in like this, we're going to be here for the rest of our lives,' I told the German. He shrugged. I guessed that he had not been in India long. We had been standing there for another couple of minutes when an Indian man and his wife came and stood in front of him. The German looked at me and I tapped the man on the shoulder.

'There is a queue,' I said. 'And you must wait in queue.' He ignored me, of course. I changed places with the German – effectively I had pushed in ahead of him too.

'There is a queue, and you must wait in queue,' I repeated. 'Behind me and behind this man and behind the people behind him.' He smiled and shook his head. The guard was oblivious. His job was to be a guard and stand here in his blue uniform. His duties did not extend beyond that.

'You will go to the back of queue,' I said to the man who, having pushed in, had now taken his card out in readiness. 'There is no point in taking your card out. Your turn has not yet come.'

'I am in hurry, sir.'

'Everyone is in hurry.'

'I am in hurry, sir. I will be quick.'

'Everyone is in hurry. Everyone will be quick. No one will be quick, if no one waits their turn.'

He was still ahead of me. I shouldered my way alongside him. I was becoming angry. He was perfectly calm, smiling. I made sure my face was arranged in something that could be construed as a smile.

'I am in hurry, sir.'

'Everyone is in hurry, sir. You will not go in to this bank ahead of me.'

'Sir, I am requesting you.'

'But your request, sir, has not been granted. So you must go to back of queue.'

'Sir, I am requesting you.'

'And your request has been categorically refused.'

In other circumstances I might have found this wearying, but I had been in India long enough, now, to realize that there is no limit to the number of times the same thing can be said. The fact that a point has been made does not mean that the same point does not need to be made again and again. There was scope, however, for enlarging and varying the point.

'Furthermore, your request will never be granted,' I said. 'Never. Do you understand me?'

At some level, he did not. The idea of absolute refusal with no scope for a special dispensation or exemption made no sense. He continued standing where he was. We were neck and neck. Physically, he was not ahead of me in the queue, and I was not ahead of him, but I had, by now, established a crucial psychological advantage. My rival was not interested in the etiquette or principle of queuing. He simply wanted to use the bank machine quickly. That was that. Whereas for me, my place in this queue – indeed the continued existence of the very idea and principle of the queue – was at stake. Nothing in my life mattered more to me than not letting this man in ahead of me. I had found a cause I could die for. Or kill for.

'Sir,' I said. 'Look at my eyes.' I took off my sunglasses. 'Look at my eyes and listen to me.' I had no idea how my eyes looked. I hoped the fact that they were blue lent the person glaring angrily through them an air of implacable purpose and unshakeable will. In a sense it did not matter, because the queue-barger was not looking at them. He was looking at the door to the bank and he was still smiling. My own smile had by now become a death's head grin, a rictus of suppressed English rage, the product of years of rainy summers, ruined picnics, cancelled trains and losing at penalty shoot-outs. 'You are not going into that bank ahead of me. The only way you will go into the bank ahead of me is by stepping over my lifeless body. Do you understand?'

The moment of crisis had arrived. The fleshy, sari-clad woman who had been ahead of us was emerging from the lobby. Before she was properly out of the door, my rival tried to move past her, but I wedged myself between them and shouldered my way in. When he tried to come in as well, I shut the door in his face. I had made it. Pumped-up and exultant, I pumped my fist like a man who has made his point, achieved his goal, won.

I keyed in my PIN. My hands were trembling. Perhaps that's why the machine rejected my number. I must have keyed in the wrong PIN. I tried again, slowly, carefully, deliberately. The bank rejected my card a second time. And a third.

Everything that happens in India is a parable, even if the meaning of that parable is unclear. In this instance I took it to mean that there is no such thing as a pyrrhic victory, there are only pyrrhic defeats.

The fact of the matter is that I came out empty-handed, cashless. The man who had tried to get in ahead of me came in next, unperturbed, unrepentant and un-grudge-bearing. His wife was standing outside. So was the German, but he was not the next in line. Yet another person had managed to get between him and the door.

'You are a fucking Kraut pussy,' I hissed at the German, before striding off.

I took a cycle rickshaw back to the hotel. As we jolted and heaved through the jammed streets, I realized that, weirdly, the episode at the bank had restored my good spirits. I laughed aloud as I recalled the shocked expression on the face of the much-put-upon German as I'd abused him. I admired the way the man who had tried to queue-barge had stuck, smilingly, to his game plan, had refused to allow that anything was at stake other than his desire – to his credit, he had never attempted to make it his right – to get at his cash quickly. Viewed in a different light, everything irritating about India could become a source of pleasure and instruction with implausible speed. Suddenly I understood why there had been something strangely familiar, almost reassuring, about the irritation that had been assailing me for the previous weeks: it was how I felt all the time in London, the default setting for a life in which a constant drizzle of frustration, annoyance and rush-hour Tube travel was the unremarked-on norm.

All around was honk and blare. The din, the dust, the noise were unbelievable, but wasn't it great that there was a place on earth where dust, din and blare thrived? What a clean and dull planet it would be if everywhere became a suburb of

Stockholm, where citizens queued patiently and the cash machines dispatched crisp, high-denomination, fraud-proof notes, where there were no elephant-headed gods who rode around on mice, where there were no beggars waving their bandaged, pus-stained stumps in your face, no janitors claiming they were priests, no cows solemnly manuring the streets, no monkeys running riot and no kids scrounging rupees? And beneath all one's irritation and annoyance, in any case, was the knowledge that the demand for money was a straightforward expression of the inequality of economic relationships. We, the tourists, were immensely rich and they, the beggars and the boatmen, the masseurs and the hustlers, were unfathomably poor. The pestering was a persistent, but still voluntary, tax on luxury. You didn't have to pay. You could say no. This 'No' would be ignored, but if you kept saying it, if you said it over and over, then . . . it would still be ignored. But eventually, after the twentieth time, it would be accepted. Either that or it would have turned into a 'Yes'. Given the gulf between what you had and what they did without, it was a miracle, really, that you didn't get robbed every time you left the hotel, the compound, that your feet were not ripped off simply to get at your sandals, that you weren't torn limb from limb and eaten, or your liver sold for dog food.

As we laboured along Shivala road, I saw Isobel, wearing a faded yellow T-shirt and jeans, about to cross the street as the rickshaw bore down on her. She looked up, startled. I waved, smiled – 'Careful!' – and she smiled and stepped back. It was the first time I had seen her on her own and the first time we had acknowledged each other's existence. In Hinduism karma builds up and unfolds over several lifetimes, but in my speeded-up, occidental mind it was impossible to regard this accidental encounter as a sign of anything other than instant karmic payback. Two days ago – or half an hour earlier – I had been so at odds with the world that such a meeting could never have happened. Even if it had, I would only have grunted at her; if she'd noticed me at all, she'd have seen only a scowling familiar face bearing down on her from the orientalist perch of his rickshaw. But now, with my equanimity regained, I was a nice, smiling person obviously concerned for her safety.

We arrived back at Assi ghat. As I climbed off, the rickshaw driver tapped me on the leg and angled his foot back so that his sandal flipped down, revealing the sole of his foot. There was a raw hole in the arch of his foot, as if he had been crucified, except the hole was not bloody. It was whiteish, an ulcer of some kind, presumably. I gave him a hundred rupees, for which he showed no gratitude – and who can blame him? For someone whose job involved pedalling all day long, pressing down on his foot, this was a terrible affliction. But not a whole lot worse – quite a bit better, in fact – than some of the other ailments, injuries and illnesses afflicting people here. The amount of pain, discomfort and agony people were able routinely to bear without complaint, without any expectation of getting better (let alone cured), without hope even of the quantity of pain being lessened, was immense. Did this mean that it wasn't pain, wasn't anguish? Perhaps in the west our capacity for pain had been heightened as it had become more avoidable. Anguish was the expectation that whatever was ailing us could be reduced and treated. Anguish was the outrage that the expected outcome wasn't achieved immediately. Anguish was the delay in getting the right treatment, waiting for the medicine to kick in. Anguish was waiting.

And here in India we westerners rarely had to wait for anything. We moaned about the constant pestering, the constant offers of 'boat' and 'rickshaw', but when we wanted a boat or rickshaw we expected someone to be there, providing a boat or rickshaw immediately, at rock-bottom prices. Accustomed, at home, to the dismal wait for a bus, here we were slightly put out if we had to wait more than a minute. At some level, the poorest backpacker enjoyed the privileges and perks of the Raj.

I walked for a while along the ghats. A boy ran up alongside me.

'School pen,' he said. I smiled, continued walking. 'School pen,' he said again. 'School pen.' As it happened, I did have a pen with me, a high-quality roller-ball pen from London. I gave it to the boy, who ran off quickly. A holy man was sitting by the river, in the shade of a mushroom umbrella, looking at me nicely.

I came to the 'I LOVE MY INDIA' sign, was happy to see it.

Laline said, 'What are you reading?'

I was on the terrace and had not heard her approach. She was barefoot, wearing very faded jeans and a T-shirt that looked white and clean-smelling. I held up the book: *Women in Love*, an old Penguin edition.

'Strange choice.'

'I only started it because someone left it in the hotel. But there's a lot of Lawrence here in Varanasi: the river of dissolution, the Ship of Death . . . ' I ran out of steam. Lal pulled up a chair and sat down next to me, waited. Her toenails were painted pink and she had a silver ring on her little toe.

'That's only two things.'

'I know, but two can be a lot. In certain circumstances, *one* can be a lot.'

'And zero, sir, can be everything,' she said, Indian-wise. 'Actually, to qualify as "a lot", you need a minimum of three.'

'You're right, of course.'

'So, did Lawrence come to India?'

'Sri Lanka. Ceylon. Which he hated. And he sort of inferred India from Sri Lanka. But it's a shame he didn't spend time here. It would have been a source of irritation, obviously. In terms of caste, he'd have seen himself as an Untouchable Brahmin. He'd have claimed that Gandhi advocated non-violence because he secretly wanted to smash people's heads in with a hammer.'

'Especially Nehru's?'

'Exactly. He got ill everywhere, but he could have got iller here than everywhere else combined. And he'd probably have written an Indian novel. In about eight weeks. Full of inaccuracy and wild speculation, but right in all sorts of strangely prophetic ways. He'd have seen that one day tandoori chicken would become the English national dish, that his hometown, Eastwood, would have several restaurants with the word Mahal in them.'

Laline had ordered tea. Kamal brought a pot on a gleaming tray and set it on the table. I put down my book and went inside to get a banana. Since getting a stomach upset, I had taken to eating mainly bananas.

'You're living like a monkey,' said Laline when I sat down again. 'Next, you'll be stealing bananas from people's plates. Creating a commotion.'

'One day, if I'm just an orange blob, would you still recognize me then?' I said.

'If you're just an orange blob? No, of course not. But I don't think that's going to happen. You're one of those men who get skinnier and skinnier. And you're not orange. You're kind of off-white, pinkish. You should put some sun cream on.'

'You are denying the god in me,' I said. 'Bingo! That's a sort of Lawrentian idea: denying the god in yourself or someone else. I've got the three I needed to qualify as a lot.'

'It sounds a bit general to me, but I'll let it go.'

Darrell appeared on the terrace and Lal waved him over.

'Just in time,' she said. 'I was getting an interminable lecture on *Seven Pillows of Wisdom*. And you wouldn't believe what he just said. He called Ganga a river of dissolution.'

'Did he tell you how he pissed in it?'

'No!' said Lal. 'Blasphemer! Evil-doer!'

Darrell drew up a chair and sat with us. There were three of us now: enough to be a lot. Like Lal, he was wearing a white T-shirt. He didn't kiss her, but now that he was here, I saw that she had the glow of a woman in love. Darrell didn't glow in that way – men don't, especially men like him. But something else about him had become more pronounced (in an infinitely discreet way): the certainty that he could be relied upon, that she was not making a mistake. Perhaps that is one of the reasons why the fact that he and Laline had become involved had no effect on their relationship with me.

'How's your tummy?' Darrell asked.

'OK,' I said. 'You know what they say. Whatever doesn't kill me makes me weaker.'

For a few days we were joined by Sayoko, a young Japanese woman. She was eating dinner at a table on her own and Darrell asked if she wanted to join us. She spoke very little English and so, when she had sat down at our table, he began speaking to her in Japanese – which, even by his standards, was pretty cool. Sayoko and I couldn't say much to each other, but she was easy to be around. Her way of being in the world was unlike anyone else's I had encountered. Having worked in London, in journalism, often interviewing artists,

I had pretty well accepted that the sole point of existence – especially for artists, but among journalists too – was to make a mark, a splash, to draw attention to oneself. Sayoko was the opposite. She moved through the world as though the idea was to have a minimum impact upon it. Like a skilful driver, she negotiated her passage through things without collisions or near-misses. In the context of Varanasi the comparison made no sense, but to be in her company was to be reminded of how relaxing it was not to be honking your horn and constantly expecting a crash, not to have your attention strained to breaking point. I wondered, naturally, if this quality was unique to her or if there was something distinctly Japanese about it.

There were a lot of Japanese in Varanasi, both the slightly idiotic-looking groups who photographed everything in sight and obeyed their tour leader unquestioningly, as if he were the Emperor, and the younger trance types, sometimes dread-locked and often wearing interesting T-shirts. Sarnath, where the Buddha gave his first fire sermon, was one of the attractions for them. It was only six or seven miles north of the city and I don't know why I never got round to going. I should have gone with Sayoko. She was a Buddhist and went there on her own one day. She didn't ask me if I wanted to go, but there was no reason not to go, and it's not like I was averse to the idea or uninterested.

Sayoko was with us only a short time. We walked along the ghats a couple of times, had pancakes and coffee at the Lotus Lounge. On the way there we saw two dead rats, lying side by side on the promenade, the implication being that the Ganges was too filthy even for them. Once we were at the Lotus Lounge, we didn't speak. We'd hardly spoken before, on the way there, but while we were walking, seeing dead rats and stuff, it didn't matter. It didn't matter once we were there either, waiting for our coffees and pancakes, but it was a new thing for me, sitting silently with someone, unable to speak, communicating only at the vibe level.

I barely got to know her and then she was gone, to Bodhgaya. I told her about the change, the ten per cent commission, but I'm not sure she understood. I was sad when she left, which was strange because, once she had gone, it was as if she had never been here.

An exhibition opened at the Kriti gallery: photographs by Dayanita Singh. We – Darrell, Laline and I – went to the opening along with Shashank and a few other guests from the Ganges View. Decorated in the international art style of plain white walls, the gallery would not have been out of place in London or New York. (This was it: the modernity found everywhere else in twenty-first century India *was* here in Varanasi after all!) Although the opening was quite crowded, it was very different to equivalent events in either city: there wasn't any free booze – or even a pay bar – so, once I'd eaten a few samosas and looked, in vain, for Isobel, there was nothing to do except concentrate on the art.

The pictures were not big, about the size of LP covers, arranged in a single row around the gallery, and hung with Indian visitors in mind (I had to stoop slightly to look at them). They were black and white, but had none of the torsion, the psychological malaise and shock of Ackerman's Varanasi pictures. There were people in some of them, others were of empty rooms. Reflections. Shelves of things. The forecourt of a building at dusk. Cracked paving stones that refused to offer any sign of being a path. Light reflected in a swimming pool so that it looked like a tennis court under water. Gloves hanging on a rack. A death mask in a bell jar. Two white jackets, the sort worn by Nehru, hung up in some kind of display case.

237

The absence of people was not a universal principle. People were there or not there, there in some pictures and not there in others. A hand-out said that all the photographs had been taken in India, but there were no individual captions, nothing to tell you where anywhere was, or what anything was, or when it had been. There were just these pictures of places, pictures of places that were in these photographs. There was nothing to help you get your bearings and then, after a while, once you accepted the idea, you realized that you didn't need these things that you so often relied on, that there were no bearings to get. A given picture had no explicit or narrative connection with the one next to it, but their adjacency implied an order that enhanced the effect of both.

A curving row of cinema seats, or seats in a concert auditorium, gleaming slightly. From the seats' point of view, the cinema was always packed, even when empty; it didn't make any difference what was playing, or even if anything was playing. Windows in a tower. Light coming through windows. Without the pictures, until they were taken, you might have thought there was nothing in these places to see. Being photographed left them as they were, unchanged, altered. Did the idea of *darshan* come into play here? Was there a form of *darshan* in which there was nothing to be seen?

In the visitors' book on the desk someone had written out three lines of what I presumed was Hindi. I showed them to Laline, who read the lines out loud. They were from a poem by Faiz, she said, a Pakistani poet. Faiz had written in Urdu, but whoever had written the lines here had translated them into Hindi. Moving her finger along the pattern of flowing script, she translated them again, hesitantly, into English.

"'All that will remain is Allah's name,

He who is absent but present too,

He who is the seer as well as the seen.'"

I stared at the incomprehensible pattern of words, letting their revealed meaning sink back into them. Lal said, 'It might have been better without the first line.'

'In this context, yes, we could have done without the context,' I said. 'But I like the rhyme: "remain" and "name". Or near-rhyme, at any rate.'

People did not stay long at the opening – as with dinners at the Ganges View, the lack of booze was a powerful disincentive to linger. Once the gallery had thinned out, it was possible to see all the photographs at once – captioned now, by Faiz – arranged around the white room in a single line. A receding hallway, the wet floor reflecting doors and windows. A tower with surrounding sky. A grid of lights under water, like something that was a reflection of itself.

Two musicians came to stay at the hotel: a tabla player and a French guitarist. The guitarist was studying Hindustani music in Kolkata and his guitar had been modified by the addition of sympathetic strings, which gave it an Indian sound. The tabla player was Indian, from Mumbai, but lived mainly in Europe, in Germany. They did not know each other, but after dinner they jammed together on the small enclosed terrace at the very top of the hotel. It wasn't a public performance, but anyone from the hotel who wanted to could sit and watch.

Even if you listened intensely, it was impossible not to feel excluded from the little cocoon the musicians wove for themselves. Watching them play was like watching two lovers, attentive and responsive to each other's every move, and oblivious to everyone else. While they were playing they had ears and eyes only for each other, and when they were not playing they were not interested in anything, or only interested in talking about music. It was difficult not to envy their absorption. For years I'd earned my living as a journalist, even though

239

I hated writing. When I had a piece to write, there was nothing – nothing – that I would not rather have been doing instead: tennis, television, drinking, washing up, having a bath, reading the paper, even just staring into space. Anything was preferable. Perhaps it would have been different if I'd done my 'own' writing – whatever that meant – but I doubt it. It would still have been writing, something to be put off and avoided. Whereas all these two wanted was to play music. I'd hear them in their rooms, practising separately, going over stuff they'd hit upon together the night before or preparing some kind of structure they could improvise around later that evening. I wished there'd been something in my life like that. Convinced that there must have been, I tried to remember what it was. It took a long time to accept that the reason I was having such trouble remembering was because there really wasn't anything to remember. Tennis came closest, except by the time I got serious about it there was a limit to how much my body could take: three times a week, tops. If I played more than that, I got injured. What else? Going to parties, drinking, drug-taking. Drugs were certainly something I'd always looked forward to but, as with tennis, I was conscious that if I did them too much I'd get physically or psychologically injured. Besides, taking drugs hardly constituted a vocation, or not for me at any rate; it was just a leisure activity, a hobby, not something I could earn a living from. Perhaps the nearest I'd got to sustainable, all-consuming enjoyment was the life I was leading here, doing nothing. And it was sustainable, or could easily become so. By renting out my flat in London, I could continue like this indefinitely.

During my first weeks in Varanasi I'd checked email constantly, kept up to date with work-related stuff back in London. (By the time I read my piece about Varanasi on the *Telegraph* website, I'd begun to take as normal things that had once made me feel like a package tourist from Mars.) Since then I'd let things slide, had failed to respond to various offers of work. Nothing was so urgent that it could not wait, and if you waited long enough then that which had been urgent became – by virtue of its urgency – irrelevant. Gradually the reciprocal momentum of email diminished, faded, petered out completely. The only thing I still kept up with was the football, possibly because there was no point in doing so. Without access to the games – without seeing the highlights on TV – they were irrelevant, might as well never have been played. The scores might just as well have been invented. (So what if Chelsea lost eight-nil to Watford?) But I still found it difficult to let it go, especially now that the European Championship had, allegedly, resumed. I didn't support a particular team, but I missed the support of football. It wasn't just the games themselves; it was the whole structure that football lent to one's life, the shared belief system, the stories and controversies that reinforced it.

I'd come to Varanasi because there was nothing to keep me in London, and I stayed on for the same reason: because there was nothing to go home for.

Darrell was on his way to a yoga class. I walked with him as far as Niranjani ghat, where I spotted the friendly-looking holy man I'd seen after the confrontation at the ATM. He was in the same spot, sitting in the shade of a mushroom parasol, looking out at the river.

'Let me talk for a while with this philosopher,' I said to Darrell, who hurried on. I'd said 'talk', but since he had no English, I gave him fifty rupees just to look into his eyes. He was happy to oblige. We sat in the shade, cross-legged, facing each other. His head was framed by the brick red of the wall behind him – almost exactly the same red as the *tilak* on his forehead, so that it seemed as if a hole had been bored straight through his head. At first I felt a little self-conscious, but soon I got used to just gazing at his kind, brown eyes. He sat and stared. It wasn't like that childish game of not blinking – though he did seem possessed of an uncanny ability not to blink. There was nothing aggressive about it. We just looked. He looked like he wasn't seeing anything. I tried not to have any thoughts, tried just to look. I'm not sure what I was looking for, what I expected to see – that's why I was looking, to find out what I was looking for. What I didn't see was any affinity between us. He was in his world and I was in mine. My world-view would never be his and vice-versa. That was what we had in common. What distinguished us from each other was that he had no interest in mine – it meant nothing to him – whereas I was intensely curious about his. What was it like to be him? I wished we could have changed places, for a while at least. If I looked closely, I could see my own face reflected in the dilated pupils of his eyes. It was as if I was there, a little homunculus. And then, after a while, as I concentrated on it, so that little image of me came to fill my vision. I zoomed in on it so that instead of seeing his face, all I could see was my own, staring back at me as from a mirror. That was one way of seeing it. The other was that I was actually seeing what he was seeing and, contrary to what I'd originally thought, there was no real difference between the way I saw him and the way he saw me. He saw what I saw, a man in his mid-forties, grey-haired, thin-faced, the mouth set in an attitude of some glumness. The face was not unkind, but there was a rigidity about it, the same rigidity that I had noticed among other travellers of the same age. It was not a stupid face, that was obvious, but, equally obviously, once you moved beyond a narrow idea of intelligence, an abundance or lack thereof counted for nothing. The face I saw, the face that was my face, was full of something, trembling like a glass brimful of water, trembling like a whippet. Not out of fear, but out of the simple fact of being alive. To be a whippet was to tremble and to be me was to tremble like a glass full of water. What was it full of, this face, this face that was my face? I stared harder, straining to see, to know, and as I did this, so the face that I was seeing acquired a look of straining intensity. What the face was full of, I could see now, was yearning, desire, in this case a desire for knowledge, but it could quite easily have been a desire for chocolate or sex. This was the fundamental difference between myself and my new friend, the holy man. His face was free of desire. How had he got there? How had he managed that? Did he just happen to be that way? Unlikely. More likely it was a state he had acquired, worked his way towards through meditation, yoga, smoking charas or what-have-you. It seemed a great state to be in, to attain. But for the idea of desirelessness to take root, to set off in that direction, to try to free yourself of desire, surely that must manifest itself as a desire, a yearning, an urge. How, then, does desire transcend itself? As I was thinking this, so, without my intending it, my focus broadened. Having zoomed in on the pupil of my friend's eye, I zoomed out and the sight of my face, which had been full-frame, in tight close-up, receded and took its place as a single detail within the larger picture of his face. I saw his eyes and hair, the *tilak* on his forehead, the *tilak* that was the same red as the wall behind him. I saw his nose, his teeth and the gaps where his teeth were missing. He was smiling. I smiled back.

That night a concert was held on the terrace of the Ganges View. It was a clear warm night, full of listening stars. The terrace was lit by candles, flickering in a breeze that was hardly there. An audience of perhaps thirty people had gathered to hear a middle-aged woman on violin, accompanied by a thin man with white hair and thick glasses on tabla. The tampura was played by a woman whose shy manner seemed perfectly adapted to her instrument. The violinist explained that they were going to play the *raga Malkauns*. I had heard it before, in several different versions, on my iPod, but I still did not know what made it the *raga Malkauns* rather than another, similar-sounding *raga*. The bits that I thought identified and fixed it in one performance were nowhere to be found – nowhere to be heard – on another.

Night had fallen hours before, but the violin was dusk-laden, twilit. I knew that the violinist was exploring the *raga*, bringing it into being, could feel myself becoming gradually immersed in a geometry of sound, but I could not identify it. But I did, at least, have an inkling of why I couldn't. Melody depends on time. Played a little faster or slower, it remains recognisably itself. Whereas here the heart of the *raga*, the melody in which it had its origins, had been completely taken out of time. An entire dimension of listening had been removed. I began to lose myself in the infinitude of something I could not recognize or understand.

This may have been music of the spirit, but there was no attempt to disguise the physical fact of how it was produced. In the midst of the most lyrical touches there was no fear of the rasp, the friction of the bow being drawn across the strings. It could be left behind, that rasp, at a moment's notice, but it never was, or not for long. Even as it soared free, it dug itself more deeply into the earth. The violin was as thick as the night lying over the river, indistinguishable from it. Every move forward was tugged backwards and yet, irresistibly, the music advanced and accelerated. A pulse was making itself felt. It was impossible to say when this pulse had started. I became aware of it – the return of time – only when it had been there for a while, as if it had been there, inaudibly, imperceptibly, even before it was there. The stars lay on the river. At first something had taken shape; now it was coming to life. There was a feeling of brooding accumulation and of subtle realization: melody could be made more lovely if it was not left to be itself. By being forced to leave itself behind, it would become more than itself and, eventually, more purely itself. The pulse had become stronger than anything else, so strong that it was generating a need – for rhythm – it was incapable of satisfying.

At that moment the tabla kicked in. You could feel the sense of relief spreading through the night. A flight of birds flitted past, quick shadows of themselves. In the unaccompanied *alap* there was an immense yearning, a yearning, on the part of the violin, to achieve the incomparable sob of the sarangi. The fact that this was impossible had added greatly to the sense of longing, but that longing had been answered by the tabla, and the violin grew familiar again. For stretches now, there was a foot-stomping, shit-kicking, hillbilly quality to the music that was not at odds with the mood of meditation and transcendence. It was like discovering some universal template of music, extending from the Appalachians to the Indo-Gangetic Plain. The rasp, the squawk, grew more pronounced, but so too did the glide and swoop of melody, the abandoned melody that had never been left behind. The tabla was tying the beat in knots, more and more tangled, more and more intricate – and untying them just as quickly, faster and faster, but always with time to spare. At the heart of the gallop of the tabla was a gong, ringing out. I could not follow the rhythmic cycles, not consciously at any rate, but however far the violin and tabla strayed from each other, there was always a place they could return to and, at some level, I began to know where this place was, to recognize

245

it, to know how it sounded, to expect it even if I did so only after it had once again been left behind. The darkness flowed over the river and into it. The river was dark. The sky over the river was as dark as the river, but did not move, unlike the river, which moved constantly. Darkness was hidden by darkness.

Although I had looked at it every day, I had never crossed over to the other side of the Ganges. Then, one afternoon, I did. The boat nudged into the soft mud, directly opposite Jain ghat, and I stepped out. It was deserted, but not completely deserted; a few other tourists had also made the trip and were strolling around. What had looked appealing from a distance turned out to be abysmal up close. There was nothing remotely holy about it. For the most part, it was sandy and dry. In places it was like a boggy moon, with pools of brackish water, patches of moss and slime. At the edge of the water pretty wading birds picked at bubbles of scum-foam. By any normal standards, it was litter-strewn; there were crushed packets of cigarettes, squelchy plastic bags, the odd animal bone, brown fragments of pottery, an old sandal, a couple of broken, muddy Biros. Several dead kites lay in a pool of brown, greenish water. A dog came padding towards me, more hyena than dog. There was a strong sense of standing amid the aftermath of something, but of what? The aftermath of a rubbish dump, a dump where the best bits had been cherry-picked so that what remained was detritus – rubbish – even by the low standards of garbage: stuff that, even according to the Indian habit of maximum utility, could not be recycled and reused. There was nothing to do here, no point in staying.

I wished I hadn't come. It had been possible, beforehand, to believe that this other shore was the place where souls came to rest. If this was the case, then eternity now seemed a polluted, defiled place. One would have been better off being reborn, having another punt on the roulette wheel of Samsara and hoping for an incarnation-upgrade next time around, for nothing, surely, could have been worse than ending up here.

Especially if you died here and – as I had repeatedly been told – were reborn as a donkey. If that happened, would you know, even if only for the split-second in which the transmigration occurred, that you had been you in a previous life? Would any of you survive in this new incarnation or would you just be a memory-less donkey? If the latter then there was no need to worry about reincarnation. Lacking all consciousness of previous or future lives, you might as well never have been born before. If it had no idea of ever having been anything other than a donkey, then the donkey was oblivious to the fact that it was a donkey. So, through ignorance, the donkey had escaped from Samsara – though it probably didn't feel like it when it was dragging loads or being beaten with sticks and forced to do things against its will, when all it wanted to do was lie down in the soft mud, looking back towards Varanasi, thinking, *Now that rings a bell . . .*

I started to feel sleepy. I thought about the perfect shots I had played at tennis and the games when I had made mistakes on key points and, as a result of those mistakes, had ended up losing the whole match. I thought of games I had played and the tens of thousands of pints of beer I had swilled and the hundreds of lines of cocaine I had snorted, and I realized that my life was flashing before my eyes, as we are told happens at the moment of your death. That's always taken as meaning your whole life unfolds before your eyes, and maybe there was a time when this was the case, but now, in the age of soundbites and highlights, a degree of selectivity is in order. You don't have to re-live every moment of your life, every detail of desire, temptation and surrender, all the hours and hours watching TV, waiting for buses, picking your nose. That's just padding. No, there are only a limited number of moments that count for anything, that make up and define a life. And one of these moments, I realized, was this one, the one when I realized that my life was . . . I jolted awake, suddenly afraid that I was on the brink of dying, that this had been my destiny, to die here and be reborn as a donkey, a donkey with a brain, a donkey troubled by a stubborn but inadequate inkling – not a memory, just a nagging doubt, really – of what it meant to be human.

I got to my feet uncertainly, like a newborn foal. The other tourists had gone. I was alone on the far bank of the Ganges.

I checked that the boatman was still here – he was – and walked for a while, looking back at Varanasi. As I did so, the feeling that it had been a mistake to come here gradually reversed itself. I was glad, now, that I had: it was a reminder that since this life – the one back on the other other side, over there in Varanasi, back in the world – was the only one you got, the only real crime or mistake was not to make the most of it. The idea of the afterlife or eternity was just what it was revealed to be here: rubbish. Rubbish that no one wanted, that no one could set any value by. What was here was the aftermath of life itself, what was left when your time was up.

At Harishchandra ghat some kind of happening was in progress. A group of five drummers were thrashing out a hectic rhythm. A bunch of old guys were freaking out, alternating between dancing and fighting. It was a combination of Bum Fight and a festival for brain-damaged veterans of the trance scene. Did the music placate or incite them? Impossible to say. At one moment they were all leaping around, throwing themselves on the floor. Then, without provocation, they hurled themselves into each other and the whole thing turned into a brawl. There were no obvious alliances or sides – or, if there were alliances, they changed too swiftly for the neutral observer to keep track of them – but, at some point, a few of the other participants tried to break it all up. Wrestling turned to embracing. A man who, a few minutes earlier, had been fighting was now gyrating like a belly dancer, stroking an invisible phallus into a state of massively imagined engorgement. Then the music started again and it all kicked off again. Or the music stopped and it all kicked off again. Those who had tried to calm things down now became the instigators of a further round of hostilities. The longer I watched, the more difficult it became to detect any order, pattern or loyalties. It was a little bit of mayhem that, while constantly threatening to get completely out of control, never quite did. Everyone involved was having a good time.

I had to walk around the participants to get back to the Ganges View. As I did so, one of them came lurching back into me. On impulse I shoved him back into the mêlée. No one seemed bothered by this retaliation. At close range the banging of the drums was intense, hypnotic. I nodded my head for a bit and then began dancing. After a few minutes another guy bashed into me and I lurched back into someone else. I didn't let go completely, took care not to reel and lurch into the really crazy guys, but once you were in the midst of it, all this lurching and reeling was actually less dangerous than it seemed from the outside, to an onlooker. It was really just an open-air mosh pit, located – inappropriately to western sensibilities – ten yards from where a funeral was in progress.

Shortly after making my trip to the other side, I did something else I'd intended doing for ages: I went into the temple at Kedar ghat. In the time since I had been in Varanasi, the pale blue stripes had faded to the white I'd originally taken them to be. I remembered how, on my first day here, Varanasi had looked like a decrepit seaside resort. With its pink and white horizontal steps and vertical stripes, Kedar was the epicentre of this impression: it seemed to have taken inspiration from a stick of rock and a deckchair. Such a possibility was not so far-fetched. Nothing if not accommodating, Hinduism could easily incorporate the idea that Shiva once spent a long weekend – about ten thousand years, say – in Brighton, before there were mods and rockers, when even the humblest B&B was the size of the Pavilion.

The roof was rimmed with statues of the gods, bright and cheerful as garden gnomes. The sun was pounding down on the pink and white steps. It was the hottest day of the year so far, by far. Relative to how hot it would be two months from now, when it would be unbearably hot, it was not hot at all, but this did not make it feel any cooler. I walked up the pink and white steps towards the pink and white stripes of the temple, where horizontal became vertical. I took off my sandals and stepped inside. The darkness flickered with candles. Just being inside, out of the sun, was nice. Bells were being rung. My eyes adjusted, grew accustomed to the dark. The walls were painted the same mauvey blue as the steps outside, before they faded. There was a Pollock-splatter of the same blue on the tiled floor, some yellow columns. The green and white tiles on the walls would not have been out of place in an old dairy.

The temple was dedicated to Shiva – there he was, gold-hatted, all blue and all-powerful – but this didn't mean the other gods and their consorts were excluded. On the contrary. They were all here; all different, all the same, all one. All for one and one for all. I walked clockwise round the temple. At the back, in what looked like a jail cell, a holy man with a knotted mane of white hair and beard mumbled words and tended a small flame as if it were a frail bird to be coaxed back to life. He was focused intensely on the flame and the words he was saying. It didn't sound like an incantation, or only like the vestiges of one at any rate, as if the words he'd used to get him to where he was now could only be dimly recalled and lacked the power to bring him back. Not that he had any desire to return. He spoke the words as if asleep, words that suggested that wakefulness was a kind of sleep and only those who slept deeply could awake to the dream of life. Completely oblivious to my presence – and, I suspect, to his own – he would have looked equally at home in a madhouse as a place of worship. He shuffled along in his cell, which was not a cell at all, any more than the universe itself is a cell. Bounded in a nutshell and a king of infinite space! A shame, in a way, that *Hamlet* had not been translated into Sanskrit – though it's quite possible that an audience of sixteenth-century Brahmins would have dismissed the 'To be or not to be' soliloquy as a lot of mumbo-jumbo on the grounds that being and not being were one and the same, that non-being was the highest form of being, that being was itself illusion. A boy was saying hello, asking 'Where from?' I smiled, said 'Mars,' and walked on. I wanted to be on my own but that idea made no sense either. Why be on my own when I could be giving someone money to tell me things I already knew? A dusty pole of sunlight poked in from the outside, illuminating a piece of Sanskrit written on a wall. The boy pointed at the light, which pointed at the sacred text like the finger of a slow reader moving across the page of a difficult book. I continued moving too and the boy tagged along, keeping fractionally ahead of me, thereby subtly suggesting that he was being employed to guide me. He named the various deities tucked into their little niches, many daubed with fresh vermilion or garlanded with flowers. A white marble Vishnu and a grey stone Vishnu lived next to each other, in adjacent petal-scattered shrines. I found myself momentarily outside, visiting a three-eyed Ganesh, tangerine-coloured, sunlit.

There were flowers everywhere, including around my neck. Unlike those in the Durga temple, these smelled as they were meant to, were fragrant as flowers. Back inside again, I handed twenty rupees to the old man who had put them there, the old man to whom the young boy had guided me, the old man whose place the young boy would one day take, or had taken, fifty years earlier. Everything in India was so much easier as long as you had plenty of change. The air was heavy with the smell of flowers and the heavier smell of incense. More people had crowded in and more bells were being rung. It was incredibly loud, loud as a nightclub – the original Escape from Samsara. The boy was still at my side. His lips were moving, but I couldn't hear what he was saying. (Was this what it was like to be deaf? To be trapped in a storm of noise?) I gave him five rupees and he walked away. It was impossible to say where the noise of one bell stopped and the sound of another began. If you had to choose a single word to describe the noise of the bells, it could only be 'din'. The bells were making the most incredible din. At the heart of this din a drum was pounding, adding to the din, deepening it, lending it focus. Deeper within the temple, in a sanctum, a sinewy priest in a white *dhoti* was tracing patterns of fire with a kind of candelabra. The flames sent shadows lurching and reeling up the walls. The bells were louder than ever, so loud they seemed to be emanating from inside my head. Not that this meant that they were loud enough. The louder the bells became, the more people wanted to ring them. The worshippers formed two rows as if someone or something – a bull? a god? a bull-god? – was about to be released and would come charging out, out of the candle-shadowed darkness and past us, out into the unimaginable sunlight. But no, nothing was coming out; we were being ushered in, into the sanctum. The bells were deafening. And that pounding, I saw now, came from a mechanical drum pounding, pounding, pounding. Boom! Boom! Boom! The bells were demented, delirious, deranged. In this, the shrine in the deepest recess of the temple, people were reaching out to touch the *lingam*, a lump of brown rock, festooned with orange and yellow flowers. The boy who had insinuated himself into my employment reappeared, indicating that I should make an offering of my garland. No one else was paying me any mind. They were all absorbed in reaching out and touching the *lingam*. I chucked the garland, unceremoniously, onto the heap of flowers. Nothing changed as a result of this gesture, this faithless bit of *puja*, but the sense that I was at the heart of something was irresistible, and in any case I had no desire to resist. The drum kept pounding. Boom! Boom! Boom! The bells were a molten clamour of din. Within the multi-din, the din of all the different bells, another sound was taking shape: round, glowing, expanding, golden. *Aum*.

If there is one episode from my time in Varanasi that I would like to have on film, it is the one with the monkey and the sunglasses. I'd like to study it, to analyse it more closely. I was on the terrace, the only person there, reading Darrell's copy of Ginsberg's *Indian Journals* (I'd given up on *Women in Love*). My sunglasses were on the table, along with the remains of the soup and tea I'd ordered for lunch. I'd got over my stomach upset and was eating normally again, was no longer subsisting on bananas. There was a sudden crash on the corrugated iron of the roof behind me and a monkey leapt down onto the table. I jumped backwards, scared. The teacup fell to the floor and smashed. Unsure what to take, the monkey grabbed my sunglasses and bounded off with them, over the wall, in the direction of the temple.

Relieved that I hadn't been touched, scratched or bitten, I walked over to the wall where the monkey had made his getaway. He was sitting a couple of feet away, holding my glasses in both hands. I thought for a moment that he was going to try them on, but he just sat there, on his haunches, clinging to a pair of sunglasses – they had prescription lenses – that were useless to him. We watched each other. He was holding my shades with just one hand now, waving them in my direction. It occurred to me that an idea was forming in his head, a more advanced notion than any he had yet conceived. He had snatched the sunglasses on impulse, because they were shiny and because they were there. But he had not stolen them, we both realized now; he had taken them hostage. Worthless in themselves, they nevertheless had considerable exchange value. I made a gesture I'd seen in statues of the Buddha: hand raised, dispelling fear.

'Wait,' I said. 'Just wait.'

The monkey made no acknowledgement. I walked backwards, to the covered part of the terrace where there was a tray of fruit, a bunch of three bananas. I stuffed a couple in my back pocket and came out holding the third. I held it in one hand, at arm's length, ready to drop it if he rushed me, with the other closer to my chest, still raised in the *mudra* dispelling fear. The monkey was holding my sunglasses. Moving slowly, not taking my eyes off him, I put the banana on the wall separating us. When I had done this, I made sure that both my hands were visible, raised, palms facing him. He did not move. He just sat there, poker-faced or oblivious, it was impossible to say. I reached into my back pocket, took out a second banana and put it down beside the first. I retreated again, palms raised. The monkey looked away, swatted at a fly with my glasses. He shook his head, a gesture that might have had no connection at all with my improved offer.

'You really want to play hardball, don't you?' I said. 'OK, I'm through shitting around.' I took out the last banana and put it next to the other two, forming a bunch. Keeping my eyes on him, I turned slightly so that he could see that I had no more bananas in my pocket. 'That's my last offer,' I said. 'Take it or leave it.' My hands were still raised, but now I crossed them over each other in what I hoped was a universal, trans-species gesture of finality, closure. I took a step back. If the offer was not accepted, if negotiations broke down, I had no intention of snatching the bananas back. It was a matter of honour now. The ball was in his court. I wanted my sunglasses back. Of course I wanted my sunglasses back, but I was conscious, also, of the historic importance of this encounter. In terms of the development of his species, the step the monkey was about to take – the step I hoped he would take – was on a par with Neil Armstrong's giant leap from the Lunar Module to the dusty surface of the moon.

'It's down to you,' I said. 'You've got a straight choice. You can leave the sunglasses and take the 'nanas. In other words, you can start evolving. Or you can grab the 'nanas and make off with the glasses as well. But if you do that, you'll just be a fucking chimp for the rest of your days. And one other thing too. If you do that, I swear I'll hunt you down. Like a dog. So make your play.'

In the course of this speech, my hands had gradually lowered. They hung at my hips now, like a gunslinger's, or an ape's. The monkey twitched slightly. Then he nimbly bounded over the wall and snatched up the bananas, quickly but carefully. He bounded off again, dropping – whether by intention or by accident was impossible to say – my sunglasses on the table.

Events in Varanasi often assumed a kind of symmetry. The monkey and the sunglasses episode was still on my mind the next morning when I went up to the terrace for breakfast. Darrell was there already, eating porridge.

'How are you, Darrellji?'

'A bit discombobulated. Last night I dreamed I was attacked by a kangaroo.'

'How weird.'

'I know. It's the only dream I've had here, or at least the only one I can remember. And the only reason I remember it is because it's so ridiculous, so irrelevant. In the course of an average day here you see more animals than you do in a year in New York. It's a zoo and a city farm. Walking along the ghats is like going on safari.'

'A kangaroo is one of the animals you can be guaranteed not to encounter.'

'Exactly. If they weren't practically extinct, I wouldn't be surprised to bump into a tiger. But what's a kangaroo doing, turning up in a dream and attacking me?'

I shook my head. I had no idea about the kangaroo, but he was right about the lack of dreams. Varanasi was surprisingly unconducive to them. You'd have thought that all the stuff encountered during the day – stuff that scarcely made sense in the normal run of things – would have felt quite at home in the crazed swirl of the unconscious, could have pasted itself in with little or no editing. But it didn't. You shut your eyes and slept, dreamlessly, and because you didn't dream it was not like being asleep.

'I had a long nap here the other day,' I said. 'When I opened my eyes, it wasn't like waking up. It was like coming into

256

existence again. While my eyes were shut, I was not alive. I could just as well have been the chair I was sitting in, or the tile beneath the chair; or the foundations of the hotel, or even the mud, the earth it was built on.'

'At least you weren't attacked by a kangaroo.'

'I know. Maybe it's time for Hinduism to become more international, to reach out to Australia. A kangaroo god could be really popular. Ganoona could ride in its pouch, peeking out.'

'Who is Ganoona?'

'Ganoona is all that which is not anything else. But it's also that which is everything else.'

'Ganoona?'

'Yes. Nietzsche proclaimed the coming of the *ubermensch*. I proclaim the coming of Ganoona. In a kangaroo's pouch.'

I don't know where this idea of Ganoona came from. It would have made sense, in the context of a conversation about being attacked by a kangaroo, to have said that yesterday afternoon I had been involved in hostage negotiations with a monkey, but instead I had come out with this nonsense about Ganoona. I had never heard or thought of the name Ganoona before saying it, before it made itself said. But now that I had said it, Ganoona was a fact. It was real. It was Ganoona.

At the Nepalese temple near Meer ghat, just beneath the edge of the wooden roof, was a wooden frieze, decorated with erotic carvings. The figures were rounded, curvy, ambiguous. Sometimes it was difficult to tell exactly what was going on, sometimes you could see plainly: a woman masturbating a man while he caressed her breasts. Or a man fucking her from behind while one of her legs extended vertically, like a ballet dancer being stretched by a demanding trainer. Or his prick merging into her face. I knew about the famous erotic carvings at Khajuraho, but had not expected to find such things here. They were like visions of a lost world I could only vaguely recall: the world of desire, of answered passion. Looking at them made me feel content and sad, homesick for a place to which I would never return.

That afternoon I lay on my bed and thought of sex. Or tried to. I have never had fantasies, only memories, memories that occasionally got slightly improved and embellished. But my memories of sex had become weirdly non-corporeal. I thought, guiltily, of Lal, of how her skin might feel beneath my hands, but could not make the idea tangible enough to feel aroused. My dick was not hard. I'd not had a hard-on in weeks. Perhaps I was losing the ability to get one. I tried masturbating, but found it difficult to concentrate. Images of Varanasi, the ghats, crowded in and blocked out everything else. It was a relief, in a way, to be free of the torment of sexual desire, but this lack was in itself a form of torment. What if this desire went away and never came back?

Such concerns soon appeared irrelevant luxuries. I'd had a slight cold and cough for weeks. Nothing unusual about that. Inhaling a mix of dust, pollution and the smoke of the dead meant that everyone who stayed here for more than a few days developed a cough. Once you were reconciled to that, walking along the ghats and hawking up green lumps of phlegm became one of the routine pleasures of life in Varanasi. I'd had a couple of bouts of diarrhoea but, considering all the things that could have gone wrong, they, like the cough, seemed nothing to worry about.

Then, late one afternoon, walking in the confused network of streets behind the riverfront buildings, I was involved in a freak accident. The lanes were tight and dark enough for the yellow, diamond-shaped phone signs – STD – to glow hospitably, as if taverns in this area also provided opportunities – whether for treatment or contraction was unclear – of sexually transmitted diseases. Cauldrons of milk were being boiled and stirred to make sweets so sweet that dentists would caution against even looking at them too closely. I stepped into a quiet temple: green and cream walls, ochre pillars, mauve shrines. It was empty, just one other person there, sitting, not even asking where I was from. The presence of this single person made the temple emptier than if there was no one around.

A few yards from the temple I came to an intersection. The way ahead was temporarily blocked by a cow swaying down the lane that crossed the one I was on. Our eyes – one of its, two of mine – met. On its part there was no sign of comprehension, no evidence that my existence was even registered. Well, fine. The cow was in its cattle-trance and I was in my state of eager receptivity to everything that was going on around me, but there was room, even in this narrow lane, for all God's children, be they man or beast. The cow lumbered on. Its shit-caked tail was as drenched in shit as an artist's brush in paint. But just because I was me with a nice clean bottom and she was a cow with an ass caked in shit did not mean that I had not been her – or she me – in a previous existence. We could trade places in an instant. The value of your shares in the great Samsara-NASDAQ can go up as well as down. Still, all in all, a cow was a pretty odd thing to revere. I saw no reason to be cruel to them, had not eaten one for years, but apart from the fact that it was harmless, stupid and did not bite, a cow had nothing much to recommend it, or no more than a goat. Oh, well, live and let live. As I passed behind it, the cow flicked its tail, swatting me in the face with its tail, with its shit-drenched tail. There was a sharp intake of breath – mine – as my mouth opened in shock. I sort of shrieked. The cow must have heard me. It looked back, its expression unchanged, and then lumbered on. I began spitting frantically, but not spitting as you usually do, using the tongue to propel spittle out of the mouth (that would have brought my tongue into contact with the slime). Keeping my tongue curled back in my mouth, I was blowing saliva out of my mouth, using my mouth like a whale's blowhole. There were a lot of people around, quite a few of them laughing. One old man even patted the cow on the haunches, as if to congratulate it. I pulled a wad of tissues from my pocket and scoured my nose and chin, all the time spitting and hawking. A kind woman pointed out a tap to me and I bent down to wipe my face properly, taking care to keep my mouth firmly closed so that whatever infection I may have picked up from the cow's shit would not be complicated by whatever infection I might pick up from the tap water. I walked on without saying thank you. I did not want to be ungrateful or rude, but in the circumstances I was worried about the hygienic consequences of forming words.

In the west, it's considered good luck if you get dog shit on your shoe, so, in Hinduism, getting swatted in the face by a cow's shitty tail might be regarded as super-auspicious. That was one way of looking at it; but another, more sinister possibility flashed through my mind. Did the cow know what it was doing? Was this an accident or was it a targeted assassination attempt, divinely bovine retribution for pissing in the Ganges? Impossible to say. Impossible, as well, to prove a connection between this incident and what happened later, but the fact of the matter is that, later that evening, I exploded.

I went to bed with my stomach tight as a drum. I farted horribly and often, farts that smelt as disgusting as other people's. I began to feel nauseous but, since I had taken my weekly and daily dose of malaria tablets only a few hours earlier, resisted the temptation to throw up. Within half an hour it all came up, up and out, out and up. I was on my hands and knees, puking into the toilet, the smell of vomit instantly making me gag again. As soon as I had rinsed out my mouth, I was shitting yellow ooze into the toilet. There was barely time to flush the toilet before I was on my knees puking again. My body was engaged in such a frenzied attempt to get rid of whatever it was that had got inside it that it was in danger of tearing itself apart. I puked ten times in the course of the night and shat constantly. There was even shit on the bed sheets. It wasn't that I'd shat myself in the bed; my bowels had turned so watery that my asshole was not tight enough to seal it all in. I lay in my shit-spotted bed. Every hair on my head was a spike nailed into my skull. My stomach had a viper flexing around inside it. The taste in my mouth, from the vomit and, even worse, the malaria pills that I'd thrown up, was appalling. Anyone who has ever taken a dab of MDMA knows how unpleasant that taste is. My tongue tasted like I had sucked a lozenge of MDMA for several hours in order to make it last as long as possible. I had some Coke in the fridge and gargled with it. It made no impact on the taste and, within minutes, I was back on the toilet, splatting it out again.

The doctor came in the morning. He gave me anti-nausea pills and antibiotics. I spent the day in bed, falling asleep, waking for a few horrible minutes and then drifting off again. It hurt to move my eyes even fractionally. My head pounded. After several days I got up and shuffled around like a patient on a drip. I couldn't eat anything. I drank water and took Dioralytes, shitting occasionally. I was between a rock and a hard place. I'd stopped using anti-mosquito spray weeks ago because it had made my skin erupt in a rash. I had thrown up my malaria tablets. I could not start taking my malaria tablets again until the diarrhoea died down.

Gradually I recovered but, in a way, I never recovered. I'd always been skinny; now it seemed as if my bones were on the outside of my flesh – and they felt brittle as glass. My eyes still hurt if I moved them suddenly. Attacked by waves of dizziness, I was disoriented, altered. When I saw the goat I'd seen ages ago, the one with the clean white coat and the black socks, I thought he was going to start speaking to me. The sight of lentils made me nauseous. The smell of curry made me queasy. The thought of Indian food made me gag.

The evolutionary principle behind this aversion was obvious. Years ago, when we were plucking food from trees and had to learn which berries were edible and which were poisonous, it made sense if the body acquired its own infallible, instinctive memory, if, however hungry you became, you recoiled from the attractive, alluring red berry that had made you puke your soul up months or years earlier. A modern, teenage version of the same mechanism meant that I had stayed away from cider or Cinzano Bianco for thirty years. But how was I going to survive in India without eating Indian food? How was I going to put on weight again if I was living on water, Dioralytes and bananas?

Just outside the hotel there was a cute little puppy, shitting dark gouts of blood. There but for the grace of God . . .

I felt so weak after this bout of illness that I travelled more frequently by boat, especially if I was going all the way to Manikarnika ghat. As we rowed back from there, back to the hotel, I saw a water-bloated book floating in the river, being drawn to the small whirlpool created by the water-processing plant. Was this the most auspicious place for a book to end up? Did this guarantee its author immortality of a kind that rendered critical acclaim and months or years on the best-seller charts irrelevant? Or was the book destined, as it began to move more quickly towards the whirlpool, never to be reprinted or reissued in new, contemporary-looking editions? Would it never be read again? I tried to make out the title of the book. It was written in English, but that was all I could see.

We continued rowing towards Assi ghat in the fading light. I had a terrible tickling in my nose. I jammed a finger in my right nostril and the tickling turned into a tingle. I thought I could hear a buzzing, in my nose. When I dragged my finger out I saw, amid a smear of snot, the still-twitching body of a mosquito. After a few moments my nostril began to itch. When the finger went in again, I could feel a small lump. I had been bitten in the nostril by a mosquito.

At a stall in the lanes behind Kedar ghat a little Hanuman had taken my fancy. It was hand-painted, orange, in a blue container that looked like a cross between a kennel and a sentry box on Horse Guards Parade. There was nothing special about it, nothing to distinguish it from the rest of the Indo-tat on offer in the neighbouring shops, but I bought it and set it up on the chest of drawers in my room. I didn't pray to it – didn't know how – but, at some point each day, I sort of *acknowledged* it. I put my hands together and . . . I can't say exactly what I did. I tried meditating but, because I didn't know how to do that either, I thought of sex. Or tried to. I tried imagining Isobel, naked, on her knees, with shampoo'd dreadlocks and expensively laundered underwear, but the sequence refused to cohere, became confused and dispersed. It took such an effort of will to concentrate that I gave up. There was not the faintest stirring of desire. Because I couldn't think about sex, and did not know how to meditate or pray, I took, for a mantra, the only word I could think of. I intoned the name Ganoona. I said the name Ganoona, over and over, and by saying it over and over I was also asking for something – even if I did not know what that something was.

Near Lalit ghat, only a metre above the river, was a mauve-white shrine. Filled with the shadow-flicker of reflected sun and water, it was visible only from a boat. I knew that in the rainy season, when the Ganges was in full flow, the riverside temples sometimes flooded. I had seen the famous photograph, by Raghubir Singh, of a boy diving off the spire – he's completely horizontal, as if flying – of one such temple during an especially heavy flood. This particular shrine was so low-lying that it must have been completely submerged every year. Not that this stopped people paying homage to it. Daring boys dived down to offer *puja*, carrying torches in polythene bags. They swam down and shone the torches at the walls, murky through the silt-heavy water. The gods were still there, safe and sound, glad of the visit, amphibious, able to breathe underwater like fish or at least able to hold their breath for months. When the waters receded their abode would be stained, alluvial, cleanable.

I made another trip to the other side, this time from Manikarnika. I had got up even earlier than usual. It was night still, but the stars were pale in the sky, and day was at hand. The sun came up just as I passed Kedar ghat. I kept on walking. After spending an hour at Manikarnika, I accepted the offer of a boat, intending to return to the Ganges View for breakfast. The river was completely calm, flat as wrinkled glass. On an impulse, I asked the boatman to row across the river instead. The bottom of the boat was painted dull red and leaked slightly. Halfway across I pointed to the inch or two of water sloshing around and asked if there might be a problem.

'No problem,' he grinned. He paused in his rowing, held up a tin mug – it was the size of a half-pint beer glass – and made jokey baling gestures with it.

The bank at the other side was quite steep. Walking over it was like cresting a low sand dune. As I did so, a dark bird flapped noisily into the air. To my right, in a small bay, two dogs were eating something at the river's edge.

A dead man.

Was being chewed by two dogs. One was eating his left forearm, the other his right wrist. The dead man was intact. He was lying face down. I could see his hair and one ear. He was wearing a filthy pale blue T-shirt, torn in several places, and shorts. The dogs looked up, looked at me, then resumed their meal. It seemed a strange place to start, the arms. Maybe they started there because it was easy to get their jaws around limbs.

I could not see the dead man properly, but I recognized one of the dogs.

I told Darrell about the body. He took a boat out to see it the very next day. (Laline didn't want to go, but she didn't disapprove of his desire to take a look.) The dogs were still eating the dead man, who was still largely intact. The dead man being eaten by dogs had become a tourist attraction. Darrell was shocked, but said he would have been still more shocked if the dead man was being eaten by dolphins. That, he said, would have been seriously weird shit, even by Varanasi standards.

On the third day I went to take another look, to see how things were progressing, but the dead man was no longer there. There were dogs, eating bits and pieces of something, but nothing to indicate that this something – just a general mess – might once have been human.

I had been warned that the *bhang* lassis were strong, far more potent than the strongest grass, but because Darrel and Lal were having one I thought I'd join in. Things started weirdly, in that they were prepared for us not in a café, as one might have expected, but by a tailor who wanted to throw in a couple of suits for good measure.

For the first half an hour it was like being stoned, the early stages of a trip. The three of us walked with our arms around each other's shoulders, laughing at everything, at the river for instance, solid and grey as a motorway, busy with amphibious traffic. Then it was like being completely deranged. We weren't sure exactly where we were, but we had sense enough to stay away from Manikarnika and not to linger near Harishchandra where, in Darrell's words, 'all the death could really bum us out'. At one of the ghats we saw a thin man with a pale snake draped around his neck like a boa, like a feather boa, except this boa, plucked smooth, was a pet snake. The air grew so still it seemed about to congeal. Mountains of cloud swelled as if a storm were crouching over the city – only to disperse without a drop of rain falling.

Then it was like being a ghost. Darrell wandered off and it was just Laline and me on our own, wondering where he'd gone, and then I was wandering round on my own, wondering where Lal had wandered off to too. I was not unduly alarmed, but I wished they'd been around when I came across the baba with the road atlas and the wild beard. I thought something was wrong with my hearing, then I deduced that it was only him I couldn't hear and the reason I couldn't hear him was because there was something majorly wrong with his voice, in that it had gone completely and he was completely inaudible. Because he had no words, he gesticulated wildly. Expressing himself solely through gestures, his method of communicating was a form of seated, silent dance. Watching closely I could make out, from these gestures, odd phrases, even an occasional sentence. As I watched I began to piece together parts of what he was narrating. After a while, without conscious effort, I was able to understand him perfectly. He had come here, he said, to find something he had lost. What was the thing he had lost? An umbrella, apparently. And several Biros. Did this strike us as absurd? It did, yes, but I took this as meaning that the things most of us cared about – iPods and favourite T-shirts – were scarcely more important than the things we routinely lost, things like brollies and Biros to which we attached no value whatsoever, useful though they were for keeping one dry in a storm or jotting down thoughts and phone numbers. I thought that's what he was saying, but then it dawned on me that this metaphorical interpretation was too literal, because although he thought he had come here on the pretext of finding his lost property, it dawned on him that what he had lost was precisely the reason for coming here, that he was here to find out why he had ended up here. He paused, sat motionless for a while, letting the complex simplicity of his message sink in, and then, in a superb bit of theatre, he picked up and flicked open an umbrella. But not just any old brolly. No, this was a very old, totally useless, busted flush of an umbrella. Entirely devoid of fabric, it was no more than a spindly metallic skeleton, incapable of providing shelter from rain or shade from sun.

Later, as the light faded, I saw the goat again, the one with the clean white coat and the cute black socks. The one I had thought was going to speak to me. As I passed by, he began walking beside me. He smelled a bit of cheese, goat's cheese.

I felt something touch my leg. He was butting me gently with his head. I looked down at his goat-face.

'Sah, boat?' he said.

'No, thank you,' I said.

'Very cheap, sah.'

'No, thank you,' I said.

'Sah want boat?' the goat repeated.

'I walking. No want boat.'

'Very cheap,' said the goat.

'No, thank you,' I said.

I had slowed down and the goat, sensing my hesitancy and interpreting this as a willingness to be detained, tried a different approach.

'Sah, you think is nice being goat here in city? Life here hard for me. I have children. I offer you boat, but what I most want is to engage in conversation, a little philosophical discourse.'

I stopped walking so that I could give the goat the attention he obviously craved and deserved.

'OK. What would you like to talk about?'

The goat paused and then said, 'You take boat, sah?'

'I thought you wanted a philosophical conversation.'

'Joking, sah. What I want is ask what it is like, having thoughts in human head. How human consciousness different to goat consciousness?'

'Well, that's a very difficult question. To answer it, I'd need to have a clearer idea of what it was like to be a goat. I'll be honest, I assumed you were just kind of lost in your goat-world.'

'That is problem, sah. Because I am goat I do not have tools to explain what it is to be goat.'

'Well, you see, that is probably the difference. The ability to articulate things. Language. Self-examination . . . ' I didn't

268

know what else to say. It seemed that I was lacking exactly the qualities I claimed distinguished me from my interlocutor. The more I tried to articulate the difference between myself and the goat, the more we had in common. 'You know, I'm really going to have to think about this. You've taken me by surprise. Also, to be frank, I'm somewhat past my philosophical best at the moment. Could we talk about it another time?'

'Tomorrow, sah?'

'Yes, maybe tomorrow.'

'One other thing, sah. Ganoona appear soon.'

'Ganoona? How do you know about Ganoona?'

'I know only that Ganoona will appear soon. In pouch of a kangaroo. But only those who are Ganoona will be able to see him.' With that the goat turned and trotted off and I heard people calling someone's name. The name sounded familiar, but it took a while to cotton on: it was my name, and the people calling it were my friends, whose names, for the moment, escaped me.

'Well, I don't think we'll be doing that again in a hurry,' one of them (Darrell, that was it!) said the next day. He said it as though it was over and done with, but I suspected that part of me was still doing it.

In a way Laline had been proved right: I wasn't creating a commotion, but I was living like a monkey. It was nice, eating bananas under the dome of the sky, looking out at the river. The river flowed east, from right to left, but it didn't keep flowing to the ocean as any sensible river would. Here, at Varanasi, it changed its mind and returned to the source (another notion that I'd first encountered in a trance club in London). It turned back towards the Himalayas, where it came from, where the gods lived, where they had started out from and gone back to and would never leave. That was where the Ganga was heading. Did this mean that it made sense to throw a plastic bag full of marigolds into it, as an offering? What was the point of that? Every day I saw people doing this. It was obviously a stupid thing to do. If everyone did nothing but throw plastic bags into the river, it would be nothing but a river of plastic bags and it wouldn't be so sacred then, would it? I had finished my banana. It had not looked that great but, taste-wise, it was one of the best bananas I had ever eaten, so I immediately unpeeled another and started eating that too, and it was every bit as good, almost, as the one I had just finished.

Yum.

Sitting just up from Panchakot ghat, facing the risen sun, some kind of holy man or fake holy man was addressing a handful of listeners. At his feet, staring at the Ganges, were two human skulls, yellowish. Just decoration or was some larger point being made? Difficult to tell, but clearly they weren't paying much attention to what was being said. They looked pretty vacant. Whatever he was saying they had, presumably, heard it all before. He summoned me over and I went and sat with him and his mates or followers or whatever they were. One of them was wearing a Chelsea shirt with John Terry's name on the back. It was dispiriting, that shiny shirt, in the same way that it was depressing when Indian boys tried to show off their English by saying things like 'lovely jubbly'. The holy man's eyes were incredibly bloodshot, not surprising, given the size of the chillum he was toking on. He exhaled a mighty cloud of smoke – with his dreadlocks it was like an iconic reggae photograph – and passed me one of the skulls so I could take a closer look. I'd never held a human skull in my hands before, so it was quite interesting to do that. It didn't give me any thoughts about mortality or the soul or the futility of all human endeavour in the face of inevitable death, but I did start to worry that by examining the skull I had expressed a tacit interest in acquiring it. Well, there were worse things to end up buying. I had a momentary urge to boot the skull, goalie-style, into the Ganges. It would have been possible, I think. Instead, I put the skull on the ground again carefully. Feeling that I had to say something – as you do when someone shows you their poems or photographs – I said, 'Et in Arcadia ego.'

The holy man nodded and I stood up. As I did so, I saw Isobel, on her own, walking by the river. I said goodbye quickly to my new friends and ran down to intercept her. She was wearing dark, three-quarter-length shorts, with lots of pockets and zips, and the same pale yellow T-shirt she'd had on when I'd almost run over her on Shivala Road.

'Hi. How are you today?' I said.

'I'm fine. How are you?'

She had an accent, but I was unable to place it. Her shorts, I saw now, were not plain black, but discreetly camouflage-patterned: camouflaged camouflage! I tried not to stare at her stomach, tanned, flat. She was tall. Her thick dreads fell to below her shoulders. Up close she looked even younger than I had realized. The corollary of this was that I must have looked even older. Nothing is stranger, more delicate, than the relationship between two people who know each other only by sight – and nothing is more awkward than the transition from looking to speaking, when words finally come into play. Unsure what to say, I almost asked again how she was. With slight variations of emphasis – 'How are *you* today?' 'How are you *today*?' – we could have been trapped in this loop of pleasantries for the rest of time. At the last moment I asked, instead, 'Are you walking this way?'

I gestured in the direction of Manikarnika and, as if the word 'walking' obliged me to check that she had a pair, looked down at her feet. She was wearing sandals, an ankle bracelet. Her toenails were painted silver.

'Yes.'

'Me too. Shall we stroll?'

We began walking along the busy ghats, exchanging basic information about where we were staying, how long we had been in Varanasi. She was staying in a place I'd not heard of. When I said I was staying at the Ganges View, she said she had heard it was very nice, but expensive.

'I suppose it is,' I said, feeling pleased with myself for residing in such high-end accommodation.

'Where are you from?'

'England. London. What about you?'

'Switzerland.'

'Switzerland?' I was going to say *I thought you were Israeli*, but feared this might seem anti-Semitic. I almost said *I thought Swiss people were really tidy and smart*, but feared this might seem anti-Swiss or anti-scruff. While I was thinking all of these things and not saying any of them, she explained that her friends were from Israel. She said 'friends', plural, not boyfriend, singular. She had met them in Goa. I was listening, but I was also plotting, plotting what we might do in order to do something – I had no idea what – more than stroll. The sun was glinting off the river to our right, busy with boats. We had come to the steps leading up to the Lotus Lounge. Out of the blue, Isobel said, 'Have you been to Venice?'

'Yes, of course. Quite a few times.'

'Doesn't Varanasi remind you of Venice?'

The opportunity to respond seriously resulted only in the impulse to say something glib: 'Because they both begin with V?'

She punched me on the arm. 'Tiny lanes, crumbling old palaces. The water . . . '

'No, you're right.' We had stopped walking. I turned to look at her. 'They're incredibly similar. Versions of each other, almost. Twinned.'

The air was quite still, but the moment – whatever it is that makes a moment a moment – had already passed. In spite of this, I said, 'Would you like to have a coffee here? Or a juice or something?'

'I have to meet someone,' she said.

I could have said OK, *let's keep walking* but, in case her rejection of the idea of coffee or juice was meant to be construed as a larger refusal, I said, 'Oh, well, it's so nice to have met you at last.' Then, in case it *wasn't* meant to be construed as a rejection of anything other than coffee or juice, I added, 'Perhaps we could meet again.'

'That would be nice,' she said. 'But tomorrow is my last day in Varanasi.'

'No!'

'Yes. I go to Hampi the day after tomorrow.' I couldn't believe the cruelty of the timing, the way we had been here all this time and were only talking now, when there was no point in doing so.

I was standing there, digesting the implications – the non-implications of all this – when someone called out her name, 'Isobel!' We both looked towards the river, where the voice had come from. A boat was passing by. In it, someone was waving.

Ashwin.

She waved back. At first I stood with my hands hanging by my sides, as I had when confronting the monkey who'd snatched my sunglasses. Then, to cover up my embarrassment, I waved too. Ashwin waved at me. Everyone was waving.

We were all drowning in a sea of waves. Ashwin was calling out, asking if she wanted a ride.

'It's OK,' she shouted back. 'I'll see you there. I have to stop off at my room first.' There was a final flurry of waves and then Ashwin continued downstream towards wherever 'there' was.

'So, you know Ashwin,' I said. She said yes, smiled in a way that I had not seen before. 'Nice guy,' I added.

We stood there a little awkwardly until she said, 'I should go.'

'Yes, of course. Well, I'm glad we at least got a chance to speak,' I said, suppressing the urge to ask if Ashwin was going to Hampi as well. We shook hands and she turned to go. I watched her as she continued walking along the ghats. Then I climbed the steps to the Lotus Lounge. Leaning out over the wall of the terrace, I could just about see her – her thick locks and yellow T-shirt – disappearing into the crowd.

I ordered a cappuccino and a pancake. As I sat there, looking out at the Ganges, I felt obscurely that my last chance – of what, I was not sure – had just gone begging. Gone begging: the phrase flashed through my head, like a sign on a shop door saying *Gone Fishing*.

Not such a good idea, having that cappuccino. A few minutes after leaving the Lotus Lounge, I had a violent urge to take a crap. I started running, hoping I could make it to somewhere with a toilet. But it was impossible. Crouching down by a wall, I squirted vile-smelling ooze over a pair of old, sun-dried turds.

Two time schemes co-existed in Varanasi. My days passed without direction or purpose. The city's calendar, meanwhile, was plotted and marked by a rigidly co-ordinated schedule of festivals. There were so many festivals, I had given up trying to keep track of what was being celebrated or ushered in. An abundance of weddings meant that even the days that weren't festivals were extremely festive. The childish longing, 'I wish it could be Christmas every day' (imprinted in my memory by Slade), had been pretty well realized by a combination of Islam, Sikhism and Hinduism. So it was no wonder that I began to drift free of the usual demands of time and dates. Unsure of precisely how long I had been here, I checked the visa in my passport – or would have done, if I could have found it. I rummaged through all the drawers and all the clothing in the drawers where I might have hidden my passport. I tried to remember the last time I'd seen it, the last time I'd taken it out. I'd had it with me during the altercation with the queue-barger in the bank, and I thought I had a memory of putting it away after that, but the more I thought about it the less sure I became if that was a memory or just the hope of a memory, and the more likely it seemed that I *had* taken it out with me on other unremembered occasions since then. Surely I'd had the sense not to take it out on the day we went bananas on *bhang* lassis? The more I thought about that, the less sure I became that I hadn't. I sat on the bed and did not know what to do, and then I decided that not knowing what to do was a form of knowing what to do, which was to do nothing, so that is what I did.

On a day that may or may not have been particularly auspicious, Laline handed me a package wrapped in delicate pink paper, tied with red thread.

'Present for you,' she said. I untied the string and unwrapped the paper carefully. Inside was a copy of *The Painted Veil* by Somerset Maugham. On the cover she had carefully painted out the 'I' in VEIL and squeezed in a slim 'A'.

'Thank you,' I said. I kissed her, I was grateful. It was a

lovely present, but I didn't read the book because reading books was no longer something I did.

The weather grew hotter. Occasionally a line of thin cloud appeared in the sharp sky.

Walking in the lanes behind the ghats, I came across a man pushing a barrow in which he seemed to be carrying some kind of gourd. Squeezing by him, I realized that what I had taken to be a pumpkin were actually his testicles. Swollen monstrously by disease, they had become unsupportable and it was his destiny to lug them around in a wheelbarrow. Everything in Varanasi was taken to a delirious extreme. In Europe we had the myth of Sisyphus and his stone. In Varanasi there was the fact of this man and his balls.

I took a rickshaw to the museum at the Hindu University. It was a spacious, dusty place with calm statues of the Buddha and trancey bronzes of Shiva in the guise of Nataraja, the cosmic dancer. There was also an impressive array of Indian miniatures, some of which were actually quite big. I had no sense of the relative merits of any of the individual paintings, but one seemed particularly lovely. It was painted by Shivalal – the name meant nothing to me – in 1893, but looked, to my untutored eye, as if it could have been done two or three hundred years earlier. An expensively upholstered procession of horses and riders was crossing a flooded bridge or causeway, in single file, in the monsoon. Rain arrowed into the wet-look river, which had climbed up trees and into houses built, fatalistically, on the flood plain. In the background conical hills – one of them with a castle perched on top – blazed greenly. Clouds sagged. Lightning flashed – a gold snake wriggling through the soggy, indigo sky.

Down at the actual river, the real, unpainted one, the funeral of a *sanyasin* was in progress. He was not cremated. His body was carried into the Ganges, weighed down by a stone and let go.

So far, I'd not bumped into anyone from what I now regarded as my prior life – my previous incarnation – in London. Then, at Kedar ghat, I ran into Anand Sethi, who had given me the advice about not staying at the Taj Ganges.

'You've got an explorer beard,' he said. It was true. I hadn't *grown* a beard, I'd just stopped shaving – and, as a result, I'd become a man with a beard. The young Sikhs with their dark beards and the backpackers with their wispy goatees looked young, handsome; I looked like a slimmed-down version of Dougal Haston or Chris Bonnington. Anand was wearing a striped Paul Smith shirt and Prada slacks. He looked like a banker in a heatwave, which is what he was. That made me conscious of the extent to which I had gone, not native so much as ageing backpacker. I was wearing an old Rip Curl T-shirt and frayed shorts. My hair was long, uncombed, grey, like my beard.

'How long have you been here?' I said.

'Just yesterday. What about you?'

'I've been here for ages. Since I last saw you, at that opening for Fiona Rae. I never went back. I've sort of taken root here. Are you staying at the Ganges View? I'm surprised I haven't seen you.'

'No, the Taj,' he said. 'The Ganges View was full.'

'I'm sorry,' I said, trying not to smirk. 'That's where I've been all this time. I've probably ended up taking your room.' I suggested that we meet up for a drink or dinner, but he was leaving for Agra the following night. After that he was going to Bombay, to buy a painting by Atul Dodiya.

As we parted he said, 'You know, I'm really not sure about the beard. You look like a castaway. Or Terry Waite on hunger strike.'

'You're right,' I said. 'I'm going to do something about it.'

I walked straight to a place I'd long had a fondness for because of its name – the Decent Barber, on Shivala Road – to have my head, beard and eyebrows shaved. I asked the barber to leave a little pigtail at the back of the head, as I had seen on mourners. I wondered if he would object, if aping the ritual of bereavement in this way might be considered offensive, but he went ahead and did it without question or complaint. Several people watched. There must have been a number of tiny nicks; my head stung afterwards. It felt white as an egg, as a skull. I could feel the sun boiling it as I walked back to Assi.

On the way, I ran into Ashwin. I was as surprised to see him as he was surprised by me.

'I thought you'd be in Hampi,' I said.

'No. Not . . . But, I mean, what's happened?' he asked

'I am in mourning for myself,' I said, reprising the old Chekhov joke. 'My old self refuses to die. The new is struggling to be reborn. In this interregnum a great variety of morbid symptoms appear.'

I had become almost a fixture at the hotel. Though I still enjoyed a laugh and a joke, I was no longer on the lookout for friends, for people I could eat dinner and make jokes with. Everyone I met was just passing through. They were simply guests, people who came and went. My attitude was like that of the staff, except that I was never faced with the final, definitive judgement, made on the day of departure, that overruled all previous feelings about how courteous or pleasant the guests had been: the judgement determined solely by the size of the tip. (I'd been here so long that my eventual tip must have been anticipated as though it were my last will and testament.) It was a relief to be free of the tyranny of my own likes and dislikes. How could it have mattered so much what I thought of X or Y? I mean, how could it have mattered so much to me?

I don't want to sound like some kind of pseudo-*sanyasin*. We think of renunciation happening formally, definitively, possibly as a result of frustration, anger or disappointment (*'This world I do renounce* . . . '), but it can happen gradually, so gradually it doesn't feel like renunciation. The reason it doesn't feel like renunciation is because it's not. I didn't renounce the world; I just became gradually less interested in certain aspects of it, less involved with it – and that diminution of interest was slowly reciprocated. That's how it works. The world stops singling you out; you stop feeling singled out by the world.

Some people stop believing that happiness is going to come their way. On the brink of becoming one of them, I began to accept that it was my destiny to be unhappy. In the normal course of things I would have made some accommodation with this, would have set up camp as a permanently unhappy person. But what had happened in Varanasi was that something was taken out of the equation so that there was nothing for unhappiness to fasten itself upon. That something was me. I had cheated destiny. Actually, the passive construction is more accurate: destiny had been cheated.

I remembered how personally I used to take everything. Two years previously, I'd been given tickets for the opening day at Wimbledon, Centre Court. It rained, off and on, all day. We kept waiting, looking at the sky, hoping. At three o'clock the covers were rolled back and it looked like play might commence. There was a big, soggy cheer, but within twenty minutes the covers were back on and the awful drizzle returned. We didn't give up hope. We kept looking at the sagging clouds. At one point it seemed to me that the sky was brightening up and growing darker at the same time. By the end of the day, not a shot had been played. It was as if there was a curse on me. No one else – not the players or anyone else in the stadium – suffered to the extent that I did. It was my day, my Wimbledon, my parade that was being rained on. The weather had come between me and what I wanted – which was to watch tennis. The pain and the rain were intolerable because they conformed to a broader climatic pattern: something was always coming between me and what I wanted. That afternoon at Wimbledon it was the rain; another day it was another thing. But there was always something. I realized now that that thing was me. I was in my way. I was ahead of me in the queue. I was keeping me waiting. Everything was a kind of waiting. When I drank beer, I was waiting for the glass to empty so I could have it filled and start drinking again. Rather than simply enjoying the high of cocaine, I was also monitoring it, to see if the effect was wearing off, so I could top it up, have more, start monitoring again . . . I really don't want to come on like someone who has gone through rehab or undergone a conversion or awakening. All I'm saying is that in Varanasi I no longer felt like I was waiting. The waiting was over. I was over. I had taken myself out of the equation.

When I first came to Varanasi, like all the other tourists, I had treated the Ganges with extreme aversion. It may have been a sacred river, but it was a filthy one too, awash with sewage, plastic bags and the ashes of corpses: a sacred, flowing health hazard. Now I felt the urge to take a dip. I say urge, but that is not the right word at all. I had no desire to bathe in the way that I desired a cold beer – and I did still desire cold beers, just as I still enjoyed a laugh and a joke, especially now it was so hot. It was more as if I knew that one day I would bathe in the river and so there was no point not doing so. Dillydallying was just postponing the inevitable. Since there would come a time when I had bathed in the Ganges, not doing so made no sense: like trying to avoid doing something I had already done.

Just after sunrise, at Kedar ghat, I took off my shorts and T-shirt and stripped down to my underwear. All my life I have been self-conscious about being thin, but surrounded by the endlessly varied shapes of Indians – fat as Ganesh, skinny as whippets – I felt quite comfortable. I walked down the steps and entered the water. Relative to the air, it was surprisingly cold. The sun patterned the surface with wriggles and sparkles of light. I was up to my knees in the water and had got used to the cold. Now the water felt quite warm, but other than that it did not feel like anything. It did not feel dirty and it did not feel sacred; it just felt like water. I waded a little further out, on tiptoes, to avoid the moment when the water touched my balls and stomach. Then I was in the water up to my chest. I could feel the push of the current, but there was nothing treacherous or dangerous-seeming about this slight exertion of its will. Now that I was in the water, I didn't know what to do. The sun was pounding down already, not causing any problems. It was quite nice being in the water, as it always is on a sunny day. On either side people were washing or praying or just standing. Some kids were playing, splashing each other, but they did not splash me. No one paid any attention to me. No one said 'Good for you', or 'You see, it's not as dirty as these fussy tourists always claim.' I was the only non-Indian, the only westerner in the water, but I knew there were several on the steps behind me, watching. I gazed at the opposite bank, that empty world. It was easy to believe that if you swam there you would leave your present life behind.

I felt something touch my leg and glanced into the water,

fearing it was something horrible, a form of sewage, but it was just a sodden coracle with a few dead flowers in the bottom. The water may not have been clean, but it didn't look or feel dirty. I could hear voices, the voices of the people behind and beside me. The risen sun was in my face. After standing in the river for a while, I walked back to the steps and dried in the sun. I had not got any water on my face, not even a drop. I put my T-shirt and shorts back on. They felt warm and clean and it was nice to have sandals on my feet again too. I was not sure whether I'd had a wash or was now in need of one, but I was sure that the Indians regarded me differently, that I had made a significant move towards becoming one of them. As for my fellow-tourists, they probably thought I was showing off, reckless, stupid, but that, I realized now, was a form of fear and envy. When they saw me, they saw a rebuke to their own timidity.

My cough had not got better, but I had grown so used to it that I scarcely gave it a thought. Coughing was just a form of breathing, a slightly noisier function of being alive. I had got into the habit of crapping, liquidly, after every meal. My asshole felt red as a monkey's. Living mainly on bananas again, I lost weight. Thought bore a curious resemblance to a headache. It was impossible to say whether these were the varied symptoms of a single sickness or a coalition of individual illnesses that had formed an alliance to do me harm. Either way, my whole system was under siege – from within. As happens, I adapted to these new conditions, got used to them. At first, I'd kept wishing I was better. Then, after a while, my notion of what feeling better felt like grew a little hazy. I forgot there was even this state called wellness. Feeling well was indistinguishable from feeling unwell. If I felt only slightly ill, then I felt perfectly well.

It grew hotter by the day. I may have said this already, but it kept getting hotter. The heat meant that every kind of bug and germ was well placed and perfectly adapted to thrive and multiply. On top of everything else, sun- or heat-stroke seemed a distinct possibility. To combat the heat, I bought a *dhoti*. At first I wore it only in my room, practising how to tuck it into itself so that my thighs were left bare. Then, on one occasion, I actually sat on the roof terrace wearing it, relieved that no one else came up. When they did – a French couple who had only checked in that morning – I was surprised that I felt comfortable, at ease. I said, '*Bonjour*' and gave them a smile, one of those slow, semi-guru smiles that people who had been here a while felt entitled to bestow on new arrivals. They remained on the terrace only a few minutes, just long enough to show that they weren't embarrassed by this skinny holy man, and then went back to their room and had audible sex. I even heard her saying, '*Je viens.*'

'Stick it in and waggle it about,' I thought to myself. And then, because thinking this phrase was so enjoyable, I said it aloud several times: 'Stick it in and waggle it about!' If I'd known how to translate it, I would have said it in French.

A few days later I ventured out on to the ghats, wearing just the *dhoti*. As a teenager I had been so ashamed of my skinny legs that I played squash in jeans; now, skinnier than ever, I walked out in this bit of cloth, as skinny as Gandhi. My legs were perfectly white above the knees and deeply tanned below them. I look completely ridiculous, I thought to myself, but no more ridiculous than some of the other people around. What was the point in feeling absurd in a town where you could lug your testicles around in a wheelbarrow? There was no such thing as being ridiculous in Varanasi. The very idea was ridiculous. I was much further gone than any of the backpackers. They had dreadlocks and wore turbans made of sarongs, but no one looked as ridiculous as me. I didn't avoid their eyes, I met their eyes. The owner of one of these pairs of eyes, Micky, whom I'd spoken with a few times at the Lotus Lounge, was so obviously torn between his desire to ask what was going on and his fear of giving offence that, to put him out of his misery, I said, 'So, what do you think?'

'About what?'

'This,' I said, raising my arms, doing a slight twirl, as if showing off a new outfit from Topshop.

'Looks good,' he said. 'But what does it, like, signify?'

'You've heard of *sadhu*s, right?'

'Sure.'

'Well, this is my version of it. A sadd-o,' I said, beaming as I made this feeble little joke. I walked on. I concentrated on rearranging the resting expression of my face. Habitually glum-looking, I kept smiling, hoping that my face would come to reside in this more upbeat style.

Looking like this – like a freak, frankly – served another useful purpose in that, while I attracted stares, I was pestered less frequently by hawkers and hustlers. I certainly didn't look like I was in the market for buying anything. At Harishchandra ghat a tourist with a German-sounding accent asked if he could take my picture. I said yes, certainly, and stood beaming by the yellow and black lifeguard's tower that was not a lifeguard's tower. We spoke afterwards. He wanted to know my story. I said I didn't have a story and he asked where I was from.

'Where are you from?' I said.

'Switzerland,' he said.

'Switzerland?' I said. 'Then you must know my friend Isobel.'

He shook his head, no.

'Man, I'd like to have got my spoon into that chick's pudding,' I said. 'Stuck it in and waggled it about! Anyway,

Switzerland. Neutral Switzerland. I once stood in front of the fountain at Geneva. I had my picture taken there, smiling with friends, the fountain behind us. An establishing shot. I was a Champion. You see?'

He nodded, but it was obvious that he did not see. He saw me standing before him, but he could not see. The notion of *darshan* meant nothing to him.

'My story is your story,' I said. 'If you were from Swindon, then that is where I am from. It doesn't matter. There is nothing to choose between Swindon and Geneva. To me, they might just as well be Bourton on the Water. Have you been there?'

'To Bourton on Water? I don't think so.'

'If you had, you would know. A charming Cotswold village. I went there with my parents when I was a boy. There was a Tea Shoppe where we had teacakes. I remember my father's chin, how it was shiny with butter. The Tea Shoppe is now probably a cappuccino bar. In essentials, it is exactly the same as Geneva.'

The Swiss nodded.

'Another time we went to Longleat, to see the lions of Longleat. A very hot day and, contrary to the instructions on the many signs, we unwound the windows of our car slightly, a sky-blue Vauxhall Victor. No more than a couple of inches, but I began to cry because I was frightened of the lions.

'Have you heard of Mike Summerbee, the footballer? He played for Manchester City and went to the same primary school as me. Even back then, my father said that footballers earned too much money. More than anything, my father hated spending money, so holidays were a kind of torture for him and he preferred to stay home and concrete our drive or something like that. When we did go on holiday, we went to Weston-super-Mare or Bournemouth, but when we got there it was always the monsoon and so we would have to go to the cinema. The only time we went to the cinema was when we were on holiday and it rained. It always rained and we always saw the film versions of our favourite television shows: *Steptoe and Son*, Morecambe and Wise in *That Riviera Touch*. We never went to see the great works of the medium: Antonioni, Satyajit Ray, Godard. We didn't even see *Thunderball*, but to be fair I did see *Where Eagles Dare* and *The Italian Job*, films that had a profound effect on my then-young mind. I don't want you to get the wrong impression. I know this seems hard to believe as you look at me now but, in my time, I was somewhat of a lady's man. Stick. Waggle. Speaking of stream of consciousness, have you seen *In the White City* by your fellow-countryman, Alain Tanner? It's one of the first films to use Super-8 footage, to exploit the curious way Super-8 seems saturated by memory itself. It stars Bruno Ganz. At the simplest level, he plays a sailor on leave in Lisbon, who jumps ship and just stays there, wandering around, but for me it is an allegory of the attractions of Bourton on the Water, the eternal village, in the holy Cotswolds. There is a bridge there, a crossing place, a *tirtha*. It is said that if you cross this bridge, you will come to an auspicious ice cream van – Mr Whippee – selling choc-ices and raspberry Mivvis. Let be be finale of seem.'

The Swiss, understandably, was showing signs of wanting to move on.

'Wait,' I said. 'I have a question, a question about your other countryman, Roger Federer. A great tennis player. A god, in his way. But why did he persist in wearing that absurd cream-coloured blazer at Wimbledon? Do not wear a cream-coloured blazer with shorts or a *dhoti*. It is one of the most elementary rules of clothing. So, why did he do it? Answer me that. It is the question that will answer all other questions.'

The Swiss said he did not know. I was not surprised. It defied understanding. That is why it was the question that would answer all other questions.

Thereafter I always went out walking in my *dhoti*. My white thighs soon became as brown as my calves. I stopped being conscious that I was dressed like this. It felt good, it felt natural, and I felt as cool as it was possible to feel in an environment in which it was only possible to feel hot. Passing a couple of *bhang*-addled hippies, I heard one say, 'Christ, it's Shuman the Human!' A little further along I saw my friend, the friend whose eyes I had looked into. I waved to him, but he didn't seem to recognize me, possibly because I had changed beyond all recognition even though, to my mind, I was still recognizably myself. More plausibly, he didn't remember anything, didn't even have a memory. Even to have memories was a form of attachment and a form of desire. Personally, I had no need of them.

Speaking of memories, I have forgotten to mention that Laline and Darrell left Varanasi. They went to Rajasthan, to Jaipur and Jaisalmer, a city in the desert. They were flying, flying or taking a train, to Jaipur or Jodhpur. Laline asked if I wanted to go with them, but I had no desire to leave Varanasi.

'To be in Varanasi is to be everywhere,' I said. 'The city is cosmogram and mandala. When all is said and done, it is probably the least boring place on earth. And, most importantly, the pancakes at the Lotus Lounge show no signs of deterioration.'

'We're worried about you,' Laline said.

'About me? How sweet, but I can't think why. I'm just beginning to find my feet here.'

'It's just. You seem . . . '

'What? You're not going to accuse me of living like a

287

monkey again, are you? Those days are gone, I promise. I'm even thinking of learning Sanskrit. You wouldn't catch a monkey doing that now, would you?'

'You've still got your sense of humour,' she said.

'Actually, I'm the one who should be worried about you.'

'Why?'

'Darrell.'

'What about him?'

'He's with the CIA.'

'The CIA?'

'I suspected it from the moment I saw him. Now I'm sure.'

'Well, he's a terrific advert for it,' she said, apparently unperturbed.

'I know. I'm tempted to join myself.'

'They wouldn't have you. You're a security risk.'

'What if Darrell put in a good word for me?'

Lal smiled, ran her hand through my hair. 'Your hair is growing out. It's all fluffy. Like a gosling.' I thought that was a lovely thing to say.

'Fluffy as a gosling and sleek as an otter,' I said. 'That will be my motto from now on.' We moved to hug goodbye.

'Ouch!' I had trodden on her sandaled foot.

'I'm sorry,' I said. 'I'm so clumsy.'

'That's alright.'

Darrell and I hugged too. I did not tread on his foot and he did not stroke my hair or say it was fluffy as a gosling's. But I did say to him that, now that they were an item, Laline should start wearing the veal. Because they were leaving, I took a picture of them both, on the terrace of the Ganges View. They took off their sunglasses and stood with their arms around each other, smiling. Birds skittered by. It was a good picture and a quite ordinary one. In the background the great river flowed, unmoving, vast. They were my friends, I was sad to see them go, but I was indifferent too. Like everyone else, they were just passing through, just guests. The same was true of me. Even though I was still here, had no plans to go anywhere, I was a guest, just passing through, fluffy as a gosling, sleek as an otter.

I bathed every morning in the Ganges, which kept passing through and staying, passing through and staying put. Some days I even swam in it, not far, just a few strokes. I took care not to swallow any river-water but, inevitably, a few drips splashed into my mouth. One morning I saw the dolphins that were rumoured to live in the river. Two of them, black and sleek in their wet suits, surfacing and diving and with long smiles. It seemed hard to believe that they really existed, but the fact that they did tells you something, about dolphins and the Ganges and existence generally. It tells you that there are dolphins in the Ganges, and if there are dolphins here then there can be other creatures too, otters, for example, and not just here, but in other rivers also, and not just in rivers either.

'Passing through, staying put,' I chanted to myself. 'Passing put, staying through.'

On the occasion of my first dip, I had stepped gingerly into the water; these days I dived in from the ghats. Diving makes it sound far more spectacular than it really was. It was more like just leaning forward, leaning on nothing and letting go, otherwise known as a belly-flop. The sun was so powerful that I was dry within moments of clambering out of the water. After that I went and had my lemon and sugar pancake at the Lotus Lounge or went back to the hotel and generally went about my lack of business. I may have walked slowly, but I took everything in my stride. Anything seemed possible. It would not have surprised me to learn that I had left Varanasi and was now a war criminal living in Buenos Aires in the

1950s. If it had turned out that I was at home on my sofa, watching a documentary about Varanasi or playing a video game called *Varanasi Death Trip*, that would not have altered my assessment of the situation because my situation would not have changed significantly. When someone said that I had been at Charterhouse with them, in the 1970s, I did not bat an eyelid even though the only thing I knew about Charterhouse was that it was a school and that Pete Hammill or Peter Gabriel had been a pupil there. If someone had come up and said they had no idea who I was or what I was talking about, I would have agreed and said, 'Me neither.' Actually, one day that did happen, someone really said that – or something along those lines – but the person who said it was Ashwin. Back from Hampi, dumped by Isobel presumably, and, although it had taken far longer than expected, finally having the nervous breakdown for which all that overbrimming of love had predisposed him, poor kid. All I could do was give him my blessing and a few rupees.

Time passed, or maybe it didn't. All of time is here, in Varanasi, so maybe time cannot pass. People come and go, but time stays. Time is not a guest. The days, though, they passed, and eventually the day came, the day of days, the most auspicious of days. At Kedar ghat a kangaroo came boinging along. It caused quite a stir, as you can imagine, but, in the hospitable Hindu way, it was immediately welcomed and absorbed into the pantheon of interesting events. Rather than astonishment, the attitude was more like, 'Well, why *not* a kangaroo?' People threw bright flowers as a greeting, touched its big feet, draped a marigold garland round its drooping Victorian shoulders. A sandal-paste *tilak* was applied to its forehead. The kangaroo held its paws together and bowed slightly in an approximation of the *anjali* greeting. It was a nice quiet kangaroo, everyone said, glad of the attention and company. Not at all aggressive, not like the one that had attacked Darrell in his dream. I say 'everyone said' because I could not see it. I was in its pouch, you see, peeking out, fluffy as a gosling, sleek as an otter, passing through and staying put. I saw what it saw, not what the people looking at it saw. What I saw was the people seeing it. When the kangaroo came to the river's edge, I saw the heavy water of Ganga brooding slowly by. People thought the kangaroo might jump into the Ganges, but it seemed reluctant to do so. Probably it had read in the *Rough Guide* about how dirty the water was. It just stood there, right at the edge of the water, using its tail for balance. The name 'Ganoona' was being chanted. The many names of Ganoona were being intoned, but there was only one name and that name was Ganoona. I could hear it all around, coming from the people and coming from the river and coming from me. There was no difference between hearing the name Ganoona and saying the name Ganoona. To hear the name was to say the name and to say the name was to answer to the name and that name was Ganoona. Ganoona may have looked like a kangaroo, but at some level Ganoona was more otter than kangaroo. Unlike the kangaroo, Ganoona had no qualms about the Ganges. This was the otter in him. Clambering over the warm rim of the pouch was easy, like climbing onto a low wall, hearing the chant of Ganoona, leaning forward and letting go, leaning on nothing.

'What is here is also there, and what is there is also here.'
Katha Upanishad

Notes and Acknowledgements

For the record, my wife, Rebecca, and I attended three Biennales, in 2003, 2005 and 2007. Weather-wise, 2003 was the scorcher. The geography of both Venice and Varanasi in these pages is fairly reliable, I hope, but I have taken some liberties with the art, only one example of which was in the 2003 Biennale: the Africans selling knock-off bags near the Arsenale ticket office were actually part of Fred Wilson's installation at the American Pavilion, 2003. Other stuff mentioned in the Venice part of the book – Gilbert & George, Ed Ruscha, the red castle and the blue space of light – is from 2005; the rest is from 2007.

In the Giardini the wall of dartboards (*I, The World, Things, Life*) was by Jacob Dahlgren, the video shower in the Russian Pavilion was by Alexander Ponomarev and Arseny Mescheryakov, and the trippy Swiss paintings were by Christine Streuli (all from 2007).

In the Arsenale the bouncing-skull video was by Paolo Canevari, the photographs of academics were by Rainer Ganahl and the shadow-boxing video was by Sophie Whettnall (all 2007). Like Turrell's *Red Shift*, the video of the woman standing by the river (*Laundry Woman – Yamuna River, India* by Kimsooja) was part of the wonderful exhibition 'Artempo: Where Time Becomes Art' at the Palazzo Fortuny, which, though running concurrently with the 2007 Biennale, was distinct from it.

Needless to say, Jeff's opinions about art are not Geoff's, or not consistently at any rate. About the excellence of the Ganges View, however, there can be no debate. I am grateful to Shashank and all the staff for their endless hospitality and kindness when Rebecca and I stayed there in 2006–7. (That reminds me, Jeff's and Laura's hotels in Venice are both invented.)

The miniature by Shivalal in Varanasi is on imaginative loan from the City Palace Museum, Udaipur, in Rajasthan. Dayanita Singh's photographs at the Kriti gallery are from the series *Go Away Closer*. The lines from Faiz were translated for me from the Hindi (having already been translated, anonymously, from the Urdu) by the photographer.

There are some unacknowledged quotes in the text, most of which are too obvious to need acknowledging here. However, Jeff's idea (p.154) that we don't need to be 'bullied' into paradise is derived from 'Paradise Poem' by Dean Young – his exact word is 'threatened' – in his collection *Embryoyo* (Believer Books). 'People say it's not what happens etc . . .' (p.53) ; more precisely, John Lanchester says it in *A Family Romance* (Faber). The philosopher who asked where logic came from (p.173) was Nietzsche, in *The Gay Science*. The sentence beginning 'It was night still . . .' on p.262 is from *The Razor's Edge* by W. Somerset Maugham. 'Darkness was hidden by darkness' (p.244) is from *The Rig Veda*. The version of the Chekhov joke on p.276 is followed by a few lines from Gramsci's *Prison Notebooks*. 'Cloud-swollen sky', 'losing his bearings in [the] labyrinth of alleys, narrow waterways, bridges and little squares that all looked so much like each other', 'returned to the hotel and took the lift up to his room', 'inner disintegration', 'confused network of streets', 'attacked by waves of dizziness', 'Nothing is stranger, more delicate, than the relationship between two people who know each other only by sight' are all from *Death in Venice* by Thomas Mann, translated by David Luke.

Two books about Varanasi were particularly helpful: *Banaras: City of Light* by Diana L. Eck (Penguin India) and *Benares from Within* by Richard Lannoy (Callisto).

This is a work of fiction. The fact that certain figures from the art world – Fiona Banner, Richard Wentworth, Bruce Nauman etc. – are mentioned by name or spotted at parties does not mean that they were actually in Venice in 2003 or any other time. With the exception of the charming Shashank in Varanasi, any resemblance between characters in the book and actual people is entirely coincidental.

I would like to thank Ethan Nosowsky, Eric Simonoff, Dan Frank, Bill Hamilton, Victoria Hobbs, Lorraine McCann, Stephanie Gorton, Francis Bickmore and Jamie Byng for their advice and help.